Scarlet Scars Book Two

J.M. DARHOWER

ISBN-13: 978-1-942206-22-4

To Jar Jar Binks.
I'm sorry everyone in the universe seems to hate you.

Grievous

griev·ous
/ˈgrēvəs/
adjective
adjective: **grievous**
1. (of something bad) very severe or serious.
synonyms: grave, dreadful, terrible, crushing

"a grievous wound"

1

"I have something for you."

Those words rang out from the open doorway of the bedroom... and not for the first time, either. *I have something for you.* The little girl slowly turned in the chair at the desk, turning away from the window with snow falling outside, away from the blank paper and pile of mixed up, broken crayons.

The Tin Man stood there, dressed in a dark suit, his hand hidden behind his back.

"Is it Buster?" she asked, trying to ignore the swelling in her chest that really hoped it was. It had been another week without him. Another week without her mother. *Too many weeks.*

The Tin Man's face twisted, like her question made him angry. *Not Buster.*

The little girl frowned, turning back to the frosty window. "No, thank you."

"But it is Christmas today," he said, "so you get a present."

Her brow furrowed. It wasn't Christmas. Not anymore. They'd *missed* Christmas. Santa hadn't come. "It's the new year now."

"True, but it is still Christmas."

She just shook her head, staring at a bare red crayon on the desk, all of the paper peeled off and scattered around in front of her. Red crayon wax was caked under her fingernails from picking at it that morning.

The Tin Man made no sense.

How could it be Christmas still?

"Use your words, kitten."

Use your words. He always said that, like she wasn't allowed to have any thoughts that just belonged to her. She had to make them into words and give them to him. He was always taking *everything.*

"I don't have no words," she said. "I just wanna go away."

"You want to go away?" he asked, his footsteps coming through the room as he approached. "Or would you like me to go away?"

He stopped behind her, his shadow covering the desk like a storm cloud had moved in and blocked all the sunshine. He touched her shoulder and little girl froze, whispering, "I want *you* to go."

His hand darted over as soon as she said that, gripping her jaw so hard she cried out. It felt like a metal claw. He yanked her face up, forcing her head back, banging it against the chair as he made her look at him. His expression was hard, his eyes as cold as ice as they glared down at her. His rough touch left finger-shaped marks on the pale skin she'd gotten from her mother.

Tears stung the little girl's eyes, her throat burning.

"You think I will not hurt you because you are small?" His hand moved to her chubby cheeks, squeezing them hard, making her purse her lips. "You think I will not hurt you because you look so much like the woman who has my heart?"

"She has your heart?" the little girl tried to ask as tears fell down her cheeks, the words sounding like a muffled sob, but he understood.

"She has all of me. I love that *suka* more than she could ever understand. I love her *to death*, kitten. The moment I saw her, I knew she would be mine. I gave her everything, and all she had to do was love me back."

He closed his eyes, like those words hurt him, as his hand shifted again, pressing against her throat until she couldn't breathe. She tried, sucking in air, but it felt like her lungs were broken, like they had a hole in them so everything leaked out until she was choking.

Choking.

The little girl struggled, grabbing his hand with her own. His eyes opened when she touched him, something flickering in them, like flames roared inside of him.

He let go right away.

The little girl inhaled sharply, touching her neck as her whole body shook. *Why did he do that?*

From behind his back, the Tin Man pulled out a stuffed cat. Small, and calico, with a red bow around its neck. He tossed it on the desk in front of her, on top of her broken crayons.

"Merry Christmas, kitten," he said as he turned away. "I love you."

2

Morgan

"You know, when you mentioned *breakfast*, I kind of thought you were going to go home and make pancakes again."

Lorenzo laughs, standing on the street corner in the Chelsea neighborhood, just down from a little hole-in-the-wall Mexican place that stays open twenty-four hours. He clutches a Styrofoam container, at eight o'clock in the morning, eating the most gigantic burrito I've ever seen in my life.

Four bucks, cash only.

He made me order one, too.

Or rather, I said I wasn't hungry and he said, 'fuck that, I'm getting you one and you're going to eat it,' like the gentleman he is. I'm grateful for it, even though I pitched a fit.

Turns out, it's *delicious*.

"Can't believe you've never eaten there," he says. "I thought it was a requirement to be a New Yorker."

"I'm not your typical New Yorker," I point out. "I never really got the *experience*. Too busy slinging pussy, I guess."

A woman walks by as I say that, clutching her chest and casting me a look, like she might catch something by walking near me. *Yeah, like some fucking human decency, maybe.* I scowl at her, chomping on my burrito, waiting for the light to change so we can cross the street.

The old battered teddy bear is tucked beneath my arm. I probably look ridiculous, I know, like I escaped from some hospital's mental ward. People cast looks at me like they're genuinely concerned about my sanity, which is funny, considering I feel more at peace in this moment than I've felt in a while. "You ever worry you might really be crazy?"

"Worry? No. I'm pretty sure."

"You're pretty sure you're crazy?"

"Yes."

I laugh, looking at him, seeing he's watching me curiously. The light changes and people go around us, but he doesn't move. Not right away.

"There's nothing wrong with being crazy," he says. "It's all just a matter of perception. Hell, I think my brother's crazy, working some bullshit job with his beauty queen girlfriend studying whatever she's studying, spending tens of thousands for a little piece of paper that'll declare her competent enough to get her own bullshit job where she'll make not even a fraction of what I make, when I didn't even finish high school. But the world thinks that's normal, and really, that's all normalcy is—it's whatever fucking brand of *crazy* has the majority."

He goes on so long, staring at me, that the light changes again and people gather around us.

I stay quiet, waiting until it's safe to walk.

"Besides," Lorenzo says, turning to cross the street, "crazy gets shit done, Scarlet."

We stroll along, finishing our burritos, neither of us saying much of anything after that. He's right, I guess. Maybe we're all crazy. Maybe the trick in life is just to find someone whose crazy plays well with your own.

After we discard our trash, Lorenzo heads for the subway. It's packed with commuters at this hour, so there aren't any seats left, even standing room scarce. Lorenzo grabs a pole, pulling me in front of him without a word. It's cozy. *Warm*. His arm drapes around me as I rest my head against his chest.

He's so warm I almost fall asleep standing there.

It takes forty-five minutes to make it to his house. As soon as we walk inside, we come face-to-face with Leo and Melody, who are dressed for the day and heading out. Leo works in some fancy ass restaurant, one that requires he wear a tuxedo, whereas Melody is carrying her backpack full of books for class. It's all so picture-perfect.

Normal.

Leo eyes us. "Long night? You both look like hell this morning."

"Don't you have somewhere to be?" Lorenzo asks right away. "Somewhere that doesn't include talking to me?"

Leo laughs at that, slapping Lorenzo's shoulder. "But I always have time for my big brother."

"Go to work," Lorenzo says. "You get fired, you're fucked, because I'm not paying for Firecracker's wining and dining, so all romance will be off."

"Oohhh," Melody says, making a face as she grabs Leo's arm. "You know what no romance means..."

"No pussy?" I guess.

Now *Leo* makes a face.

"Good," Lorenzo says. "Maybe then they'll keep their clothes on and stop playing *Slip 'n Slide* on my damn couch all of the time."

"Speaking of the couch," Leo chimes in, "you were just kidding, right? You didn't really steal the new couch from some strip club."

As soon as he says that, I glance into the living room, seeing a familiar black leather couch with gold accents. *Oh god, did he seriously...?*

"Do you think I'd *really* do that?" Lorenzo asks.

"I'm hoping not," Leo grumbles.

"Go to work," Lorenzo tells him again before turning to Melody. "And you, go wherever it is you go when you're not in my house, breathing up all of my oxygen."

They grumble goodbyes and head out, while Lorenzo stands there, staring at the door, making sure they're gone before turning to me.

He looks like he has something to say, but I beat him to talking.

"You stole a couch," I say, "from a strip club."

"So?"

"So do you know what *happens* on those couches?"

"Probably the same ooey-gooey shit my brother does on it, but it doesn't matter. I disinfected it."

"You *disinfected* it."

"Yeah, got a can of Lysol and sprayed the fuck out of the thing."

I scrub my hands over my face. "I, uh... I'm too tired to think of a response to that."

"Then come on," he says, stepping past me. "Let's go to bed."

I don't argue with that. Bed sounds like a beautiful place to be, so I follow him upstairs. As soon as we reach his room, I kick off my shoes and yank off my hoodie, falling into the bed with a sigh, still clutching the damn bear.

Lorenzo strips down to nothing, as usual, before climbing in beside me.

Thirty seconds, if even that. My eyes drift closed, exhaustion taking over. Lorenzo's already snoring. Sleep hits me hard.

Out like a light.

I don't know how much time passes before I'm jolted back awake, but my body is sore and the room is dim, growing darker, so I sense it's late. I slept all damn day. Groggy, rubbing my eyes, I pull myself up to a sit as something falls into my lap.

Buster.

It hits me again then, as I pick up the bear. The pressure in my chest makes me feel like I'm suffocating. My fingers explore the bear's beat-up face, caressing the filthy fur and shoving stuffing back into the holes.

I wondered if I'd ever see the thing again. I wondered where it ended up and hoped—no, *counted on*—it being with Sasha. She doesn't have me, I'm not there to protect her, but I thought she'd at least have her best friend Buster.

She doesn't, though.

She's all alone.

So am I.

In the literal sense, on my part.

Lorenzo's not here.

I reach over, running my palm along the cold sheets. He's been gone so long that the bed's no longer warm.

Sighing, I get up, trudging over to the closet to pull out my duffel bag that's tucked in the back, along the bottom. I shift through it, grabbing the small black cell phone, plugging it into the charger using the wall socket as I sit down on the floor.

After a few minutes, as I hold onto the bear, the phone powers up, coming to life again. There are only a few numbers programmed into it, and I hit the button to call the top one, bringing it to my ear.

It rings a few times, as I inwardly panic, a voice in my head screaming for me to hang up *right the fuck now*, but the devil on my shoulder isn't having that. The line picks up, a voice calmly greeting me, the Russian accent still thick despite him living in America for years. "I have been waiting for you to call."

He knows it's me. I'm not sure how. I keep my number blocked for this reason, but yet somehow, he always *knows*.

I don't say anything.

I can't find the words.

My voice doesn't want to work.

I used to have a lot to say, but my pleas always fell upon deaf ears, so I rarely say anything anymore. I just sit, and I listen, hoping one of these times he'll say something of value, that he'll slip up and I'll hear her in the background.

It has never happened.

These calls used to be as frequent as the visits to the precinct, but trying to rationalize with Kassian is a lost cause. It's like trying to civilize a caveman. No matter what I say, it's never enough to get him to act human for just a moment and let me talk to my daughter.

He's never even acknowledged to me that he *has* her.

The sound of his voice makes my insides ache, but I shove the feelings down and absorb every syllable he's willing to offer, like maybe this is all a riddle that I can eventually solve.

"Did you enjoy your present? I know Christmas was months ago, but it is better late than never, no?" There's a lightness to his tone, like he's amused by all of this. "I am assuming your scarred plaything gave it to you, since you are calling... unless you are simply missing me today."

I stretch my legs out along the floor, Buster lying in my lap, as I rest my head back against the wall.

I still say nothing.

"It is a shame about the condition of the bear," he says. "I had to teach a lesson on obedience. I am sure you remember those. We had *so* many of them, you and I, but *you*... you never did learn. No matter how many times I showed you, you still thought you could have things your way. But I, of course, had to get creative this time, since I could not teach her things the way I taught you."

He laughs, like it's the funniest thing in the world, while I grow dizzy, the room starting to spin.

I have to close my eyes.

"I miss your lessons," he says, sounding almost wistful. "Striping you bare, fucking you raw, letting them all watch. Do you remember? The way they would fall all over themselves to see you, hoping I was in a generous mood and would let them have a taste. Do *you* miss that? You can admit it. I will not tell anyone. I will not tell them how much of a good girl you used to be, how you would cry *so* quietly, so not to disturb them when they took turns—"

"*Stop.*" My voice cracks as that word forces itself from my lips, tears stinging my eyes. "Just... *stop.*"

"Aw, pussycat, are you crying *now*?"

I bite my lip to keep from making a sound.

"It is okay," he continues. "Come back home, and I will make it all better. *Promises.* And maybe, if you are a good girl, once you finally learn your lesson, I will tell you what happened to your kitten."

It would be a lie to say I don't consider his offer.

Because for a second, a moment of weakness, I think '*okay*'. I think '*I can do it*'. Nothing Kassian could put me through would ever be worse than living in this void, existing in the unknown,

18

without my little girl. I think maybe if I go to him, maybe if I give in, I can find her, get her back, and maybe that way I can protect her. But reality is that I couldn't even protect *myself* from this man, and if I surrender now, nobody will ever save either of us.

And it's stupid, I know, because his '*maybe*' means nothing. His promises are bullshit. He'd teach me my lesson, sure. He'd find a way to break me.

He'd do it, and then he'd kill me.

"No more to say?" he asks.

I don't respond.

"Then goodbye for now, pretty girl. I am sure we will see each other again soon. *I love you.*"

The line goes dead.

I sit here for a minute, those words stabbing at me, before I snatch the charger out of the wall and throw it all in the duffel bag, shoving it back in the closet.

Carrying Buster, I march downstairs, finding Leo and Melody in the living room on the couch.

Not having sex, thankfully—looks like he's helping her with homework—but ugh, *that* couch.

If they only knew...

"You guys are back already?" I ask. "What time is it?"

"After nine o'clock," Leo says with a laugh. "Did you *just* wake up?"

"Ugh, yeah." I scratch my head, my hair a knotted mess. "Guess I was really tired."

I can't remember the last time I slept *twelve* hours.

"Is Lorenzo still in bed?" Leo asks. "If so, you might want to check his pulse. He never sleeps more than two or three hours. Might be dead."

I blink a few times. "He's not down here?"

"Haven't seen him," Leo says. "We got home about three hours ago, so he must've left before then if he wasn't upstairs with you."

"Is his car outside?" I ask, stepping into the living room, walking over to the window to look out. The black BMW is still parked in the driveway. "Guess he walked, or maybe he took the subway..."

"Or someone picked him up," Leo says.

Weird.

Staring at his car, I try to ignore the strange feeling brewing inside of me. *Ugh.* Lorenzo is an adult. He's under no obligation to check in with anyone before he goes out, much less tell *me* his business.

Frankly, I'm not sure I want to know half of the places the man has been.

But still, a feeling twists my gut, something dangerously close to worry, like I'm concerned about his well-being.

"Can I ask you something, Morgan?"

Leo's voice draws me from those thoughts before I can dwell on them too much. Turning, I glance at where he sits on the couch. Melody is reading something out of a thick textbook, while he eyes me peculiarly from beside her. "Ask me something?"

"Yeah, something, I don't know... personal?"

Oh no.

Inwardly, I'm on edge about that, because personal questions never lead anywhere good, but I plaster on a smile. "Sure."

"What's up with you and my brother?"

Uh... "What do you mean what's *up* with us?"

"I'm just wondering what your plans are," he says. "Do you see this thing with him actually going somewhere? Do you *want* it to go somewhere? Or is it just, you know, convenient—"

Melody slams her book closed, interrupting him with a glare. "Leonardo! I know you are not trying to have the '*what are your intentions?*' talk with her!"

My eyes widen. Is he?

Leo turns to his girlfriend. "What? I'm just asking..."

"You can't just *ask* somebody that," she says. "Don't you remember when we first started dating and you got the third degree about your intentions? Didn't like that so much, did you, buddy?"

"That's different."

"No, it's not," she says, rolling her eyes. "They're grown ass folk, so mind your beeswax."

"But—"

She points him in the face, her finger jabbing him in the nose as she makes a screeching noise to cut him off, loud enough to startle even herself.

I step closer, perching on the arm of a chair near the couch, as Leo grabs her finger and playfully pretends to bite it.

"I get it," I say. "I show up out of nowhere, and here I am, doing all the crap he complains about, like eating his food and breathing his air, yet he tolerates it."

"Yes!" Leo throws his hands up, shooting Melody a smug look. She scowls, shoving his face away as he laughs. "It's just not like my brother."

"Yeah, I don't know," I say. "Sorry to disappoint, but I don't really have an answer. I'm just trying to survive, and your brother? Well, I don't even know what to say about Lorenzo. He's an asshole a lot of the time, completely unyielding, but in a refreshing way... I kind of like it. As for why he puts up with *me*? He's been bored and the sex is good. Or well, that was his reasoning when *I* asked."

Leo doesn't look disappointed. Quite the opposite, in fact. He grins like a maniac. Melody, on the other hand, opens her book again, muttering, "talk about romantic."

"Anyway..." I stand back up, holding Buster out. "You wouldn't happen to know if there's a sewing kit around here anywhere, would you? A needle? Some thread, maybe?"

"Check the kitchen," Leo says. "Or the library... or the bathroom... or maybe Lorenzo's room..."

"So check everywhere?"

"Pretty much."

I go to walk out when Melody glances up, her brow furrowing. "Is that a *teddy bear*?"

"Yep," I say.

"It's, uh..." She hesitates. "Nice."

"It's falling apart," I say. "I need to fix it back up."

"Why do you have a teddy bear?" Leo asks before turning to

his girlfriend. "Wait, am I allowed to ask that?"

Melody just rolls her eyes at him.

"Oh, it's not mine," I say. "It belongs to my daughter."

I step out into the hallway just as my words seem to strike Leo. "Your *what?*" he shouts, but I don't answer, hearing Melody stop him from following me with another line about '*beeswax*'.

I scour the kitchen, finding a hell of a lot of utensils, enough knives to potentially qualify Lorenzo as a one of those *Doomsday preppers*, but no sewing kit anywhere. I move on to the library, scanning the shelves, squatting down to search a row of built-in cabinets beneath them, and am about to give up and move on when a loud voice cuts through the room. "What the fuck are you doing?"

I jump up, banging my head on a cabinet, and wince as I get to my feet, rubbing my scalp. Shit, that *hurt*. Lorenzo stands in the doorway, dressed impeccably in a fitted suit, wearing black from head-to-toe, looking... *whoa.*

"Yo, bro, what the hell?" Leo hollers, coming down the hallway. "Was that a *cop* that dropped you off?"

Before Leo can barge in, and without acknowledging his question, Lorenzo grabs the library door and slams it right in Leo's face. I wince again, this time from *realization*. I was so distracted by the look of Lorenzo in a suit that it didn't strike me that he just caught me searching through his library.

His library.

You know, the room nobody goes into without his permission?

He caught me all up in the cabinets, digging through his shit.

"I'm looking for a needle and some thread," I tell him, shutting the cabinet doors. "You know, a sewing kit?"

He watches me incredulously as he comes closer. "Do I look like I fucking *knit?*"

"Actually, you knit with—" I cut off abruptly when he raises an eyebrow. "Well, *you* don't knit with anything, because you don't knit, but needle and thread, come on... you've never had to sew up a cut? Give yourself a few stitches?"

"No," he says, "that's why we have doctors."

"Whatever," I say, holding up Buster. "A doctor's not going to perform surgery on this guy."

Lorenzo pushes his chair around to face me as he sits down. His expression wavers, some of the anger melting as he reaches down to untie his shoes. "I've got duct tape."

"I'm not so sure that'll work, but thanks."

He kicks the shoes off, leaning back in his chair. "Suit yourself."

"Speaking of *suits...*" I wave toward him. "What's got you looking so snazzy tonight?"

He undoes his suit coat, shoving it off, and starts rolling up his sleeves. "Had a meeting."

"With a cop?"

"There was a cop involved, yes. A detective."

My stomach sinks. "Gabe?"

Lorenzo shoots me a confused look. "Who?"

"Detective Jones," I say. "You know, the one you call my *cop friend?*"

"Ah, no, not the one you're fucking."

I cringe at how he says that. "*Fucked*. Past tense. Not currently fucking, nor will there be any future fucking. That battleship has *sunk*."

"Fucked," he repeats, running his hands down his face, letting out a deep sigh. "This is one you've never fucked. Name's Jameson, works Organized Crime in the city."

"And that required a suit? Not that I'm complaining, because *whoa...* just haven't seen you wear one before."

"Sometimes you've gotta play the part, Scarlet. You know that. When most people think of guys like me, they still imagine someone like Michael Corleone, so that's what they get. It's kind of funny, really. They're more terrified of me in a suit with shiny dress shoes than they are when I'm wearing combat boots and carrying a loaded gun."

"Maybe they're not more terrified," I say. "If they're trembling, heart racing, *sweating*, I'm saying there's a chance they might just be turned on."

He laughs, loosening his collar. "Do you piss your pants when you get turned on, too?"

I step to him, shrugging. "Depends on how turned on I am."

He reaches out, grabbing ahold of me, pulling me down for a kiss. It's soft, slow, and doesn't last very long before he breaks from my lips. "When's the last time you *showered*?"

I push away from him. "Are you saying I stink?"

Before he can answer, I tilt my head down, sniffing, trying to be subtle about it, but he catches on to what I'm doing and laughs.

"If you have to smell yourself, Scarlet, there's a pretty good chance you're due to be hosed off."

I roll my eyes, ignoring how he words that. *If you only knew, man.* "Right now."

"Right now?"

"Yep, that's the last time I showered," I say, skirting past him. "Right now."

Look, I know you're probably over there cringing. I'm filthy, and yeah, I kind of *stink*. I'm wearing the clothes I slept in, and I haven't fixed my hair in a few days, just throwing it up in a sloppy bun. So yeah, whatever, cringe all you want, but I've had a pretty fucked up *life*, you know, so don't judge me.

Trudging upstairs, I haul myself straight into the shower, scrubbing and shaving and shampooing, using all of Lorenzo's stuff since all I've got is my lotion and a toothbrush. Afterward, I brush my hair, slathering on lotion from head to toe before putting on some fresh clothes and heading back downstairs.

He's gone again. Lorenzo. It has only been about thirty minutes, but the library is empty. *Seriously?* Sighing, I go to the living room, finding Melody sitting there by herself.

No Leo, either.

"Have you seen Lorenzo?" I ask.

"He left," she says, glancing up from her schoolwork. "He had to go do something, made Leo drive him. Said it would only take a few minutes."

Well then...

I approach her, curiously glancing at her book. *Elements of Moral Philosophy.* I'm not even sure what that means. "Philosophy."

"Yeah," she says, making a face. "I thought it would be fun to major in."

"A degree in philosophy, huh? What kind of job can you get with one of those?"

"Probably the kind that involves a stripper pole."

She's being sarcastic, grumbling under her breath, but I laugh at that answer because it's not far-fetched. "Well, hell, you could've saved all that tuition and just gotten a job with me at Mystic."

She cuts her eyes at me as I sit down. "Mystic?"

"A club I used to dance at," I say. "Definitely didn't need a degree to work a pole there."

Her eyes widen. "Seriously? You're a—"

"Stripper, yeah... or well, I *was.*"

"Wow, I'm sorry, I didn't mean..." She cringes. "Ugh, I'm such a dumbass. I shouldn't have said that. I'm not trying to say, you know, that there's anything *wrong* with stripping..."

"It's fine," I tell her.

"That's just... *wow.* I mean, I guess I can see it, you know? You look like... well..."

"Someone who takes her clothes off for money?" I ask, taking a guess at where she's going with that.

Her face turns red as she shakes her head. "I mean like someone who doesn't give a crap what anyone thinks about her."

She stares at me like she wants to ask something, but before she can find the words, headlights flash through the window as a car pulls into the driveway.

"Yeah, well, it doesn't really matter what people think," I say, getting back to my feet. "Only *I* have to live with my consequences."

Walking out, I nearly run into Leo when he steps through the front door. He stalls, looking at me, his expression falling somewhere between surprise and confusion. "Seriously? A *daughter?*"

Before I can respond to that, Lorenzo steps in behind him,

grabbing ahold of Leo by the head and shoving him past me, to the living room. "*Fa ti cazzi tuoi.*"

Whoa.

"*Geesh,* fine," Leo grumbles, walking off. "No need to get your panties in a twist, bro."

Lorenzo waves him off. "Suck my nuts."

I stare at Lorenzo, surprised by the exchange, as he steps toward me, right up against me in the hallway. His suit isn't put together anymore, his shoes untied, shirt hanging loose.

"You speak *Italian?*" I ask.

"Some," he says, leaning down like he's going to kiss me, but instead he runs his nose along my jawline. "Why? You want me to talk dirty to you?"

"I, uh..." He's got me flustered as he grabs my hip, pulling me even closer. I shiver, feeling his warm breath on my skin. It's like he's breathing me in. "Well, I *didn't,* but I kind of do now."

He laughs. "Let's go upstairs, and I'll teach you all the dirty words you want."

I hum, tilting my head as his lips trace along my cheek. "All of them?"

His breath is against my ear as he whispers, "Every single one."

He doesn't have to say that again.

Pushing away, I snatch ahold of his hand, grasping tightly as I drag him up the stairs. As soon as we reach his bedroom, he slams the door, shrugging off his coat again and tossing it onto the dresser.

It hits with a thud, something in the pocket.

I cast it a curious look but shake it off, distracted when he pulls a gun out from his waistband to set it aside. He reaches for me, tearing at my clothes, but I slap his hands away. Instead, I go for his pants, unbuckling them as I sink to my knees in front of him. Lorenzo stands still, not moving at all.

I pull his cock out and stroke it.

He's already rock hard.

I don't hesitate, bringing my lips right to the tip, my tongue swirling around the head before slowly, I take it into my mouth, his cock sliding down my throat.

"Fuck," he growls, grasping the back of my head as I suck him. "That feels so good."

Lorenzo's hands tangle in my still-damp hair, his head tilting back and eyes closing. Soft groans escape his throat, and he stays like that for a moment, just enjoying it, letting me do what I want to do without saying another word.

It's a few minutes—three, maybe four at most—before he pulls his hand from my hair, reaching down further to nudge my chin.

I look up at him.

He's watching me now.

We lock eyes, and I keep sucking as he gently runs his fingertips along my face, caressing my hallowed cheek. His expression makes my chest tighten, a softness in his eyes as he tucks some wayward hair behind my ear. His breathing picks up, chest rising and falling faster as he swallows hard, the only signs that let on to him getting close. *So close.*

"*Il mio piccolo dolce trombamica,*" he says, his voice low and gritty. He cups my chin, thumb grazing the corner of my mouth, tracing my lips as they slide along his cock. "*Vedere il mio cazzo tra quelle belle labbra è una fantasia che mi ha perseguitato dal momento in cui ci siamo incontrati.*"

I have no idea what he's saying, not a fucking clue, but the sound of those words sends sparks through me as they roll right off of his tongue. I stroke him faster, sucking harder, a smirk on his lips as his eyes again drift closed.

Once more, he tilts his head back, jaw going slack, as his hand again tangles into my hair.

He grips harder this time, though, fisting handfuls.

A few seconds pass before he bucks his hips, my nose pressing into his stomach as he holds my head still, fucking my throat. A few thrusts, as I gag, before I feel him spilling. I swallow, grasping his hips to brace myself, but breathing is becoming difficult.

I give him a few seconds, holding my breath, but my chest is tight and he's not letting go, so I pinch his inner thigh. *Hard.*

He flinches, shoving away. I fall back onto my ass and inhale sharply.

"Christ, that *hurt*," he says, rubbing the spot I pinched.

"Oh, quit whining," I mutter. "I could've just bit you... or, you know, punched you in the balls."

He glares at me when I say that, giving me an *'I'd like to see you fucking try'* look, trying to be intimidating, but it's kind of hard to take him seriously when his cock is just hanging out of his pants.

I smirk. "You know, you'd probably be a lot scarier if your junk wasn't dangling all up in my face."

Before the last syllable is completely out of my mouth, he steps toward me, grabbing his cock. "Keep talking shit, I'll fucking *slap* you with it."

Laughing, I throw my hands up defensively, warding him off as he swings it, shoving it right at my face, smacking me in the forehead.

"Oh my god," I yell, still laughing, shoving him so hard he staggers. "What is *wrong* with you?"

He shrugs, tucking himself away, zipping his pants up. "You sucked the brain cells right out of my dick with that goddamn *Dyson* mouth."

Turning, he starts to walk away from me when I grab his leg. "Whoa, where are you going?"

"To take a shower," he says, trying to shake me off.

"Oh, hell no," I say, tugging him back toward me. "I'm not done with you yet."

He thrusts his leg out, damn near kicking me so I'll let go. "What do you want?"

"Some *reciprocation* would be nice," I say, "but I'll settle for just knowing what you said in Italian."

He pauses as he starts to undress, stripping out of his suit, like reciprocation may not only happen but that it might go even further. "I said I've been fantasizing about those beautiful lips wrapped around my cock since the moment I met you."

"Seriously?"

He crouches down in front of me, wearing only his unbuttoned black slacks. "Yes, seriously, my sweet little *trombamica*."

"What does *that* mean?"

A slow smile spreads across his face as he leans closer, kissing me softly, quick pecks on my lips, before he stands back up, saying, "Figure it out, Scarlet."

"*Figure it out, Scarlet*," I grumble mockingly as he goes into the bathroom and shuts the door, leaving me kneeling here. Rolling my eyes, I get up and head straight downstairs to where Leo and Melody still hang out in the living room.

Leo looks up at me when I appear. He has questions, I know, but I'm not in the mood to talk about those things, so I beat him to speaking.

"Hey, Leo, you know what a *trombamica* is?"

His eyes widen. "Uh, yeah..."

"What is it?"

"It's a... friend."

"A *friend*."

"Yeah," he says, "one with benefits."

"A friend with benefits."

"Just a, uh, more vulgar term."

My eyes narrow.

Leo's about to say something else, but I don't give him the chance, walking back out and stomping upstairs. *Unbelievable.* I hear the water running in the bathroom and don't even hesitate, opening the door and walking right in since he never locks *anything*.

Grabbing the shower curtain, I fling it open, glaring at a naked, soapy Lorenzo. "A *fuck-buddy*? Really?"

He stands beneath the spray, water cascading down his bare chest. It distracts me momentarily, detracting from my anger, as I follow the trail of water down his body.

"Didn't take you long to figure it out, *trombamica*."

I scowl, looking back at his face. He's grinning. Smug son of a—*ugh.* Before I can respond, he grabs me, yanking me beneath the spray. I nearly trip over the edge of the tub as he pulls me into it with him, fully dressed.

"What the hell, Lorenzo? You're getting me wet!"

"Don't I always?" he asks with a laugh, grabbing my drenched clothes and tearing them off, flinging them onto the floor before drawing the shower curtain closed again. He shoves me back against the tile wall, and I gasp as he grabs my thighs, lifting me up. I wrap my legs around his waist, my arms around his neck, holding onto him. "Guess I owe you some reciprocation, huh?"

"You're damn right you do," I say. "You better make it good, too."

He grins, kissing me, whispering against my lips, "I'll do my best."

3

Lorenzo

"You son of a bitch," I growl, squinting, hunkered beneath the glowing lamp in the library with my gaze fixed to my lap. "I swear to God, if you don't go in that fucking hole, I'm going to lose my shit..."

Carefully, I aim, lining up for what feels like the twentieth goddamn time, but my hand slips right past my target, once again, instead somehow making me stab myself in the thumb.

"Fuck!" I yank my hand back, watching as a bead of bright red blood bubbles up on the surface. I pop my thumb in my mouth and shove up out of my chair, sending it flying halfway across the room. "Mother*fucker!*"

The word's jumbled, since I'm sucking my damn thumb, sounding more like a bitch ass shriek than anything resembling English. Frustration builds up inside of me as I kick the table, lashing out, making it screech along the floor.

"Boss?"

Seven's hesitant voice calls out from the doorway just in the knick of time, because I was three seconds away from pulling out my gun and shooting *something*, which would've probably just pissed me off more. *Goddamn bullet holes.*

I turn, regarding him. He looks like his usual self, fresh-faced and wide awake, despite it being around five o'clock in the morning, the sun not yet shining. He has probably already eaten breakfast. Probably fucked his wife before leaving his house. Probably got some extra snacks stashed in his pockets. Probably did it all while I sat here like a fucking schmuck, struggling to thread this stupid ass needle.

"Everything okay?" he asks. "What happened?"

What happened?

His favorite goddamn question.

"What happened," I say, pulling my thumb from between my lips, "is I can't take Tab A and stick it in Slot B properly because my brain thinks the world is fucking flat so nothing appears 3D."

He stares at me cautiously, like how you regard a wild animal, like he's afraid of what I might be getting myself into this morning.

"Come thread this fucking needle," I say, throwing the sewing kit down on the table, pieces of it scattering, "before I stab myself again."

Seven approaches, assessing things, picking up the discarded needle and cutting a fresh piece of black thread, since the one I used is knotted and frayed. Three seconds, just like that, he holds the needle up in front of him and slips the thread right through it, securing the ends before handing it back.

Three seconds.

I've been at this for thirty minutes.

"Bullshit," I mutter as I snatch it back. "Thanks."

"Anytime, boss," he says. "Is that all you needed? Is that why you called?"

"Do you seriously think I'd make you come to Queens just to thread a fucking needle for me at five o'clock in the morning?"

"Yes."

I cast him a glare.

He's right.

I would.

But I didn't.

Shaking my head, I reach down, snatching the damn stuffed bear from the floor where I tossed it earlier after swiping it out of Scarlet's clutches in bed. I motion for Seven to have a seat in my chair, while I slide up onto the table, sitting on the edge of it, beneath the lamp.

I don't know where to start.

With *any* of this shit, really.

When building a puzzle, you always start with the border, since those pieces are the easiest to pick out and put together. From there, depending on the puzzle, you either separate by color or you use the picture as reference, if there's something unique to pinpoint. Regardless, you hit what's most obvious first, breaking it down into manageable chunks. *Divide and conquer.*

Start at the border and work our way in.

I push the needle through the side of the bear, to close a hole some fluffy guts are spilling out of.

Seven sits down, still watching. "You ever sewn before, boss?"

"Sewed someone's lips shut before when they wouldn't shut the fuck up," I say. "Why? Do I look like I don't know what I'm doing?"

I'm asking that genuinely.

I'm trying to *not* screw this all up.

"Your technique is a bit... unusual."

"What's so unusual about it?"

I'm shoving it in and pulling it back out, winding round and round and round as I go, forcing the hole closed. Makes sense, right?

"You're using kind of like a double overcasting basting stitch instead of a blind stitch... or maybe a ladder stitch would've been better."

"What are you going on about?" I ask, brow furrowing. "Stitches are *stitches*, are they not?"

"Well... sure, I guess."

"You *guess*."

"It's just that certain stitches work better in different circumstances—like, for instance..."

He rambles, babbling on and on and on about stitches and fabrics and techniques, while I just keep shoving the needle through the bear, back and forth, until the hole is no more. *Poof.* I cut the thread and knot it the best I can, looking up at Seven when I'm done.

Not even kidding. He's *still* talking.

"How the hell do you know all that?" I ask, cutting him off. "Get your rocks off in *home ec*? Spend your free time whittling out coats for the homeless?"

He laughs. "The wife is a seamstress."

"No shit? Didn't think she had a job anymore since you got set loose and started making money again."

"She still does a bit of work here and there," he says. "Mends costumes for a couple shows when they need it. She enjoys it, and well, not gonna turn down extra money, you know?"

"Yeah," I mumble, examining my sewing job before moving on to the next hole, making Seven rethread the needle for me.

Extra money is a bullshit concept, when it comes down to it. For most people, the more they make, the more they spend. Bigger houses, fancier cars, more recognizable brand names. It isn't like they get to a point where they think, 'yep, I've got enough now, I'll pass on the rest.' Which means there's no such thing as *extra*. Money is money. It's a necessary evil.

"Speaking of money," I say, sewing up another hole. "I met with Jameson and a few of his guys over in Midtown yesterday."

"Why didn't you call me? I could've driven you."

"Wasn't necessary," I say. "I just had Jameson swing through and pick me up. Got the guns from storage unloaded. Banked about a hundred thousand. His guy wants more, though, so I'm going to have another shipment put together in the next few days and have it brought up."

Seven lets out a low whistle. "*More?* That's a lot of guns for one man. What's he doing, starting a war?"

"Probably," I say. "Not my problem, though. What they do with it all is their business."

"And the rest of the stuff?"

"It'll all be out to market in the next few days," I say. "Three can handle it, like usual."

Look, while I'm sewing this hole closed, let me give you a rundown about how all of this works:

I help acquire shit. Illegal shit, mostly, some of it that way because of where it comes from. You see, a long time ago, when I was still swimming around in Charlie Gambini's nutsack, the government said '*fuck Cuba*' and banned everything to do with the place. No imports. No exports. Couldn't even step foot on the island without going through a bunch of bullshit. And people, you know, when the government tells them they can't have something, it just makes them want it even more.

Hence, the blackmarket boomed.

After my stepfather wreaked his havoc and took over the groves, he decided to capitalize on that demand. The convenience of having property in Florida meant they could slip shit in and out from Cuba under everyone's noses. After he died and I took it all back, I kept the market running. Most of the product still stays down south, and some guys run it all as they keep up with the groves, but special orders are brought to me up here.

You want it, I can probably get it.

Whether or not I *will* depends on how much you're willing to pay and if I like you that day.

So in summary, we bribe a bunch of motherfuckers to look the other way as we funnel the good shit in from Cuba. I deal with our connections and handle the money. Three distributes the inventory, while Seven makes sure I keep my head on straight through it all. *Eye on the prize.* The rest of the guys, well, they mostly do the brunt work, and it pays pretty damn good, so they don't complain.

You bored now? Yeah?

Can't say I blame you.

That part of it bores the shit out of me, too. I wouldn't bother doing it, except I rely on that money to keep the groves running, since there isn't much money to be made in oranges. I'd break that reality down for you, but it might put you to sleep.

All caught up now? Good.

Back to sewing.

"Anyway, so I asked around about the Russian, figuring one of them would have an in with the guy since most are undercover with that crowd." Oh yeah, did I mention most of the *select group* that buys my illegal shit up here works in law enforcement? I have Seven to thank for those connections. "They say they can't get near him. They've tried. He keeps it all close to the chest, but *somebody* has to have an in with him since he's always a step ahead. So I'm figuring, you know, I've got Jameson in my pocket because he works organized crime, but *they* aren't building a case, the locals are, which tells me whoever's supposed to be investigating the Russians has gotta be bending over for the guy."

"Makes sense," Seven says. "Most likely a detective in the area."

"*Ding, ding, ding,* we've got a winner." I finish sewing up that hole, assessing the bear's leg, the bottom part of it pretty fucked, a chunk burned away. "How am I supposed to fix *that?*"

"Cover it up," Seven suggests.

"What, sew a sock onto it or something?"

"No, make a patch," he says, "like when you get a hole in your pants."

I glance down at my jeans, covered with holes.

They were made that way. No patches.

"Sometimes you seem *a lot* older than me, Seven."

He laughs. "You're just young at heart."

"Is that your way of saying I'm immature?"

"I'm just saying you don't seem to be in any hurry to grow up," he says. "Which there's nothing wrong with. But me? I've settled into my life. You're still finding yours."

"Well, I appreciate the validation, but that's not helping get this goddamn bear fixed."

"Why *are* you fixing it?"

Man… that's a good question. The only answer I've got is, "Who knows?"

He laughs. *Again.* "Look, find some fabric, cut it to fit the space, finish the raw edges and sew it on."

I toss the bear down on the table beside the sewing kit when he says that. It sounds like a lot of work with a high probability of something going wrong. Can't do much about the rest of the bear, either. Can't replace its ear. Can't put it in the washer without it falling apart. And certainly can't give it back its missing eye, considering I've only got one myself.

It's just fucked.

"She had a file on me, you know. *Scarlet.*"

Seven's eyes widen.

"She swiped it from a detective's office. Gabriel Jones. You know him?"

Seven makes a face. "Unfortunately."

"Any chance he could be our Senator Palpatine?"

"Who?"

Sighing, I stand up, taking off my glasses and setting them on the table. "I'm only giving you a pass on that because of the prequels, but if you tell me you've never seen *Empire Strikes Back*, I'm shooting you in the face."

"Seen it a few times."

"Good, now come on," I say, pulling my keys from my pocket and tossing them to Seven. "We're gonna have us a little rendezvous with our little Sith detective this morning."

* * *

"I'm not sure this is a good idea, boss."

Those are the first words out of Seven's mouth when we step foot into the precinct down near Coney Island. I sort of expected it, though, being who he is. He's more uncomfortable here than at a strip club, and that's saying something, since the man has an aversion to any naked woman that isn't his wife. *Allergic to unfamiliar pussy.*

"You can wait in the car," I tell him. "Won't hold it against you."

"I'm fine," he says. "Just letting it be known so when things go haywire you can't blame me."

"Oh, I can still blame you. Probably will, too."

He shakes his head, stepping by me, naturally taking the lead on this since he's all too familiar with the procedures in these places. He approaches a woman in uniform sitting behind a desk, clearing his throat before saying firmly, "We're here to speak with Detective Gabriel Jones."

Ohhh, his *cop* voice—no bullshit, no humor. I guess if we're playing the good cop/bad cop routine, that makes me the good one. *The irony...*

The officer regards him warily, like she might have an idea of who he is. "Name?"

"Bruno Pratt," he says.

Recognition flashes in her eyes.

"I'll let him know you're here," she says, motioning toward the lobby. "Have a seat, someone will—"

"Don't worry about that," he cuts in. "I can find his office myself, no problem."

Seven pushes away from the desk, immediately heading for a nearby elevator. The officer at the desk shoots me a look next, that all-too-familiar expression of dread washing over her as she averts her eyes.

My reputation must precede me here, too.

"Officer," I say, nodding in greeting as I walk past the front desk, trailing Seven.

The elevator opens and we step inside. He presses the number three button.

"Third floor, huh?" I ask.

"Just a guess," he says.

A damn lucky guess, it turns out, because we find the detective's office in the back against the wall, blinds drawn, his name prominently displayed on the door.

"Doesn't look like anyone's home," I say.

"Oh, no, he's here," Seven says. "Should probably look away unless you wanna get an eyeful."

"No shit?"

Seven shoots me a look that says just that: *no shit.*

I don't avert my gaze, because well, I'm nosey. Besides, I've seen it all before. *Nothing's* going to shock me. Seven grabs the door, shoving it open, a high-pitched yelp ringing out from inside as we interrupt whatever's happening. *Uh-oh.*

"Whoa buddy!" I say, letting out a laugh as the detective scrambles to pull himself together. His pants are down around his ankles, damn near tripping him, his awkwardly hairy ass on display. "Might wanna shave that shit, Sasquatch."

He's cursing under his breath as he yanks his pants on, the woman on her knees shoving him away to stand up. Blonde, sickly skinny, which I'm guessing is courtesy of coke judging by the *high-as-fuck* look on her face. She flees the office, and I grimace as she rushes past me, getting a whiff of something *rank*.

"Christ," I grumble, walking into the office, not awaiting an invitation since I'm probably not getting one. "I don't even know what to say right now, detective."

"Nothing was happening," he says as he fumbles with his belt. "It wasn't what it looked like."

I drop down into a chair in front of his desk, stretching my legs out, making myself comfortable. "I sure hope not, because I thought you had better taste than *that*. I mean, don't get me wrong, I've fucked my fair share of questionable women, but that's like sticking your dick in a trash compactor."

He glares at me. "I don't have time for visitors today. I'm busy."

"I saw," I say. "You working on something for that girl? A little head, a little pussy, and what? You'll give her case a little extra attention?"

"Sounds like him," Seven says, still lurking in the doorway.

The detective seems to *just* notice Seven's presence, a look of contempt passing across the man's face. "Pratt."

"Jones."

"I see your choice of friendships hasn't gotten any better."

"And I see you still get your rocks off fucking with people."

"That was always *you*, Pratt. Quick to sell out everyone for a dollar."

"Me?" Seven comes further into the office, leaving the door wide open, his quick advance making the detective step back. "You want to talk about selling people out?"

I glance between them as they shoot daggers at each other.

"Are you two... *flirting?* Because it's kind of turning me on."

Okay, now those daggers are being shot at *me.*

"Sit down, Seven," I say, shoving the chair beside me toward him before I point at the detective. "You, too, Detective Fuckface. Plant your ass in a chair. Let's chit-chat."

Neither man listens to me right away, but Seven's common sense kicks in after a moment. He sits down, not saying another word.

The detective follows his lead, taking a seat behind his desk, his eyes fixed on me. "Lorenzo Gambini, I presume? Or would you prefer to be called—"

"Sir," I cut in before he can say *Scar.* "You can call me *sir*, if it gives you the tingles. Otherwise, let's just stick with Gambini."

He sits quietly for a moment, stewing, before he asks, "What do you want? Huh? You think you can show up here and threaten me?"

"*Threaten* you?" I look to Seven. "Did I threaten him and already forget about it?"

"I didn't hear a threat," Seven says.

I glance back at the detective. "Didn't think so. I'm just here to check up on a case."

"Make an appointment," he says.

"I'd rather not," I say, "so I'll just sit here and wait."

I think he thinks I'll give up and go away, or that I'll do something to justify him having me thrown out of the building, but I'm smarter than that, and I'm stubborn as shit. I'll sit here for a fucking week in silence if it means I win.

It doesn't take a week, though. Hell, it only takes a few minutes. A few minutes of him trying to ignore my presence before he gives in. *Weak.*

"Fine!" He throws his hands up. "Tell me what you want from me and then get the hell out."

"Kassian Aristov."

He blanks.

Full on, no fucking poker face *blanks.*

There's this thing people do when death is imminent, this

40

look that comes over them. Sometimes it only lasts a second. All color drains away. Eyes widen. Jaw goes slack. They almost look dead already, life non-existent, when the realization hits them that they're completely fucked and there's no way to stop it from happening.

That's the look he gets on his face right now.

Dead man walking...

"I can't talk to you about a case that doesn't involve you," he says, choosing his words carefully.

"Oh, do you have a case that *does* involve me? Because I'd love to hear about that one."

He glares at me, still as white as a ghost.

"Well then, in that case, we can stick to Aristov," I say. "I'm actually here on behalf of someone else, so don't you worry your pretty little mind... you can tell me all about it."

"You're here on *whose* behalf?"

"Morgan Myers."

There he goes blanking again. *Panicked.*

"Well?" I snap my finger at him. "The sooner you get with it, the sooner I'll go."

He clears his throat and looks away, absently shifting things around on his desk. "Miss Myers can't speak for herself anymore? She has to send you to rough me up?"

"Jesus *fuck*." I look at Seven. "Did I miss myself roughing him up now? What's happening here?"

"Beats me," Seven says, arms crossed over his chest. "I'm surprised he hasn't told you everything. He's always been good at ratting people out."

Something strikes me then, something in Seven's clipped tone, and I laugh as I turn back to the detective. *Motherfucker.* Turns out I might be dealing with backstabbing *Lando.* "No way, *you*? Tell me you didn't snitch on a fellow officer."

"He shouldn't have been working for the Italians," the detective says. "He betrayed the badge."

"Ask him how he knows," Seven chimes in. "Ask him how he found out I was on their payroll."

"Oh, I don't have to ask," I say. "He sold you out to save his own ass."

Nobody says anything, which really says everything.

"And you didn't return the favor?" I ask Seven. "Didn't take him down with you?"

Seven shakes his head.

"He would've," the detective said, "if he thought for a moment that they would've *believed* it. They hailed me a hero for that arrest. How else do you think I got this cushy private office?"

"Sure as hell isn't because you're good at helping people, huh?" I laugh again, sitting up in the chair, getting pretty tired of dealing with this jackass already. It's no damn wonder Scarlet faded out whenever he touched her. I ought to break every fucking bone in his hands for doing what he did, despicable piece of shit. "Morgan Myers... you're going to tell me what's going on with her case."

The detective is quiet, like he's thinking about how to answer, before saying, "There isn't one."

Did I just hear that right? "What did you just say?"

"There is no case," he says. "We investigated, nothing panned out. Miss Myers was advised to handle it herself, since it's a civil matter."

It's not often I'm rendered speechless, but it's been happening quite a bit lately, and it always seems to have something to do with *Scarlet.*

It's blowing my goddamn mind.

"A civil matter," I say. "Which part? Because I'm just wondering whether murder or kidnapping is the *civil* matter, legally speaking. I might be interested in partaking in one or the other, if that's the case."

"Look, I don't know what she told you, Gambini, but there was no kidnapping. Aristov has a right to his daughter. Morgan kept the kid from him for years prior to this, and she wasn't charged with kidnapping, either. So like I said, it's a civil matter. If she wants us to do anything, she needs to sue for custody and get an order filed with the courts, something that can be enforced. And last time I checked, Miss Myers was still very much alive, which means there wasn't a *murder*."

"Attempted murder, then."

"There's no proof he tried to kill her," he says. "At most, with just her testimony to rely on—if she'd even testify, which she *won't*—it gets pled down to simple assault. He pays a fine, takes anger management, and that's the end of it. She's also welcome to petition the courts for a restraining order. Again, that's something we can enforce."

He's got an answer for everything, an excuse as to why they're not doing a damn thing to help her.

"Fair enough," I say, "but riddle me this: if she gave birth at sixteen, which is under the age of consent, why wasn't he charged for *that*? Pretty sure that's one hell of a cut-and-dry felony."

"There was never any complaint of statutory rape."

"Not even when a man over twice her age signed the birth certificate?"

He stares at me in silence.

"Huh, so either you ignored that little fact or he never signed the birth certificate, which means he's either guilty of statutory rape or he's guilty of kidnapping her child. Which one is it, detective?"

He still says nothing.

Knowing what I know, I'm betting it's the kidnapping. Some bullshit piece of paper issued by the government would mean nothing to Aristov. He doesn't need the validation.

But it also means he's got no *legal* right to her.

"Do you like it?" I ask after a moment of strained silence. "Does it make you hard, bending over for the Russians, letting them fuck you?"

He glares at me.

"It's okay, you can admit it," I continue. "We've all got our kinks. Bet you love it when they come all over your back and treat you like a little bitch."

"Fuck you," he growls. "You don't know anything."

"I know you sold out a grieving mother, and I know you fed her a bunch of bullshit about how you were going to help. I know she let you stick it in, because she loves her kid, thinking you were a good guy that was going to help her with this. But you never planned to do a goddamn thing for her, did you?"

"I'm doing all I can for Morgan," he says through gritted teeth, his nostrils flaring. He looks like he wants to tear me to pieces. *Awesome.* "You think I don't *wish* I could get the kid back for her? If it was in any way possible, I would've done it, but my hands are tied. You just don't cross Aristov."

"Careful, detective," I say. "You're sounding a bit like a coward right now."

"I'm being *realistic*," he says, running his hands down his face. "Unlike Morgan, who seems to think she can go up against him and not lose *everything*. I mean, Christ... what does she expect? She's alive. She escaped with her life. She ought to be grateful for that! The kid... the kid is *fine*. I get that it sucks, but she's with them, and she's... fine."

"And you just took the Russian's word for that?"

"Of course not," he grumbles. "I'm not an *idiot*. I made him prove it. And the kid, you know... she's fine. He has her. She's fine."

I'm beginning to question if he believes his own words. He's said she was fine so many goddamn times that I think he might be trying to convince himself of that.

"I take it that means you've seen her?"

He looks at me, going white again. *Uh-oh.*

"Where's he hiding her?"

"I don't know."

"What *do* you know?"

"Nothing."

Lying son of a bitch...

I shove up to my feet, towering over the desk. "You wanna know what *I* know, detective?"

"What?"

Snatching ahold of his shirt, I fist the collar and yank him up out of his chair. He grabs the desk when he slams into it, bracing himself as I pull him to me. I stare him right in his eyes, face-to-face, so damn close our noses almost touch.

"I know if you ever lay another finger on Morgan, I'll cut your dick off and fuck you with it," I say. "And then, when I'm done, I'll shove it down your mother's throat while *I* fuck *her*. You got me?"

Blinking rapidly, he nods.

I shove him back into his chair, and he damn near falls right out of it, alarmed. Man, you don't even know how much I want to shoot him in the crotch right now, just pump bullet after bullet into the man's puny balls.

"I'll be seeing you around, Detective Fuckface," I say. "Next time, though, you might not like me so much."

"See, *that* was a threat," Seven chimes in, getting to his feet. "I heard it that time."

I laugh, walking out, leaving the precinct without bothering with anybody else.

Stepping outside onto the sidewalk in front of the precinct, I pull the small tin from my pocket to grab a joint.

"Uh, boss," Seven says, pausing beside me. "Might not be the best place to light up."

I shrug that off, lighting it, inhaling deeply and holding the smoke for a moment before saying, "What are they gonna do, arrest me?"

"Probably."

I take another hit of it, nodding, before strolling away from the entrance, heading to where the car is parked. I lounge in the passenger seat, steadily smoking, letting it soothe my nerves and clear my mind as Seven drives. The windows are rolled up, so he's probably getting a bit of a high, but he doesn't complain about it.

"He saw the kid," I say after a moment, "which means Aristov kept her around here."

I can feel Seven's gaze flicker my way as he says quietly, "His refrigerator."

His refrigerator.

What the fuck?

"Seriously? You think he's keeping her in his *refrigerator?*

Jesus Christ, Seven, who is he, Jeffery Dahmer?"

"No, I'm not saying he... *you know*. But when we were at his house, when I went to the kitchen to wait... there was a picture on the refrigerator. A drawing, stick figures and a house. You know, stuff kids draw."

"And you didn't think to mention that before now?"

"No," he admits. "I didn't know we were even looking for a *kid*. You didn't tell me, so I didn't realize it was important."

I'm thinking about that as we head back into Queens, approaching my house, my gaze steadily watching the mirrors, making sure nobody is following us. *Can never be too sure.* It's bothering me, what Seven just said. "How many stick figures?"

He pulls into my driveway, casting me a curious look. "What?"

"How many people were in the drawing?"

"Uh... two. A guy and a kid, it looked like."

Shit.

I sit there, even after he cuts the engine to the car, staring out the windshield at my house. It's after sunrise now, which means Scarlet is probably awake in there, roaming around.

"What are you thinking, boss?" Seven asks.

I'm thinking life is going on without Scarlet, the world is still turning, and that's going to hurt the fuck out of her. You see, that's the thing about grief... it feels all-consuming. It makes it feel like time stops, because for you, it does. Life as you know it ceases to exist, but for everyone else, it just keeps going on. And sometimes, you know, if it stops for too long, there's not much chance of you ever catching up.

Because by the time your world moves again, everyone else is already too far gone.

"Thinking I might make some pancakes this morning," I say. "Maybe some bacon, too."

Seven follows me inside. The moment I open the front door, music greets me, rattling through the house from upstairs. *Tupac.* I make my way up there, the noise blaring from my brother's room, loud despite his door being closed. I'm pretty sure I know what other noises the music is drowning out, so I don't bother him, instead strolling over to my room.

The door is cracked open, and I push it further, leaning against the doorframe.

A smile slowly turns my lips.

Scarlet's making my bed, dancing around as she flings sheets across the thing, trying to get the corners to stay put but they're a bitch to secure. Too big T-shirt, lacy panties, and a pair of socks tugged damn near to her knees is all she's wearing, her hair all over the place. *I Get Around.* She tries to rap along to the song, only knowing half the words, fucking up the rest by just making shit up.

Her eyes shift my way after a moment, and she startles, the singing stopping as she freezes. It only lasts a few seconds before the chorus kicks back in and she shrugs me off, singing along again as she finally gets the fitted sheet into place, moving on to the rest.

I say nothing, just watching her. The song changes to *Hit 'Em Up*. She knows even less of his one, spewing out part of a line every now and then, violent and vulgar, so damn out of place with her honeyed voice that I laugh.

"You laughing at me?" she asks, cutting her eyes my way. "That's foul."

"It's cute," I say, "you trying to sound hardcore."

She scowls as she struts over to me, pausing when we're toe-to-toe, not even hesitating as her arms go around me, her hands meeting at the nape of my neck, fingers running through my hair.

She stares me dead in the face, her expression stone cold serious as she says, "I will *cut* a motherfucker."

"I don't doubt that for a second," I tell her, leaning over, kissing her. "My wicked little *belladonna*, beautiful, deadly, so tempting to keep tasting but so goddamn toxic every touch is just *too much*."

Something flashes in her eyes, her cheeks growing pink, a flush taking over her warm skin.

"Is this foreplay?" she asks. "Because I'm not really in the mood."

"Liar." I laugh, running my nose along her cheek. She smells

47

like warm vanilla and maybe even a bit like *me*. "Are you forgetting what happens to people who lie to me?"

Rolling her eyes, she pushes away, walking back over to finish making the bed. "How do you know I'm lying?"

"You look like you might enjoy a good pounding," I say. "Besides, fresh sheets... no better time than now to fuck the bed all up."

She throws the comforter on top of it, doing a half-assed job at the rest, before dropping to the floor on her hands and knees, looking *under* the bed.

Walking over, I reach down, running a hand over the curve of her ass before slipping further down, rubbing her pussy through her panties. "You assuming the position?"

She laughs. "I'm looking for Buster."

"Ah, its downstairs in my library."

She stands up, giving me a weird look as she pushes past me.

"Where are you going?" I ask, catching her arm.

"To get Buster," she says.

I stare at her as she pulls away, leaving the room.

Un-fucking-believable.

Cock-blocked by a one-eyed teddy bear.

Are you seeing the irony here?

The song changes, *Picture Me Rollin'* blaring through the house, but in those three seconds it takes for the music to kick back in, I hear the unmistakable sound of moaning.

Walking over to my brother's room, I bang my fist against the door, hard enough to rattle it, before snatching ahold of the knob and shoving the fucking thing open.

"Whoa, Pretty Boy!" I tilt my head as the door slams into the wall. "I didn't know Firecracker was so *bendy*."

Shouts, panic, as they scramble, throwing blankets over themselves, Firecracker covering up entirely as she pushes Leo off of her. Truthfully, I saw nothing, but if I'm getting cock-blocked, so is my brother.

Yeah, whatever... no one ever said I was *mature*.

"Jesus, bro!" he yells. "Do you mind?"

"Keep the fucking noises down," I tell him. "Some people are busy *not* fucking and don't want to hear that shit."

I walk away as he yells something at me, something that has something to do with me being an *asshole*, as if I don't already know that little fact about myself. I make my way downstairs, heading to the library, damn near slamming into Scarlet.

She thrusts the bear at me, shoving it right in my face. "What the hell, Lorenzo?"

I push her hand away. "What?"

"Who did this?"

"Who did what?"

"This… *sewing*."

I look at the bear in the dim morning light, at the thick lines of black thread knotted together, before my gaze turns to Scarlet, who clutches the thing so tightly it looks like she might bust the holes right back open.

Tears swim in her eyes.

My skin starts to crawl.

I should've known better.

This is why I don't do shit like this. Why I don't try to help people. Why I don't fucking *bother*. I think, *hey, it's important to her, let's do something about it*, because maybe I'm not always an asshole, maybe I can be a nice guy sometimes, but I should know better than to think anything the nice side of me does could ever be good enough for somebody else.

"So, what, I can't sew worth a damn," I say, pushing past her into the library.

She turns in the doorway, staring at me. "You sewed it? *You* did this?"

"Yeah, so what?"

I sit down in my chair, regarding her as she blinks rapidly, like she suddenly doesn't comprehend English, staring at me like I'm a stranger, like she doesn't know who I am.

"Look, be pissed all you want, Scarlet. Go boo-hoo in a fucking corner, if that's what you want to do, but if you start in on me because I fucked the thing up even more, I'm liable to flip out

49

and give us *all* a reason to cry, so go do that shit somewhere else."

"Seriously?" She gapes at me. "Are you fucking with me, Lorenzo?"

Closing my eyes, I run my hands down my face, muttering, "I wish I was..."

The door slams, and I look up, tensing. She's still standing in the room, still staring at me.

She comes toward me, clutching the bear. "I changed my mind."

"About what?"

"I'm in the mood now."

"What?"

She climbs right onto my lap, forcing her way on the chair, tossing the bear on top of my puzzle on the table as she straddles me. No hesitation, the woman rolls her hips, grinding against me, as she runs her fingers through my thick hair.

I need a haircut. *Desperately.*

It's falling into my face.

Grasping tight to the locks, tugging to the point of pain, Scarlet yanks my head up so I'll look at her.

"How are you so fucking *dense?*" she asks. "You think I'm mad right now? Seriously?"

There are still tears in her eyes. "You look like you might cry."

"Because it's the nicest thing anybody has ever done for me, Lorenzo. You're trying to *fix* things."

I grasp her cheeks, framing her face with my hands, and stare her straight in the eyes, dead serious, as I say, "If you're going to start crying, I need you to *not* do it while you're sitting on my lap."

She lets out a light laugh, grabbing my wrists, pulling my hands away from her face, forcing my arms around her.

"I'm not going to cry," she says, fumbling between us, undoing my pants. "I'm going to show you my appreciation instead."

"You don't have to give pussy to show gratitude," I tell her.

Grievous

"A simple '*thanks*' will suffice."

"I know," she whispers. "*Thank you*. But I *want* to give you pussy to show you I'm grateful, because the way I feel when you're inside of me? There's nothing else like it. You make me feel *alive*."

Those words twist me up, and I want to say something about it... about how I need her to not put so much stock in me and get so damn sentimental... but my cock beats my voice in terms of springing free, and the second she starts stroking me all I can think is '*fuck... fuck... fuck it*'.

Like I'm gonna turn down pussy...

She shifts lace aside to sink down onto me, riding me, no hesitation. Fuck, it feels like *Heaven*. Warm, and wet, and so damn tight wrapped around my cock. I always thought it would get tedious, fucking the same woman over and over, but nothing about Scarlet is ever boring.

Thirty seconds. That's all the time I get before somebody shoves the library door open without knocking. *Son of a bitch.* I'd pull out my gun on principle, as usual, but Scarlet's kind of sitting on it, so I'd have to throw her off first.

That's out of the question.

I look over, seeing my brother in the doorway, just in time for shock to flash across his face as he throws his hands up. "Seriously? How do you like being interrupted? *Huh*?"

"Doesn't bother me," I tell him, but he knows that. My gaze turns to Scarlet, who is still looking at me. "Does it bother you?"

She scoffs, not stopping what she's doing. "I can't count how many times I've been watched."

The door slams closed again about ten seconds later as my brother shouts, "You're both *crazy*!"

"Guess he didn't want to watch, after all," Scarlet says.

I let her stay in control, letting her do what she wants to do. Reaching between us, I rub her clit, getting her off before I finally let loose. Closing my eyes, grunting, I come inside of her. *Fuck*, it feels good, nothing at all between us.

She stops moving after a moment, her forehead resting against mine as she breathes deeply.

51

"You're welcome," I say after a bit of silence.

She laughs, climbing off of my lap.

I tuck myself back away, fastening my pants before shoving up out of the chair.

"So, are you hungry?" I ask as she stares at the bear. "I'm going to make pancakes."

"Uh... sure."

I walk out, letting her pull herself together, and head to the kitchen to find Seven sitting at the table, reading today's newspaper.

Look, I'm going to be honest with you—I forgot the guy was here. He's good at being unassuming. "Your wife cook for you this morning, Seven?"

He glances up at me. "Of course."

Of course.

I get the shit together to cook, and yes, before you ask, I indeed wash my hands. *No pussy juices in the pancakes.* I'm whipping together the batter, tossing some damn chocolate chips in for the hell of it, when Seven speaks again.

"He would've kept something, you know," he says quietly, still flipping through the paper.

"Who?"

"Jones," he says. "He'll have something on Aristov, something incriminating, just in case."

I almost ask how he knows that, but it's a stupid question, and I try to never ask those myself.

Been there, done that.

"A file, maybe pictures, maybe a recording... *something.* And he'll keep it somewhere where Aristov can't get to it. At work, probably... hiding in plain sight. That way if anything ever happened to him, the police would find it. Something that could take down Aristov, so Jones would get the last laugh. Might be beneficial to get our hands on whatever it is."

Movement in the doorway catches my eye. I glance over, seeing Scarlet lurking, listening to our conversation. *Nosey little witch.* Seven looks her way, averting his eyes quickly when he sees her standing there in just a t-shirt and underwear.

She's not even naked and his *allergy* is acting up.

"I saw the file Gabe has on Kassian," she says. "It was on his desk with all the others. I looked through it, but there was nothing worthwhile."

"He'll keep the real goods somewhere else," Seven says. "A desk drawer, a locked box... he had some pictures stashed in his locker on a flash drive last time."

Scarlet's brow furrows. "Last time?"

"Ah, Seven here and Detective Fuckface are old friends," I explain. "We paid him a visit this morning, discovered he's been taking it up the ass from your Russian."

"Wait, *what?* He's working for Kassian?"

"Seems so," I say. "He gave me some bullshit spiel about no proof of a crime, *blah blah blah*, be grateful you're alive, *yadda yadda yadda*, but hey, it's all good because the kid, she's fine, so *whatever whatever.* I wanted to shoot him in the fucking face, but then I'd have to blame it on Seven, so I kept my cool for his sake."

"I appreciate that, boss," Seven says. "I'm sure you'll have plenty chances later to shoot him."

I start making pancakes, dishing out the batter, as Scarlet wanders away, disappearing.

"I don't think she took that well," Seven says after she's gone. "Maybe you should go talk to her."

"And say *what?*"

"Tell her it'll be okay, that things will work out. Maybe it'll make her feel better."

"The only thing that'll make her feel better, Seven, is having her problem solved, so that's what I'm going to do."

"And then what?"

I flip a pancake before turning to him. "And then she gets the bullshit fairy tale life she wants with her daughter."

"And you?"

I laugh dryly. "And I might *finally* get to finish my fucking puzzle."

4

More months.

More weeks.

More days.

So many hours.

The little girl couldn't count so high, even though the Cowardly Lion still tried to make her learn all the time. She didn't talk much, doing as she was told, eating her porridge and using her words. She didn't cry anymore, like she'd used up all her tears, and she faced the Tin Man whenever he was around, because she didn't want him to scare her.

Face your fears and wipe your tears.

She remembered those words, even though she didn't hear them anymore in her mind. She couldn't hear her mother's voice, no matter how hard she tried.

Money scattered along the bar top as the Cowardly Lion emptied his pocket, dropping it all in front of the little girl. She caught a silver coin before it rolled away, shoving it back onto the pile.

"Well?" He sat down across from her. "What is it?"

The dice game got too easy for her, he claimed, so now she added up his money every day. Most days it was dollars and quarters, but some days it was more colorful paper. *Funny money*, she called it.

This day was a mixture.

It was going to be *hard*.

She started sorting it into piles, the stuff she knew and then everything else. She picked up one of the bills—a red colored one—and her eyes widened at the big number. "Whoa! What is this?"

"Five-thousand," he said.

"Five-thousand *dollars*?"

"No, it's more like eighty dollars."

"But why's it say a five and the zeroes?"

"Rubles."

"What?"

"It's rubles."

"Like rubies?"

He laughed at that as footsteps headed into the kitchen where they sat. The Tin Man. He was carrying something, but the little girl didn't look, minding her own business so she didn't set him off.

"*Pindos*," the Cowardly Lion said, motioning toward her. "I swear it, *Vor*, she's *so* American, just like that mother of hers."

The Tin Man didn't respond to that as he shoved in at the bar beside him, across from the little girl, setting something down beside the money she was counting. Curious, she peeked at it, her eyes widening as he tore the top off of a plastic container that held what looked *a lot* like it could be cake. "What's that?"

"What does it look like?"

"Cake," she said.

"*Medovik*," the Tin Man said. "Honey cake."

"What's it for?"

"Your birthday."

The little girl watched him with surprise as he pulled out some candles, shoving them through the top layer of the crumbly tan-colored cake. It didn't look like the birthday cakes she saw before, but it was still cake, and *that* mattered. "My birthday?"

"It is your birthday today."

Her brow furrowed. How could that be? She thought her birthday came before Christmas. Was it already almost another year *again*? "How do you know?"

"Because I was there when it happened," he said with a laugh. "How do you *not* know?"

She shrugged. "I don't know what day it is."

He lit the candles. "Make your wish."

"Are you going to sing?"

"No."

"I'll sing," the Cowardly Lion chimed in before launching into a raunchy song, loud and vulgar.

"That's not the right song," she said, reaching across the bar and slapping her hand over his mouth, trying to stop him. "Don't sing that!"

He laughed, pulling her hand away, still singing.

"Enough," the Tin Man said, silencing him with that simple word. "Blow out the candles, kitten."

She looked at the flickering candles, sighing. *I want to go home, with Mommy and Buster.* It was the only thing she wanted.

She blew hard, extinguishing them all with one breath. The Tin Man plucked the candles back out, tossing them in the trash before walking away.

As soon as he was gone, Cowardly Lion grabbed a pair of forks, tossing one to her as he pulled the cake closer. He took a bite right out of the container, shoving his mouth full. "Well, what are you waiting for? Eat up!"

The little girl hauled herself up onto the bar again and took a bite of cake. It wasn't so sweet, and it didn't really have frosting, but it tasted *a lot* better than everything else he made her eat.

She sat there, with the Cowardly Lion, tearing the cake apart, stuffing themselves full of it, leaving none for anyone else.

"Do you think Daddy wanted some?" she asked, crumbs *covering* her.

"No," he replied. "He doesn't like sweet things... not even his women, *especially* your mother."

He laughed at his own joke, but she just made a face at him as she tossed her fork down. Sometimes he could be nice, but other times he said mean things the little girl didn't like.

"Ah, don't look at me that way," he said, putting his hand on her face and playfully pushing her. "I only speak the truth."

"Why are you here?" she asked, snatching his hand away.

"You're always here."

"Why are *you* here?"

"Because he's my daddy. He makes me be here."

"Yeah, well, he's my brother," he said. "And he kind of makes me, too."

The Cowardly Lion started collecting his things as she gasped. "Does that mean you're my family?"

"I'm afraid so," he said, shoving his money in his pocket before handing her the red 5000 bill. "Happy birthday, sweet Sasha... although, just between us, your birthday was months ago. I just told him it was today so you could make another wish."

He strolled out, leaving her there, clutching the money and utterly confused, covered in cake.

5

Morgan

Sasha would've liked chocolate chips in her pancakes.

That's what I'm thinking, as I sit at the kitchen table beside Lorenzo, slowly chewing a small bite. I've never made pancakes from scratch. Hell, I've never made *anything* from scratch. I wish I would've at least tried before, though.

Sasha would've eaten them every morning, if she could've, and I know, without a doubt, she would love Lorenzo's pancakes.

I wonder if Kassian has made them for her.

I wonder what Kassian is making her.

I wonder if Kassian is even feeding her.

All day, every day, it's in the back of my mind.

Is she eating?

Is she sleeping?

Is she breathing?

Will we make it through this?

Will I ever see her again?

Will she still remember me?

I get lost in my head, drowning in those thoughts, forcing down bites, so consumed by these torturous unanswered questions that I almost don't hear the words spoken from across the table.

"I'm moving out."

Blinking a few times, pulling myself out of my stupor, I glance over at Leo and wonder if I'm imagining things, because *whoa...*

Leo stares down at his plate, at his untouched breakfast. He looks *nervous*.

"What did you just say?" Lorenzo asks, his tone clipped.

"I'm moving out," Leo says again.

"The hell you are," Lorenzo says, dropping his fork with a clang. "You're not going anywhere."

"I am," Leo says. "Mel and I, we're going to get a place together. Our *own* place. We've been talking about it for a while, and well, I think it's time."

"You think it's time, do you?"

"Yes."

"And how are you going to do that, huh? How are you going to *afford* that?"

"I've got my job," Leo says. "I can pick up extra shifts, if I need to, but I've got some money saved up. And Mel, she's about to graduate, so she'll be getting a job soon, which means there's no reason we can't—"

Before Leo can finish, Lorenzo slams his hands against the table, the loud bang echoing through the kitchen, rattling plates and knocking drinks over. "There are plenty of reasons why you can't. Do you need me to fucking *name* them for you, Leonardo?"

A strained, painful silence swells through the room. Nobody moves. Nobody speaks. Hell, I don't know if anyone is even *breathing*. Lorenzo glares across the table at his little brother... a brother whose name he just used. I've never heard him do that before. The sound of it is downright chilling.

I shiver.

"I should go," Melody whispers, rubbing Leo's arm as she stands up from the chair beside him. "I'll let you guys talk."

"We should all probably do that," Seven says from where he lurks across the room. "Morgan?"

I glance at him when he says my name, watching as he walks out of the kitchen, realizing he's pretty much telling me to get my ass up and leave, too. My gaze flickers around the room, landing on Lorenzo, who looks seconds away from flipping the table over. *Shit.*

I get up without a word and walk out of the kitchen, barely making it into the hallway when chaos erupts. I head toward the library, where Seven stands in the doorway, looking worried as he stares back at the kitchen.

"What are the odds that ends well?" I ask.

"Depends."

"On what?"

"On who you want it to end well for."

I think about that for a moment, as Lorenzo's furious voice echoes out from the kitchen, followed by Leo shouting right back.

"What are the odds it ends well for *anyone?*"

"Not very good," Seven admits, turning to me. "I should head home. Take care, Morgan."

He walks away, heading for the front door, as I go into the library. Buster lays on the table, surrounded by a scattering of needles and thread. He bought a sewing kit. *Unbelievable.* Shaking my head, I pick up the bear, running my fingers along the rough knotted stitches on its side and chest.

Grabbing a needle, I carefully thread it, tucking what remains of Buster's damaged ear in before doing my best to sew it closed so no more stuffing escapes. I'm trying to ignore the fighting in the kitchen, but neither guy is holding back.

Even the happiest homes aren't always *happy.*

The angrier they grow, the more uncomfortable it feels, so after a while I snatch up the rest of the sewing kit and take the bear upstairs. Leo's bedroom door is open, Melody sitting on the end of the bed, listening to the sounds from downstairs.

Look, I know I'm not any older than her, but I've been through so much that it feels like I've got a few lifetimes under my belt. When I look at Melody, I very much see a *kid*, one who has spent her life sheltered from the world, and at the moment, she looks scared.

It stirs up the mother in me, the woman who taught her little girl to face her fears. Monsters are real, but they only really have power if you let yourself be *afraid.*

"It'll be okay, you know," I say, stalling in front of the bedroom, capturing Melody's attention.

She sighs. "I hope so."

"It will," I say. "No matter what."

"Leo knew he wouldn't take it well," she says. "That's why he hasn't brought it up until now, but I pushed him to... I feel like it's my fault."

"It's not your fault," I tell her. "Leo's allowed to have his own life, so don't feel guilty. Lorenzo's just..."

"Insane," Melody mutters.

I laugh. "Well, yeah, but mostly he's just worried. He'll calm down."

"You sure about that?"

"Pretty sure," I say. "He might not *like* it, but he'll deal with it."

She smiles when I say that, but it doesn't last long, as a loud noise echoes through the house, the sound of something banging, things clattering.

Yep, flipped the table over.

Bye-bye, pancakes.

Melody looks worried again, but I laugh lightly, turning away. "Of course, he has to throw his little temper tantrum first, but it'll all work out in the end."

I head to Lorenzo's bedroom, making my way into his bathroom, searching drawers and cabinets for a first aid kit. He *at least* should have one of those, right? He might not give himself stitches, but he ought to have bandages. I manage to dig up a roll of gauze and take it into the bedroom, sitting down on the bed to finishing fixing up the bear. I wrap the gauze around his burned leg, covering it like a makeshift cast, and stitch a line of thread along the edge of it to secure it to the bear.

I hear stomping on the stairs eventually before Leo's bedroom door slams, followed moments later by another set of footsteps. I listen as they hesitate at the top of the stairs, like he's deciding where to go or what to do, whether to drop it or keep the fighting going up here.

"Don't do it," I mutter under my breath. "Just let it go."

Lorenzo stands there for an entire minute, debating, before he exhales loudly, almost a frustrated growl, and makes his way to the bedroom where I am. He appears casual, *unruffled*, but I can tell it's all an act.

My heart races, skin tingling when his gaze meets mine. He's teetering on a brink. I know what it's like to detach from reality, to shut down to keep from feelings things. I pity whoever might cross this man if he ever truly lets the coldness consume him. He's clinging to a life raft right now. The moment he says *fuck it* and lets go, everyone's going to drown in the waves he creates because he's not going down alone.

Should that scare me? *Probably.*

Does it? *Nope.*

"I know how you're feeling," I say quietly.

"I'm fine," he says, sounding fine, but I know he isn't. He's so damn far from *fine* there isn't even a word for what this man is.

"I have a kid."

"I'm aware."

"So I know how you're feeling," I say again. "You want to wrap them in bubble wrap and protect them from the world, but you're only human. We can only do so much for them."

"Your kid is what, *four?*"

"Five," I say. "She turned five after he took her."

"Five," he repeats, strolling into the room. "Pretty Boy is in his twenties. And besides, he's not *my* kid."

"True," I say. "Doesn't change how I know you're feeling, though. You raised him. You want to keep him from harm."

"I want him to not be such a fucking fool," Lorenzo says, sitting down beside me.

"He's just hopeful," I say, "and he's in love."

"He's a fucking fool," Lorenzo says, lying back on the bed, covering his face with his forearm.

"It's sweet," I tell him. "Just because you don't want all of that doesn't mean there's no worth to it. And really, lets be real... did you expect him to live with you *forever?* He's grown, and you and him... you're different people. He wants to cuddle and watch rom-coms with his girlfriend. You want to shoot at things and steal couches that were molested by strippers. This was kind of inevitable."

His arm shifts. I can feel his gaze.

I don't look at him, though, only getting a slight glimpse from my peripheral. If what I said pissed him off, he doesn't say a word about it, just staring at me in silence as I tinker with the bear.

After a moment, he reaches out toward me, his hand on my back, gently rubbing it, sending sparks up my spine. I turn, caught off guard by the tender touch, and finally look back at him.

"Are you trying to fuck right now?" I ask. "Because we just had sex, like, an hour ago, before you ruined breakfast."

He laughs, sitting up, his hand leaving my back to instead ruffle my hair. *What the hell?* He pushes up off the bed, strolling toward the bathroom.

"I need to shower," he says. "I smell like pussy."

"You go do that. I'm gonna... do something, I don't know."

"Do whatever you want, Scarlet," he says, which is quickly becoming his favorite sentence—even though he totally regretted it last time he said that. "Just do me a small favor and keep yourself out of trouble, because I'm not in the mood to play *White Knight* right now."

* * *

Kassian used to tell me I was stupid.

So pretty, yet so stupid. That is why you cannot be trusted to make decisions, suka.

How many times had he told me that? How many times had he used those words to justify the brutality he inflicted upon my life?

So many times I lost count.

I never once bought it, never once believed his bullshit, but sitting here at a wooden picnic table on the Coney Island boardwalk, I'm wondering if maybe he was onto something about me.

Stupid. *So stupid.*

I shouldn't be here.

The boardwalk is packed, despite the weather still being cool, the amusement park not far off behind me, so close I can hear the rumbling of the Cyclone and the faint noise of the Wonder Wheel running, excited screams and children laughing and music playing... the sound of *happiness.*

I can still remember the first time I felt it, the first time I saw the lights illuminating the Coney Island night sky and heard the laughter and thought *'this is where I'm meant to be forever'.* Standing right here along this boardwalk, dirty and tired, having no food or money, fourteen years old and on my own.

Still so much a child at heart but looking way too much like a woman on the outside.

Enough to capture *his* attention.

Enough to pique his interest.

The late-July air had been sweltering, a touch of sunburn on my sweat-sticky skin, sand clinging to my legs beneath my cut-off jean shorts. I was thirsty, and hungry, my stomach angrily growling as I walked along, passing vendor after vendor on the boardwalk, the array of smells assaulting me.

I just wanted some food.

"Excuse me, do you have some change you can spare?" I asked, again and again, to people who passed, getting a nickel here, a quarter there, but most offered me nothing more than repulsion. *Get a job. Get out of my face. Fucking scum. Disgusting piece of shit.* The words bounced off of me, never getting under my skin, because I was in the city of dreams.

And dreams? I had plenty of those.

It took more than an hour for me to amass a pocket full of change. I sat against a railing in the darkness, out of the way of the crowd, counting it.

I needed four dollars for a coveted hot dog at *Nathan's.*

I only had a little more than three dollars collected.

Sighing, I shoved the change back away. I tried to be a good person, I *did*, but desperation has a way of bending morals. Lying, cheating, stealing... I hated doing it, but sometimes, I ran out of options, and I had to do what I had to do, blurring the lines. Begging relied on the compassion of others, and I'd learned quite quickly that people weren't always compassionate. I had to look out for myself.

Shadows moved along the boardwalk as I contemplated my next move. A pair of shiny black dress shoes appeared in front of where I sat. Before I could react, a flash of crisp green paper dangled in my face.

I thought it was a dollar... until I saw the zeroes.

A hundred dollar bill.

My eyes darted to the man holding it. He was handsome, almost like a work of art, dark ink coating his fingers and part of his neck, wearing a dark fitted suit, despite the heat.

"Take it," he said, waving the money at me, his foreign accent thick.

"I, uh... I can't." I shake my head. "That's *way* too much money."

He curved an eyebrow. "Too much?"

"I just need like, another dollar. Just enough to buy a hot dog tonight."

He crouched down, still holding the money. "What will you do tomorrow? And the next day?"

I shrugged. "Same thing I did today."

"But you will not take my money?"

"No."

He laughed, like that amused him, before standing back up. "Come on, I will buy you that hot dog you want, pretty girl, and I will not take no for an answer."

Right there. *Right there.* Just a few feet from where I sit right now. Kassian Aristov had watched me for over an hour as I begged for change, hungry, before he waltzed into my world and took over my life.

He told me once it was my tenacity that intrigued him. I was steadfast, determined to take care of myself, and that got him curious.

He knew, right then, that I would be his. He wanted nothing more than to break me.

"Excuse me, is someone sitting here?"

I look up at the sound of the male voice... New York accent, *thank God.* A man stands there—dark hair, light eyes, five o'clock shadow along his jawline. There's a little girl with him, clutching hold of his hand. Four, maybe five years old, with bright eyes and a big smile, her dark hair French braided.

"No," I say quietly, offering a smile. "Help yourself."

"Thank you," he says as they sit down across from me at the picnic table, settling in with hot dogs and an order of cheese fries with two forks.

"Daddy, look!" the little girl says excitedly, grabbing the sleeve of his shirt and tugging on it as she looks past me, toward the rides. "Look at those things going all round and round still!"

He laughs. "I know, Jenny. I see. We need to eat now, so we can get home. We'll come back another time, I promise."

The little girl is too excited to eat, rambling on and on about the amusement park, climbing all over the table, giving her father a hell of a time. She's not careful at one point, waving her arms all around, smacking her drink over and sending it spilling across the picnic table, splashing me with it.

"Jesus, Jenny, you need to calm down!" the man says, grabbing napkins, trying to clean up the mess, as he shoots me an apologetic look. "I'm so sorry. She got you, didn't she? She's just excited..."

"It's okay," I say quietly, looking at the little girl, who seems to be on the verge of tears. "I've got a daughter. I know how it is."

"Yeah?" He laughs. "How old?"

"Five."

"Ah, so you *do* know how it is."

"I'm six!" the little girl chimed in.

"Wow, *six?*" I feign shock. "I bet that means you can count pretty high, huh?"

"To a hundred!" she exclaims. "You wanna hear me do it? I can!"

I'm about to say yes, because you don't turn down a proposition like that, when her father chimes in. "As much as we'd *all* love to hear it, baby, we've got to get going."

"Next time," the little girl tells me, nodding. "I'll do it when we come back because Daddy said we would!"

I give her a smile. "Make sure you practice."

"I will," she says.

Her father shoots me a look that says he might not be too fond of my suggestion, like maybe she already *practices* too much, but I don't feel bad for him, not at all.

He doesn't know how lucky he is.

He doesn't know how good he's got it.

What I wouldn't give to live in a house again swaddled with the incessant chatter of a little girl who just wants you to share in her excitement...

I sit here after they're gone. Others come and go, resting for a bit before moving on, a few people politely greeting me but for the most part, I'm left alone. Six o'clock approaches, the beach closing.

Getting up, shoving my hands in my hoodie pockets, I keep my head down as I head down the boardwalk. It's only a few blocks to the police precinct, darkness falling by the time I reach it. *Shift change.* Officer Rimmel, who usually works the front desk, is walking out, a young guy sitting there instead, one I've never encountered.

I always come in the mornings.

I've never been here at this hour.

"Hey there," I say, smiling sweetly, trying to turn on the charm. "Any chance Detective Jones is still in the building? I meant to stop by earlier, and well, I got a little caught up with things and just made it."

"I'm not sure," he says, picking up the phone. "I can call up to his office. Who should I tell him is here?"

"I, uh... Scarlet." *Shit.* "Any chance I can just run up there quick? It'll only take a moment. It's sort of a surprise, if you know what I mean."

Gabe's antics are notorious. Even a front desk rookie would know all about the way he is with female visitors. The officer hesitates before hanging up the phone, scowling and motioning toward the elevators. "Go ahead."

I don't linger, not wanting him to change his mind, hitting

the elevator and heading straight up to the third floor. Gabe is locking up his office to leave when I get there, and I watch, following him to the locker room on the floor.

I slip inside behind him.

His locker's in the far back, tucked away in the corner. He approaches it, starting to undo the combination lock as I creep closer. He turns the knob, glancing back, a look flashing across his face when he spots me. My stomach drops at the sight of it. Anger. *Hunger.* Something I don't like. There's a sinister twinkle in his eyes. He doesn't raise any alarms, though, continuing what he's doing, taking the lock off to open his locker.

It's a fucking *mess* in there.

"Well, if it isn't Miss Myers," he says, his eyes flickering all around me. "You alone?"

"Of course," I say. "Thought I'd catch you before you left. I felt bad about how I acted last time, bad about how we left things."

He's so easy. That's all it takes. I can see the distrust in his eyes, but he's not going to pass up an opportunity if he thinks one might exist. As soon as I'm within reach, he grabs ahold of me, dragging me closer. I wrap my arms around him, grimacing when he buries his face in my neck, kissing and biting at the skin.

Ugh. Ugh. Ugh.

I know, I know... *ugh... look away.*

"Where's your little attack dog?" he asks, a bitter bite to his voice. "You know, the mutt you sent here to threaten me this morning?"

"Who?"

"Scar," he says—although not long ago he claimed to have never heard of anybody called that. "Tell me you haven't taken up with that guy, Morgan. I told you—"

"Anyone named *Scar* is trouble, I know," I say. "He's got his own motivations, though. It has nothing to do with *me.*"

"Sure seemed to," he says. "Told me he'd cut off my dick if I ever touched you again."

My eyes widen. *He said that?*

Gabe pulls back some to look at me, his hands roaming. It

makes my skin crawl, and I ball my hands into fists, keeping myself from punching him.

"Doesn't matter," Gabe says, grinning. "Kassian... Scar... doesn't matter who *thinks* they own you. Won't ever stop us. Isn't that right?"

"Right," I whisper when he turns me around, shoving me against the row of lockers as he fumbles with his pants. *Fuck. Fuck. Fuck.* My heart races as I panic, my body shaking, wedged between him and the cold metal. "Wait... Gabe, wait... *condom.*"

He sighs, reaching past me, shifting things aside in his locker but coming up empty. "Damnit."

"Don't you have some in your office?"

"Yes, but—"

"Just go grab one."

He groans, pushing away and saying, "Wait here."

My stomach twists as he walks away, leaving me here alone. The second he's out of sight, I dive right for his locker, knowing I've only got like thirty seconds until he gets back and then I'm fucked.

Figuratively. Maybe literally, at the rate I'm going.

I'd rather *neither* way happen, to be honest.

So I grab stuff, sorting through it, looking for anything that might be *something*, but it all seems to be nothing. No files, no papers, no journals, no flash drives. *Shit.* I'm about to give up, on the verge of panicking, when my hand hits something wedged along the back at the bottom.

A DVD.

I yank it out, heart racing. It's tucked into a worn protective sleeve, a lone word written on the front of it in faded black marker: *Aristov.*

"Thank you God, and Jesus, and even fucking Krampus," I mumble, shoving the DVD in my hoodie pocket, gripping it tightly as I scurry away.

I get to the door of the locker room just as it swings open. *Gabe.*

"Whoa, where are you running off to?" he asks, grabbing my

arm to stop me. "Come here."

"I can't do this," I say, trying to pull away. "I'm sorry, I just... I can't do it. I thought I could, but I can't, so I'm just going to go now."

"What?" He grips tighter to my arm. "What are you talking about?"

"*This*," I say, shoving away from him. "Don't touch me. I told you before... don't *ever* touch me again."

"What the fuck? What the hell is wrong with you?"

"I'm sorry."

I find part of me means those words. God knows I probably shouldn't. I shouldn't be *sorry* about anything, especially if he is working for Kassian, and this DVD in my pocket is certainly suggesting that might really be what's happening.

But still... I'm sorry.

I'm sorry for whatever led us to this moment.

I used to believe in him, and the sorry part of me still thinks part of him might be *good*.

But it is what it is, and I can't stick around here, so I shove out of the locker room to get away from the precinct... *fast*. I've got probably about a minute before Gabe figures out what I'm up to.

I don't have time to wait on the elevator, so I head for the stairs, scaling them as fast as my legs will carry me down to the first floor of the building.

I almost make it out, am already past the desk officer, when Gabe's frantic voice rings out from the stairwell. "Stop her!"

Shit.

I run, shoving past people. I can hear others following, shouting for me to stop, but I keep going, out of the precinct and down the block, away from the subway, running into the first alley I come across.

They're right on my heels.

Shit. Shit.

Looking around, frantic, my mind works fast. I could hide, but they'd find me. I could run, but they'd catch up. My gaze shifts toward the nearby dumpster. *Ugh.* Heart racing, I yank the DVD out and fling it beneath the dumpster, turning away from it just as somebody rounds the corner.

Shit. Shit. Shit.

Officers appear, my hands are in the air, and I don't know what's happening, but guns are in my face out of nowhere.

Guns.

Okay, it's not the first time someone has aimed a gun at me, and being as my life has gone to hell, I'm guessing it probably won't be the last time, either. But right now there are three of them, and they're kind of looking like they might want to shoot.

Gabe shoves past them, into the alley, and comes right for me, breathing heavily, his face bright red. Oh, man, he's *pissed.* Instinctively, I take a step back, my hands faltering, until the officers start shouting, "Don't you fucking move!"

"Okay, okay!" I freeze. "Geez, relax."

Gabe grabs ahold of me, roughing me up as he pats me down, searching places his hands ought not go, before he shoves me against the side of a nearby building, slamming my face into the bricks so hard my vision blurs.

"Geez, detective." I cringe as he yanks my arm behind my back, standing flush against my body, pinning me there. "I'm pretty sure this breaks protocol."

"Where is it?" he asks, his free hand still searching. "Where'd you put it, Morgan?"

"I don't know what you're talking about."

"Don't play stupid with me," he growls. "I swear, if you don't give it to me *right now*—"

"You'll what?" I ask, cutting him off. "You'll fuck me right here, in the alley, in front of these officers? Teach me a lesson? Show the world what a big, powerful man you are?"

"No," he whispers, his mouth near my ear. "I'll call Aristov so he can come pick his little runaway up... just like I did with your daughter when she found her way to my office last month."

Those words knock the breath from my lungs.

Or maybe it's the fact that he shoves me harder against the building.

I nearly black out.

"You wouldn't," I say. "Tell me you *didn't...*"

"Oh, but I *did*," he says. "She ran away from him, crying about how she wanted her mommy. You missed her by about ten minutes that morning. Pity, really, since that's probably the closest you'll ever get to her again, you dumb *bitch*."

Something in me snaps when he says that, my last shred of civility toward this man gone.

I'm not sorry anymore.

I shove off of the wall, throwing my head back, slamming him right in the fucking nose with the back of my skull.

BAM.

He loosens his grip on me, grunting, caught off guard by the blow, and I twist my own arm, damn near yanking it out of socket to get away from him. He pulls himself back together, but not fast enough, because I raise my foot up and kick him right in the nuts.

BAM.

He hunches over, letting out one hell of a screech, as I shove him out of my way, barely making it three steps before reality slams into me.

Guns, remember?

Oh, fuck me...

I put my hands up again, surrendering, but it's too late to go peacefully. Someone tackles me, throwing me face-first to the alley, knees in my back as handcuffs secure my wrists. My cheek stings, asphalt scraping the skin on my face, guns still aimed at me as men shout orders I can't possibly comply with since I'm pinned to the ground.

I'm yanked to my feet after a moment and come face-to-face with Gabe. Blood pours from his nose, his face contorted with a mix of anger and pain, but he doesn't feel even an ounce of the hurt I feel.

Fuck him.

"Book her," he says, staring me dead in the face as he tries to stop the bleeding. "*Assault on a police officer.*"

73

* * *

The arrest process is bullshit.

I answer what I have to, but I have the right to remain silent, so screw the rest of their questions.

I'm not in the mood to talk.

They transfer me to Central Booking in another part of the borough, where I'm moved from cell to cell, from place to place, in a piss-scented building filled with a lot of nosey-ass people.

Hours.

So many hours.

Signs posted everywhere guarantee the process will be over within twenty-four hours, but as I surpass hour twenty-three, I start to think the signs are lying to me.

Finally... fucking *finally*... I'm allowed to make a call, dragged to a room by a disgruntled officer and shoved in front of a phone.

My charge doesn't seem to elicit friendliness from their kind, that's for sure.

"You get three calls," the officer says, glaring at me. "Make them quick."

There's really only *one* number I can think to call.

I dial it once. *No answer.*

I dial it twice. *No answer.*

So I try for a third time, thinking I'm out of luck. Either it's coming up blocked on his caller ID, or he recognizes the number and doesn't accept jailhouse calls. It rings and rings and rings, and I frown, about to give up when the line clicks and his voice cuts on, annoyance in every syllable. "*Gambi—*"

"Don't talk," I say, cutting him off. "I'm being recorded. There's a big sign right above the phone that says so. So I wouldn't have called, but I kind of needed to, okay?"

He says nothing, but I know he's listening.

Or well, he hasn't hung up yet, so I know he's still there—pretending to listen, at least.

"I went on sabbatical to my favorite precinct and got arrested in the alley near it. I'm going to be arraigned tomorrow sometime. But really, that's beside the point. I just..." *Shit*, how do I say this without giving up the goods? "Remember the time at my apartment where we went falling off the roof of the building and I played a bit of Hide & Seek? My hiding spot was so good they didn't find me, but you did... you found me easily. I was hoping to play again, you know, if you want to go do some seeking, same basic spot this time."

He's still quiet.

I don't know if he understands.

I don't know if I'm making sense.

But I can't just say 'look at the fucking dumpster beside the precinct' because who knows who else is listening and might go look themselves?

"I got you," he says after a moment, his voice low.

"You got me?"

"I got you."

He hangs up without another word.

I don't know if he's got me, really, but I'm hoping like hell he does. Hanging up, I look at the officer, who watches me curiously, like I'm speaking in riddles and he's trying to crack the code.

"So, any idea when I'm getting out of here?" I ask, motioning to one of those 'twenty-four hours' posters. "Pretty sure time's up."

"Time's up when we say it's up," he says. "We can hold your ass here for as long as we want... especially if we *misplace* your paperwork."

"Ah, so you're one of *those*..."

His eyes narrow. "One of *what*?"

"Those big guys that get off on picking on women. What, your mommy didn't love you enough, so you've gotta take it out on us?"

He looks like he wants to punch me, but being as there are cameras everywhere, he can't. Instead, he roughly grabs my arm and drags me back to a holding cell, whispering, "you should probably get comfortable," before shoving me in.

More hours.

So many more hours.

I doze off, lying on the filthy concrete floor, but it doesn't bother me much, considering I used to live on the streets. Do you know how many nights I slept on the cold ground when I was fourteen?

Pffft, that's nothing.

Do you know how many days I survived chained up in a basement?

I'm eventually woken, taken to yet another cell. Time passes, almost another entire day, before someone shouts my name. "Morgan Myers!"

"Showtime," I mutter, staggering off to a little room, where I see a bald guy behind plexiglass with a file on me. *Public defender.*

"They're offering a deal: plead guilty to misdemeanor disturbing the peace and you walk right out of here a free woman, the rest of the charges dropped."

"Wait, what? What other charges?"

The man rattles off a whole host of offenses, like they're trying to nail me for every teeny-tiny infraction they could possibly think of.

"Okay, wait... so what if I don't *want* those charges dropped?"

He looks at me like I'm crazy. "You'll probably end up in Rikers for years."

Ugh, don't want that, either, but I'm not sure just walking out of here is something that's possible. I've been stationary for too long under my real name, which means Kassian has had forty-eight hours to sniff out my very public location.

And my suspicion is confirmed a few minutes later when I'm ushered into the courtroom and see him.

Him.

I come to a halt.

My feet won't move anymore, cementing right into the floor. *Shit.* Kassian stands in the back corner, dressed impeccably in a dark suit. I've heard his voice, and I've breathed his same air, but this is the first time, in so many months, that the two of us have come face-to-face. The first time I've looked at him the same time he was looking at me, our eyes meeting for no more than a few seconds, but it feels like an eternity.

I'm pulled away, forced to keep going, and avert my gaze as I'm lead to the front of the courtroom.

The District Attorney and the judge exchange words, but I'm not paying them much attention. I keep glancing over my shoulder, toward the back corner. I can't help myself.

Kassian isn't smiling. He isn't laughing.

He just stares at me, his expression a blank mask.

"Miss Myers?"

I turn to the judge when he calls my name. "Yes?"

"You need to plead on the charge of disorderly conduct."

"Oh." I hesitate. "Guilty."

He says something else. I don't know. My ears feel clogged, everything foggy as my heart crazily pounds. I glance behind me again, stalling this time when I find back corner empty.

Kassian is gone.

The judge is still talking but all I keep thinking is Kassian is here somewhere, lurking in the shadows, waiting to pounce.

"Miss Myers is hereby ordered to be held for pick-up by the seventeenth precinct..."

Whoa.

I look at the judge, confused, before turning to the public defender. "What?"

"You have an outstanding warrant," he says.

That only confuses me more. "A warrant? For *what?*"

He shrugs.

The man *shrugs.*

Like he doesn't give a shit at all.

I raise my hand, trying to get the judge's attention before he can bang his gavel.

"Put your hand down," the public defender hisses. "He'll hold you in contempt if you disrupt his proceedings."

I ignore that, because really, at least *those* charges would make sense. The seventeenth precinct is in Midtown, Manhattan. There's *no* reason for me to have charges there.

"Excuse me?" I call out. "Your honor?"

The judge looks at me.

Man, he looks like he'd like to smack *me* with the gavel, but instead he says, "Yes, Miss Myers?"

"A warrant?" I ask. "What kind of warrant?"

"Conspiracy," he answers.

That's it.

Conspiracy.

"What kind of conspiracy?" I ask, but it doesn't matter, because the man bangs his gavel and I'm dragged away.

Hauled back to another holding cell to wait again.

Back to being watched by the disgruntled officer, who personally seems to be monitoring me, a fact that isn't really surprising.

He's probably on somebody's payroll.

A hundred bucks says it's Kassian's.

"So, any chance you know what a 'conspiracy' charge is?" I ask him.

"It means you conspired to do something."

"Well... no shit. But *what?*"

He shrugs.

Another shrugger.

Awesome.

It's only an hour this time before someone comes for me, two men in plainclothes, only their badges giving them away as officers. Big, and built, the rough-and-tumble types. The officer that had been watching me steps back, letting out a low whistle. "The violent felony squad, huh? Must be a doozy."

My stomach is in knots as a sinking feeling consumes me. None of this ever felt right, but this without a doubt is *wrong*. These guys hunt down the bloodthirsty murderers. I've never even fired a gun.

Although, okay, I probably would, if I had one.

But I don't, so I haven't.

Which means there's no reason for them to come for *me*.

I'm handcuffed and shackled, like a hardened criminal, before being led out of the back of the building, where inmates are loaded up to be taken over to Rikers. An older white man in a gray suit lingers in the darkness, casual as can be, waiting beside an unmarked Crown Vic, a black SUV parked right behind it at an angle, blocking my view of the exit of the underground garage.

The man in the suit opens the back door of the car, and I'm immediately shoved into it, the door slammed. It's like a little prison, a cage separating me from the front, the windows all obscured.

"We'll follow, just in case," one of the plainclothes says. "Any problems, radio us."

"You know I will," the man in the suit says.

The man climbs behind the wheel and pulls out of the garage, not saying a word to me at all. It's nighttime, well past sunset, maybe even pushing midnight. It's hard to tell. I look around, glancing behind me, seeing the SUV is, in fact, following.

"Is all of this really necessary?" I ask, my shackles jingling as I turn back to the man in the suit, glaring at him through the bars of the cage.

He glances in the rearview mirror. "You broke a detective's nose two days ago, did you not?"

"His nose is *broken*?"

"Yes."

"Huh." I'm pleasantly surprised. "Well, I mean, in my defense, he deserved it... off record, of course. You can't *double jeopardy* that, right? Wait, shit, that's not the *Conspiracy* charge, is it? Is this like some special prosecutor thing, making an example out of me for assaulting your prized detective?"

The man laughs. "I have no interest in seeing you prosecuted."

Those words rub me wrong. "What, exactly, *are* you interested in doing?"

"Just delivering you where you need to go."

My heart races so hard my chest starts to hurt. I look out the windows at the neighborhood around us, but it's hard to see much of anything. I know we're not in the city, though. We haven't crossed a bridge, but we should've by now, I think, so we're still deep in Brooklyn.

"Oh, *fuck me*," I mutter, leaning forward, smacking my head against the cage. He's delivering me somewhere, but it sure as hell doesn't seem to be Midtown for a warrant.

"What did you say?" the man in the suit asks.

I look up, meeting his eyes in the rearview mirror. "You know he's a terrible person, right?"

His brow furrows. "Who?"

"The asshole you're taking me to."

A look of surprise passes across his face. "How do you know—?"

"Oh, give me a break," I say, cutting him off. "Contrary to popular belief, I'm not stupid. Give me some credit here, *officer.*"

"Detective," he corrects me.

"Detective. Of course. Well, detective, you're not the only one that can *detect* shit, you know, and I'm detecting this little field trip we're taking isn't to the seventeenth precinct for a *Conspiracy* warrant."

"You'd be correct," he says.

"So you're going to take me to him instead, huh? How much is he paying you? Whatever it is, I'll double it. *Triple* it. Just let me out right here and the money is yours."

"Nice try, but no."

"Why?"

"Because he'll kill me if I don't come through."

"Yeah, well, he'll kill *me* if you do."

He laughs at that. *Laughs.* "He's not going to kill you... or, well, I don't think so. I hope not. He said he wouldn't, anyway. I told him I wasn't getting involved if this was leading to a murder."

I sigh, exasperated, as I lean back in the seat, trying to wiggle out of the handcuffs but they're too tight, cutting into my wrists.

The SUV is still right behind us, riding our bumper.

There's a crackling then, the sound of a radio, but not the

police radio, no… a fucking Walkie-Talkie.

They're talking off the airwaves. *Of course.*

"We've had a car tailing us for a few minutes," a voice cuts in. "Could be a coincidence, but we're going to double back and run a traffic stop, to be safe."

"10-4," the detective says. "We're almost there. Meet at the spot."

Almost there.

That means I'm running out of time. I need to figure out something fast. The SUV backs off, and I can see lights flashing, but before I can get a good look at what's happening, we make a sharp turn.

Then another.

And another.

A few turns later and we're whipping into an old parking garage. We follow the arrows, going round and round and round, making our way to the very top. The unmarked Crown Vic pulls onto the roof, the cars growing scarcer with each level we navigate. There are none up here *at all.* The car creeps along the empty spaces, coming to a stop somewhere along the edge of the space where there are no lights.

I'm guessing no cameras, either.

No witnesses.

As the detective puts the car in park, a thought passes through my mind, something I couldn't bring myself to entertain until that moment.

Sickness swells up inside of me.

A lump forms in my throat.

He said he was delivering me where I'm meant to be, but what if where I'm meant to be is… *dead?*

Before I can even wrap my head around that possibility, lights flash onto the roof, cars approaching. *Cars,* plural. I spot the SUV but the others are a blur. Two more, I think. I can't really tell. My vision is blurring and it's too damn dark.

The detective gets out, no hesitation, and opens up the back door, reaching his hand in. I pull away, shifting along the seat.

"Don't fucking touch me."

I hear doors slam nearby, footsteps approaching. Sighing, the detective reaches further in, snatching ahold of my arm and dragging me out. Panic bubbles up inside of me. He's right there, in the doorway. I've got little range of movement, but more right now than I will have in a few seconds.

Fuck this.

Now or never.

Lying back, I move quickly. As soon as the man reaches for me again, trying to force me from the backseat of the car, I thrust my legs out, my feet slamming against him.

BAM.

He staggers backward, gasping, wide-eyed as he clutches his chest.

I knocked the air right out of his lungs.

I rock myself out of the car, springing to my feet. Shadows move around me. I can't escape them, not while shackled, but I'll be damned if I'm going down without fighting.

Before the detective can catch his breath, I tackle him, knocking him onto his back on the parking deck. I land on top of him with a grunt, and he tries to shove me away, tries to shove me *off*, but I'm not giving up.

I can't punch, can't kick, but hell, I can head-butt, so I slam my forehead right into his face. BAM. All that extra security he brought and I'll *still* break his fucking nose like I did Gabe's. The detective screams, and my vision blurs, the pain echoing through me, so I know *he* has to hurt.

"Jesus, fuck!" a voice calls out as arms wrap around me, tearing me off of him. "I told the guy nobody would die tonight, so don't *kill* him."

That voice rushes through me as I'm set on my feet. I'm dizzy, but I manage to shove away from those arms to turn around, to look at him.

Lorenzo.

"Seriously?" I yell, staring at him with disbelief as he stands in front of me. "This was *you?*"

"Yes," he says, grabbing the detective's hand to help him up. "Why? Who did you think it was?"

I just gape at him.

"Some asshole who wants to kill her," the detective mutters, covering his face with his hands. "At least, that's what she said."

Lorenzo's eyes widen before he lets out a laugh. A laugh. He's *laughing*. What the fuck?

"This isn't funny!" I growl, lunging at him, slamming into him, shoving him back, nearly knocking him down.

His guys, all present, come right at us, like it's an instinctive reaction to protect the boss, but Lorenzo stops them with a raised hand, his other grabbing my hip. "Whoa, stand down, fellas. We're still all friends here. Scarlet's just a little upset. No biggie."

He stares at me, his hand still touching me, his face inches from mine. I kind of want to break *his* nose, too, while I'm at it, because of the amused twinkle in his eyes.

But I can't deny the relief that rushes through me at the realization that I probably won't be thrown off this roof tonight, the realization that someone jumped through hoops to get their hands on me but that someone wasn't Kassian.

Lorenzo saved my ass. *Again.*

"It's still not funny," I say. "I thought he seriously had me."

"I got you," Lorenzo says. "How many times do I have to tell you that before you believe it?"

"Probably a few more times."

"And I thought I told you to stay out of trouble," he says, scolding me. "I even asked *nicely*."

"Yeah, well, the trouble with trouble is that it doesn't always *look* like trouble, Lorenzo."

"This was very obviously trouble, woman."

Woman. He flings that word at me like it's a term of endearment. "Can't help myself, I guess."

He reaches out, pushing the hair from my face, brushing the back of his hand along my tender cheek. He doesn't look angry. He doesn't even really look amused anymore. No, he looks *concerned*. "You look like hell."

"I feel it."

His hand drifts down to my neck, his fingertips stroking a spot there. "Tell me what happened."

"Can you, uh... I don't know... uncuff me first? Remove the shackles, too, maybe?"

Lorenzo pulls his hand away, motioning for someone to help me. One of the officers in plainclothes pulls out a set of keys and removes my restraints. I flex my wrists, rubbing them, relieved to be free. The detective casts me a cautious look as he moves to lean against his car.

He's still breathing kind of funny.

"Is he okay?" I ask, worried he might be having a heart attack or something.

"You okay, Jameson?" Lorenzo calls out.

"Fine," the detective mutters.

"He's fine," Lorenzo says. "Now tell me what happened."

Ugh, I don't want to, but I know I need to tell him, so I just spill the whole shebang, starting with going to Coney Island and faltering when I recount the confrontation in the alley.

Lorenzo absorbs every word, waiting until I grow quiet before he says, "I'm going to kill him."

Matter of fact. Just like that.

I'm going to kill him.

The detective groans. "Really, Gambini? I wish I hadn't heard that."

"Why? You gonna arrest me for it?"

"No, but now I've gotta pretend you never said it."

Lorenzo laughs, turning to the officers, thanking them for their assistance, telling them to get on out of there. He twirls his pointer finger around in the detective's face when the guy pushes away from the side of the car to climb in it. "Send me a bill for the nose, Jameson."

"You know I will," the detective says. *Oops.*

The Crown Vic drives off, followed by the SUV, leaving me here with just Lorenzo and his guys, who seem to be watching me warily for some reason. Even Seven is more tense than usual, off to the side, sort of behind Lorenzo. *Standoffish.*

I'm not sure what to make of it.

"Seven, I need you to find Detective Fuckface," Lorenzo says. "I want his address. I want his *mother's* address."

"Yes, boss," Seven says.

"The rest of you... I want you on Aristov. I want to know where he goes, what he does, and who he talks to. I know where he lives, and I know where he works, but I want to know everything else the man does. You got me?"

They murmur in agreement.

"Good, get out of here," Lorenzo says. "Report back when you've got something."

The guys disperse without another word, piling into the cars and leaving us here all alone, up on the roof of the parking garage with no car.

Lorenzo reaches into his back pocket once they're gone, pulling something out and holding it up.

The DVD I tossed under the dumpster, Aristov written on it in faded black marker.

"You found it?"

"I did," he says. "Took me a minute to riddle out what you were babbling about, but I put the pieces together and there it was."

"I wonder what's on it," I say, reaching for the DVD, but Lorenzo pulls it back from my grasp before I can get my hands on it.

"Something you don't want to see."

My stomach sinks. "You've looked?"

He nods once.

"What is it?" I ask. "Tell me."

Lorenzo says nothing for a moment, just staring at me, before carefully holding the DVD out so I can take it this time.

"Watch it, if you feel the need," he says, his voice quiet. "Just don't say I didn't warn you, Scarlet."

6

Lorenzo

I've always preferred getting lost in silence, but people, I've found, like to hear their own voices. *Blah blah blah*, just spewing bullshit; doesn't matter what it is, since nobody hears it.

You see, people don't really listen anymore, no… they just sit around waiting for everyone else to shut up, waiting until it's finally their turn to talk. Back and forth, an endless cycle that gets us nowhere, because nobody really gives a shit about what's being said.

Silence, though… silence speaks in ways that words just can't.

We've been in my library for well over an hour now, just me and Scarlet, the room cast in light from the glow of the lamp. No sound, unless you count the soft whirling fan from the laptop in Scarlet's lap, one she borrowed from Melody.

White noise.

The silence speaks volumes.

I warned her. I told her she didn't want to see, but against my advice, she popped the disc into the drive and looked at the little home movie.

A fucking horror flick, really.

A young Scarlet—maybe sixteen or so—being tormented by the Russians, the men taking turns brutalizing her. A baby cries in the background, screaming bloody murder, but Scarlet doesn't make a sound.

No, she's faded out. *Gone.*

I could barely sit through a minute of it. It turned my fucking stomach, and that's saying something, because I've watched men be slaughtered before without flinching.

What do you say to that? It'll be okay? Chin up, buttercup, at least you're alive? *Fuck that.* Words don't mean shit, they won't erase what's on that DVD, so I just stand here, working on my puzzle, pouring myself into it.

"Boss?"

I look to the doorway. Seven stands there, clutching my phone, waving it toward me.

"The guys are on their way over," he says. "Just wanted to give you the head's up."

"I appreciate it," I say, looking back away. "Any luck on that address yet?"

"Still working on it," he says.

I nod, picking up a puzzle piece, trying it a few more places. Silence again takes over the room when Seven walks away.

"Did they watch it?" Scarlet's words are quiet as she breaks her silence. "The guys... did they see?"

I snap a piece into place before grabbing another. "I didn't let them watch it. I stopped it when I realized what it was."

"But they saw."

"They saw."

She's quiet for another moment before asking, "Did *you* watch it?"

"I didn't pop some fucking popcorn and make a night of it, if that's what you're asking. I saw enough to know that it's not something I care to ever watch happen to you."

"Thank you," she whispers.

I turn, looking at her with disbelief. She sounds genuinely grateful, sure, but there's something else in her tone, a dejected note. I don't like it. That's not the woman I've come to know.

"You're thanking me," I point out, "for not making a movie night out of your borderline *snuff* film. You realize that, right? You're thanking me for not getting off watching you be fucking violated."

"I'm thanking you for being a decent human being."

"I wouldn't go *that* far, Scarlet."

"I would," she says. "Think what you want about yourself, Lorenzo, but there's decency in you."

I scoff, turning back to my puzzle. "I ought to shoot you for saying that shit."

"But you won't."

"I won't," I agree, "because I assured Jameson tonight wouldn't lead to murder."

"How *decent* of you."

Shaking my head, I try my puzzle piece in a few places, forcing it where it doesn't belong, nearly ripping half the puzzle apart as I yank it back off. Frustrated, I throw it down, watching as it bounces onto the floor, and run my hands down my face, pulling my glasses off and tossing them onto the table, too. "I like you more when you don't talk."

She laughs. "I bet you say that to all the girls."

"I do," I say, turning toward her as I lace my hands together on top of my head, surprised she can be *laughing* right now, with the night she's had. "But most of them I don't even like when they're quiet. You, I can tolerate."

"You can tolerate me."

"Yes."

"Well, for the record, I can tolerate you, too, Lorenzo," she says, staring at the laptop screen. "Most guys I know would've watched it."

"I've told you before... you surround yourself with the wrong people."

"Yeah, I'm trying to get better about that," she says. "I think I might've found a few decent ones."

I glare at her but don't respond, hearing noise echo through the house as others arrive. I walk out of the library, leaving Scarlet to whatever she's doing, and meet the guys in the living room. They're riled up. That's what I like most about them, why they've survived so long in my company... they're just as fucked up as *me*. Money, sure, they love it, they want it, but the excitement and adrenaline is priceless. They'd take the chance of a thrill over the promise of a dollar in a heartbeat.

Well, with the exception of Seven, maybe. He's got a wife and kids, remember? He's much more cautious than the others.

"Gentlemen," I say, greeting them as they settle in and secure bottles of rum, noticing right away that somebody is missing. "Where's Three?"

"Ran off to see some woman," Five says. "Said he had to take care of something quick."

"Yeah, his *dick*," Four says with a laugh.

Shaking my head, I sit down on the couch and turn on some music before retrieving a joint from the tin in my pocket. I light it, inhaling deeply, holding it in my lungs, before passing it over to Five as he sits down beside me.

"Always letting pussy get the best of him," I say. "Will he ever learn?"

"Not likely," Five says, taking a hit of the joint before passing it back. "If getting chained up in a basement wasn't enough to stop him from fucking around with those women, nothing short of a bullet to the brain is going to teach him that lesson."

I laugh dryly, taking a deep drag, exhaling slowly as I say, "I could arrange that."

Five casts me a look. He knows I'm dead serious, but he laughs, regardless. "You could."

Seven slides into a chair nearby and clears his throat. "Love is blinding."

"Love is blinding," I say, repeating his sappy ass proverb shit. "And what, Three loves pussy, so it excuses his behavior?"

"Doesn't excuse it, just explains it," Seven says. "Declan's a sucker for a woman in stilettos. He doesn't think straight where they're concerned. We're all knocked off-kilter eventually, and usually what does it is a woman. That's how I ended up married so long ago. Love, it makes us forget ourselves sometimes."

"I'll fucking drink to that," Four says, raising up a bottle of rum.

"Goddamn women," Five says, raising his own bottle. "They're cyanide to the senses."

Shaking my head, I look around at these idiots toasting, my

gaze stalling at the doorway, seeing Scarlet lurking.

"How about you, Scarlet?" I ask as the guys take sips, clinking their bottles together. "You gonna drink to pussy-blindness, too?"

She pushes away from the doorframe, strolling into the room. "Love is a terrible excuse. It's dangerous to lose yourself in someone else."

"Ah, that *I'll* drink to," I say as she slides in front of me, sitting down on the coffee table, her knees touching mine. Five smacks my arm at those words, passing me a bottle of rum, and I take a swig before offering it to Scarlet.

She stares at it for a second before snatching it from my hand, taking a big swallow, enough to make her grimace.

She seems nervous, looking around at the guys... not worried so much as maybe feeling vulnerable. I offer her the joint, which she happily takes, waving her off when she tries to give it back.

"Keep it," I say, retrieving another one from my tin and lighting it. "I've got more."

I kick my feet up, planting them on each side of her on the coffee table, penning her in between my legs. The guys are laughing, joking around, bullshitting, acting like their usual selves, which helps Scarlet relax a bit.

Seems she thought they'd treat her differently, but they won't. They're not like that. I wouldn't let them in my house, around my brother, if I thought they might be the backstabbing variety. They'd seen no more than thirty seconds of the DVD, and it had gotten every single one of them furious beyond words, tense and on edge and ready to kill someone for it.

It doesn't take long before smoke fills the room, my eyes bloodshot, burning, as my muscles tingle. I feel like I'm floating, sky fucking high, a sense of euphoria settling into my chest.

I feel no pain.

It's nice not having a jackhammer going off in my head for once.

Doesn't last long, though.

Headlights flash as a car pulls into the driveway. Seven gets up to look, glancing out the window, saying, "Looks like Declan... and a woman."

And a woman.

Eyes turn to me, awaiting my reaction, but I just sit here, not doing a damn thing yet. Three barrels his way on into the house, dragging a skinny little brunette along with him, red high heels clattering along the floor as she drags her feet. She doesn't look happy to be here. Quite the opposite. He pulls her into the living room, shoving her in front of him. Her terrified gaze skitters around, settling on Scarlet, her dark eyes widening with recognition. *Uh-oh.*

Scarlet averts her gaze, turning her back to the girl, staring down at her hands as she picks at the chipped red polish on her fingernails.

"Fellas," Three says casually, greeting everyone, his attention turning my way. "Boss."

The guys mumble in response.

"Nice of you to join us," I say, studying the woman. "I see you've brought a guest along."

"Yeah, this is, uh... *shit.*" Three snaps his fingers, like he's trying to remember, before giving up and nudging her. "Tell them who you are."

"Alexis," the girl says, her voice shaking.

"That's it! Sexy Lexie..." Three grins, like he's proud of himself for remembering that nickname. "Lexie works down at Limerence. I ended up in a basement because of her."

"I'm sorry," she says right away, looking back at him. "I told you, I—"

"You didn't have a choice," Three says, cutting her off. "Yeah, I know, I heard you."

"I didn't *want* to do it," she says defensively. "I swear I didn't. I like you, Declan. You've always been so nice, but Mr. Aristov—"

"Is your boss," Three says, again cutting her off before he looks at me, raising an eyebrow. "You hear that? She works for the Russian."

"I heard," I say.

"I don't have a choice," she whispers, eyes turning to me.

"We know," Three says, putting his hand on her shoulder. "What Aristov says goes—no *ifs*, *ands*, or *buts* about it, huh? He tells you to fuck someone, you do it, no question. Get on your knees for him? You'll do that, too, like a good little girl. He tells you to put something in somebody's drink, to drug them, and you don't hesitate, huh? You'll do whatever he says. He makes the rules."

The more Three talks, the more the woman looks like she wants to collapse... but she's not the only one. Scarlet tenses, and before the last syllable is even from Three's lips, her voice cuts in. "That's *enough*."

Everyone looks at her.

"That's enough," Scarlet says again. "We get it. Just... leave her alone."

Gazes shift to me, again awaiting my reaction. You see, around here, *I* make the rules, and they don't follow orders unless they come from *my* mouth.

"Get to the point," I say, motioning for Three to continue. "I'm sure you mother taught you not to play with your food."

Three squeezes the woman's shoulder as he leans closer to her, saying, "Tell them what you told me about your boss, Lexie."

The woman opens her mouth before closing it again, over and over.

"Just spit it out, Tweety Bird," I say. "Tell me what the *Puddy-Tat* did."

"He has these parties at his house sometimes, him and the guys that work for him... they get together and some of the girls are brought in, but they don't always come back out. Sometimes... well, *sometimes...*"

"Sometimes they're never seen again?"

She nods, taking a moment, not continuing until Three nudges her once more. "A few months ago, I went to one of his parties. I didn't *want* to, but none of us really do. He's been... different. Colder. And we knew... we *heard* he found Morgan." Her gaze shifts to Scarlet, her voice dropping lower. "They told us he found you, that he killed you. We all thought you were *dead*."

Scarlet's bottom lip trembles, but otherwise, she doesn't react, still not looking at the woman.

"Hey, yo, eyes on me," I say, snapping my finger, getting the woman's attention again. "As much as I'm thrilled by story hour, I need you to get to the point before my high wears off and I stop listening."

"There was a girl there," she blurts out, "a *little* girl. His daughter. She was there. He's been keeping her out of sight, so none of us even knew she was around, but she drew him a picture and she wanted to give it to him, so she snuck downstairs."

"You saw her?"

She nods.

"She was okay?"

She nods again.

I glance at Scarlet, wondering how she's taking this, but she's just sitting, listening in silence, still picking at her fingernails.

"Well, I appreciate you chirping for us, Birdie," I say, looking back at the woman as I sit up, my left hand coming to rest on Scarlet's knee. "*Truly*. It's been enlightening. So thank you."

"You're welcome," she whispers.

"You got anything else you want to share?" I reach into my waistband and pull out my gun, cocking it and aiming it at her. "Any parting words?"

Three jumps back a few steps, moving away, because he knows my aim is shit and if he stands too close, he's liable to get shot. Besides, I think he's still traumatized from being splattered with brain matter last time. The woman tenses as terror rushes through her. I can see it, the horror in her eyes, her body trembling. She doesn't raise her hands, doesn't move, staring straight at me, but the floodgates open. Tears coat her cheeks, words spewing from her lips.

"Please, don't do this," she cries. "Please... I'm *begging* you... you don't have to do this!"

"But I do," I say. "I let you walk out of here, you run back to your boss, and then what? Huh? I'll tell you what—you'll spill your guts."

"I won't," she says. "I swear. I'd *never*. Morgan... please... Morgan, *tell him*."

Scarlet squeezes her eyes shut.

"Boss," Three chimes in as he takes a step back toward the woman. The second he does, I aim the gun at him instead. At least he has the sense to raise his hands. "Maybe you *don't* have to do this..."

"You brought her to my house, Three," I say. "You know better. Maybe I should be shooting *you* for this."

"But maybe you don't have to shoot *anyone*," he says. "She's an *in*. We can use her somehow."

"How?"

Three blanks when I ask that.

Might be the gun pointed at him.

Hard to think while that's happening.

Tick-tock. Tick-tock. Pressure's on, motherfucker.

"Next month," the woman blurts out. "There's another party. I can go. I'll volunteer. I can help you, whatever you need me to do. I'll do it. I *swear*."

"See?" Three says. "Problem solved."

Problem *not* solved, contrary to what he thinks.

He just made it domino into a whole host of other problems for me. Slowly, though, I lower the gun, taking the bullet out of the chamber, my finger leaving the trigger. "Fine."

Three lowers his hands.

"This is on you, though," I warn him. "She fucks me, I fuck you... and I mean that in *every* sense of that word, Three. I will fuck you while *fucking* you, so you better keep an eye on her."

"I will," he says. "Don't worry."

I slip the gun back away, waving him off. "Get her out of my house before I change my mind and kill you both."

"Yes, boss."

He grabs her shoulder, pulling her away, dragging her back out of the house just like he dragged her in. Grabbing the bottle of liquor, I take a big swig before slamming it back down on the coffee table beside Scarlet.

"Well, that was something, huh?" Five asks, shoving to his feet. "We ought to go, too, make sure he's not fucking us all up too much here."

"Yeah, you go do that," I say, scrubbing my hands down my face with frustration. *Pussy-blind.* That's Three, without a doubt. He's going to get himself killed over a woman. "Keep in touch."

The guys filter out, although Seven lingers.

"I'm not sure this is a good idea," Seven says. "This whole thing... it's a big risk. Are you sure this is what you want to do?"

"About as sure as I usually am, Seven."

Which means not sure *at all.*

I'm just making shit up as I go here.

Nodding, like he's not surprised, Seven walks out, leaving Scarlet and I alone. My head is starting to pound again, throbbing building up in my skull behind my eye, colored splotches marring my vision. *Fuck.* Hunching over, elbows on my knees, I lace my hands together at the back of my neck, closing my eyes as I lower my head.

The last thing I need right now is a migraine.

Right away, I feel something, a tingle along my scalp, rugged fingernails scratching as Scarlet's fingers run through my hair, sending a chill down my spine.

I can't help it.

I *moan.*

"Fuck, that feels good."

Scarlet laughs lightly and keeps on doing what she's doing, gently stroking my hair, the sensation damn near putting me to sleep. Voodoo, I swear... I'll never not believe it.

The woman's touch is witchcraft.

It's a sin to give in, but seeing as sinning is my specialty, I let her dark magic consume me, because what do I have to lose? My head? I want to chop the fucking thing off most nights, anyway.

I'm jolted eventually, eyes snapping open, head darting up as noise echoes through the house. I look up, blurry eyes going straight to my brother as he appears in the doorway with his girlfriend. I must've dozed off, maybe just for a second, because the sudden movement makes me dizzy.

I lower my head again, covering my face with my hands as everything starts to spin.

"Hey, Morgan," Leo says. "Haven't seen you in a few days."

Scarlet's hand grips my thigh as she turns around. "Yeah, I was a bit indisposed."

"Good to have you back," he says. "Is, uh... is he okay?"

"Uh, yeah... sure."

"I can answer for myself," I grumble. "I'm right here, you know."

"I'm well aware," Leo says. "Rough night?"

"Rough life," I counter, looking up at him, grateful everything stays still. "I'll survive."

"I'm sure you will," Leo says, frowning, glancing at his little firecracker, who looks extremely nervous right now for some reason.

I sit up straight. "What is it? Spit it out."

Leo hesitates. "We found an apartment."

"You found an apartment."

"Yes, in Manhattan... *Midtown*. It's kind of small, just one bedroom, but it's got a great view. We put in an application. I think we've got a good shot."

He stares at me, like he expects me to have more to say, but seeing as there are more than a million apartments in New York City, this isn't exactly shocking news that they found one, is it?

Any schmuck with a few bucks could find an apartment if he wanted one.

Sighing, I stand up, snatching up the bottle of rum as I move past Scarlet, strolling out of the living room. I pause near the foyer, looking at my little brother... not so *little* anymore, frankly. I've only got about two inches on him and maybe ten pounds, but maturity wise, he surpassed me long ago, with his pretty blonde girlfriend and his bullshit job and now his inky-dinky apartment that probably overlooks Times Square.

"Congratulations," I say, heading for the stairs.

"Seriously, bro? That's all you're going to say?"

"What do you *want* me to say, Pretty Boy? That I hope you're not allergic to cockroaches, because God knows with what *you* make you're probably splitting the fucking rent with thousands of them."

"Ah, yes..." Leo throws his hands up. "*There* it is."

"Rats, too. And fucking *bums*. Good thing Firecracker has had practice with people listening to you *fuck* her every night, so the paper-thin walls and nosey neighbors won't be a problem, huh?"

I start up the stairs, my footsteps heavy, hearing my brother mutter, "I knew you'd have something shitty to say about it."

"Of course you did. Of course I *would*, right? Not like I'm a *decent* person." I laugh dryly. "Only spent the past twenty fucking years taking care of you after your piece-of-shit parents tried to put me in the ground."

He says something in response.

I don't know. I'm not listening anymore.

I make my way to my bedroom, guzzling rum, and slam the bottle on the dresser before falling into the bed on my back. I stare up at the ceiling fan, watching as it goes round and round, hoping it'll lull me to sleep, but I'm tense and wound tight.

I want to kill something.

I want to fuck someone.

I want to fuck someone after I kill something.

"He doesn't deserve that, you know."

Scarlet's voice is matter-of-fact. She's standing in the doorway. I didn't hear her follow me, but I'm not surprised she did.

"What I'm hearing here," I say, "is that I *do* deserve this."

"That's not what I said," she argues, stepping into the room. "You're only *pretending* to listen again."

"I heard you, Scarlet, loud and clear."

"You only heard what you wanted to hear, Lorenzo. You didn't hear what I said."

"I'm reading between the lines."

"No, you're twisting shit," she says, sitting down on the edge of the bed. "I hate to break this to you, and you might not like it, but the sun doesn't rise because of *you* every morning. You're not this all-powerful entity the world revolves around. Not everything has to do with you. Leo, he's got hopes and dreams, and he deserves to be able to follow them without you pissing all over things."

"Look, can we not do this?" I ask, throwing my arm over my face as I close my eyes, because her running her mouth is getting in the way of the ceiling fan doing what it's supposed to do. "Let's just skip the part where we argue over bullshit, like we actually give a fuck about each other, because I'm not in the mood for it tonight."

"You're an asshole," she grumbles, laying down beside me, close enough to touch but we're not touching. She feels miles away right now, coldness settling in that space between us.

"Yeah, well, at least you know..."

"Yeah, and it's a pity, really, because I found myself starting to give a fuck about you."

She says nothing else.

I don't say anything, either.

We lay there in silence.

For once, I don't prefer it.

I want her to say something else, anything else, just to erase those words now assaulting my mind.

I found myself starting to give a fuck about you.

I don't like it, not at all, because as she says those words, I come to realize, in the moment, that feeling might be mutual.

* * *

"When's the last time you slept?"

That question is like nails on a chalkboard. It's like Jim Carey in *Dumb & Dumber*. It's like a boojie little blonde talking about her fucking wardrobe.

It grates on my every nerve.

I *twitch* at the sound of it.

Seven stands beside me in the old warehouse, eyeing me with caution, awaiting an answer to his question. It's approaching noon, and we've unloaded a few crates, a truck coming in this morning with the guns for one of Jameson's connections. I couldn't get ahold of Three, but Five showed up in his place, a fact that *also* irritates me.

"This morning," I tell him, leaving out the fact that it wasn't for more than an hour. I had too much on my mind. "You gonna ask me about my feelings next, doc? Maybe prescribe me a tranquilizer to keep the nightmares at bay?"

"I'm just looking out for you," he says, not at all ruffled by my attitude.

"Yeah, well, I don't need my hand held, thanks," I say, snatching up a crowbar to pop the top off of a crate, figuring I'll just inventory it all myself.

I left Scarlet at home, in bed, asleep.

She could probably use the extra money, but I need some space to clear my head so I can try to think straight when it comes to all of this. There's work to be done, things that need handled, and I can't be worrying about the people around me when I need to be concerned about the ones standing in my way.

My phone rings as I start sorting through the guns. I pull it from my pocket, glancing at the screen. *Three.* I hand it to Seven, saying, "Deal with this bastard before I kill him."

Seven nods, taking the phone and answering it, saying everything that needs to be said, minus the threats I'd be spewing if I had to deal with him directly. He lectures the kid like he's his fucking father, which is kind of funny, you know.

That's how Seven acts. Like a father figure.

Like he knows what's best for us.

He usually does.

Seven hangs up eventually, sighing, still clutching my phone. "He said his phone was dead, he forgot to charge it because he was preoccupied dealing with that woman."

"That sounds a lot like an *excuse* to me."

"That it does," Seven says. "He apologized."

"He's got two strikes already," I say. "If it so much as even *rains* on me, he's catching the blame and that's it for him."

"Understandable."

I go back to inventory, popping open the other crates before dismissing Five, paying him for the manual labor. I'm nearly finished with it all when ringing once again shatters the silence.

"If that's Three again..."

Seven looks at my phone, expression guarded as he holds it up. "Brooklyn number."

Son of a bitch.

"Put it on speaker," I order, waiting for Seven to press the buttons, knowing right away it'll be none other than Aristov. "Gambini."

"Ah, Mister Scar, I was hoping you would be accepting calls today."

"For you, Yogi? *Anytime.* Now tell me what you want so we can both get on with our days."

"I am curious if you are with Morgan right now," he says, "if she is there, wherever you may be."

"You don't seriously think I'm going to tell you that, do you?"

"I am hoping so."

"Well, tough shit, because you're not getting anything from me."

He lets out a dramatic sigh. "That is a shame. You could have made a little girl very happy, but instead, you choose to break her heart." The phone shifts, his voice dropping lower as he says, "I am sorry, my kitten, but you cannot talk to your mommy on her birthday."

This conniving son of a bitch...

"Do you think I'm stupid?" I ask. "Do you think I'm going to fall for this bullshit? That I'll actually believe you have the kid right there with you?"

The phone shifts again, his voice sharp as he says, "Say hello to the man."

I shake my head, snatching a lid up and slamming it back onto the last crate, the bang echoing through the warehouse so loud that I almost miss the sound of the soft voice coming through the line. "Hello."

Time feels like it stops.

I turn, looking in the direction of my phone. Seven still holds it, wide-eyed, staring at me. Guess he didn't expect to actually hear the kid, either.

"Hello," I say, having no idea what else to say, if I should even say *anything*.

"Is Mommy there?" she asks, a hopeful edge to her high-pitched voice that I know I'm about to crush.

"No, she's not," I say, "but she misses you."

"I miss her, too," she says, and I can hear her voice as it quivers, hope replaced with devastation. "Do you know where Mommy went?"

"Put your father back on the phone," I say, because I can't answer those questions for her, but she doesn't listen to me any more than Scarlet ever does.

"Please!" she says, starting to cry. "I want Mommy! I don't wanna be here no more! *Please don't*—"

She lets out a shriek that is muffled damn near instantly. I can hear a struggle through the line, frantic sobbing, coughing, like the girl can't catch her breath. My stomach sinks. Seven looks at me with horror, like he expects me to do something, but what the hell am I supposed to do about *this*?

I'm suddenly grateful Scarlet isn't here, that she isn't hearing it.

"Quiet, kitten," Aristov says, getting back on the phone. "Daddy is talking to Mommy's new toy."

The girl grows quiet.

I don't hear a fucking peep from her.

"Did you just hurt her?" I ask, trying to keep calm, when I want to reach through the line and rip his fucking balls off.

"I shushed her."

"You *choked* her."

"Nonsense," he says. "They must be taught or else they run wild. It is for her own good."

For her own good.

"What do you want?" I ask. "I'm starting to lose my patience with you, and you're really not going to like me when that happens."

"You know what I want," he says. "I want my little kitten to have her mommy back."

"Well, then, we're on the same page," I say. "I'll gladly come pick up the kid and reunite them so they can go on their merry way."

"*Tsk, tsk.* You know it will not work like that." He laughs. "Tell me where to find the *suka*. I, also, grow tired of this game, and I will not play it much longer. If you do not give me what I want, everyone you know will pay the price. Your friends, their families... even your own brother. Yes, I know about him, Mister Scar. I do not want to hurt them, so do not make me. All I want is my pretty girl back home so we can be a family."

Before I can respond, the line goes dead.

He hung up on me.

"I'm gonna enjoy watching that man die," I mutter, shaking my head.

"Boss..."

"Not now, Seven," I say, hearing the worry in his voice. "Save it, whatever it is, until I've had more sleep and can handle this shit."

I walk out of the warehouse, pausing in the alley to pull out a joint and light up as Seven secures everything, locking the doors.

"Call Jameson," I say when he joins me. "Tell him to meet me at that bar, the hole in the wall..."

"Whistle Binkie," he says.

"Yeah, that one," I mutter, heading toward the car. "I need a fucking drink."

Seven does as I ask, not questioning me anymore, driving into the city, to the Lower Eastside, where the bar is. He pulls up to the curb right out front, finding that rare street parking.

Maybe my luck is turning around.

"Need me to come in?" Seven asks, cutting the car off but leaving the keys dangling in the ignition.

"You can wait out here," I say. "Catch a nap for me or something."

He laughs. "I'll see what I can do."

The place isn't that busy so early in the afternoon, a few people sitting along the bar but most of the tables are empty. I slide up onto an empty stool, and the bartender looks at me, doing a double-take. It's the same guy as every other time I've been here. Do they even *have* other employees?

"Haven't seen you in a while," he says. "Bottle of rum, right?"

"Right."

He hands it over, no argument, tearing out the pouring spout for me. I drink straight from the bottle, just sitting in silence, tinkering around with a coaster until Jameson appears.

He pulls out the stool beside me to sit down. "Thirsty?"

I take a swig from the bottle, shrugging, before looking his way. The second I see his face, I *laugh*. His nose is swollen and bruising, tape covering it.

I offer him the bottle. "You look like you can use some of this."

He waves me off, saying, "I can't mess with that hard stuff," before motioning toward the bartender, asking for whatever's on tap.

He sips his beer when it's delivered, sighing, hunched over along the bar.

"So, how'd you explain your face?" I ask.

"Told the guys at work my grandson hit me with a ball, but I told my wife the truth," he says, cutting his eyes at me. "Got head-butted by a perp."

"A *perp*, huh? That about sums her up."

"Tell me about it," he says. "Got the judge to rescind the warrant this morning, got it wiped out of the system. Heard the Russian showed up and made a stink when nobody could tell him where she went."

"He called me a bit ago."

"Yeah? What did he want?"

"To use the kid to get me to cooperate," I say. "He had her ask me for her *mommy*."

Jameson makes a pained face. "He must be getting desperate."

"He is, which means it's probably going to get ugly soon. I'll try to keep it all under the radar, so you're not pulled in, but I wanted to give you the heads up so you're not blindsided."

He nods, sipping on his beer. "Do what you've gotta do for your girl, Gambini."

"She's not my girl."

"Could've fooled me," he says. "You're sure going through a lot of trouble for a girl that's not *yours*."

"It's principle," I tell him. "The sooner this is over, the sooner my life can get back to normal."

"Normal." He laughs at that. "When the hell has your life ever been *normal?*"

I cut my eyes at him but ignore that question.

We drink in silence for a while.

Jameson shoves his glass aside when it's empty. "I need your assurance that Aristov is the end of this."

I look at him but say nothing.

"I've looked the other way on a lot of shit, Gambini," he says. "I've buried a lot of evidence for you going back *years*. I let your friend walk for taking out all those bosses, because you came to me, a favor for a favor, when I had more than enough to lock him away for the rest of his life. So I need *this* particular situation to end with the Russians, okay?"

He's not spelling it out, but I know what he's getting at. "You want me to leave Detective Fuckface alone."

"We had a deal, you and I... *no cops*. You remember that, don't you?"

I don't make promises, but I did tell him years ago that I wouldn't target any boys in blue. It was his hard limit. I could raise as much hell as I wanted, but if I ever killed a cop, it would be all over, our arrangement off.

"You really want to cash in your favor for *that* scumbag?"

"No," he says, laughing dryly. "I felt safer, knowing you owed me, so I hoped to keep that card for a long time, but I haven't got much of a choice unless I want a fellow cop's blood on my hands."

"I can make him disappear, no blood at all."

He cuts his eyes at me.

Apparently, he doesn't like that idea.

"Okay, then. If the guy stops breathing, it won't be *my* doing. Is that what you want to hear?"

"Yes."

"Fine. *Deal.*" I take a swig of rum before shoving the bottle aside, tossing some money onto the bar to pay as I stand up. I take a few steps away, pausing to glance back at him. "Just so we're clear... do ventilators count? Because I can do *a lot* of damage if we let a respirator do his breathing for now on."

Jameson's eyes narrow. "Don't lay a finger on him, Gambini. I mean it."

I hold my hands up. "Just checking. Have a great day, detective."

He mutters something before motioning for the bartender to bring him another beer.

I walk out, seeing my car still parked along the curb, Seven behind the wheel, tinkering with my phone. I climb in beside him and he cuts his eyes my way, carefully setting the phone down.

"Someone call?" I ask, picking it up.

"Yeah." He starts the car. "A rental agency. Your brother put you down as a reference on his application for an apartment."

"Did you handle it for me?"

"Of course," he says. "Told them he was a great kid, a hard worker, responsible and respectable."

"Good," I say with a nod, settling in. "Thanks."

7

Buster was still sitting on the mantle.

A layer of dust covered him, some soot from the fireplace streaking his patchy tan fur. He looked so sad, covered in darkness, the fireplace not lit and the lights not on.

The little girl crept closer, walking through the empty room, and stared up at him, frowning. She wondered if he still smelled like her mother, or if he'd just smell all dusty. Standing on her tiptoes, she reached up, her fingertips grazing the bear's scorched foot.

"What are you doing?"

The sharp voice pierced the room, instantly knocking her back flat on her feet. She swung around, facing the doorway. "Nothing."

The Tin Man stood right inside the room, arms crossed over his chest as he stared at her.

"Nothing," he repeated, starting toward her, his steps measured. *Uh-oh.* He stopped right in front of her, crouching down, eye-level. "*Nothing* sounds like a *lie*, kitten. Do you want to change your answer?"

"I didn't touch him," she said. "I *swear!*"

"Another lie," he pointed out. "I watched you."

Her voice was quiet as she said, "But I just miss him."

"Tell me, why is he so special to you? He is old, and ugly, and he *stinks*. Why does he matter?"

She shrugged. "I don't know."

"Yet another lie," he said. "One more time and you will live to regret ever opening your mouth to me, so be very careful. I will ask you again, and I want an answer... what makes your Buster so *special?*"

She hesitated before whispering, "Mommy gave him to me."

"She gave you your life, too, but you do not seem to care about that," he said, cupping her chin, squishing her cheeks with his fingers like he sometimes did. "Do you not take me serious? Is that the problem? Do you think I am just joking with you? Because what did I say would happen if you touched that bear?"

She trembled, her knees all wobbly. "That you'd burn him."

"And?"

"And…"

And… she didn't know.

She couldn't really remember.

Remembering was getting so hard.

"And I would burn you, too," he said, raising his eyebrows, his face so close their noses almost touched. "What makes you think I will not shove you in that fireplace and light you up?"

"You love me," she whispered, her voice shaky.

"I do," he said. "You are special to me, kitten, for the same reason... your mother gave you to me. You are *my* Buster. And oh, how I wish I could set *you* on the mantle, keep you from trouble, but there is a fire in you. You are the *suka's* daughter. She had a fire, also, and you want to know the best way to put out fire?"

"How?"

"You *smother* it."

Before the little girl could say another word, he pounced. His left hand grasped the back of her neck, pinning her in place, as the hand on her chin shifted, fingers pinching her nose closed as his palm covered her mouth.

She tried to inhale, but she *couldn't*.

Eyes wide, she struggled, clawing at his arms, trying to rip his hand away so she could get some air, shoving him as hard as she could, nearly knocking him back.

Groaning, he stood up, his hold loosening long enough for her to take a breath, letting out a piercing shriek that he silenced by snatching her up. Yanking her over to a black leather chair, he threw her down on it, his knee bracing him, pressed into the cushion, as his hand went over her mouth again.

"*Vor!*"

The Cowardly Lion's voice shouted from the doorway. The little girl recognized it. His sudden presence didn't stop the Tin Man, though. He kept smothering her.

"*Kassian!* Stop before you kill her!"

The Tin Man let go at those words, and the little girl inhaled sharply, her vision blurry. She blinked, trembling, as he leaned down, his nose close to her nose again. "You will *never* have your Buster back, kitten, and you have no one to blame but yourself."

The Tin Man stood up and walked away, stalling near the door, where the Cowardly Lion lurked.

"You are forgetting your place again, Markel," he said, glaring at him. "I make the orders. If you do not like it, go somewhere else."

The little girl curled up in the chair, crying, as the Tin Man walked out, disappearing. After a moment, the Cowardly Lion turned her way, carefully approaching. Stopping by the chair, he reached down, brushing the hair from her face, wiping the tears from her cheek.

"I always hated when he made your mother cry," he said. "So many nights, she would cry, but she found courage with you. And I know you want that bear, sweet girl, but it is not the bear you love. It is your mother."

"I miss her," the little girl whispered.

"I know," he said, sighing. "And in his own twisted way, he misses her, too."

8

Morgan

The front door opens just as I step off of the stairs and into the quiet foyer of the house. My gaze flickers that way when Lorenzo walks inside. He's alone, and nobody else is home, which means it's just me and him at the moment.

I pause there, cautiously watching him.

He was gone when I woke up, even though I beat the sunrise. The air in the house was stifling last night, and it doesn't feel any more comfortable this morning. I'm not sure if it's leftover tension or if maybe I'm just projecting.

Either way, I don't like it.

I don't want to wear out my welcome.

Lorenzo glances my way, hesitating a moment before he shuts the door. "You look nice."

I glance down at myself, at the casual little black and white striped dress with long sleeves. It goes almost to my knees. I bought it because it has pockets, which is damn near a miracle for women's clothing. Pockets are kind of like men who eat pussy for fun—*unicorns.*

"Yeah, I've been setting the bar crazy low lately, with all the sweats and junk, so I just thought, you know, why not give looking like myself another go?"

His gaze slowly scans me. "You're beautiful no matter what you wear."

"Thanks," I say, the compliment surprising me. There was not a stitch of sarcasm to it. *Weird.* He's wearing faded jeans and loosely laced combat boots with an unbuttoned black Henley shirt and a black coat. It's strange, how the man can look so well put-together with whatever just thrown on, no thought given to it at all. "You look nice, too."

Lorenzo glances at himself, making a face, before cutting his eyes my way. "Don't make this shit weird, Scarlet."

I laugh as he shrugs off his coat, draping it over his arm. He takes a few steps away, toward his library, before pausing in the hall.

He lingers there, his back to me, like something has him torn, before he slowly turns around again. "You going somewhere?"

"Yeah, I figured I'd get some air," I say, motioning toward the front door. "You know, get out of your hair for a while."

"Get out of my hair for a while."

"Yep."

"Pity," he says. "I kind of like you in my hair."

He walks away, disappearing into his library, leaving the door open behind him. I stand here for a moment, my gaze shifting between the hall and the front door, before following him, my black heels clicking against the wooden floor, so I know he hears me approaching.

He's sitting in the chair, hands laced together on the top of his head, the sleeves of his shirt shoved up to his elbows. His legs are stretched out, crossed at the ankles. While he *looks* relaxed, I sense the tension. It rolls off of him like waves, written in his silence.

I stall there, mostly still in the hall, and lean against the doorframe as I regard him.

He stares at me for a moment before saying, "You can come in, you know."

"I know."

"Yet you're standing there," he says, "making shit weird."

I smile softly. "I was just wondering if maybe you'd want to come along."

"Come along."

"Yes."

"To get out of my hair."

"Yes."

He doesn't say anything.

It's still tense. And awkward. I can feel it. *Can you?* I mean, look, I know how stupid I'm probably sounding at the moment, but I'm so out of my element here. It's not like I'm exactly *fluent* in relationships. I've got no friends... no family besides my daughter... never even had a *boyfriend*, if we're being technical. Just a string of men who used me for my body and now I have him, and whatever this thing is, and it's all just so foreign. But things feel weird, he's right, and I don't really know how to make it better.

"I mean, no offense, but you're a bit of an asshole," I say. "Figured you might want to get away from that dude for a while."

Again, he says nothing.

"Or not," I mumble, giving him a small smile that he doesn't return before I push away from the doorframe, going back out into the hall. I head for the front door, opening it, and am about to walk out when I hear movement behind me.

Glancing over my shoulder, I see Lorenzo as he slips on his coat, coming toward me, moving *past* me, walking right outside without a word. I join him, shutting the front door as I eye him peculiarly. It's seventy degrees out, yet he's bundled up like it's still winter.

"You hungry?" I ask as we start to walk away from the house, leaving his car parked in the driveway, since I figure the subway will suffice. He follows my lead, like he's just tagging along.

"Depends," he says. "You offering?"

"Of course," I say. "You ever *dine and dash?*"

He laughs at that. "All the time."

"Awesome."

We head into the city, switching trains twice. It takes almost an hour before we finally get off around Broadway. I'm not sure where we're going, or really even *why*, but somewhere along the way Lorenzo takes the lead like he's got a destination in mind.

We end up at a restaurant near Central Park, one of those fancy ass billionaire call girl places, the *wine* and *dine* and *sixty-nine* kind of gals, where you treat her to champagne and caviar before turning her out at The Plaza until your Viagra gives out.

You get where I'm going with this?

Me, with my face all scraped up from the alleyway scuffle, and him being, well... *him*. We're out of place here, but Lorenzo doesn't seem to notice. He waltzes on in the door as if he owns the place, approaching the hostess and saying, "need a table for two," as if barking that will negate the *'by reservation only'* sign hanging up near us.

The hostess impatiently mutters the reservation policy before she looks up, silencing mid-sentence. She's quiet for a second, caught of guard, before she says, "Sure thing, Mr. Gambini. Coming right up."

Oh-kay.

She shows us to a small table in the back corner, dropping off two tiny one-page menus full of shit that's foreign to me, like Miyazaki Wagyu (some fancy ass kind of steak, according to Lorenzo). I'm reading through it, making faces as I try to decipher it. "Have you eaten here before?"

"All the time," he says.

Of course, makes sense, since they recognized him. "You know, dining and dashing only works if you're able to get away, which doesn't really bode well for us, since they know your fucking *name.*"

He laughs. "I know."

"So why are we here?"

He doesn't have to answer that, no, because the universe tells me exactly why we're here when I glance up and come face-to-face with Leo. He's wearing his tuxedo work uniform.

I realize right away that he's our waiter. *Oh boy.*

"What do you want?" he grumbles, stalling beside the table, staring at his brother. He's kind of adorable, with that little black bow tie, especially with him pouting at the moment.

Makes me want to pinch his cheeks.

"Is that how you greet all of your customers?" Lorenzo asks. "Because if so, I would've fired your ass long ago."

"Look, it's been a long day already, and I'm working a double, so can you cut me a break?" Leo asks. "I'm doing my best here."

"I know," Lorenzo says, snatching the menu from my hand, discarding it. "We'll just take the tasting menu."

I scowl. "You're ordering for me?"

Lorenzo cuts his eyes my way. "Is that a problem?"

"Depends," I say. "What did you order?"

"Tasting menu," Leo chimes in. "It's a little bit of everything, like a sampler or whatever."

"Oh, well then..." I wave toward Lorenzo. "Not a problem."

"You want some wine or something?" Lorenzo asks.

"Or something," I mumble, picking up the drink menu, which is a hundred and fifty times bigger than the food one. Not even joking. A hundred and fifty pages of alcohol. I flip through it, scowling some more. *Wine. Wine. Wine.* Red. White. Locations and years and who the fuck knows what all the French means. My eyes skim along the price list. "Oh geez, who can afford to even *smell* half of these?"

"I can," Lorenzo says.

"Does that mean you're buying?"

He shrugs.

I take that as a *yes.*

"Well, in that case..." I close the drink menu, shoving it aside. "A bottle of your most expensive whatever the hell is on that menu, *thanks.*"

Leo laughs, while Lorenzo snatches the menu up. "Whoa, whoa, I'll be *goddamned...* that's like twenty-thousand dollars, Scarlet. Drop some fucking zeroes, woman."

I roll my eyes, turning to Leo. "You got anything fruity, like the crap that comes with little umbrellas?"

Leo nods.

"Give me one of those," I say. "Surprise me."

Leo looks at his brother again. "What do you want?"

"Rum."

Rum. *Of course.*

"Glass of our best rum," Leo says.

"*Cheapest* rum," Lorenzo says. "And the whole bottle will be nice."

"Glass of our worst rum," Leo mutters. "Whole bottle, my ass..."

Leo walks away, while Lorenzo glares at him.

My drink doesn't come with a little umbrella, it turns out, but instead is decorated with some fancy orange peels in curly shapes. I pluck one out, looking at it peculiarly while I take a sip of the whatever-it-is. Sweet and fruity and *strong*.

"Those are my oranges," Lorenzo points out as he takes a swig of his rum from the small glass Leo brought him. *No bottle.*

I eye the peel. "Straight off the Gambini groves?"

"Yes."

"Huh, isn't that something," I say. "Must make you proud, having such a successful business."

"It's all right."

"It's all right," I say, repeating him. "Geez, man, contain your enthusiasm."

He smiles slightly. "Forgive me for not squealing like a little bitch about it. It's a lot of work for not much pay off. It's kind of depressing, having spent over fifteen years working sun up to sun down, busting my ass to keep the family business going, and not banking even a *fraction* of what I've made since coming to New York. And I don't even break a sweat here, you know. It pays to be a non-sentimental asshole."

"But yet you keep the groves," I point out.

"They're my home."

That response surprises me. *Home.* "You think of that as home?"

"Why wouldn't I?"

"Uh, I don't know," I say. "Maybe because of what you went through there, with your stepdad and your mom and—"

"Doesn't matter," he says, cutting me off. "My father built the place and left it to me. Nothing they could do would ever ruin that. I refuse to let it."

"So why are you *here?*"

"I already told you why," he says. "Same reason as you... I saw a movie."

I know he's bullshitting. How do I know that? Because *I* was when I said that to him on the roof all those weeks ago, that I'd come to Manhattan because of the Muppets.

"There are, what... eight million people in New York City?" I ask.

"Something like that."

"I just thought, you know, *that* many people, I was bound to find *somebody* to give a shit about me. So that's why I came. I was young, and lonely, and sick of being ignored and overlooked. I wanted to matter to someone."

Lorenzo stares at me, like maybe he doesn't know what to say to that. It starts to get weird again, with him not speaking, so I'm damn grateful when the food starts to arrive. *Thank god.* Leo drops off two plates, and I make a face when he explains what it is—some kind of cream sauce with oysters and caviar.

It looks more like art than something to eat.

I try it, though, because *fuck it.* I don't like letting food go to waste. It's salty, and fishy, and *ugh...* no thanks. It gradually gets worse, with more fish and some artistic-looking artichokes, some funky beef in strong-tasting broth, before there's even more seafood. And more. And more. *And more.* There's a salad with dressing that tastes like sweet and sour sauce and a fucking celery and leek something that's been grilled with truffles.

Truffles.

The only truffles *I* eat are the chocolate ones.

Lorenzo, though, devours it all.

We don't talk.

The last course arrives, and I breathe a sigh of relief that the dessert looks like *dessert* and isn't some weird fish shit. Cookies and ice cream and chocolate, oh my god... I shovel it all in, no hesitation at all. I'm still *starving.*

"I got bored," Lorenzo says eventually, not touching his dessert.

I glance at him, brow furrowing. "What?"

"That's why I'm here," he says. "I know that sounds like bullshit, but it's true. I got bored, and I wanted a change. Oranges weren't my father's only legacy. He grew up in the mob, ran these streets for years, until the Genova family drove him out of town... that's how he ended up in Florida. But even then, they wouldn't let him be. So I thought, you know, why not pick up where he left off? So I showed up, took them all out, and here I am, bored again... or at least I *was*."

"Not bored anymore?"

"At the moment, no."

"That's good to know," I say. "What happens when you get bored again?"

"I go back home."

Leo shows up again before I can respond, dropping off the check, which I promptly pick up. It's damn near *eight-hundred* bucks. For *lunch*. "Whoa, buddy..."

Lorenzo snatches it from my hand and tosses it back on the table before standing up. "Come on."

He starts walking away, and I just gape at him, because he's legitimately leaving, like we're actually dining and dashing, because he's not paying the check, and I certainly can't do it. I don't *have* that much money. I shove up out of the chair, following, keeping my head down and not making eye contact with anyone, while he looks people dead in the face.

He's fucking *insane*.

The second he steps outside, he pulls out his tin and grabs a joint, flicking a match to light it, smoking it right here on the sidewalk as he looks around. "So, where to now?"

"Jail, probably," I say, pausing beside him, scowling as he blows smoke in my face. "I don't know how the hell you've evaded lockup so far, because you're *terrible* at flying under the radar."

"Who says I'm trying to fly under the radar?" he asks. "I mean, come on, baby... look at my face. There's no point in me sneaking around."

I look at him, not because he just told me to, but because of the word he used. *Baby.* It does the kind of thing to my chest that makes me feel uncomfortable—the squeezing, tightening, pitter-pattering bullshit. Ugh, knock it off, heart. You've got no business reacting to him.

I point at his face, waving my finger around. "Yeah, well, that doesn't mean you have to flaunt it."

Lorenzo grabs my hand, pulling it away from his face, still holding onto it as he says, "But that's what makes it all so fun."

I roll my eyes. "There's something wrong with you."

"I know," he says. "So, where to?"

He's looking at me like he wants an answer, but I just shrug, because I'm not sure. I didn't really leave the house with a *plan*, you know?

Besides, he's touching my hand. Holding my hand. *Weird.*

Lorenzo sighs, finally letting go and continuing to smoke, motioning with his head down the street before he starts to walk. I don't know where he's going, and he sure as hell doesn't tell me, but I follow along regardless.

"So your Broadway story was bullshit?" he asks. "The Muppets didn't make you want to join the chorus line?"

I smile. "It wasn't bullshit, per se. I *did* fall in love with Broadway."

"Yeah?"

"Yeah," I say. "I wish I had that kind of talent... the kind where someone would pay me to dance around with my clothes *on*... but I don't, so I leave it to the professionals."

"What's your favorite play... musical... *whatever?*"

"*The Lion King.*"

"Yeah?"

"Yeah."

He laughs, like he finds my answer funny. "I saw the cartoon a few times."

"Me, too." *More* than a few times. "Never actually saw the musical, though."

His footsteps falter so much that I almost run right into him. "How is it your favorite if you've never seen it?"

"I've never really seen any of them," I say, "but I heard it's good, and I've seen clips."

"You've seen *clips*."

"Yes."

"That's just..."

"Pathetic?"

"I was going for more like *bullshit*."

"It's life," I say, "which, contrary to what *you* seem to think, can't always be fun."

"See, now that *is* bullshit."

He pulls his phone from his pocket and starts tinkering with it, like the conversation is over now, nothing else to say about it. We stroll along for who knows how long, wandering the streets until my feet start to hurt. I kick my shoes off and carry them, because fuck it, which earns me a peculiar look from Lorenzo. He shoves his phone away eventually, but we still don't really talk.

I let him lead, and maybe it's weird, but I'm kind of enjoying the silence. It's peaceful in a sense and sets me at ease.

I needed that today.

Needed this.

Serenity.

We end up on Broadway in the middle of the afternoon, and I look up, gazing at the yellow *The Lion King* signs along Minskoff Theater. Lorenzo heads right for the place, getting closer... closer... closer, but I grab his arm to stop him as he nears a gathered crowd. "What are you doing?"

"Going to see *The Lion King*."

"I, uh... *what?*"

I start to argue, but he doesn't stop to listen to a word of my complaint, heading right inside just as others filter in. The man working the door looks at Lorenzo, averting his eyes quickly in reaction.

I tense. It makes me sick to my stomach.

Lorenzo, though, doesn't seem bothered.

The guy asks for our tickets, but Lorenzo talks his way right out of it, weaseling past two more workers and an usher inside, like they're all just too afraid to say '*no*' to him. We find some empty seats in the back, way up top, but I'm not going to complain a bit. I'm just too damn shocked I'm actually in the theater. Intermission is ending, the second act starting up. We missed the whole beginning, but *fuck it*... I never thought I'd see *this* much.

The music starts, and I'm entranced as we *second-act* the son of a bitch, ignoring the looks of people around us who know damn well we weren't here earlier. The first few minutes, I'm on edge, waiting to be thrown out, but eventually, the draw of what's happening on stage is just too much.

I watch, tears in my eyes that I struggle to hold back, pressure in my chest like my heart wants to explode. I'm bursting at the seams with *feelings* and I don't know what to do about it. It's like being swept up in a tornado and I'm just waiting for it to drop me somewhere.

And I land *hard* the second it's over.

I'm up out of my stolen seat, cheering loudly, clapping and screeching and crying, because it's the most beautiful thing I've ever witnessed outside of my daughter. *Nothing* will ever be more beautiful than her, but this moment is a close second, and all I can think as I stand here is how much she'd love this, how happy it would make her to see something so touching.

I turn to Lorenzo. He's just staring straight ahead. He cuts his eyes at me, like he can sense my attention, and makes a face because I'm crying.

"Come on, fuddy-duddy," I say, shoving against him. "Let's get the heck out of here."

He doesn't have to be told twice. He's out of the chair and heading through the crowd while the performers are still taking bows. I wipe my face as we go outside, knowing my makeup has to be a mess.

"That was... *wow*," I say when we walk away from the theater. "I don't even have words right now."

"Yet you're talking." He makes a puppet out of his hand as he holds it up, right in my face, saying, "*blah, blah, blah, blah, blah...*"

I shove his hand away with a laugh. "Fuck off."

He looks at me and smiles. He *smiles*. It's genuine, no more than a flicker of happiness, but it's there, and I see it, and it does something to me.

There's that damn pitter-pattering again.

"There's something about you, Lorenzo," I say, shaking my head as I look away, unconsciously returning his smile. "Sometimes I think you might just be *human*."

"You're making shit weird again, Scarlet."

I roll my eyes. "Whatever."

"So, where to now?" he asks, stopping on the nearby corner, waiting for the light to change to cross the street.

"I don't know... *nowhere*, I guess?" I shrug, waving back toward the theater. "I'm not sure how *that* could be topped."

He looks at me, raising his eyebrows. "Is that a challenge?"

"Uh, no…"

"It sounds like one."

"Well, it isn't."

He grins, a sly kind of smile just as the light changes, leaning closer to whisper, "challenge accepted," before walking away, crossing the street.

I'm not sure what he's thinking right now, but my stomach twists all up in knots. *Shit.*

I've got a bad feeling about this.

But I've got to admit... *I kind of like it.*

* * *

Seven lives in a little brown cookie-cutter townhouse. Potted plants line the steps, the flowers in them starting to bloom.

Purple. And pink.

Seriously, he's got purple and pink flowers leading to his front door.

He stands there in the doorway, dressed like usual but yet barefoot, his eyes scanning us with confusion, like we're the *last* people he expected to see when his doorbell rang a moment ago.

"Bruno, love, who is it?" a woman's voice calls out from

behind him inside.

"It's, uh..."

Seven doesn't finish, but he really doesn't have to, because the woman pops up in the doorway beside him. She's everything you'd expect from someone with potted plants leading to her door, the kind of woman that just *looks* like she'd pack her husband healthy snacks before sending him off to work—burgundy ruffled blouse, black pencil skirt, with perfectly straight blonde hair, wearing the kind of makeup that doesn't *look* like makeup.

You know what I'm saying?

She looks out at us, eyes widening only slightly. She's either got one hell of a poker face or she's gotten used to Lorenzo. "Oh, hello, Mr. Gambini."

He merely nods at her.

Her gaze shifts to me as she smiles. "Hi, there! I'm Sarah. You are...?"

"Morgan," I say, a little caught off guard by her politeness. "Morgan Myers."

"Nice to meet you, Miss Myers," she says.

"You, too," I say, because I don't know what else to say to that.

"Morgan is, uh... Lorenzo's girlfriend."

Oh, whoa, buddy...

My eyes dart to Lorenzo, stunned, and see he's making a face similar to the one he makes when he sees me crying. He's *disturbed*. That should probably offend me, right? Should probably want to hit him. Instead, it makes me laugh.

"Oh, wow, that's great," Sarah says, still smiling at me. "I was just finishing up dinner. We're having tacos. Would you like to join us? There's plenty to go around."

"Oh, Jesus, *yes*," I say, the words flying out of my mouth without me even thinking about them.

Sarah laughs. "Well, then, come on in!"

Seven looks insanely nervous, watching his wife as she walks away, before he turns to Lorenzo. "Boss?"

Lorenzo just stands there.

He says nothing.

I don't have it in me to try to figure out their exchange, because my stomach is growling and the woman said *tacos*. Shrugging it off, I head up the steps, my movement bringing Lorenzo back around to reality.

"Relax, Seven," Lorenzo says, following me inside. "It'll be fine."

I don't know if Seven agrees with that, because he says nothing, too preoccupied as his wife calls out for him to set two more places at the table.

I start to follow, but Lorenzo grabs my arm, stopping me right in the entryway to the town house. His voice is low as he says, "Do me a favor and be on your best behavior."

My brow furrows. "What do you think I'm planning to do here, straddle the woman's lap and motorboat her titties? It's *dinner.*"

Lorenzo lets out a laugh of disbelief, not letting go of my arm. "They're Mormon."

Okay, that stalls me. "What?"

"Watch what you say," he continues. "Don't talk about stealing, or killing, or fucking..."

"What are we supposed to talk about?"

"I don't know," he says. "Whatever people talk about that aren't those things."

"Wait, hold on," I say when he finally lets go. "If she's super-conservative, how does the dude get away with working for *you?*"

It strikes me, as soon as I ask that, that she doesn't *know*.

"We deal in oranges, Scarlet," he says, turning away. "It's a lucrative business."

I head to the kitchen, because well, there's no getting out of this now. Tacos, it turns out, aren't the kind of tacos I'm *thinking* about. They're fancy homemade chicken tacos with some kind of yogurt sauce. We sit down at the table, and they bless the food with a prayer.

Yeah, I got us in deep here...

"So, tell me about yourself, Morgan," Sarah says as we start to eat. "What is it you do?"

Oh, boy.

I'm waiting for one of the guys to chime in for me, but nope. I'm on my own here.

"I'm kind of in between gigs right now," I say. "Still trying to figure out what I want to do with my life."

"You're young. You've got plenty of time." She smiles. *Always smiling.* "How'd you two meet?"

She motions toward Lorenzo, who is eagerly eating like the guy has never eaten before, avoiding having to talk. *Figures.*

"Just ran into him on the street one day," I say. "It's kind of a funny story, actually... you see, he lost his wallet and I happened upon it and he tracked me down to get it back. I never expected to see him again, much less somehow become his *girlfriend.*"

Lorenzo chokes.

Not even kidding.

He starts choking, *coughing*, his face turning red.

Seven jumps up, like he's about to give him CPR, but Lorenzo pulls himself together before the man can touch him.

"I'm fine," he grumbles, waving him off. "Sit back down."

The subject changes, thanks to Seven, who finally decides to chime in and distract his wife, taking the attention off of us. I slouch in my chair, leaning toward Lorenzo, whispering, "It's just a word. They're only *words*, remember?"

Lorenzo cuts his eyes my way. I know he's got some choice words for me right now, but he stays on his best behavior.

Dinner is over quickly, and Lorenzo makes an excuse about having work to do in order to flee the house. Sarah draws me to her in a hug... a *hug*... before telling me to stop by anytime I'd like.

Seven walks us out, stalling near the potted plants as I head down onto the sidewalk to wait. *So weird, their perfect little life.* I didn't expect it.

"I need that address," Lorenzo tells Seven. "You got it for me yet?"

"Yeah, hold on." Seven goes back inside, returning a

moment later with a slip of scrap paper, something written on it. "Do you need me to—?"

"No, I got it," Lorenzo says, fisting the paper. "Tell the missus we appreciate dinner."

"Sure thing, boss."

Seven goes back inside, closing the door, visit over.

Lorenzo turns to me, slowly approaching, and says nothing, although I know there's so much he could say at the moment.

"That totally didn't top *The Lion King*," I tell him.

"Yeah, well, you did that shit to yourself, Scarlet."

He walks away.

Again, I follow.

I don't know where we're going, and he doesn't ask me for ideas this time, so I'm pretty sure he's got another destination in mind.

As we head deeper into Brooklyn, my nerves grow more frayed. We end up down in Manhattan Beach after sunset, in front of a decently sized gray house. Open and airy, modern architecture with massive windows and a second-story terrace. The lights are all off, nobody home that I can tell.

"You ever been here before?" Lorenzo asks.

"Uh, no." I look at him with confusion. "Should I have?"

He shrugs.

Oh-kay.

Before I can question that, he scales the fence surrounding the place and heads for it. *Shit.*

I follow, not nearly as gracefully, keeping my head down. Lorenzo circles the outside, surveying the house, before focusing his attention on the terrace.

I've snuck into enough abandoned buildings in my life to know exactly what he's doing.

"You want me to, like, give you a hand up?" I ask. "Maybe get down on my hands and knees and let you stand on my back?"

"Would you?" he asks.

I shrug. "Why not? Won't be the first time a guy stepped all over me."

He laughs, shaking his head. "Actually, it might be easier if I helped *you* up there."

"To do what, break in?"

"Yes."

I sigh, staring up at the terrace. *Fuck it.* "Fine, let's do this."

He has the audacity to look surprised, like he doubted my commitment to delinquency (*seriously?*), but he kneels down, saying, "Climb on my shoulders."

It's awkward, but I do it, straddling his neck while wearing a dress, sitting on his shoulders like we're playing a game of *Chicken.* I grip him tightly, holding on, as he stands up again, lifting me just high enough to reach the terrace.

Look, I'm not even going to pretend that swinging on poles day after day doesn't have its benefits. As soon as I get my hands on the railing, I pull myself up, no problem. Climbing is a breeze. Getting *down* is usually a different story, though. Gravity can be a bitch.

I approach the terrace door, tugging on it.

Locked. *Of course.*

"Just wiggle it," he calls up to me. "The locks on those are usually shit."

"Yeah, yeah," I mutter, reaching into my bra and pulling out my knife. What, you didn't think I stopped carrying it, did you? *Pfftt.* I open the blade, sliding it in the crack, toying with it for a moment before it pops open. "Ha!"

"Good girl."

I swing around, scowling at those words as I look down at him. "*Seriously?*"

He waves me off. "Just come let me in, woman."

I mock salute him, slipping inside what turns out to be a bedroom. A very clean bedroom. *Spotless.* I tiptoe through the house, making my way downstairs where Lorenzo waits.

I unlock the back door, letting him in.

He locks it right behind him again.

Lorenzo starts searching the house. I don't know what he's looking for, but I just roll with it, wandering through the kitchen and finding a stack of mail on the counter. I glance at the top envelope, freezing as my eyes gloss across the name on it.

Gabriel Jones.

"*Seriously?*" I hiss, turning to Lorenzo as he opens drawers, glancing inside of them. "We broke into a detective's house? Do you *want* to get arrested?"

"Not sure," he says. "Never been."

"Never been arrested?"

"Nope."

"*How?*"

He laughs.

He's been laughing a lot tonight.

"Maybe I'm just good at what I do," he says.

"That's insane," I say. "It's like you cast some spell that makes you invincible. You're a fucking *wizard*."

He cuts his eyes at me. "Voodoo?"

"Yes!"

He laughs. *Again.*

"What are we looking for, anyway?"

He shrugs. "Figured I'd take a peek around while I was here, but really, I just wanted to fuck you in his bed."

He says that so flippantly that it almost doesn't register with me.

"We broke into Gabe's house," I say, "so you could fuck me in his bed."

"Yes."

I blink at him, and I know he's about to laugh again as he heads my way. "You're insane."

"You're starting to sound like a broken record with that shit," he says, grabbing my arm and pulling me to him. "Is it *so* wrong that I want to take you upstairs and turn you out where that asshole lays his head? Make you come, over and over... make you scream my name into his pillow? I want his bed sheets to smell like us... want them to smell like that beautiful pussy, the one he'll never again know, the one he never *deserved*. Is that really *so* bad?"

"Yes." I wrap my arms around his neck, gazing at him. "It's demented."

"You think?"

"Absolutely," I say, "but that doesn't mean we shouldn't do it."

He grins, leaning closer, kissing me softly before whispering, "I knew there was a reason I tolerated you."

Now it's *my* turn to laugh.

Grabbing my hand (seriously, he's holding my hand again), Lorenzo leads me upstairs, straight to the bedroom with the terrace. The second we're inside, he's all over me. Lips and fingertips explore hidden places, kissing and touching, as I paw at his clothes. We strip down quickly, because who knows how long we have before Gabe shows up, and he shoves me down onto the bed, on my stomach, not being gentle about it. He strokes me before shoving between my legs, raising my ass up off the bed just enough to slide right in.

"Fuck," I moan as he fills me. "*Lorenzo.*"

He kisses my back, biting along my shoulder blades, sucking on the skin. I know he's leaving marks, I can feel the sting, and I know he's doing it intentionally, like he's marking his territory, but I don't mind. Gabe will never see it, but I let him have his moment. If anybody deserved it, it sure as hell would be *him.*

"Rub your clit," he says, his voice strained as he thrusts. "Make yourself come."

"Pretty sure that's *your* job."

"Aren't I doing enough of the work here?"

"Seriously?" I laugh. "You lazy son of a bitch."

I reach beneath me, to touch myself, but he beats me to it, smacking my hand away. His touch is rough, borderline painful, as he strokes my clit hard and fast. My breath hitches, a shrill cry escaping.

I come damn near instantly.

"Oh god. *Fuck.*" Pleasure rushes through me as I fist the sheets. "Christ, I take it back. You're *not* lazy. *Jesus...*"

He fucks me. There's no other way to describe it. This way, that way, upside down, inside out, he fucks me until my muscles quake and my body aches, my senses all jumbled. I'm covered in sweat, utterly exhausted, and I think it has probably only been minutes but it feels like *hours*.

"Lorenzo?"

"Yeah?"

"Make yourself come."

He laughs, mocking me as he says, "Pretty sure that's *your* job."

I clench around him, squeezing his cock.

He groans.

That does it.

He comes.

He doesn't pull out, coming inside of me, grunting as he fills me, thrusting a few more times before stilling. His lips find my back again, kissing along the sweaty skin, as he slowly pulls out. He starts to say something, but I don't know what, because noise outside silences him.

The sound of a gate opening.

The sound of a car door.

Gabe's home.

"Fun's over," I say, shoving Lorenzo off of me to get to my feet, scrambling for my clothes as I throw Lorenzo's at him. We dress, and I'm looking around, tossing the comforter. "Fuck, where's my underwear?"

"Leave them," Lorenzo says, grabbing me as a door unlocks downstairs. "We have to go."

I want to argue, but I can't, because we need to get out of here *right now*. Lorenzo shoves the terrace door open, motioning for me to go, and he follows me outside, again closing the door.

"Shit." I glare down. "I have to jump, don't I?"

Lorenzo doesn't answer, because he doesn't have to. The man swings himself over the railing, just leaping, landing on his feet in the grass.

Asshole makes it look *easy*.

Me? I fall.

Lorenzo tries to catch me, but there's no helping it as I hurl through the air, landing on my back with a thud. I flash him all the goods, since my underwear is gone, nearly taking him down with me.

"You're a fucking mess," he says, yanking me to my feet before shoving me toward the fence. "Now you get to do it again."

I do it again, because I have no choice, managing to land on my feet this time since the drop is lower. Lorenzo lands beside me, not hesitating at all, snatching my hand and dragging me away from the place before anyone sees us.

I'm distracted as he pulls me along, staring down at our hands. It's not some gushy interlocking fingers handhold, but still, he's holding my hand yet again, and that's just... *whoa*.

"You know he's going to figure it out," I say, shaking off whatever feelings are stirring up, because it's neither the time nor the place for it. "I mean, he's going to find my underwear tangled up in his sheets or something."

"So?"

"So? So he'll *know*."

"Doesn't matter," he says. "What's he going to do, call the police? *Wah-wah*, nothing got stolen, but someone broke in and fucked in my bed."

I laugh, because he's right.

Nobody would give a shit but him.

It's late, so we make the trek back to Queens. Lorenzo finally lets go of my hand when we hit the subway. The house is dark, Leo still at work, Melody off wherever, so it's again just the two of us.

"Thank you," I say, stalling in the foyer. "I'm glad you came along."

"Yeah, me, too," Lorenzo says, taking a few steps toward the library before pausing, like he's waiting for something.

"I had fun," I say, "and you know, while the sex was great, nothing topped getting to see *The Lion King*. I think the only thing that would *ever* be better than that is getting my daughter back."

I head for the stairs, needing to shower, when Lorenzo's quiet voice stalls me. "I talked to her."

Turning, I look at him as he lingers in the hallway. "What?"

"Your daughter," he says. "I talked to her."

I gape at him. I'm not sure what to say, what to think, what to *do*, so I just repeat myself. "What?"

"Aristov called while I was at the warehouse this morning," he says. "She was with him."

"And you talked to her?"

"He put her on the phone," he says, "made her ask for you."

I feel like I'm being suffocated. It hurts to *breathe*. "What did you say?"

"I said you weren't there, but you miss her. Then I told her to put her father on the phone, because he was using her to try to get your location, and I wasn't having that shit."

None of what he's saying wants to sink in, like I can't comprehend it. *He talked to her.* He heard her voice. "She was with him this morning?"

Lorenzo nods.

How many times have I called Kassian, desperate for a moment just like that?

I'm going to cry. I know it. I can feel the tears building up, stinging my eyes. So I turn away, walking away, going upstairs so Lorenzo doesn't have to watch when it happens.

9

Lorenzo

"Seriously, bro?"

I know, the second I hear those words, exactly what Leo's going to say to me. I left the restaurant without paying the check. *Blah blah blah whatever whatever.* Sure isn't the first time it's happened.

I scrub my hands over my face, groggy, trying to wake up, as I glance toward the library doorway at where my brother lurks. I'm not sure what time it is, but it's dark in the house, eerily quiet.

I fell asleep sitting here in my chair, giving Scarlet some time to process shit after she went upstairs.

"Did you use my credit card?" I ask.

"You're damn right I did," he says.

"Good." I shove up out of my chair, staggering his way. "Figured you would."

I'm not going to stiff my little brother or fuck up the good thing he's got going on at that place. He keeps one of my credit cards on him, for *emergencies*, and he always just swipes it whenever I do this shit.

He gives me hell for it, of course, but he handles things like the respectable adult he is.

So no *dining and dashing*, technically speaking, and truth be told, I would've even paid for *The Lion King*, but the show had already started and tickets were no longer on sale, so I said to hell with it, we were going anyway.

"What time is it?" I ask, heading past him, out into the hallway.

"Around eleven."

Not even midnight yet. *Huh.*

I go upstairs, because I'm too tired at the moment to deal with Leo's lecturing, but I stall when I reach the bedroom doorway.

My bed's empty.

A glance toward the bathroom tells me there's nobody in there, either.

"Goddamnit, woman," I mutter as I lean against the doorframe, covering my face with my hands. "Why can't you make shit *easy* for a change?"

Sighing, I shove away from the bedroom, heading back downstairs.

Scarlet's not here anywhere.

She's got a head start on me, but I've got a pretty good idea where I might find her.

I hope like hell I'm *wrong.*

Leo watches me from the living room as I pull out my keys. "Whoa, you're driving?"

"Yes."

"In the dark?"

"Yes."

"Just... don't kill anybody."

"No promises."

He doesn't like that answer, but I don't stick around and make it better for him. He's a big boy. He can deal with the shit.

I drive south, straight into Brooklyn, only sideswiping one other car as I make my way toward Brighton Beach. Scarlet is impulsive, and she's desperate to see her daughter, so I'm pretty sure I gave her just enough ammunition to have her gunning for these motherfuckers.

Without a *gun*, mind you.

There's a thin line between ballsy and boneheaded, and she's toeing that line going at this alone.

I park far enough away not to draw attention to my car and stroll through the darkness to Aristov's house. It's dark, no lights on inside, no cars parked out front, so I'm assuming he's not home.

There's no sign of Scarlet, though, either.

It makes me nervous.

I don't like it.

I circle the property, eyeing it, and stall when I reach the back corner, spotting a ladder leaning against the side of the house. *Fuck.* My gaze darts to the top of it, to the small offset roof along the second floor, seeing her right away.

She's just sitting there.

Alone.

I'm assuming that means she didn't find what she came for, which means she's probably upset at the moment. Part of me wants to leave her here, to walk away and give her some space, but most of me knows she's acting fucking crazy so if I leave, I may never see her again.

And *all* of me doesn't like that thought.

Before you ask—no, I don't want talk about what's up with that, because *fuck you.*

Strolling over, I grab the ladder, climbing it up to join her. She doesn't look at me. She doesn't greet me. I might as well be Casper, the friendliest fucking ghost you know, with the way she doesn't react to me *at all.* She just sits there, staring off into nothingness, so I let her have her silence as I sit down beside her on the roof. There's a window behind us, and I turn, glancing through it.

Broken crayons cover a small desk *right there* with a stack of blank paper and a stuffed cat toy beside it. Looks to be a bedroom. *Hers,* I'm assuming, but she's not in it at the moment.

"You followed me," Scarlet says quietly, "*again.*"

"It's kind of our thing, isn't it?" I pull out my tin, grabbing the last joint from it. "You run from me; I track you down. *Wash, rinse, repeat...*"

"How long is that going to go on?" she asks. "How long until you stop coming for me?"

Look, I know that's a sex joke waiting to happen, but now isn't the time for it, so keep it in your fucking pants.

"I guess when the story's over," I say. "When we hit the *blah blah blah* picket fence bullshit."

"What if we never do?"

"Then I guess we spend the rest of our lives being the coyote and the fucking roadrunner."

She laughs. It's a sad kind of sound, like the shit isn't funny, but it's either laugh or cry and she's cried enough tonight.

I light the joint, passing it to her, and we smoke it in silence. It burns too quickly, gone in what feels like a blink, which means our little moment is over and I've got to get her out of here while I still can.

"Happy birthday, by the way," I say. "Or hell, it's probably after midnight now."

She turns her head, eyes wide. "You knew?"

"Yeah," I say. "Kind of pissed *you* didn't mention it, though, that you were just going to let it go by without acknowledging the shit."

"Didn't seem important."

"Fuck that," I say. "My birthday's August the ninth. I expect a cake and some presents."

She laughs... *again*... but this time, it's more genuine. "I'll remember that."

"I'll even let you throw me a party," I tell her, standing up. "First, though, we need to get you the fuck out of here before Aristov shows up."

"But what if he shows up with *her*?"

"And let whatever's going to happen go down in front of your little Pearl? Not a good idea. It's going to require some coordination, Scarlet, and this shit?" I wave all around us. "This isn't coordinated."

"But—"

"The only 'but' I want right now is your butt getting the fuck off this roof."

She just stares at me.

"Chop-chop," I say, grabbing her arm, yanking her to her feet. "Your princess is in another castle, Scarlet. Time to keep going."

She's still staring at me.

"What?" I ask. "Why all the fucking staring? Do I got something on my face?"

Ha-ha.

Fuck you.

"That whole thing sounded almost fatherly," she says. "It was kind of hot."

Seriously?

"Look, as much as I'd love to fuck you in Aristov's bed, too, I'm going to need you to control your hormones. We'll deal with your *daddy issues* later."

She rolls her eyes, looking quite annoyed, but my obnoxiousness gets her ass down the ladder and off the roof, so I'm calling it a win.

I follow her down, leading her off of the property and to my car down the block.

"You drove?" she asks, surprised, stalling on the sidewalk.

"Yes," I say. "The quickest way from point A to point B is a straight line and not taking trains C, J, F, and a fucking cab like a dumbass, you know?"

"I know," she says, holding out her hand. "You want me to drive?"

"Unless you maybe want to die tonight, it's probably a good idea."

I drop the keys right in her palm.

She drives in silence, away from the Aristov residence, straight to my house back in Queens. She cuts the car off after she parks and starts to say something, but her stomach cuts her off.

It growls. *Loudly.*

It sounds like an angry lion.

She clutches her stomach. "Guess I'm still hungry."

"Come on," I say. "There's plenty of food in the kitchen. No need to starve."

"You're not sick of me eating your groceries?"

I turn, looking at her, *scanning* her. "Getting close, but not quite yet. Ask me again tomorrow."

She laughs.

Scarlet heads straight for the kitchen once we're inside, scouring through cabinets, snatching up a fresh bag of trail mix and chowing down on it as she says, "Can I ask you a question?"

If there's one question I hate most, it's that one. *Can I ask you a question?* What a waste of fucking words... "Just ask."

"All this stuff we did today," she says, motioning around with the trail mix bag. "Was it just because you knew it was my birthday and you didn't want me to spend it alone?"

"That's a stupid question."

"I never said it wasn't," she says, pulling herself up onto the counter. "I'd still like an answer, though."

I stroll over, sitting down in a chair at the table, and glare at her as she swings her legs, her heels banging against a cabinet below her. "Do I look like the kind of guy who would just humor someone?"

"Maybe."

"Maybe?"

"You look like you might enjoy toying with people," she says, "in the *playing with your food before you eat it* kind of way."

"That's different," I tell her, my muscles coiling as her heels continue to hit the cabinet. THUMP. THUMP. THUMP. "I'm not going to spend an entire day doing shit with somebody if they're not somebody I enjoy doing shit with."

"So you enjoy being with me?"

"Sometimes."

She's still kicking her feet.

"Just sometimes?"

"Well, right now, I'm getting pretty fucking aggravated," I tell her. "Is there's a *reason* you're banging against my cabinet like it's a goddamn bass drum?"

She stops, just like that, jumping down from the counter to shove the trail mix back away. "I wondered how long you'd tolerate it."

"Seriously?"

She shrugs, looking at me.

Playing with her food.

138

That's what *she's* doing.

Taking a page right out of Leo's book and pressing my buttons intentionally, like she thinks I won't shoot her.

Fuck you, over there, shaking your head at me. I *will*. Just because I don't doesn't mean I won't. Just because I haven't doesn't meant it'll never happen.

"I'm going to bed," I say, shoving out of the chair.

"Without me?"

"Fuck you."

She laughs, following me out of the kitchen, not put off at all by my attitude as she joins me in bed.

* * *

Seven is munching on a carrot.

He gnaws away at it, like he's goddamn Bugs Bunny, sitting on the top of a crate of guns in the warehouse. Second morning in a row, we find ourselves here, this time for a delivery of oranges.

I should count them.

I *always* count them.

But I forgot to inform Three, to let him know to come do inventory, and I'm not in the mood to do it myself. It's tedious work. And Scarlet, well... I left her in bed again, sleeping so hard she was snoring.

Didn't feel like waking her.

I mean, part of me felt like *smothering* her with a pillow, maybe, but I left her snoring away, not disturbing her slumber.

Reaching into my pocket, I pull out my phone and toss it to Seven without warning. He attempts to catch it, but he's too far off. It hits the filthy concrete with a thud. My fault, since I can't really judge distances. Could be three feet from me. Could be the whole way in fucking Tahiti. Hard to tell.

"Call Three," I say, "and tell him to come count these oranges."

Seven grabs the phone. "Yes, boss."

I reach into my pocket, to pull out my tin, and flip it open.

Empty. I glare at it, having forgotten to roll more joints, and snap it back closed, shoving it away. "I'll be right back, Seven. I'm heading to the car for a moment."

I walk out of the warehouse, leaving him there on my phone, and make it barely halfway down the alley before coming to an abrupt stop. My feet, they're not moving any more, my gaze fixed straight ahead, right at the end of the alley where a familiar man stands.

Aristov.

My instinct is to reach for my gun. I grab a hold of it, but I don't pull it out. No, something stalls me. I'm not entirely sure what that *something* is, but I let it go for the moment, remaining calm.

I don't move any closer, and he doesn't approach me, both of us just standing here.

"Boss, Three said he was—"

Seven steps out of the warehouse, freezing when he sees what I see.

"Three said *what?*" I ask.

"He said he was on his way," Seven says, his voice low. "He'll be here in a minute."

"Good."

I stroll away then, because *fuck it*, I'm not intimidated. A little put off by Aristov's presence, wondering how he found this place, but he doesn't scare me, personally, so I walk right up to him.

"Mister Scar," he says, greeting me. "I must admit... I expected *more.*"

I glance at the warehouse as he motions toward it. It's non-descript, unassuming, looking like a piece of shit, but it does everything I need it to do, and I got it for cheap, so what more could I ask for?

"What are you doing here?" I ask.

"I was in the neighborhood," he says. "Quite the coincidence, is it not?"

"I don't believe in coincidences."

"That is a shame," he says. "I am a big fan of *happy accidents*, myself."

"What are you doing here?" I ask again. "I'm not really in the mood for chit-chat, so spit out whatever it is so I can go on with my day."

"I am curious... were you at my house last night, Mister Scar?"

"Why would I go there?"

I answered his question with a question.

The man's not stupid. I'm waving the red flag of *evasion* over here.

"You will not find her there," he says, not beating around the bush anymore. "She is gone now."

"Where'd she go?"

A smile tugs his lips. "I could ask you the same, could I not? Seems we are *both* hiding someone."

"Oh, I'm not hiding anyone," I tell him. "Like I told Doodlebop, you're welcome to check my pockets if you'd like. You see, *me*? I'm not a runner, nor am I a hider. I'm more of a wolf than an armadillo."

Another round of animal metaphors.

Cut me some fucking slack here.

It's still early.

What's important here, in case you haven't done the math, is the man managed to locate my warehouse, which is just a step away from finding everything else. Nothing I own is in my name, no... most of it's under an alias. *Oliver Accardi.* But all it would take is a simple search of this property to stumble upon every other deed I have, including the one to my house in Queens.

You know, where Scarlet's at...

"Not in the mood to strip search me, huh?" I ask. "Maybe next time."

"Next time," he says. "Are you certain there will be one of those?"

"Pretty goddamn sure."

Aristov glances all around me, like he's contemplating what to do. Before he can do anything, though, Three struts into the alley, interrupting.

DARHOWER

"Ah, Mister Jackson," Aristov says. "It has been a while!"

"Not nearly long enough," Three growls. "What are you doing here?"

"Just saying hello to your boss," Aristov tells him. "I thought I would give him one more chance to return what belongs to me before I start helping myself to what does not."

Three's eyes narrow. "Is that a *threat?*"

"Does it sound like one?" Aristov asks. "I am merely saying if I do not get what *I* want, I may have to settle for something else. In fact, there is a pretty brunette already on stand-by, a sexy little one we call Lexie... she is not my Morgan, but I suppose I can make do with a substitute for now."

Three looks damn close to snapping, about to lunge at the guy for that, which is what Aristov wants, so yeah... *not happening.*

"Three," I say, "get to work."

"Yes, sir," he mutters, making his way into the warehouse.

"Go help him, Seven," I order, knowing the man's still lurking behind me, "so we can get out of here."

"Yes, Mister Pratt, go help your friend," Aristov chimes in. "I am sure your wife will be happy to have you home early. Lovely woman, that one."

"What did you just say?" Seven asks, stepping closer instead of going away.

"I said she is a lovely woman."

"Go, Seven," I order. "*Now.*"

Seven listens that time, storming into the warehouse.

"Threatening a man's family doesn't make you a bigger man," I say. "It makes you a *disgrace.*"

"Do you think I care about the names you call me?" he asks. "Besides, it is not a threat. I do not *make* threats. I am a man of my word."

"Your *word* being...?"

"I will do unimaginable things to that woman, lovely or not. It would not be hard. She is very trusting. Most women are. But I will leave her alone, I will leave you *all* alone, if you return my Morgan."

142

"She's not yours."

"Do you think she is *yours?*"

"I didn't say that."

"So why does it matter so much to you whether or not she is *mine?*"

I don't answer that, because fuck him.

I don't owe this man a goddamn explanation.

"I will give you a chance to think on it," he says, taking a step back, "but your chance will not last long, so think quickly, Mister Scar."

He leaves, disappearing from the alley, just as Seven bursts back out, unable to contain himself. I know he was still listening. It's written all over his face.

"Go ahead," I say before he can even ask. "Check on your wife and make sure he doesn't show up there."

"Thanks, boss," Seven says, his steps brisk as he rushes away.

I stroll back into the warehouse, finding Three sitting exactly where Seven had been earlier, munching on one of Seven's carrots.

"What are you doing?" I ask him.

"Imagining that jackass dying a horrible death."

"That's all well and good, but there's still work to be done," I say, "so let's count these fucking oranges so we can *all* go home."

10

There was a time, less than a year ago, when the little girl still believed in fairy tales. Not those shocking ones from the storybooks, no... she believed in those *happily-ever-after, bad guys are punished as the heroes persevere* stories, the ones from the cartoons her mother watched with her.

She loved *Cinderella*. She loved *Snow White*.

Princesses were pretty, and happy, and kind.

But more than all of that, more than anything else, the little girl really loved *Toy Story*.

Be like Buzz and Woody.

She thought her toys were real, that they had feelings and came alive, too, when she wasn't looking, but all those months later, she wasn't sure anymore.

Because Buster hadn't moved at all from the mantle. The little girl couldn't save him, but he wasn't saving himself.

"Bye-bye, Buster," she whispered, being oh-so-quiet, standing in the doorway to the den in the darkness, as the Tin Man slept hunched over in a chair by the fire.

She gave the bear one last look before going back to the bedroom they called hers.

It was the middle of the night. A little bit of snow covered the ground outside, the sky cloudy, the air so cold it fogged up her window. She shivered as she shoved it open, making a face when it made a screeching sound, like grinding metal. *Like a rusted Tin Man.*

She was scared—so scared—but she didn't let it stop her. Her mother told her to name her fears, so she called it *Buzz Lightyear.* Climbing out of the window, onto the small roof, she crawled along it, teeth chattering. It was only the second story, but she felt like she was way up in the sky. But still, she sat down, scooting to the edge, and took a deep breath.

"Be like Buzz," she whispered to herself. "He can fall with style."

It took her only a moment to gather the courage to jump— or more like *roll*, just tucking and falling into a small snowdrift on the grass below. She cringed, landing with a *thud*, her whole body hurting, but she tried to be quiet so nobody would hear her.

Her arm stung, and her head felt all woozy, but she got to her feet and started walking, heading away from the palace she hated.

The little girl had no idea where she was going, no idea where the Tin Man even lived. But she remembered it was just one road to the beach, so she went that way, with nothing more than the clothes on her back and the red-colored money the Cowardly Lion had given her.

She walked... and walked... and walked, walking forever, freezing cold, her nose running, her fingers numb, before she finally came upon the boardwalk. Nobody was out there at that hour. The few people she passed along the way were too busy to even notice her. It was so dark, and she was still so scared, but she kept going, walking to the only place she knew around there.

Passing the signs that said the beach was closed, she walked out to the shoreline, the cold water touching her shoes.

Where was she supposed to go *now?*

"Hey, you there," a voice called out, light flashing her direction. "What are you doing?"

The little girl turned, seeing a man approaching—a man wearing a blue uniform. A police officer.

"You're not supposed to be here," he said, coming closer.

Uh-oh.

Panicked, she turned and ran, sprinting down the beach. The man gave chase, shouting for her to stop, but she kept running so hard her lungs burned as the air slapped her face. He was a stranger in the dark, and her mother had warned her about those. *Hide &*

Seek. Frantically, the little girl looked for somewhere to hide, but she didn't make it far before he caught her. He grabbed her arm, sending her into even more of a panic.

The little girl lashed out, swinging and fighting, kicking the officer in the ankle before trying to bite him. He subdued her, pinning her arms at her sides, as he radioed for backup.

"Let me go!" she yelled.

"Jesus, kid, *calm down,*" he said. "You're not in trouble, so relax, okay?"

"Let me go!" she demanded, yet again, still struggling. "I just wanna go home again!"

"Then relax," he said, "and I can take you home. Just tell me your name. Can you do that?"

She shook her head. She wasn't using her words for him. He was a stranger. *Stranger danger.*

"Then tell me your parents' names."

Nothing.

"Tell me where you live."

That, she didn't *know.*

"You've got to tell me something, kid," the officer said. "Anything at all."

"I wanna go home," she whispered. "There's no place like home."

11

Morgan

"Whatcha think?"

I glance toward the doorway of the bedroom at the sound of that question, seeing Melody standing there. She twirls, wearing a flowing little black dress and black tights, her lips bright red, a matching bow in her curled blonde hair. My gaze scans her, settling on her feet, on a familiar pair of red Louboutin pumps.

My stomach sinks.

"You look gorgeous," I say, because it's true. The girl is stunning. "What's the occasion?"

"Leo's taking me out to celebrate," she says. "It's our *met*-iversary."

"Yeah? How'd you meet?"

"I was walking through the park one afternoon when the beat of an old Tupac song greeted my ears, playing from his phone. It was love at first sound. I mean, of course it didn't hurt that he was gorgeous. Whoa... second I saw him, I was *his*. To paraphrase the late great—it was just like *Aladdin*, bitch... would've given him anything he asked for."

I laugh. "That's cute. You two... you're *cute*."

"Right? I think so, too." She grins, leaning against the doorframe. "So, what about you and Lorenzo? What's the story? Where'd you meet?"

"I thought he told you the story."

"All I know is you pulled a Cinderella on him," she says. "He's not exactly known for offering details."

"Ah, yeah... we met at a shitty little bar."

"Drunken hook-up?"

"More like a serious lapse in judgment."

Her eyes widen. "Oh no, regrets?"

"About him? No." I stretch my bare legs out along the cold wood. I'm sitting on the floor beside the bed, my back against the wall as my phone charges, wearing only an oversized white t-shirt and underwear. Doesn't bother me, and it doesn't seem to bother Melody, either, my almost nakedness, so I'm not in a rush to do anything about it. "I misjudged him, figured he was just like all the others I've met, so I took his wallet home from the bar instead of him."

Thought it was impossible, but her eyes somehow widen even more. "What?"

"I pick-pocketed him. He caught me, though, put me through some hell for it, but it worked out, I guess, since he eventually took me home with him."

"That's... *wow.*"

"So no, I don't regret it, but man, how stupid was I, thinking I'd get away with that?"

She shakes her head, pushing away from the door. "You're a brave, brave soul, Morgan, a braver soul than *I*. First time I met Lorenzo, I was afraid to even go near him."

"Because of his scar?"

She scoffed. "No, because of how he looks at people, namely how he looked at *me*."

"How's that?"

"Like I'm Tupac and he's Biggie."

"Ah, like you might be his enemy."

I know that look.

He has given it to me a time or two.

It's not even really a look of *anger*. It's a blank stare, devoid of everything imaginable, like he's trapped in his head somewhere. Cold, and calculating, like he's plotting how to remove you from his life. Nothing personal about it, just *bitch, be gone...*

"Bingo! That's the one!" She smiles again, turning around. "Anyway, Leo should be home soon to pick me up, so off I go to

await my chariot."

"Have fun," I call out. "Happy anniversary."

She goes downstairs, and I sit here for a moment before picking up my phone. There are only a few minutes of airtime left on it, maybe ten at most, which means I either need to refill it soon or buy another in order to continue this tiresome routine.

I don't want to do *either* option. Last time I bought minutes, I vowed that was it... I would have my daughter back before I ran out of time again.

I want this to be over.

Why isn't it over yet?

Sighing, I dial the number, bringing the phone to my ear, listening as it rings and rings and rings, ignoring the voice in the back of my mind that begs me to hang up. After the fifth ring, he finally answers, greeting me. "Ah, pretty girl, I was *just* talking about you."

"I bet."

"I was," he says. "No more than an hour ago. All good things, of course. I would never say a bad word about you. *Promises.*"

"Yeah, right."

He laughs. "That is twice now you have spoken, pussycat. You must be feeling chatty today."

I say nothing, tilting my head, tucking the phone between my ear and my shoulder as I pick the polish from my fingernails. I can tell he's in a good mood for some reason, which tends to be terrifying with Kassian, but then again, it might be my chance to weasel something out of him.

When he's in a good mood, he gets sentimental, and he used to open up to me. Sadly, though, it was also those moments when I learned what a cruel, disturbing man he could be.

"Ah, do not go mute on me now," Kassian says. "Tell me what is on your mind."

"I'm just... tired," I admit. "I'm so tired of doing this with you. It's exhausting. It's almost been a *year.*"

"I know," he says. "I am tired, too. I have been chasing you for a long time, pretty girl."

"*Too* long," I whisper.

"Too long," he agrees. "Tell me, are you happy?"

I don't answer that.

I'm not sure why he's asking.

He's never cared about my happiness before.

"Are you?" he asks again. "You can tell me. I would like to know. Are you happy with your life?"

"I'd be happier if I had my daughter, Kassian."

"I am sure you would be," he says. "Only, you do not want me along with her. No, you seem to have decided you want him."

Him. Lorenzo.

I know that's who he means.

"It's not like that," I whisper.

"Tell me what it is like then," he says. "Is this what you want? Does your little scarred plaything make you feel like a woman? Does he take you into his bed and fuck you as you cry? Does he tell you how beautiful your tears are? Does he make you feel safe in his white house with this cute little picket fence around it? Do you feel at home here, pretty girl?"

Coldness rushes through me. Sickness swells in my stomach, bile burning my throat as those words hit me. *Oh god.*

I exhale shakily.

He described the house.

"I just want to know if you are happy," he says quietly, "because if you are, I am going to *very* much enjoy dragging you out of this fucking place and taking you back home with me."

A loud chime echoes all around me. I flinch, gasping, dropping the phone as panic floods my system. The doorbell. That's the first time I've ever heard it. Nobody even bothers to *knock* here.

The clicking of high heels trails through the downstairs, heading in the direction of the front door. *No. No. No...*

Shoving up from the floor, I run out of the bedroom, screaming, "Don't open it! Melody! Oh god, get away from the door!"

She turns toward me, startled, but it's too late. *It's too late.* Her hand is on the knob and it's already halfway open before she realizes what I'm saying. She tries to close it again, reacting fast, but he's much faster. *Much, much faster.* Something slams against the door, shoving it open the whole way, nearly knocking Melody down as she stumbles a few steps, barely managing to stay on her feet.

Her eyes dart to the door, her voice loud, defensive, as she says, "Excuse me, can I help you?"

I freeze on the stairs, halfway down, my feet unable to move anymore, everything inside of me screaming to go the other way. *Go back. Retreat. Run, motherfucker. Run away from him.* I could sprint upstairs, make my way out the window, climb onto the roof, maybe even get away from here.

But I can't. I can't move. I can't run.

I blink, and he's there, standing in the foyer of Lorenzo's house. He's dressed impeccably—straight black suit, hair slicked back, shoes glistening as the light hits them. Melody's too shocked to react right away. She gapes at him as he smiles, stopping just inches from her, his eyes raking her body from head to toe. His gaze stalls at her feet, at the red heels, and he lets out a light laugh, the sound nearly buckling my knees, before he looks back up again.

Common sense kicks into Melody, or maybe it's just a healthy dose of fear, because she takes a step back, putting a bit more space between them.

It's not enough.

It's too late.

He's too damn fast.

He grabs her before she can run, his thick tattooed hands wrapping around her throat, squeezing, stopping her dead in her tracks. Melody grasps his arms, his hands, trying to rip them away as she struggles, eyes wide with terror. His grip is so strong he lifts her up, onto her tiptoes.

"Kassian!" I cry out, the sound of my voice drawing his attention. His gaze darts my way, gliding along the stairs, his eyes meeting mine.

He loosens his hold on Melody just enough that she can

breathe, but he doesn't let go entirely, no… instead, he swings her around, making her stumble as he drags her to him, her back against his chest. One hand stays on her throat, gripping, while his other arm wraps around her, his hand resting against her stomach, keeping her pinned there.

She struggles, trying to break free, but he's unwavering, *unrelenting*.

"Morgan," she whispers, voice trembling, tears filling her wide eyes.

"Just… *relax*, okay? Stay calm," I tell her, my eyes turning to Kassian again as I say, "You'll be okay."

His smile grows.

I hope like hell I didn't just lie to her.

I take a step further down, and another, and another, holding my hands out in front of me in surrender, because I know he doesn't trust me.

Not now.

Probably not ever again.

I broke any chance of trust when I ran.

"You do not look happy, pretty girl," he says, scanning me. "But you do look *comfortable*."

I'm very much aware I'm not wearing pants. The goods are covered, but not by much. I really don't need that pointed out right now. This is painful enough to deal with.

"Tell me, does he fuck you in front of everyone? Does he let them see the things he does to you? Does *he* like to watch?"

"Kassian, can you just—?"

"No!" he shouts, his anger echoing through the downstairs of the house, as he grips Melody tighter, cutting off the air to her lungs. "Answer me. *Now*."

"He doesn't," I say right away. "He hasn't."

Kassian loosens his hold on Melody again, but he's clearly furious, so I don't know how long this is going to go on before he actually chokes her.

"Can you let her go?"

"Why should I?"

"Because she has nothing to do with this."

"So?"

"So, just let her go. She's not who you want."

"No, she is not," he says, pulling her to him rougher, his hand shifting, cupping her chin, forcing her head up so he can look at her tear-streaked face. Kassian only likes brunettes. She doesn't know how lucky she is. "But she is still very pretty, this one. Melody, yes? I bet you make the most beautiful noises. My men would enjoy making you sing."

She whimpers, trembling, proving his point.

"Kassian," I say again, desperate. I can practically *see* his thought process right now, and it's all just getting worse by the second. He'll take her. I know he will. But Melody won't last a day with those guys. There's too much goodness, too much emotion, inside of her. They'll *kill* her trying to draw it all out. "Let her go."

"Why?"

"Because you came here for me, remember?" I say, approaching, stopping just within reach. My legs are wobbly, not wanting to be this close to him, but I don't have a choice, not really. He's not walking out of here alone. One way or another, he's taking someone home, so if it's not me, it's going to be Melody, and I can't let that happen. I can't let him hurt her. "Look, I'm right here."

He looks at me when I say that.

And I know what he's thinking.

He's thinking he can just take us both.

He's thinking there's nobody here to stop him.

He's thinking how he knows I'm not going to let her go alone, that I won't throw her to the wolves, because so many times he's watched me take the brunt of his violence to spare other girls.

He's thinking too much... *way* too much... and that's too damn dangerous. I need him to just react.

I take a deep breath, blurting out words on an exhale. "He doesn't fuck me in front of other people. You know why that is, Kassian? Because he doesn't *need* to in order to feel like a man. Unlike *you*, he's strong enough to handle me all by himself."

I regret it... oh, *holy fuck*, do I regret it... but I can't take it back. I won't take it back. The anger takes over just like it did that night, the night he tried to kill me, the night I damn near died. He shoves Melody away from him, pushing her hard. She stumbles, tripping, crying out when she hits the floor. I can't help her, though. No, she's on her own.

Kassian grabs me by my neck, yanking me toward him. My vision blurs right away. He doesn't cut off my airflow. No, he's not playing games, not trying to make me uncomfortable. Instead, his fingers press just the perfect spot to block the blood flowing to my brain. I go lightheaded instantly, grabbing his wrists. From the corner of my eye, I see Melody get up and run, but I can't much dwell on what's going to happen now. I've got thirty seconds at most before it all goes black.

Kassian draws me closer, his lips a breath away from my lips, the world around me fading as he whispers, "Stupid little *suka*, you will always be *mine*."

* * *

Almost a year ago, on a warm summer night, Kassian Aristov took my life.

I had gone unconscious within seconds, as he gripped my throat, hitting my head when I slammed into the floor. The doctors, they couldn't be certain, but they suspected he'd held on for minutes, letting go just in the nick of time. In the literal sense, I managed to survive, but that doesn't change the facts.

That night, Kassian took my life. And now, months later, he almost did it a second time.

When I come to, consciousness rushing through me, rousing me from the darkness, I'm surprised... surprised I'm still *alive*. It's cold, and I'm shivering, shaking, my teeth chattering as goose bumps pebble my skin. The rigid floor beneath where I lay feels like it's covered in frost. The air smells stale as I breathe it in.

Every inch of me feels heavy—too heavy. I sit up, my muscles protesting, and fuck, my throat is sore, my mouth so dry that my voice feels hoarse.

I sense right away that it has been longer than a few minutes. Hours, maybe.

Every blink is exaggerated, my head foggy, like something flows through my bloodstream, weighing me down.

Drugged.

Must've known, when I came to, I wouldn't have come quietly.

My head rattles, swimming, as the faintest thumping noise echoes from above. Even in my groggy state, I recognize where I am.

The basement.

I've been here before, under the ground, beneath Limerence, in this filthy concrete dungeon.

Been here way too many times.

I try to shift around, metal clanging as heaviness presses against my chest. Reaching up, feeling around in the darkness, my fingers graze over the cold metal wrapped around my neck, secured with a padlock.

He has me chained here, like an animal.

"Wakey, wakey, pretty girl."

My breath catches as I turn toward the sound of the voice, the chain clattering against the concrete, echoing around us. It's hard to make out much of anything down here, but I can sense his gaze on me as something in the shadows shifts.

My voice cracks as I ask, "Why am I here?"

He *laughs.*

Stepping closer, close enough for my eyes to adjust and make out the shape of him, he says, "Still so much that stupid girl."

"I thought you were taking me home," I whisper. "Not *here.*"

Kassian crouches down in front of me, eye-level, looking me in the face. He says nothing for a moment. It's unnerving.

I swallow thickly, forcing back a swell of emotion.

"Aw, my sweet pussycat," he says, reaching toward me, nudging my chin before his thumb sweeps across my trembling bottom lip. "Did you think you would just awaken in my bed, all tucked in, snuggling with our precious little kitten? That everything would just be forgiven? *Forgotten?* Maybe you are stupider than I thought."

Tears burn my eyes. I know what this room signifies. It's *sink or swim* down here. This is where he *breaks* people, his own little twisted version of boot camp. He locks you in and puts you through hell. The girls at the club, they always called it *training*. You act up, you go back through training, as if this is just some regular job, like we were being taught to run cash registers instead of being forced into submission so he could sell us off.

I'm not talking about some BDSM shit. Don't get me wrong. There's nothing even remotely cathartic about what he does. He wants you to go numb. He wants you to give up. He wants you compliant, a pretty little Play-Doh body that he can shape and form however he wants. A few he keeps for his business, but most aren't seen around again. Some he just sells off like property, while others never even make it out of this basement.

'She could not be trained.'

He said that about me, too.

Some girls break within hours.

Most take a few days.

After a week, he usually grows tired and discards them, but he's been trying to break me for *years.*

"So pretty when you cry," he says quietly when that first silent tear streams down my cheek. He brushes it away, his touch too gentle. It fucks with my brain. "She got that from you, our sweet kitten. Every time she cried, it reminded me of *you.* Those soft, shaky breaths. The way you always quivered. She did that, too. Some days, I could not even *look* at her without reliving what you put me through."

"I've done nothing to you."

"You ran from me," he says. "I gave you everything. I even gave you a part of me. Yet you *ran.*"

"You were hurting me."

He raises his eyebrows, looking genuinely curious as he asks, "Was I?"

I nod.

"Well," he says, staring at me for a moment before continuing. "I suppose, then, it makes you happy to know that you have hurt me back."

"I never wanted to—"

He grabs a hold of the chain around my neck before I can finish, his hand slipping beneath it, twisting it in his fist, tightening it to where it cuts off my words. I can't *breathe*. I grab his arm, clawing at it, trying to get him to let go.

My chest feels like it bursts into flames. *Oh god.*

"You have not felt my hurt *yet*, but you will," he says, his voice low. "By the time I am through with you, there will be nothing left for anyone else."

He lets go, and I inhale sharply, vision blurring. I'm hyperventilating, trying to calm down, but he's still right in front of me.

It's overwhelming.

"Not that anyone else wants you," he adds. "Especially not that freak. Even *he* does not want you now. He used you up and now he is done. You are not worth it to him."

"You don't know what you're talking about," I whisper. "Lorenzo isn't like you."

Something flashes in Kassian's face.

He laughs again.

He's *laughing* at me.

"Oh, pussycat, you were not falling for him, were you? Did you think he would want to keep you? Oh, this is cute, *suka*. You gave him *my* pussy, and you thought you could give him *my* heart, too? You belong with me. Even he sees that now."

"You're wrong."

"How do you think I found you? How do you think I knew where he lived? He told me, pretty girl... your scarred little plaything gave you up today."

"You're lying."

He stares at me, unwavering, as he reaches into his pocket, pulling out a cell phone. After a moment, his eyes flicker toward it, and he reads out a phone number. *Lorenzo's* phone number.

"Do you recognize it?" he asks.

I glare at him. "That proves nothing."

He presses a button before holding the phone up. The harsh glow in the darkness makes me squint, and I blink a few times, realizing he's showing me a text message.

14682 Liden Blvd, Queens
You want her, take her.
Leave everyone else alone.

"No." I shake my head, the chain clanging. "No way, that's... *no.*"

"It is right here in front of your eyes." He shoves the phone into my face, smacking me with it. "Is that not his number? Did I not find you there?"

"Yes, but..." My heart is battering my rib cage. I feel sick. "He wouldn't."

"Threatening everyone he cares for must have done the trick," he says, an edge to his voice. "Because you, *suka*, do not fall into that category. He would not sacrifice his family, his friends, for a piece of used-up pussy that half of this city has fucked!"

I snap, as he spits those words in my face, his anger slamming into me, fueling my own. I smack the phone out of his hand and send it flying across the room, hitting the concrete face-down, the glow extinguishing, the text message gone. "I *hate* you."

Kassian raises up when I say that, towering over me. I glare at him in the darkness, refusing to back down, refusing to look away.

"Hate me all you want," he says. "I do not mind. But until you *love* me again, *suka*, until you finally learn your place, you will stay right where you are. So it is in your best interest, I think, to just give in... especially since being with your kitten requires getting out of *here.*"

He walks away, snatching up his phone as he goes. I hear his shoes on the creaky wooden stairs leading out of the basement, into his office, light basting through as the door opens, music assaulting my ears.

I squeeze my eyes shut, to block it out, before everything

around me grows dark again.

There are at least a dozen locks on the basement door, all of which only *he* has the keys to open. The odds are slim of getting out of here without his blessing, which brings me to a crippling realization.

"And she never saw her daughter again," I whisper to myself. "*The end.*"

12

Lorenzo

Remember back at the beginning of this all when I told you to listen to your intuition? Your thoughts can't be trusted and your heart will fucking betray you, but your gut is one tough son of a bitch. It always senses when something is happening.

You just have to pay attention.

"The gate's open."

Seven puts my car in park and cuts the engine, pulling the keys from the ignition before turning to me, his brow furrowed. "What did you say, boss?"

I motion out the passenger side window, toward the unlatched gate on the picket fence, before repeating myself. "The gate's open."

"I see that," he says, his voice hesitant. "Does that mean something?"

"It means someone came or went in a hurry."

Getting out of the car, I head toward the house, walking right through the open gate on my way to the small porch. All seems quiet and still. The front door is unlocked, but fuck, isn't it always?

I certainly never lock it.

Seven follows me, latching the gate as he comes, right on my heels as I step into the house. I glance around, that bad feeling stirring inside of me, rising up like my gut is pulling a fucking mutiny. There, on the floor in the hallway, is a pair of familiar red high heels, toppled over, like someone kicked them off while running.

Deja vu.

"Scarlet?" I call out, my voice so loud it echoes through the house. "You here?"

No answer.

I know she gave those shoes to my brother's girlfriend, but last time I saw them hastily discarded, Scarlet was in trouble. Yeah, whatever, the trouble back then was *me*, but that little fact does nothing to pacify my bad feeling.

"Check upstairs," I tell Seven as I reach beneath my shirt, grabbing my gun. "See if anyone's here."

He hits the stairs, no question, no argument, heading off to search the house.

I walk down the hall, stepping over the shoes along the way. The living room and my library are both empty, nothing out of place. Reaching the kitchen, I pause, seeing the back door standing wide open.

Someone ran out of here in a hurry.

I hear Seven approach after a moment, stalling beside me, his eyes fixed on the open back door as he says, "The house is clear, nobody home."

Shit.

Is it too much to ask for her to have just been *asleep*?

Shoving my gun away, I search through my pockets for my phone.

"Here," Seven says, retrieving it, handing it over, knowing exactly what I'm looking for.

I hit a few buttons, calling my brother's number, listening as it rings and rings and rings. *No answer.* I call his work next, being greeted warmly by the hostess.

"Can you tell me if Leo Accardi is there?"

"Uh, yes, sir," she says. "He's actually just leaving. Would you like to speak to him?"

"No, but can you pass a message to him for me?"

"Sure."

"Tell him his brother said to hurry home."

I hang up, glancing at Seven, who looks anxious. *Not good.* I scan through my phone for Melody's number. I've never called it... never *cared* to call it... but I saved it for a rainy day.

Guess it's raining on me, huh?

I hit the button, dialing it, instantly hearing the faintest ringtone of some old rap song coming from upstairs.

I hang up. The music stops.

"You sure she's not up there?" I ask, knowing the answer before Seven even confirms it.

"Positive."

My gaze scans the backyard briefly before I close the door, not sure what to do about this. Some bullshit equations are spinning around my head, putting two and two together again.

I don't like what it's adding up to.

Errrnnnttt, wrong fucking answer.

I go to walk out when my phone rings. *Leo.*

"Yeah?" I answer. "You on your way home?"

"Jesus, yes, what the hell is going on?" he asks. "I've got like forty missed calls from one of the neighbors, saying Mel showed up there freaking out about some man being at the house? Do you know anything about this? Lady tried to call the cops, but Mel made her call *me*."

I close my eyes, pinching the bridge of my nose. "Which neighbor?"

"The blue house, like three doors down," he says. "Mrs. McKinnon. You know, the elderly lady whose groceries I sometimes get?"

No, I don't know. I've never heard of the woman. He's practically Mother Theresa, isn't he? The patron saint of fucking friendliness. Next thing you know, he'll be organizing neighborhood watches, painting people's fences like we're all Tom Sawyer and he's the little twit getting tricked, like doing someone else's dirty work is an *honor.*

"I'll see you when you get home, Pretty Boy."

"But wait, what's hap—?"

I hang up, not letting him finish that question, because I don't have an answer for it. I shove the phone into my pocket, motioning toward Seven. "Firecracker's hiding out down the street. Blue house, old woman, Leo feeds her... I don't know."

"Mrs. McKinnon?"

"Yeah."

"I'll handle it."

He walks out, his steps determined, and I shake my head, running my hands down my face. "Fuck."

Fuck.

Fuck.

Fuck.

I head to my library. My nerves are fucking shot. Rolling a sloppy joint, I light it up, smoking in silence as I stand there, in front of the table, waiting for them to return.

Melody bursts in a few minutes later, shrieking like a banshee, talking so damn fast I can't keep up, yammering about a guy with some hands and something, something, something...

Just as it seems she's about to finish, Leo rushes into the house, and the girl starts all over again from the beginning, somehow even more frantic now. Leo manages to calm her down, and I get the gist of it, hearing all I need to know—the Russian bastard showed up at my house and now Scarlet is gone.

I'm trying to get my thoughts in order, but my head is starting to throb. These people are in my library. There's crying and panic and blah, blah, blah... and maybe it makes me an asshole, but I really wish they'd all shut the fuck up. I just need a moment of silence so I can figure things out.

Absently, I reach over onto the table, picking up a puzzle piece and trying it in a few spots.

"Is he seriously working on a puzzle right now?" Melody asks. "*Seriously?*"

"It helps him think," Seven says.

Usually, we should add, because it's not much helping at the moment. Sure, Aristov might've had enough time to do his research. He might've just happened upon this address. But chances are someone told him where to find the house, spilling their guts faster than the Tauntaun on Hoth when Han Solo sliced it open with the lightsaber.

If that reference didn't make sense to you, go watch *Empire Strikes Back*.

Point here being, someone tattled like a little bitch.

"Call Three," I say, giving up on that puzzle piece and instead trying another. "Tell him to come pay me a visit."

"You think he has something to do with this?" Seven asks.

"Not him, but maybe the girl," I say. "Besides, I'm not sure it even matters. *Somebody* needs to answer for this, so unless you want to claim credit, Seven, get his ass over here."

"Yes, boss."

Seven leaves the room.

"We should... go somewhere," Leo says. "Anywhere but *here* tonight. Go stay in the city, get away, try to forget this happened."

"But Morgan," Melody says. "We have to do something!"

I can feel my brother's eyes. I don't turn around. I don't acknowledge whatever look he's giving me.

"I'm sure Lorenzo will figure something out," Leo says finally. "And whatever it is, we probably don't want to be around for it."

* * *

"Wait... wait... *wait*!"

BANG. BANG. BANG.

I pull the trigger back to back, no hesitation, no calculation, no fucking *deliberation*. As soon as I see Three's face, I shoot. The bullets fly through the living room from the suppressed gun in my hand, from where I sit on the stolen couch in the darkness to where he popped up in the doorway just now. Three throws his hands up in an attempt to stop me, but otherwise, he just stands there, frozen. A bullet rips through the wall beside him, another zooming past him, slamming into the banister for the stairs, while the last one lands God-knows-where.

Seeing as how he's not currently bleeding to death, I'm going to go out on a limb and say I might've missed my mark this time.

The fourth time I pull the trigger, the gun jams, completely locking up on me. I sigh, sitting up straight, forcing the slide to the rear, locking it so I can eject the magazine and try to clear the chamber.

Can't even fucking rely on *guns* these days.

"You've got maybe a minute until I reload," I say. "*Now* would be the time to do something."

A normal person would run right now, get the hell away while they had the chance. A smart person would find a gun and shoot me, quite frankly, since this certainly qualifies as self-defense. But a *crazy* person would just fucking stand there, awaiting their fate. One guess on what Three does.

Fucking insanity.

"Look, boss, I don't know what happened, but I swear to you, on my mother's life, that I had nothing to do with it," Three says, not moving an inch, his hands still raised in front of him as I clear the chamber. "I promised you years ago that I had your back, no matter what, and I meant that. I know I've made mistakes, so if you wanna kill me for being a meathead, go ahead, but I *refuse* to go out like I'm goddamn *Judas*."

I reload the magazine and chamber a round, eyeing the gun as I say, "You sound like you believe that."

"Because it's true," he says. "I would never betray you, nor would I stand back and let anyone else fuck you over that way. If I thought for even a *second* that Lexie would spill, I would've blown her brains out myself."

"You're thinking with your dick."

"No, I'm following my gut," he says. "She wants that rat bastard to pay just as much as we do, and she's our way in. She wouldn't have done this."

I point the gun at him, aiming center mass, finger on the trigger, and he still doesn't run. "Is that what your gut tells you?"

"Yes," he says. "So if you're gonna shoot me, fine, but use the girl. She wants to help, and she *can*."

I stare at him, far past the point where a normal person would grow uncomfortable... which, with my face, is a few seconds, at most. Three doesn't waver, though. He just stands there, like a man on death row who has come to terms with his impending execution and just wants to tell the world, one last time, that he doesn't deserve to die. Whether or not he's *innocent* is irrelevant. We're all guilty of a lot of shit.

Scarlet's a thief who sometimes used her pussy to survive.

Seven's a former crooked cop who took bribes from the mob.

Me? I've probably killed more people than Ted Bundy but with only a fraction of the charm.

"Is it raining outside?" I ask.

Three shakes his head. "Not a cloud in sight."

Huh.

Slowly, I lower the gun, setting it on the cushion beside me as I relax back on the couch.

"Boss, if I may?" Seven chimes in from where he stands near the window. I wave toward him, motioning for him to continue. "Look, I want to preface this by saying *don't shoot me.*"

That's never a good way to start a conversation.

"I just think maybe we ought to take a minute to *really* think about what we're doing here," Seven continues. "I'm not sure it's a good idea."

"Which part?"

"*All* of it," he says. "We went up against the Italians for territory, for reputation, to take over a lot of the business, and it worked. They're terrified of you, and we've made *a lot* of money off of them. But with the Russians, it's different... you're starting a war over a *woman*, and history tells us that never works out good for any man."

I turn my head, looking at Seven, seeing a flicker of fear in his eyes, like he thinks I might actually shoot him for his opinion.

I mean, yeah, I *might*, but I probably won't.

He's always been the one to play devil's advocate with motives and consequences.

Must be the cop side of the man.

"It's not about the woman," I say, and I know I'm fucking

lying the moment I say it, because it damn sure *feels* like it's about her. I can't shake the sickness in my stomach, the tightness in my chest, knowing wherever she is, he's probably there. Brave, beautiful Scarlet, she fucking buckles because of that man, and I saw enough of his little home movie to riddle out why that happens.

"It's principle," Three chimes in. "We're not exactly *The Avengers* here, but sometimes shit has to be done. Sometimes you've gotta go after a guy, to make a point, to say *'this shit isn't happening on my watch'* because it shouldn't be happening."

"Exactly," I say. "Besides, the guy came into my house today and helped himself to something that doesn't belong to him. We're a little past *live and let live* at this point. I ought to cut his balls off for stepping onto my property."

Seven says nothing else. I don't know if he's convinced, but he knows better than to press too hard after I've made up my mind on something.

"You can go," I tell Three, waving him away. "Tomorrow, I need you and all the guys back here, so we can handle this. Try to get a hold of the girl tonight and see if she can tell you anything."

"Yes, sir," he says, nodding before leaving.

"You can go home, too," I tell Seven. "I'm sure your wife is waiting for you."

He hesitates. "Are you going to be okay here by yourself tonight?"

"I'll be fine," I say. "I don't need a babysitter."

Seven leaves, finally, a minute later, saying nothing else. I sit in silence as darkness creeps in, nighttime coming. Picking my gun back up, I run my fingers along the cool metal. The gun feels heavy in my hand, heavier than usual, like the weight of this situation is pressing upon it.

I've never really liked guns.

Sure, I use them often. They do the trick, in a pinch, but it's almost *too* easy, if you know what I'm saying. You don't even have to get close to someone to pick them off, if you've got a gun. That makes it impersonal, which also makes it *boring*.

This thing with the Russians... it's as personal as it gets, which means Aristov won't get the easiness of a bullet.

Getting up, I stroll out of the living room, clutching the gun like a security blanket. I take the stairs up to the second floor, heading for my bedroom. The bed is unmade, unkempt, comforter bunched up along the end, sheets rumpled, the beat up old bear lying in the center of it. *Left behind.*

Turning, my gaze catches my reflection above the dresser, blurry in the darkness, before my attention shifts to the remnants of red lipstick on the mirror, not yet wiped off. Didn't see the point, so I never bothered. *I'm sorry.* I can make out part of the words, smeared but still there.

It grates my already frazzled nerves.

As anger rushes through me, my blood turning cold, I raise the gun, finger on the trigger.

BANG.

BANG.

BANG.

The mirror fractures, shattering, pieces of the glass flying back at me as bullets rip through it, destroying my reflection and the apology I never asked for, the one I don't *want*. I don't stop until the last bullet pierces the mirror, tearing through the wall behind it, but it doesn't matter, because there's nobody else here. The clicking of the gun echoes through the room before I toss the damn thing down on top of the dresser.

Empty.

* * *

"Seven years bad luck."

My brother's voice filters through the haze of exhaustion that keeps pulling me in and out of consciousness. I'm too tired to sleep, if you can believe that shit. My body aches and my head just keeps throbbing. Every time I doze off, I'm jarred right back to reality. *Figures.*

"I didn't raise you to be a superstitious little bitch," I mutter, my forearm covering my eyes as I lay in the bed, on my back, still fully dressed from yesterday. "There's no pot of gold at the end of the rainbow, Pretty Boy. Life isn't *magically delicious*. The consequences of breaking a mirror is that your goddamn mirror is now broken."

"Yeah, well, you didn't just break it," he says, his voice growing louder, closer, as he comes further into my bedroom. "Looks like you murdered the thing. What did it do, tell you Snow White was prettier than you?"

Moving my arm, I open my eyes and glance over at him. I'm not sure when he got here. I'm not even sure what time it is, but being as the room is bright and I can tell there are people downstairs, moving around my house, I'm going with it being *afternoon*.

"Why are you even here?" I ask, sitting up, scrubbing my hands over my face before running them through my hair, trying to wake up.

"I live here," he says, turning to look at me, "in case you've forgotten."

"For now."

"For now," he agrees, quiet for a moment before saying, "I'm worried about you, Lorenzo."

I laugh at that, getting to my feet, swaying. I grasp his shoulder, squeezing, on my way out of the room. "It's my job to worry about you, not the other way around."

I walk out before he can argue with me on that, not in the mood for the sentimental bullshit. I appreciate it, the fact that my brother cares, but I don't have it in me to deal with any of that right now. There's too much else on my mind.

The guys are all here, but I don't greet them right away, instead making my way to the kitchen. I grab an orange from a bowl on the counter and start peeling it as I stroll to the living room. The guys are chatting—*strategizing*, as it is. Where to go, who to hit, what to do, how to do it... why the hell we're all just sitting here instead of being out there, doing *something*.

It's a damn good question.

Leaning against the doorframe, I finish peeling the orange, tossing the scraps at Seven for him to discard. I eat it, still not saying a word, as they continue to bicker back and forth.

Three wants to hit the strip club.

Five wants to blow the guy's house up.

Seven looks like he wants to mediate, opening his mouth to chime in every few seconds before just closing it again, shaking his head. He knows it's not his place. The others don't seem to know *what* they want to do, but they sure seem ecstatic about the prospect of raising some hell out there, somewhere.

"I'm telling you, we've gotta hit the club," Three says. "The club is where she'll be."

"Oh *bullshit*," Five says, waving him off. "Now isn't the time to go get your dick sucked, Declan. He isn't just going to take her back to his goddamn whorehouse to work for him."

"No, but he would've taken her there to lock her up," Three says. "Are you forgetting he locked me in his fucking basement and tried to get information?"

"*Tried*, huh?" Five glares at him. "Who's to say it didn't work? Who's to say you're not working with him now?"

Three springs to his feet, furious. "How *dare* you! I'd *never!*"

Five jumps up, coming at him, bumping right into him, pointer finger jabbing against his chest. "How are we supposed to know that, huh? *Somebody* spilled their guts to him. So if it wasn't you, who was it? Huh?"

Three shoves him. "Maybe it was you, asshole!"

Five stumbles but recovers quickly, coming back at him, this time swinging. Three punches back, the two of them trading blows, sending Seven over the edge. He can't stay out of it anymore.

"Guys, guys, *relax!*" Seven says, shoving his way between them, separating the two men. "There's no need for this! The last thing anyone needs right now is us turning against each other."

"Tell that to that traitorous *bitch*," Five says.

Three tries to come back at him, shoving, but he can't get past Seven. "Fuck you!"

"*Jesus Christ,*" a voice mutters behind me, and I glance over

173

my shoulder, back at my brother as he steps down off of the stairs, pausing. "What's even going on around here anymore?"

Another damn good question.

The guys are still trying to fight, the others jumping in, choosing sides. Seven's doing a shit job playing peacekeeper on this one, unable to keep the hotheads from exploding at each other, taking a few blows himself as fists start flying again.

If I had my gun on me, if I hadn't unloaded it in the mirror upstairs, I'd probably shoot half of these assholes right now just to rid my life of all this *bickering*.

"You should probably get out of here," I tell my brother. "Might get ugly."

He laughs dryly, saying something about how it's pretty damn ugly at the moment, before heading out the front door. I push away from the doorframe after he's gone.

"If you're measuring, fellas, to see which of you has the biggest cock," I say, "I can end this easily by telling you it's neither one of you jackasses, because *nobody* has a bigger cock than I do, so sit the fuck down before I'm forced to whip it out."

I shove right through the middle of them, doing what Seven couldn't accomplish, sending the two of them to opposite corners and stopping this shit-show of a showdown.

Three wipes his mouth with the back of his hand, smearing blood from a busted lip onto his cheek. "Boss, I just think—"

"Shut up," I say. "I haven't told you to speak."

Three says nothing else, nostrils flaring as he breathes heavily, balling his hands into fists. He doesn't take well to being called a traitor.

Can't say I blame him.

I turn to Five just as he goes to step back, to turn away, thinking that's the end of it, like this is over. He, on the other hand, doesn't take well to being betrayed, but I can't say I blame him, either. Still, I grab him roughly by the back of the neck, forcing him to stay where he is, yanking him in the direction of Three. "*Apologize.*"

Five looks at me with shock.

"Three and I have already hashed that out," I say. "If I thought he was to blame, do you really think he'd be standing in my living room?"

"No."

"Then apologize," I say again. "Kiss and make up, whatever, because I don't have time to deal with the two of you whacking off when there's shit to take care of."

Five glares across the room at Three. "I apologize."

There's not a stitch of genuine meaning to his words, but that doesn't matter. I didn't tell him to be sorry. I told him to apologize.

"Fuck you," Three grumbles in response.

"Fuck you back," Five says, stepping over to sit down on the couch.

"Well, then," I say, "if you're all done being stupid and want to offer *real* suggestions, I'm listening... otherwise, get the fuck out of my house."

They throw out ideas, the same bullshit ones they spewed before, as I take a seat beside Five on the couch and pull out my phone, ignoring the guys as they start bickering once more. *Stubborn assholes.*

I guess if I want shit done, I'm going to have to figure it out myself... like usual.

13

The little girl sat in a blue plastic chair in the lobby of the police precinct. The lights were bright, blasting her like summer sunshine, the heat cranked up high in the building, but she was still so cold. Even with the thick blanket they'd covered her with, she couldn't stop shaking, her teeth chattering.

She just wanted to go home.

How many times did she have to tell them?

She said it every time they started asking their questions, but they kept ignoring her, wanting to know other things she couldn't say, things she didn't want to talk about with those people.

"What should we do?" an officer in a uniform asked, standing beside the chair. "We've been trying for an hour and *nothing*."

"I'll put a call into DCFS," another man said, this one wearing a suit. "Family services should be able to help, maybe send up someone who can coax something out of her."

"You don't think something happened to her parents, do you?" the uniformed man asked, frowning. "We checked all over the city, no missing reports matching her, but somebody ought to be missing her, you know?"

No missing reports.

Somebody ought to be missing her.

The little girl didn't like how they talked about her, like she wasn't there and couldn't hear, and she especially didn't like some of the things they said, like how nobody told them she was missing. *Was* she missing? Her mother would be missing her, the little girl was sure of it, but maybe she thought she was just still hiding.

"What's with all the commotion in here this morning?" another man grumbled as he wandered into the lobby, his suit all rumbled, the skin under his eyes dark, his hair sticking out, like he'd just woken up. He carried a huge cup of coffee, sipping on it. "Someone said Ramirez got assaulted out in Brighton Beach? Who the hell did that?"

"*This* one did," the first man in the suit said, motioning to the little girl. "He found her wandering alone at four o'clock this morning. Feisty thing damn near clawed his eyes out."

The new arrival stepped closer, regarding her, and froze a foot away, eyes widening. The little girl looked up at him, and it took her a moment, but she thought his face looked kind of familiar.

Like maybe she saw it before.

"Son of a bitch," he grumbled.

"Putting a call into DCFS," the other man in a suit said. "Going to broadcast an alert, probably blast her picture out there, hoping someone will step forward once DCFS clears it."

"Don't bother," the new man said with a loud sigh. "I know who she belongs to."

The guy in the uniform looked surprised. "You do?"

"You *don't?*" he countered. "Come on, use your eyes. Have you even *looked* at her? It's obvious."

All three men looked at her then.

The little girl didn't like their attention.

The uniformed still seemed confused, but the other one got a vacant stare as he whispered, "Oh, *fuck.*"

"*Fuck* is right," the newcomer said. She'd call him Sleepy, except he suddenly looked wide awake, so she went with Dopey instead, since it was the only other dwarf she could remember right then. "I'll handle it personally. I've been dealing with this long enough, so I ought to be the one to do it."

The others didn't argue, averting their eyes and walking away, as Dopey motioned for her to follow him to an elevator.

"Come on, kid," he said. "I'm going to make sure you get back to where you belong."

The little girl liked the sound of that.

She belonged at home with her mother.

Standing up, dragging the blanket along with her, she followed him, her wet shoes squeaking against the floor. Everyone kept looking at her. She didn't like it. She followed Dopey onto the elevator, still not saying anything, and he led her to an office on another floor, tucked in the back, surrounded by glass.

"Take a seat," he said, pointing to a chair, before he closed a bunch of blinds, which made the little girl happy. It meant people had to stop *staring.* She sat down, and he joined her, sitting behind a desk piled high with folders. "This was certainly not how I expected this to go."

He drummed his fingers against the arm of his chair, regarding her.

The little girl thought he'd ask her all those same questions, about names and parents, but instead he asked, "Are you okay, kid?"

She shrugged.

"You're not hurt, are you?" He looked her over from a distance. "Before I make any calls, I want to be sure you're okay."

"My arm feels funny," she said. "It got hurt when I fell."

"You fell?"

She nodded.

"Anything else? Did anyone else hurt you? Another person?"

Tears welled in her eyes, but she shook her head, not wanting to talk about it.

"Are you sure? You can tell me."

"He took Buster," she whispered. "He burned him, but not all up."

"Who's Buster?"

"My bear," she said. "And he made Mommy go to sleep, too. She told me to play Hide & Seek, and she would find me, but she hasn't."

"But *you're* okay?"

She nodded.

She guessed she was.

He picked up the phone, dialing a number. It rang and rang and rang, but she couldn't hear it. "Hey, it's, uh... *me*. I'm calling to let you know that we've located your daughter. We're down at the precinct."

He paused, sighing. "An officer saw her this morning wandering alone along the beach. She's okay, though. She's fine. You'll just want to get down here right away, you know, before anybody else catches wind of it."

Another pause. Another sigh.

"See you in a few." Hanging up, Dopey looked over at her. "Don't worry, it won't be long."

"Do you know Mommy?"

"Your mother?" He let out a light laugh. "Yeah, I met her when this all happened. Someone saw your front door busted down and found her on the kitchen floor."

"Sleeping."

"Sleeping," he agreed. "She told me all about you as soon as she woke up."

The little girl smiled at Dopey, taking in his expression, almost like her mother made him *sad* for some reason. He had polka dots on his face, ones the little girl thought were funny. She'd seen them before, but it was weird, because it wasn't with her mother.

"Anyway, your mother, she's made the trek to my office every week since then. And today... today makes ten months since she lost you. I'm sure it'll warrant a visit."

Ten months.

The little girl didn't know what to say, but she really didn't get the chance anyway. There was commotion outside the office, the door shoving open without a knock.

Turning, the first person the little girl saw was the Cowardly Lion, followed by the Tin Man strolling in.

No.

This was wrong.

It wasn't supposed to be *them*.

"Come on," the Cowardly Lion said as soon as she started

crying, pulling her out of the chair, scooping her up in his arms as he whispered, "Don't make a scene, sweet girl, and he'll forgive you for this."

But she didn't want the Tin Man's forgiveness. She wanted rid of him.

"I appreciate the call," the Tin Man said, "and I assure you, this will *never* happen again."

"Just... take her home, Aristov," Dopey said, covering his polka-dotted face with his hands. "Get her out of here before this gets any worse than it is."

14
Morgan

A buzzing sound disturbs the stark silence, pulling me from unconsciousness, so quiet I think my imagination might be playing tricks on me. Forcing my eyes open, I blink rapidly as the faint noise registers with my ears. A soft glow cuts through the darkness right behind me, illuminating the space surrounding me, like I'm cast in a spotlight, but there's not a stitch of warmth to it. I *shiver*.

Pushing off the hard ground, sitting up, I turn and see him. *Kassian*. Just a foot away, he sits in a rusted metal chair, so close he could've kicked me had he gotten the urge. My heart stalls a beat, alarmed by his proximity, as I shove away, the filthy concrete scraping against my bare legs.

I don't get far. It only takes him a few seconds to react, his foot stomping on the chain, abruptly cutting off my slack. Gasping, I grab where it's wrapped around my neck, my breathing strangled as I pull my knees up to protect myself, forced to stay there. He's holding his phone, the buzz coming from it.

Somebody's calling.

Kassian presses a single finger to his lips, warning me to be silent, before he answers it.

"How nice of you to call," Kassian says, his voice so loud in the vacant basement that I wince. "What can I do for you, Mister Scar?"

Scar. I let out a shaky breath, my lips parting, words on the tip of my tongue, wanting to spring free, yearning to call out to him. *Lorenzo.* I force the urge down, though, swallowing back the words.

As much as I want to scream, as much as I want to lash out, I know it's not going to help me right now.

Kassian listens in silence as Lorenzo talks, before a smile cracks his face and he lets out a laugh, the sound of it chilling. My hair stands on end, tears prickling my eyes. Laughter from Kassian isn't a sign of happiness; it doesn't signify peace or that everything is all right. Laughter from Kassian is sadistic, *dominating*, his sense of humor twisted. He laughs at others' misery.

This time, I think, he's laughing at *mine*.

"I look forward to it," Kassian says, eyeing me, the smile lingering on his lips. "Until then..."

He pulls the phone away from his ear without finishing his thought, ending the call before pressing another button, the light disappearing, leaving us in total darkness. I blink, trying to adjust my eyes so I can make him out, but there's no natural light down here in the basement.

"Come here," Kassian says, his voice so quiet that it's like the shadows are whispering, beckoning me closer.

I don't move, though.

I want *nothing* that lives in these shadows.

Kassian gives it maybe ten seconds before the chain jingles. He grabs it, yanking on it like it's a leash. I try to resist, losing my breath, digging my heels in, but he's too damn strong. I cry out as I'm dragged along the floor, the concrete skinning my knees and the palms of my hands when I try to catch myself to keep from smacking into it.

As soon as I'm within reach, he grabs where it's wrapped around my neck and pulls my face right up to his face. I can hardly make him out, even *this* close, but I can feel his warm breath against my skin.

"I said *come here*," he says, his voice still quiet, a forced kind of calm. "Have you gone deaf? Do we need to clean out your ears?"

I don't answer him.

He doesn't care about my answer.

Closing my eyes, I hold my breath as he runs his nose along my jawline, the scruff on his face rubbing against my cheek. I'm trembling. I know he can feel it, and I try to stop, but his proximity makes it hard for me to get a grip.

He makes me feel like that teenager again.

"You are still beautiful when you sleep, *suka*," he says. "I could not bring myself to wake you. You looked so at peace. You do not look that way when your eyes are open. Why is that?"

"You know why," I whisper.

He pulls back some, looking me in the eyes, the tip of his nose brushing against the tip of mine. He tilts his head ever-so-slightly, and I let out a shaky breath, knowing he's thinking about kissing me.

The thought makes me grimace.

"I came down here so we could catch up on your lessons, pretty girl," he says, just a whisper away from my mouth, "but it seems as if we will have to put that on hold for now."

He lets go of the chain, and I immediately move away, scrambling to put a bit of space between us. Just a foot or two, just enough so I can't smell his cologne, so his cruel warmth can't swaddle me in the cold, damp room.

Standing up, he starts walking away, like he's just going to leave, like he's going to go without torturing me for the moment. My stomach twists in knots, heavier than the thick metal constricting my throat. Here I am, after fighting so hard for so long, once more at the mercy of a man who isn't particularly *merciful.*

I don't trust his passive demeanor.

He's up to something. I know it.

"Oh, I almost forgot," he says, stalling. "I have something for you."

Of course.

Closing my eyes, I sigh, hearing his steady footsteps as he approaches again. Whatever he's got, I don't want it. He can keep it. He can shove it up his ass, for all I care. The only thing I want is to see my daughter, so unless he's giving me that...

Be gone.

Kassian stalls in front of me, and I peek through the

darkness as he reaches into the front pocket of his black slacks, pulling something out. A piece of paper, it looks like, crumbled and folded again and again, into a little square.

"I have been carrying this around for some time," he says, unfolding it. "I told my kitten that I would give this to you, a gift from her, whenever I saw you again."

He drops the paper, and it floats to the concrete in front of me. I don't reach for it right away, just staring at where the paper lands, unable to make out any of it in the darkness. My heart races, like the paper is a ticking time bomb, like it has the power to detonate everything inside of me that I've somehow kept together even after Kassian tried to break me apart.

"It will not bite," he says, his hand on my head, petting my hair before I even realize he's reaching for me. I instinctively recoil, expecting punishment for the snub—a blow to the face, a thump to the cheek, maybe a hand fisting my hair—but he merely pulls away, turning to leave. "I will let that go this time. Be a good girl this afternoon, and I will have a mattress brought down."

I shake my head, although I know he can't see it, whispering, "I don't want it."

There used to be a bed down here. There used to be *a lot*. The first time I found myself locked in here, all those years ago, it looked like a shabby studio apartment, dirty and dark, but yet, it had been livable. You see, since Kassian spent so much time down here, he wanted to be comfortable, but I changed that, because the only thing he cherished more than his own comfort was my suffering. He'd gladly do without if it meant I had nothing.

It went from a regular little jail cell to solitary confinement.

Slowly, piece-by-piece, it all went away. The blankets, the extra clothes, the towels, the sheets. He ripped out the plumbing after I flooded his basement, leaving just a toilet that only flushes when water is poured into it. The bath was removed after I threatened to drown myself, replaced with a hose that is now kept under lock-and-key after I blasted him with cold water when he tried to come near me.

The bed, though, was last to go. He clung to that

convenience like a dying man to his last breath, but after I stabbed him with a rusty piece of metal I tore from the box spring, he finally got rid of it.

That's when the chains appeared.

Act like an animal and I will treat you like one.

I guess getting that tetanus shot was Kassian's final straw, because after that, it wasn't a simple game of willpower anymore.

After that, he became *cruel.*

Not like locking girls in basements was nice in the first place, but a line was drawn that day. I drew blood. He decided it was time he did the same.

Before then, it was mostly mental. He didn't want to ruin the goods, so he left no permanent traces of himself. That changed with me, though, and sometimes I wonder if I brought that on myself. Would it have been easier to escape him had I not fought *so* hard?

"You will change your mind," he says. "The first time I slam your face into the floor, you will be *begging* me for that mattress, because it will muffle your cries a lot better than the concrete."

I bite my lip to keep from reacting to that.

As he starts up the stairs to leave, I reach over, carefully running my fingertips along the paper, feeling the waxy substance coating it. *Crayon.* She drew me a picture. I smile to myself at that thought, but it quickly fades, worried about what she might've drawn, if maybe it was monsters.

"I will turn on a light," Kassian calls back to me, "so you may see your present."

A bright light flicks on, harsh and blinding, hurting my eyes. I squint, trying to ward it off, and look at the paper as I pick it up.

My stomach clenches, bile burning my throat.

I hear the door open and close, locks clicking into place as he walks out, leaving me simmering under the harsh lights with tears burning my eyes. I try to exhale, but the air is trapped in my chest, pressure building until I feel like I'm going to burst. I can't seem to take a breath.

It's a picture she drew of me.

I cover my mouth with my hand, stifling a sob, my other hand shaking the paper as I grip it tightly. After a moment, I clutch it to my chest, hugging it as I pull my legs up. Tears stream down my cheeks, streaking my dirty bare legs as I rest my head on my knees and cry.

And cry.

And cry.

Please let her be okay.

* * *

I give myself twenty minutes.

Or well, at least I *think* I do.

I don't exactly have a watch here.

It's hard to judge time in a void, and it's not as if counting the seconds would make much of a difference, since I'd eventually waver and have to start over.

But it *feels* like twenty minutes before I swallow back my fears, wiping away my tears as I pull myself together, taking it one shaky breath at a time. Getting to my feet, I pace around, moving as far as the chain will let me go, stretching, trying to keep my strength up despite my soreness... despite my exhaustion... despite my thirst, my hunger, my *fear*...

You can do this. You can do this. You can do this.

I need a way out. I don't yet know what that way is, but I'm imagining it's not going to be easy, because getting out entails somehow getting past Kassian.

He said I wasn't leaving this basement until I loved him. I made him believe I loved him once. Hell, maybe I actually *did*. I remember a time when I looked at Kassian like the universe existed beneath his skin, stars twinkling in his eyes, constellations in his soul, air and atmosphere and water forming his strong, masculine body, like without the breath from his lungs, breathing life into us all, the sun would no longer burn. I thought he was the Heavens and the Earth, I thought he was my savior, but he was really just Hell in disguise. They always did say the devil was beautiful.

I know too much now, though, and so does he.

I'm not sure I could ever trick him into believing I still love him, but unless *you* have a better idea... no? Didn't think so.

Yeah, I'm totally screwed...

The basement door opens as I continue to pace, not a stitch of slack left in the chain as I move away from it as far as I can, turning to face the wall, needing a moment to dry my lingering tears before I can bring myself to look at him. There are footsteps on the stairs, too restrained to be Kassian's, my head dizzy as a soft voice rings out. "Morgan?"

Slowly, I turn.

Alexis.

I saw her just days ago, standing in Lorenzo's house. She'd been nervous then, but she seems to be even more nervous *now*. I'd already been deeply entrenched in life here when Kassian found her, another sweet little runaway girl in the city, one of the invisible, the forgotten. If you're all alone, on your own, it means there's nobody coming to save you, nobody to even *miss* you when you disappear. He exploits that, making you believe that without him, you're nothing.

You have nothing; you mean nothing.

But he made a grave mistake with me.

You see, he gave me something. He gave me someone. I'll never again be *nothing*, not as long as Sasha's out there somewhere. He thought that he was further tethering me to him, but in reality, he gave me the motivation I needed to break those chains.

"I, uh... I brought you something to eat," Alexis says quietly, offering me a small smile along with a brown paper bag. "You must be hungry."

I stare at her for a minute before my eyes flicker past her. The basement door stands wide open at the top of the stairs. I can hear voices, thick Russian accents spewing foreign words up in the office of Limerence. For a fleeting moment, I imagine making a break for it, wondering how many people I'd need to overpower, but as soon as I take a step, the chain jingles, grounding me back in reality.

Right. Kassian has the key to the lock hanging around my neck.

"Does he know you're feeding me?" I ask—a stupid question, frankly, because she wouldn't be down here without his permission.

"He wants you to keep your strength up," she says.

"Of course he does," I mutter, taking the bag from her before plopping down in the metal chair, surprised he left it in here where I could sit on it... or smack him over the head with it. "Doesn't want to fuck a corpse, right?"

"Right," she whispers, her smile falling as she glances up the stairs before turning back to me. "It wasn't me, Morgan. I *swear.* I would've never told—"

"I know," I say, dropping the bagged lunch on the floor, discarding it by the leg of the chair. "Kassian said it was Lorenzo."

She blanches. "What?"

"He said Lorenzo sent him his address."

"But why would—?"

Before she can finish, heavy footsteps come down the stairs. I look that way when Kassian appears.

"Stupid girl," he says, grabbing ahold of Alexis and pointing her toward the stairs. "Which part of 'give her food' did you think meant *gossip?*"

"I'm sorry, Mr. Aristov," Alexis whispers, rushing out of the basement.

He shakes his head, shouting, "Shut the door behind you!"

Alexis listens, the door closing, muffling the voices upstairs. Kassian turns to me once we're alone, curving an eyebrow as he strolls closer to where I'm sitting. He watches me carefully, eyes scanning my face. I don't move, don't speak, forcing myself to not react to his presence, as hard as that is. I try to look unruffled, as calm and collect as he seems to be, but my hands are sweaty and my heart is racing so hard I'd be surprised if he couldn't hear it.

As soon as he's within reach, he grabs the chain, no hesitation as he yanks on it hard, wrenching me right out of the chair. I stumble, tripping, trying to catch myself, to soften the blow, but I hit the concrete on my hands and knees, stinging tearing through my already scuffed palms, my kneecaps painfully *screaming*.

Wincing, I squeeze my eyes shut, taking a few deep breaths as I roll over, plopping down on my ass. A trickle of blood runs down my right shin, the skin around the knee sliced open.

The metal shifts as Kassian drops down into the chair, his voice firm as he says, "This is *my* seat. I did not tell you to help yourself to it."

"You didn't—" I cut off abruptly when he raises his eyebrows, like he can't believe I have the nerve to talk. *You didn't tell me not to, either.* Those words were about to come out, but I know if I don't watch my mouth, he might rip out my tongue, so I just leave it at that. "You didn't."

Reaching down, he picks up the brown bag lunch. "You are not eating, *suka*."

"I'm not hungry," I lie.

He sighs dramatically as he opens the bag and pulls out a sandwich covered in plastic. He unwraps it, tearing it sloppily down the middle, holding half out to me. *Peanut butter and grape jelly.* I stare at it with surprise, not moving, until he says, "Take it."

I take it, eyeing it warily. My stomach is churning, a battle brewing between my hunger and my anger, torn between eating it and wanting to shove it back in his fucking face.

"Not what you expected?" he asks, taking a bite of the other half of the sandwich, making a face as he chews. He has probably never had PB&J before, but he's trying to prove to me that it's safe to eat.

"No," I admit. "Expected some Doktorskaya bologna or smoked mackerel."

He grimaces, swallowing. "Either of those would be a much better choice, but kitten, she does not like my food, so sometimes, there is peanut butter to make her happy."

I stare at him after he says that.

"What is that look for?" he asks, tossing his half of the sandwich back in the bag, his point made. He's not trying to poison me. At least, not *right now*.

I take a small bite before mumbling, "I'm just wondering when you ever cared about somebody else's happiness."

I probably shouldn't have said that out loud.

I can see the amusement draining from his eyes.

He says nothing in response, though, watching me as I eat the half of the sandwich he offered, waiting until it's all gone before he says, "Come here."

I'm only like a foot away from him.

How much closer does he need me?

Swallowing thickly, I scoot closer, and closer, and closer, as Kassian leans down in the chair, closing the rest of the distance between us. Reaching into the neckline of his shirt, he pulls out the long silver chain he always wears, a set of small keys dangling from it.

My heart races, breath hitching.

His face is right up against mine, holding my gaze, as he grasps the heavy lock.

"Are you going to be a good girl?" he asks.

Carefully, I nod.

Not a chance in hell.

He sticks the key in, unlocking it, pulling the padlock off before unwinding the thick chain from around my neck. I take a deep breath, relieved at being free—at least temporarily.

The chain clatters when he drops it to the concrete beside me. Standing up, he slips the padlock into his pocket before grabbing my arm, yanking me to my feet.

The second he loosens his hold, letting go, instinct kicks in. There's nothing tethering me here.

Fuck this.

I run.

I dart for the exit, reaching the stairs in seconds, running up them as fast as my legs will carry me. As I near the door, my head grows fuzzy, the voices on the other side of it loud. *Shit. Shit. Shit.*

Grabbing the knob, I start to turn it when I'm ripped away, arms winding around me.

"No… no… no… no… *no!*"

Kassian' voice is laced with anger, a venomous growl right in my ear. He drags me back down into the basement, not wavering at all, even as I struggle. My breaths are sharp and quick, panic assaulting me. I lash out, trying to hit him, jabbing elbows into his chest, thrusting my feet back, kicking his legs, but his grip only grows tighter.

He pulls me across the room, to the area that used to be a bathroom, shoving me hard onto the drainage grate on the floor. I grimace, catching myself with my hands again, the metal clanging.

"Stay!" he yells.

Kassian uses another set of keys to unlock a nearby cabinet. I peek past him, inside of it, my heart hammering hard, watching as he shifts through supplies... none of which I could do any serious damage with if I stole it.

He pulls out a small hose, a bar of soap, and a threadbare towel.

"If you are looking for weapons, you should know better," he says, locking the cabinet before turning back to me. "Taking me out will never be *that* easy."

He hooks up the hose to the faucet on the wall before draping the towel over the back of his chair.

"Stand up," he says.

I don't stand up.

He grabs my arm again, yanking me to my feet as he yells right in my face, "I said *stand up!*"

I glare at him, staring into his stormy gray eyes. Rage simmers just below the surface, hints of it seeping out, buzzing like electricity between us. It's like a shock of static. My hair stands on end, the sensation crawling across my skin.

"Hands up," he orders, his voice low, *firm*.

I'd rather do anything but give in to his demands, but I think if I push him anymore right now, he might kill me.

For real this time.

I raise my arms as he grabs the bottom of my filthy white shirt, slowly pulling it up over my head before tossing it aside on the concrete.

"Do not move," he warns, "I mean it."

I drape my forearms on top of my head, tilting my head up, eyes moving to the ceiling right above me, fixed there as he kneels in front of me. I shudder, feeling his calloused fingers grazing against my skin. He runs his hands gently up my thighs before tugging on my underwear. I wait until he reaches my ankles before ever-so-slightly raising my feet, letting him take them off.

He tosses them aside with my shirt.

His hands settle on my hips as he pulls himself back up, standing, his clothed body flush against mine. He brings his mouth to my ear, my breath hitching as he whispers, "I can *smell* him on you."

I squeeze my eyes shut, still not moving, as Kassian turns on the hose. A cry escapes me the second the water pelts my chest, so icy cold that it stings, like needles piercing my skin. I breathe deeply, chanting silently to myself, trying to block it all out, trying to numb myself to it.

You can do this.

It'll be over before you know it.

Go to your happy place.

My happy place, in the little white house with the bright red door, blasting cheesy pop music and dancing around the kitchen with my little girl. Singing along at the top of our lungs, only knowing half the words, but it didn't matter how terrible we sounded because we had *fun*. Laughing until we cried, watching cartoons and baking cookies, as Buster stood guard, protecting us from monsters. My happy place, full of love... *so much love*. I'd do anything to have it back.

Anything to see her smile.

Anything to hear her sweet laughter.

Kassian's hands are as brutal as the frigid water, scrubbing me raw from head-to-toe, using the entire bar of soap.

"Did you let him come in you, *suka?*" he asks, his voice low, hands places his hands don't deserve to go. "Did you let him fuck you like only *I* am allowed? Do I need to rip out more of your insides to get rid of every trace of him?"

I don't answer.

Whatever I say won't make a difference.

My teeth viciously chatter to the point that my jaw hurts, my body shaking, shivering, parts of me going numb. I know I'm crying, but he can't see my tears, the water running down my face wiping away any evidence that he's getting through my defenses.

He drops the hose once he's satisfied and turns the water off. The floor beneath my feet is completely soaked, slow to drain. I lower my head, my eyes meeting Kassian's as he picks up the towel. He steps right up to me, so close we touch, not seeming to care that his suit gets wet.

In fact, looking at him, I can tell every ounce of care he might've had about *anything* is no longer there.

I might be freezing, but this man is ice cold.

"I can tell," he says.

I don't want to say anything. I want to stay silent.

My words won't change anything and he doesn't deserve to hear them.

But almost by instinct, my voice quietly responds, "You can tell *what*, Kassian?"

"That you have forgotten everything."

He's trying to goad me, to get a reaction, but I'm not going to give him the satisfaction. I know where this is leading. No matter how I respond, he's going to do what he wants.

"Beg me," he says, grasping my chin as I continue to shake, completely drenched. He's holding the towel hostage, refusing to wrap it around me. "Beg me to bring you that mattress and I will, pretty girl."

I continue to stare at him, his grip tight as he holds my face, waiting for those magic words.

He's not getting them.

I begged him that night. The night he broke into my house. The night he stole my *life*. I begged him not to do it, to leave us in peace, but none of it mattered, so it'll take one hell of a miracle to get me to ever beg him again.

The smirk that touches the corners of Kassian's mouth tells

me that's exactly what he was expecting... exactly what he *wanted*. He drags my face closer to his, fingers digging into my skin, squeezing my cheeks, his lips just a breath from my own as he says, "Concrete it is..."

15

Lorenzo

I don't know that I've ever encountered a problem that a grenade couldn't solve. Just pull the pin, toss, BOOM. *Problem gone.* I've gotten rid of a few issues that way, wiped right off the map, *bye-bye.* It's easy to forget about something once it no longer exists, when you never have to see it again.

Out of sight, out of mind.

Maybe that makes me an even bigger asshole than you thought, the fact that I'd rather erase something from my life than actually deal with any sort of fallout. Because fallout? It's messy... messier than the destruction a grenade can cause.

My brother says it's because I'm allergic to feelings.

I just think most people aren't worth the trouble.

A V40 minifrag, grenade the size of a golf ball. Weighs maybe five ounces or so. If you're within sixteen feet of the thing when it goes off, you're fucked. Up to a couple hundred feet, and it's probably going to hurt. *A lot.* Dangerous little fuckers, which is why they're out of service. Not hard to carry a few of them around in your pocket, if you're willing to risk blowing your dick off by accident.

I've tossed a few in my life, most just for the fun of it. They send one hell of a message. They get people's attention.

"You're making me nervous, boss."

Turning my head, looking away from the high-class whorehouse Aristov runs, I glance at the driver's seat beside me, where Seven sits. Yeah, he looks nervous. He's sweating fucking bullets.

"I'm not going to blow us up," I say, glancing at the little grenade in the palm of my hand. I've been running my fingers along the cold steel the entire thirty minutes we've been sitting here.

Debating.

Contemplating.

I really want to pull the pin and toss this bitch right inside Limerence. *Bye-bye, whorehouse. Bye-bye, Russian assholes.* But every time I get the itching to do it, to watch it all go BOOM, something stops me.

That something being more of a someone.

Scarlet.

You see, she might be inside, and that's a bit of a problem.

The kind of problem, I'm discovering, a grenade just isn't solving.

"Five more minutes," I say. "If something doesn't happen within the next five minutes, I'm shoving this grenade down his fucking throat."

Tick, tick, tick...

Four minutes and fifty-seven seconds.

I swear to fuck, that's how much time passes until Three appears. He jogs right over to the car, dressed in all black, blending into the darkness since night long ago fell. An entire day wasted where not a goddamn thing got accomplished.

Aristov is still happily breathing.

Scarlet is still, unfortunately, *missing.*

Three slides into the backseat, right behind me, slamming the door a bit harder than necessary.

"Three," I say, "you were *three* seconds away from getting your bowels blown out today."

He starts to talk but immediately pauses, brow furrowing as he scoots to the middle of the backseat, looking up at me. "I think Lexie's done that to me before."

I look at him. "What?"

"Yeah, isn't that where they stick their tongue—?"

Seven groans, covering his face as he leans forward against the steering wheel.

"Just tell me what you found out," I say, cutting him off before he goes into detail about the kinky shit they've done. "And it better be *something*, because if I sat out here waiting while you got your dick sucked..."

"Of course not, boss," he says. "Kept it in my pants the whole time. We were just talking."

"Well, don't keep me in suspense here. Tell me what your little Daisy Chain had to say."

He starts spilling. I'll spare you the word-for-word and summarize, since Three seems to like to hear himself talk and he just keeps going on and on and on.

Scarlet's most definitely inside. Aristov has her locked in the basement, only one set of keys to get down there, which are usually in Aristov's possession. Security is tightened at the moment, which is what took Three so long. Wasn't easy navigating past all the armed guards.

"Thursday," Three says after a moment. "I know it's a few days away, but Lexie thinks that's our best chance to get her out safely. Aristov has the party happening at his house, so we know *he'll* be gone, and by then he'll relax security again, figuring he's in the clear, you know? Lexie can keep an eye out for the kid at the house while we go after Scarlet, maybe hit them back-to-back."

"Maybe," I agree, although it sounds a lot like bullshit. Who's to say Aristov won't kill them *both* before then? Hell, maybe they're already dead because I took too long coming up with a plan.

Patience has never been my strong suit.

I'm not exactly keen on waiting for anything.

Nor am I good at planning, for that matter.

I'm the *shoot first, ask questions never* type... you know, the kind to toss a grenade in a packed room to solve a personal problem?

"*Or*," I say, stressing the word, "I can just walk in right now and make it all go BOOM."

Three laughs as he settles into the backseat, while Seven starts the car, like he thinks we're about to leave. I don't like it, though. I just can't walk away. It feels wrong, her being *right there* and me not doing a goddamn thing about it.

That's not *me*.

"Wait here," I order, opening my door and climbing out of the car.

I carry the grenade with me.

I know the guys notice, because they sure as fuck shout loud enough, yelling for me not to do anything stupid. But stupid is sort of a relative term, isn't it? Stupid, to me, would be coming the whole way here and not even dropping in to say *hello* to the Russian bastard. After all, when I called, I told him to expect to see *a lot* of me until this was settled.

What better time than right now to get the ball rolling?

I stroll right on up to the front door. The bouncers see me, *recognizing* me, suddenly all on edge, but they don't do a damn thing as I waltz past them and head inside. Music echoes through the place, masking other noises, although none of it is detectable outside of the building.

Soundproofing is quite genius, given his business.

If I didn't hate the guy so much, out of principle, I'd probably like him. He's *crafty*. I might have to start borrowing a bit from his bag of tricks.

As soon as I'm inside, right through the doors, hulking bodies surround me—five guys, guns drawn, aimed at my head like they'd get a kick out of being splattered with my brains tonight.

I raise my hands, still clutching the grenade. They could try to take it from me, try to disarm me... hell, they could even go ahead and shoot me in the face... but they'd have four seconds to save themselves before we all got blown to pieces.

They take a few steps back, but nobody lowers their weapons, like guns are going to help them in this situation.

Rock, paper, scissors, motherfuckers... you better take your pick and hope like hell you win.

"I just want to say hello to your boss," I say, "and then me and Betty-Boom here will be on our way."

For some reason, they don't look like they believe me. It kind of hurts my feelings.

Just kidding.

I wouldn't trust me, either.

A bark of angry Russian echoes nearby before Aristov rounds a nearby corner. He's *fuming*, so irate that he almost doesn't notice me, but when he does, he stops dead in his tracks. His eyes flicker around, assessing, before he simply nods his head toward his office, telling his guys, "Let him in."

I step past them. They don't look happy about it, but nobody tries to stop me as I walk over to Aristov's office, following him inside. He spews out more Russian to two guys lurking in there, who immediately vacate the room, closing the door behind them, so it's just me and him.

He heads for the vodka. "So it is true, then, that you deal in heavy weapons?"

"As true as the rumors of you kidnapping and raping women."

Instead of being offended, he laughs at that, strolling over to sit down on one of his couches, eyeing me as he sips his liquor. Doesn't escape my notice that he hasn't offered me a drink today.

I think he might be feeling some type of way about our *friendship*.

"Well, that is a shame, Mister Scar, because those rumors are not true at all."

"That's funny," I say, even though it's not fucking funny *at all*, "because I stumbled upon a little home movie you made that contradicts that, Aristotle."

He stares at me, all amusement gone. "And where, may I ask, did you acquire such a film?"

"A certain police detective had it in his possession."

There's that flash of rage I was hoping for.

He drinks in silence, guzzling the liquor as he gets his thoughts in order. In the wrong hands, or maybe the *right* ones, that video could be a serious problem for him. Even Jameson would give his left nut to get his hands on it, to use it to take down the Russians, but I'm not really big on letting the justice system do my dirty work.

I happen to *like* getting my hands dirty.

That's why Detective Fuckface had it, why he kept it hidden. He might've been working for the Russians, but in the event Aristov turned on him, he needed his own little grenade to make his problems go away.

"What is it you want from me?" Aristov asks. "If you are looking for the million dollars I promised, I am afraid I do not have it here. But being as I am a man of my word, I am happy to arrange a time for you to pick it up."

"You think I want your *money*?"

"Why else would you have given me the address of where I could find her?"

I stare at him when he asks that. I want to think he's toying with me, that he's just trying to fuck with my mind, but his expression is dead serious, almost *curious*, like he's genuinely wondering why I would've done such a thing. Problem number seven hundred and seventy-six in my life right now: *I didn't do it*. I didn't give him a goddamn thing, but for some reason he thinks I did, which means whoever did it made it look like I'd given her up. *Son of a bitch.*

"Of course, it is possible you just grew sick of the *suka*," Aristov continues with a shrug. "Since it seems you saw the video of her *sweet sixteen*, maybe you just did not want to touch her anymore, but all the same, I am grateful."

I'm not sure how to respond to that.

I kind of want to break his fucking jaw for half of the words he's spoken these past few minutes.

"Does she know how you found her?" I ask. "Did you tell her it was me?"

He nods. "She did not believe me, of course. The stupid girl *never* believes what I tell her. I showed her the message so maybe she would believe her own eyes. It upset her, but she is fine now. I have ways of making her get over things."

"I bet you do," I say, my gaze flickering around the room, settling on a door along the side—one I'm assuming leads to the basement. "Any chance I can see her, give her a proper goodbye?"

He laughs, sipping his vodka. "I think you have given her

quite enough, Mister Scar, but I will send her your regards."

I bite the inside of my cheek.

Man, I want to kill him...

"Now, if we are done here, I have other business to take care of," he says, standing up. "Seems I have a friend I need to talk to about a video in his possession."

"Seems you do," I say, not bothering to point out that he doesn't have the video anymore. *I* do. I turn to leave, still clutching the grenade, and pause long enough to say, "By the way, I think I *will* be claiming my reward. A million, cash, for her."

He doesn't look happy, because that's *a lot* of damn money, but he nods. "I will be in touch to make arrangements."

"Good," I say. "I look forward to it."

"Wait, Mister Scar," he says before I can walk out. "The grenade..."

I look at it in my hand before glancing at him. "What about it?"

"Do you think you could get me some of those?"

I laugh, because he's serious with that question. "Maybe once I'm sure it's not *me* you're going to be using them on."

"Fair enough."

I leave.

Nobody stops me.

I don't *want* to go, but at the same time, tonight isn't the night to rock the boat any further. I need to wrap my head around things before I do something I might regret.

I don't regret things often, but blowing us all up might be an exception.

The guys are still waiting in the car right down from the club, the engine running, both just staring at me like I've lost my mind. *Like they didn't expect to see me alive.* I get in the passenger seat, securing the grenade before waving. "*Now* we can go."

Seven starts driving. The atmosphere in the car is tense, wrought with unspoken words, but it doesn't last long with Three in the backseat.

"So... nothing went BOOM," Three says. "Didn't hear any

BANG-BANG, either."

"It was mostly just a bunch of *blah blah blah*," I say. "Nobody's dying tonight."

I think.

"Pity," Three says. "I know Lexie will be happy to be free of that asshole."

"You seem awfully concerned about a woman whose name you couldn't even remember not long ago," I point out.

"Yeah, well, you know how it goes," he says. "I drew a blank. But I can't help that I've got a soft spot and Lexie just happens to touch it."

"They make a pill for that now," I say. "Makes you harden the fuck up."

He laughs. "I'll be sure to bring that up to my doctor."

Thankfully, Three stops chattering, the conversation dwindling back to silence. The drive to Queens feels like it takes forever, traffic light but my thoughts heavy, Aristov's words bouncing around in the torture chamber I call my mind.

By the time I see my house again, I'm wound tight.

The last thing I want to do is deal with people right now, but my brother is home, in the living room with his girlfriend, cuddling on my couch. At least she's not singing this time, I think, as I pause in the foyer, glancing in at them. Three leaves, while Seven follows me, like he might be afraid to leave me alone.

My brother's eyes study me, looking all *around* me, like he's hoping to see Scarlet. Disappointment flickers across his face when he realizes she's not here, but he doesn't express the sentiment out loud. Melody just lays there, her face pale and splotchy. She looks like she's been crying. Not sure I've ever seen her without her face painted before.

Something tells me she's not handling this well.

"If you need me, I'll be in my library," I say, not awaiting any response before walking away.

Seven follows but lingers in the doorway as I stroll over to the bookshelf along the wall, carefully setting the grenade down. I reach into my waistband next, pulling out my gun, setting it down on top of the metal case.

"You got my phone, Seven?" I ask, patting my empty pockets before I turn to him, holding out my hand. I know he's got it. He usually does.

If it's not in my possession, it's in *his*.

Pulling the small black burner from his pocket, he approaches me, handing it right over. I lean back against the bookshelf, scrolling through the phone, finding no texts at all. As much as I'm not a talker, I'm even less of a texter, not a fan of leaving evidence of my words around. *No paper trails.* But being as we're living in the age of technology, sometimes texts come in or go out, credit card balances and other bullshit. Unavoidable. Which means those messages got erased somewhere along the way—and not by accident, I'm guessing.

Look, I'm not exactly *Nancy Drew* here, but I can do basic math. Two plus two equals four, three is the square root of nine, and only *one* person has access to this phone as much as I do.

So while there might be room for reasonable doubt, this isn't the court of law. If not me, then who? If it's true, must be the person I entrust it to.

Slipping the phone in my pocket, I reach over, snatching up my gun. Before Seven can react, I've got it pressed against his chest, right around his heart. He tenses, eyes as wide as they'll go. He looks horrified but not exactly surprised.

"Boss," he says quietly, leaving it at that, not bothering to ask what this might be about. He fucking *knows*.

"I was reminded of something tonight," I say. "Something that I damn near forgot."

"What?"

"Even your *shadow* leaves you in the dark."

My finger is on the trigger. It would be so easy to pull. Part of me wants to do it. Blow a hole in his fucking chest and watch him bleed out on my floor.

But I hear my brother's voice in the living room, just down the hall, talking to his girlfriend, who already seems to be traumatized by this all.

DARHOWER

Not that her mental state is a priority of mine, but having her play witness to a murder will probably break her beyond repair, and being as my brother seems to be fond of the girl, I'm trying to avoid that.

"Did you seriously think I wouldn't find out?" I ask. "Do you think I'm *stupid?*"

He slowly shakes his head. "I knew you'd figure it out eventually."

No denial.

No bullshit.

Just a straight up confession.

"So why would you do this?"

"Because," he says, "Aristov was coming for my family, he'd been to my house, he'd talked to my wife, but you... I knew you'd just come for *me*. I had to protect them."

I almost laugh when he says that. *Almost.* Would I kill his wife? Probably not. His kids? Doubtful. There's no point to it. I'd get nothing out of it. But the simple fact that he'd go behind my back like this makes me want to slit all of their fucking throats just to spite him.

"Get out of my house," I say. "You don't get to be a martyr. Not on *my* watch. So go home to your wife, to your precious family, and go to sleep tonight knowing there's a little girl out there somewhere, missing her mother... a mother who is chained up in a basement... because you're a fucking *coward*."

He takes a step back but hesitates, mouth opening and closing, like he wants to say something.

Whatever it is, I don't want to hear it.

"Get out!" I yell. "*Now!*"

He turns, his steps brisk, knowing I won't tell him again. I can hear him leave, slamming the front door, and I just stand there, clutching the gun, staring at the space he occupied.

If he's smart, I'll never see him again.

* * *

Silence.

That's what I'm met with, standing in the old warehouse in Brooklyn, surrounded by my guys.

Well, the guys I've got left, anyway.

Silence.

"So, wait, hold up," Three says after a moment, the first to open his mouth. *Of course.* "Bruno was Judas? Seriously? *Our* Bruno?"

"That's what I said, isn't it?"

"Yeah, but... *Bruno?*"

I turn away from him, glancing into the crate in front of me at the shipment of assault rifles. I know how he's feeling. I've been feeling it since last night. *Blindsided.*

I let the guy get too close to me.

I depended on him for far too much.

"I just... *wow,*" Three says, still the only one with anything to say. "This sucks."

The others finally chime in, mumbling in agreement.

"No, for real, it *really* sucks," Three says. "I mean, with Bruno gone, who's going to be bringing the snacks?"

A bit of laughter echoes through the warehouse.

"You're a *dumbass,* Declan," Five says. "That's what's bothering you? Who you're going to turn to when you get the munchies in the afternoon?"

"Fuck off," Three says. "It's a valid concern."

"It's carrot sticks and granola bars," Five points out. "If it makes your bitch ass feel better, I've got a knob you can slob on. Treat it like a lollipop."

I shake my head, reaching into the crate and pulling out the sleek new AR-15 as they bicker back and forth. I've stopped listening. Same ol' bullshit. I'm grateful for it, the background noise. They fight like brothers but they'd kill for each other, and that's all that really matters.

"So, wait, hold up," Three says again, raising his voice. "Boss, what did you do about Bruno? I mean, should I be sending his wife flowers or something?"

"Maybe you can shack up with her next," Five suggests. "She can pack you your own snacks."

"Huh, that idea's not half-bad," Three says. "She's kind of hot, you know, for an old chick."

"She's barely forty, Deac."

"I'm only twenty-one, dipshit, which means she's older than my mother."

"You'd still fuck her..."

"Yeah, well, *probably*."

"If you fellas are done," I say, holding the weapon out for someone to take it, "we can get on with business."

Five grabs the gun.

"For real, boss." Three steps over, pausing beside me. "Bruno?"

I pick up another gun, shoving it at Three. "Hate to break it to you, but his wife already raised two sons... she doesn't need another little boy to take care of."

The guys make noises, poking fun, as Three rolls his eyes. "Whatever."

"Besides," I say, passing guns out to the others, "you ought to save the flowers for another day, like for when her husband is actually *dead*."

They all look at me with surprise.

Again, Three's the only one to chime in. "Whoa, you kept him breathing?"

"For now."

"But not forever?"

"That's really up to *him*, isn't it?" I ask before motioning around the warehouse. "Clear the rest of this shit out, move it somewhere... I don't care... just get it out of *here*. When you're done, burn the place, leave no trace of any of us, just in case."

16

The little girl was tired. *So very tired.* She wasn't sleepy, though. No, she was the kind of tired that felt like sadness without all the tears.

Her body hurt.

The outside hurt, because her shoulder still felt funny and she had bruises all over from falling off the roof, and the inside hurt, because everything was all wrong and nothing felt okay anymore.

She went back to hiding again, even though it wasn't a game, because she didn't want to see any of those people. They all lied, and were mean, and they wouldn't let her go home, no matter how nicely she asked.

So she hid for hours, for *days.* The Tin Man acted like she'd turned invisible, like he didn't care if she was there, which was weird, since he'd added alarms and locks to all the windows so they wouldn't open again. The Cowardly Lion still hung around. He sometimes looked for her. He'd search under beds and inside closets, but he never said a word, just staring at her before going away again.

Weeks went on that way, weeks of isolation, of *silence.* Sometimes the little girl would whisper words to herself, would tell herself stories when she was alone in the dark, just to be sure that her voice still worked. Sandwiches would appear on the desk in her bedroom, or sometimes in brown bags outside wherever she was hiding. It started out as stuff like fish and bologna, but eventually, it turned into peanut butter and grape jelly.

She didn't want to eat anything from them, but she was so hungry, and those were her favorite, so sometimes, she couldn't help herself.

The little girl didn't know what day it was now, or how long it had been, as she lay curled up on the floor of the kitchen pantry, staring at the light filtering in from beneath the closed doors. Voices carried through, some that she hadn't heard before. They didn't have an accent like the flying monkeys. These were just visitors.

"Would you like a sandwich?" the Cowardly Lion asked, but he wasn't talking to *her*. One of the newcomers stood in the kitchen with him.

"No," the man answered. That was it. *No.*

The Cowardly Lion laughed at the man's clipped tone. "It's only PB&J. You have eaten it before, no?"

The man didn't answer.

"I have been in America since I was sixteen years old, but it wasn't until recently that I tried one myself," the Cowardly Lion continued. "They are not bad. I've come to enjoy them, especially—"

"I don't want your sandwich," the man said, cutting him off.

"Ah, well, your loss," the Cowardly Lion said. "There is no reason to be so uptight. Your boss is fine. *Relax.*"

"I'll relax when this is all over," the man said.

The Cowardly Lion sighed. "It will only ever be *over* when my brother gets what he wants."

There was a commotion in the house then. The little girl squeezed her eyes shut, trying to not listen, singing softly to herself... the song from *Toy Story*. It wasn't until the pantry doors moved that she opened her eyes again, coming face to face with the Cowardly Lion just as the front door to the house slammed.

The Cowardly Lion knelt down, setting a small plate on the floor, a sandwich on it. He was squinting, his eye watering, puffy and swollen, like he got poked in it. He said nothing to her, nodding in silence, before standing back up just as the Tin Man stormed into the kitchen.

"Follow them," he barked.

The Cowardly Lion was gone in a blink.

Grievous

The little girl sat up, grabbing the sandwich, her gaze shifting to the Tin Man.

He stood there, watching her.

It was the first time in weeks he'd so much as even *looked* her direction, since the morning he'd picked her up at the police station. The attention made her queasy, or maybe that was the hunger. She took a small bite, chewing slowly.

"You do not like me," he said, almost a sad note to his quiet voice. "I do not know why."

The little girl stared at him. She wasn't sure what to say. She was even queasier now, as she set the sandwich back down. It was true, she didn't like him. She hated him *so much*. But he should know that, she thought. He should know why she didn't like him. "You're mean. I want Mommy."

"And you think it is *my* fault you do not have your mommy?"

The little girl nodded.

He stared at her... and stared at her... and stared at her some more, before he let out a deep sigh. "Your mother's birthday is soon. Maybe I will let you talk to her. You can ask her to come home yourself."

17

Morgan

There are countless ways to torture someone. Whips and chains, fire and water, fists and kicks and unwanted touches... sleep deprivation, starvation, dehydration... branding and cutting and suffocating... you could rip my fingernails out with a pair of pliers, but none of it would ever be as tormenting as being sealed away in the darkness with *nothing*.

I'm not sure how long I've been here. Sleep has been my enemy. It twists time, manipulating the universe, strangling me with confusion. Nothing has made sense since the first moment I succumbed to it. I fall asleep in a black void and wake up again the same way, in and out of consciousness, exhausted and aching. Resentment flows through me, filling my battered body with indignation, the finger-shaped bruises covering my skin rooted so deep I can feel them even on the inside.

My soul hurts.

Wincing, I stretch my legs out, sitting along the basement wall, propping myself up against the cold metal cabinet. I'm wrapped up in an old blanket, the material rough and scratchy, but it's thick enough to keep me from violently shivering. I huddle here in the corner, swaddled like a goddamn burrito, awaiting his inevitable return.

Kassian took my clothes with him when he was through the first time, leaving me lying on the concrete floor. I passed out, waking later to find the ratty blanket on top of me, the chain around my neck once more, a pack of crackers nearby. *Dinner.*

He's returned a handful of times since then, in and out,

disturbing the little bit of rest I manage to get. He asks if I want the mattress yet, if I'm ready to accept his *generosity,* and each time I refuse, he gets rougher.

And rougher.

And rougher.

A blast of light tears through the room as the basement door opens. I squeeze my eyes shut, pulling the blanket further up, shielding my face. Footsteps descend the stairs, slow and methodical, like a restrained march toward an execution chamber. *Fitting.*

I don't look, keeping my head down as I hear his approach. I don't want to see him, nor do I want him to look at *me,* but I know that's wishful thinking. He'll do what he wants.

Dried blood and dirt cakes the side of my face, the skin rubbed raw, scrapes all over my body. He stormed out last time, losing his temper, leaving me to wallow alone for far too long in the darkness.

"You are hiding from me now?" His voice is calm, so close... *too close.* "Does this mean you are done fighting?"

I don't respond.

I have nothing to say.

He laughs at my silence, the sound running through me, making me shiver beneath the blanket. I can tell he's crouched down, can feel his warmth disrupting the air, his cologne wafting around me, suffocating my senses.

"I always did love that about you," he says. "You are so strong. So *persistent.* It makes you so much more beautiful when you are broken."

I pull the blanket down, away from my face, and look at him when he says that. "You'll never break me."

His mouth twitches as he fights off a smile.

Reaching over, he presses his palm to my cheek, his thumb rubbing the scuffed skin. It *stings.* His hand moves as I grimace, exploring my battered face. I tolerate his touch until his fingertips gently caress my dry lips. He leans toward me, like he expects a kiss, but I turn away, refusing him.

214

Grabbing my chin, he yanks my head back toward him, his grip so rough a cry escapes my throat. He says nothing, staring me in the eyes, his mouth just inches from mine. Slowly, he leans toward me again, closing the rest of the distance, his lips just barely ghosting across mine before he pulls back.

"I brought you another present," he says quietly. "Do you want it?"

"Not if it's a euphemism for your penis."

He laughs when I say that, like he finds me genuinely funny, and pulls his hand away from my face. He stands up, and everything inside of me tenses, because I think that's exactly what he means. I think he's going to unzip his pants, that he's going to pull it out, and I'm tired... so goddamn tired... of being just a *body*. A body with holes, but one without a heart and a soul, a body to be touched and fucked and tossed aside afterward.

But instead, he reaches into his pocket and retrieves his cell phone before crouching down in front of me once more.

"It is nothing *that* exciting," he says as he looks through his phone to bring something up on it. "It is just a little video."

If he expects me to be relieved by that, he's crazier than he looks. I've starred in his *videos* before. I know how they go. And I know there are cameras down here; I know he's recording my every move. The last thing I want is to have to relive the things he's done to me.

"I don't want to see it."

He raises an eyebrow, like that actually surprises him. "You do not want your present?"

"I want nothing you're offering," I whisper, turning away, gripping the blanket tighter to me as some of the cold seeps in.

"If you are sure," he says, standing back up with a shrug and turning away as he says, "I thought you would *want* to see your daughter, but I guess I was wrong."

I blink a few times when those words hit me, watching as he approaches the stairs, like he's just going to leave the basement. "You're lying."

He keeps walking, his steps slow, but he casually holds his

phone up, pressing a button on the screen.

Instantly, I'm hit with her voice.

It's like a baseball bat to the chest. It knocks the wind from my sails, the air out of my lungs, my heart seizing, viciously squeezing, like nothing inside of me wants to work. It hurts. Jesus Christ, it *burns*. Tears sting my eyes.

I can't see her, he's blocking the screen, but her voice sweeps through me like a wildfire. Her words are muffled from his hand over the speaker, but I can hear my name as she says it: *Mommy*.

So sweet, so hopeful, as she says that word. What I wouldn't give to see her face, to have her in front of me, calling me that again.

Tears stream down my cheeks as I stifle a sob, shoving up from the floor, away from the wall, stumbling over the blanket as I clutch tightly to it. Kassian stops the video, hitting a button before pocketing the phone again, heading for the stairs to leave the basement.

"Wait," I cry out.

He keeps going, like he doesn't hear me.

"Stop!" I yell, rushing toward him. "Wait a second!"

I catch him just as he's stepping out of reach, the chain choking me, making me gag as I grab the back of his coat, fisting the material.

Mistake.

Before I can even catch my breath, he whips around, snatching ahold of my arm and twisting it. I let go, crying out, as he shoves me back further into the basement, his grip tight, his face close to mine. His expression is dark, so goddamn angry, like he's trying to skin me alive with just his eyes.

"Don't do this, Kassian," I whisper. "Don't do this to her. Don't hurt her this way."

He curves an eyebrow. "Me?"

"She's so young," I say. "She doesn't understand. You can torture me all you want... I'll take it, *all* of it... but don't do this to her. She isn't like me. You'll..."

"Break her?" he asks when I trail off, finishing the sentence that I couldn't bring myself to finish. "You think I will break her?"

"Yes," I whisper.

"I am not the one hurting her," he says. "*You* are. All she wants is her mommy, and it is not *my* fault her mommy would rather stay here and do this than go be with her."

I don't say anything to that, because quite frankly, I don't know *what* to say. Nothing will make a difference or matter to this man who only sees the world in black and white, who views everything with tunnel vision, an Aristov-centric viewpoint where nothing matters except what he wants, and for some godforsaken reason, what he wants is *me*. He wants me broken. He wants to use me as he sees fit, and he wants me to buckle and just accept it... accept that my life is not my own, that my life will never again be my own. That my story ends tragically, locked away in his tower with no one coming to rescue me and no way for me to save myself.

And it would be easy... so easy... to just give in, to let it happen, to let him break me, so he'll grow tired of this back-and-forth. And so many times I've been tempted to let go, to let him win, but I can't, because *she* exists. This breathing little body, one *with* a heart and a soul... she needs saved from it all before her innocence is gone. Giving in to him won't spare her. It'll just doom her to a life like mine. A life of hurt, of pain, before one day he decides she, too, isn't worth the trouble she brings.

Kassian loosens his hold on my arm, and I think he might leave, but instead he reaches up, brushing his fingertips along my battered cheek again.

He thinks my silence is a sign of surrendering.

"Do you want that mattress yet, pretty girl?" he asks, his voice low as he grasps my chin. "It is up to you."

I remain silent, staring at him.

"You think, by not speaking, that you are saying nothing, but I hear you, *suka*," he says, pressing right up against me, making me take a step back as his grip on my chin tightens. "I know every thought that passes through your mind. Stupid girl, thinking you can beat me at this. Still thinking someone is going to rescue you, that maybe your scarred little plaything cares, but I am sorry, so very sorry, because nobody is coming to help. He was here two nights ago, upstairs in my office, discussing the money I promised for turning you over, all the while you were laying down here, sweaty, sticky, covered in *me*. If he wanted you, he would not have just walked out that door. The sooner you get that through your head, the easier this will be. So I will ask you once more, and this is it... I will not ask again. Do you want that mattress yet?"

Fuck you. Those words are on the tip of my tongue, desperate to spring free, but self-preservation forces them back. As much as I want to say no, that I don't want his goddamn generosity, I know I can't... but I can't say yes, either. No matter what I say here, I'm wrong. No matter what I do, I'm taking a risk, a *big* one... the kind of risk that could lead to the end of everything. So instead of answering, I just stand here, frozen, yet again refusing to acknowledge his question, which is probably the biggest risk of all.

Errr... scratch the *probably*.

I see it in his eyes, the flicker of rage that I know well, so intense that I gasp seconds before he even acts on it. As soon as I inhale sharply, his hands are around my throat, squeezing, *choking*. I lash out at him, desperate to get him to let go, scratching his face with my jagged nails before trying to pry his hands away from my throat, but he won't loosen his hold. My vision grows fuzzy, my chest feeling like it might burst, and I fight with all my strength, flailing, punching, clawing, but nothing is working.

Nothing ever works.

I grow sluggish, dizziness rushing through my body. It strikes me at that moment, the realization that consciousness is about to be gone, so in that split second, I do the only thing I've got the strength to do. *Poke.*

I jam my fingers right in his eyes as hard as I can.

He flinches. He doesn't expect it. It's not enough to incapacitate the man, but it buys me a few more seconds, buys me another deep breath. Air rushes into my lungs as he shoves me, my legs too weak to hold me. I slam into the concrete, banging my head hard, pain rippling down my spine as everything goes black.

It's only a few seconds, and I feel like I'm going to puke when I come back around, but there isn't time for it, there's only time to react, because I see his foot.

It's coming right at me, aimed straight for my face.

He's about to stomp me into oblivion.

Oh god, no.

I turn my head, curling into myself, going fetal as he kicks... and kicks... and *kicks*. I protect my head, protect my face, but my body is a lost cause. There's too much of it to shield from him as he rips the blanket away.

Russian words fly from his lips, too fast, too furious for me to understand. His leg must grow tired because he stops kicking, instead grabbing me. I don't know what he's doing as he yanks me around, pinning me down, until he fumbles with his pants, his body on top of mine, a hand around my throat again.

"I have been *nice*," he growls. "We will see how easy you break when I am not being nice anymore."

Go to your happy place.

Go to the house, the one with the red door and the white picket fence, the one where your daughter used to twirl around on the wooden floors. Go back to where nighttime meant kisses and hugs, bedtime stories and cuddles with Buster. Go to where sunrises were promises instead of just false hope. Go to where love still lives. Go to where you were happy.

Go there.

Stay there.

Don't be here anymore.

I fade... fade... fade away, trying to ignore his touch, trying to ignore the pain of his hands and the brutality of his thrusts. I try to ignore the feel of his breath on my skin and the ugliness of his words. It's hard, so hard, to block him out, when he keeps squeezing my throat, strangling the air from my lungs, making me teeter on the edge of consciousness. I try to imagine her instead, try to cling to her, but her face is lost in the shadows, her voice a fading whisper.

Blackness.

Blackness.

Blackness.

I'm choking, gagging. I can't *breathe.*

Flashes, again and again, flickers of reality as I'm in and out of it. I get lost in the blackness for too long at one point, the pain starting to fade away, a sense of peace taking over, before I'm violently yanked back to reality. Gasping, I blink rapidly and clutch the chain around my neck as I'm dragged across the floor by it. He lets go, dropping me on top of the rough metal grate, and I wince, wheezing, trying to get air, but it's not enough, or maybe it's too much, because I pass out right away.

"Wake up," he says, his voice cold, seconds before something even colder slams me in the face. I sputter, my chest on fire. He's spraying me with the hose. Violently coughing, I force the water back out of my lungs, trying to turn away, but he won't let me move. Grabbing ahold of my face, he forces something past my lips, into my mouth. Pills, I realize, as I gnash my teeth, bitterness coating my tongue. *Too many pills.* He pours them right from a little orange bottle, still spraying me in the face, before dropping the hose, forcing my jaw shut and pinching my nose closed as he demands, "*Swallow.*"

I can't. I won't. I don't want to. I fight him as he yanks me upright by my hair, but I can't breathe, my chest convulsing. The pills slide down my throat, my ears clogging from the pressure as tears stream from my eyes. Satisfied, he shoves me back against the grate, standing up to shut off the hose.

Rolling onto my side, I start heaving, forcing myself to empty my stomach.

"Throw them up if you want," Kassian says, his voice calm, "but you will regret it once the adrenaline wears off."

I ignore him, purging as much as I can, but exhaustion gets the best of me, and whatever he forced down my throat works quickly. Parts of me are tingling as numbness takes over my body. I lay down, curling up, shivering from the cold as my eyes fight to close.

"I hate you," I whisper, my voice cracking around those words.

Kassian crouches down in front of me, pushing my damp hair away from my face. "Is that so?"

"Yes," I say. "You'll never break me."

"Oh, but I *will*," he says. "You see, pretty girl, I have realized something. Being a mother is the most important thing to you. So while death would not break you, taking your daughter away will."

"You already took her," I whisper, my voice sluggish. It's getting hard to stay awake, hard to keep my eyes open.

"I merely separated the two of you," he says, reaching into his pocket, once more pulling out his phone. He presses a few buttons before holding it up, a picture of her covering the screen, a still from the paused video he played earlier. "She is beautiful, huh? So much like you, that girl. More like you than you even think, because she has not broken, either, when I have given her more than enough reason to. She hides from me. She runs away. She lies right to my face. And I know, despite what she says, she does not love me. She hates me, just as you do."

I stare at the picture through blurry eyes, a flicker of a smile on my lips as I whisper, "That's my girl."

"Yes, she is your girl," Kassian says, putting the phone away as he stands back up. "Pity I have to kill her for it."

As soon as those words hit me, I shove away from the floor, trying to sit up, but the room is spinning... spinning... spinning... and I can't stomach it anymore. I heave again, my tears coming down harder as I choke on a sob, collapsing back onto the grate. I try to scream. I try to talk. I need him to tell me he doesn't mean that, I need him to take it back, but before I can find any words, he's gone.

Darkness creeps up on me when I hear the basement door close. All I can think, as it sweeps me away, is *'this is all my fault.'*

* * *

In and out. In and out.

The darkness doesn't completely fade, refusing to release its grip on me, as I lay here, wasting away. Brief flickers of lights, the hollow sound of voices, as people come and go, more pills shoved down my throat, the cycle repeating.

I go to my happy place.

I cling to it, like it's all that exists.

I have to believe it's still possible, that the world I love is still out there, waiting for me to find it again.

I have to believe that she's out there.

That she's okay.

That I'll find my way out of this basement.

That we'll find peace together after this is over.

That some fairy tales *can* have happy endings.

I'm not sure when things change, but slowly, the darkness loosens its hold, the numbness fading as the pills wear off. And the first thing I notice, when I'm conscious enough to move, is that I'm lying on a mattress.

The mattress I never wanted.

The one I refused to ask for.

It's in the center of the basement, full-sized and soft. Memory foam, maybe. No sheets, but there is a pillow, and I'm once again covered by a blanket, like someone tucked me in. What the hell? My heart races as I sit up, groggy, blinking to try to clear my blurry vision. My eyes burn. Every inch of me hurts, but I don't think anything is broken.

Except my sanity, maybe.

I try to swallow, my throat raw, but my mouth is too dry. My tongue feels swollen. I feel around cautiously, shaky hands exploring my face. I don't know what I'm looking for... deformities, maybe? Nothing feels *real*.

I'm okay, though. *I think.*

Sickness swishes around inside of me. When's the last time I ate? When's the last time I did *anything*? I don't even know what day it is. How long has this been going on?

Why the fuck is there a mattress here now?

The basement door opens as I try to get a grip. I pull the blanket around me tighter, alarmed, like the flimsy material can shield me from harm. The overhead lights flick on, and I wince, hearing footsteps on the stairs coming closer. I expect to see Kassian when I peek over, but instead I'm met with the guarded look of a curious brunette. *Alexis.*

She clutches a brown paper bag as she approaches.

My stomach clenches at the sight.

"Are you hungry?" she asks, holding the bag out. "I brought you something to eat."

I just stare at her.

My head is pounding.

Frowning, she opens the bag, reaching inside of it, pulling out the contents: a piroshki wrapped in plastic, a small container of pickled cabbage, and a bottle of water. It isn't hard to tell who packed this lunch, and it wasn't the young American girl in front of me.

I pick up the bottle of water, cracking the lid and slowly sipping it.

I expect her to leave, but Alexis just stands there, fidgeting nervously as she glances behind her. After a moment, she sits down on the edge of the mattress. "Are you holding up okay down here?"

I look away from her, sipping more water. "I'm alive."

"I'm glad," she says. "And don't worry, it's going to be okay."

She sounds like she believes that, but what does she know? *Nothing.* She lives her life at Kassian's mercy just like the rest of us.

"What day is it?" I ask, taking one more sip of water before screwing the cap back on.

"It's Thursday morning," she says. "You've been here almost a week now."

Before either of us can say anything else, there's noise on the stairs, more footsteps approaching. Alexis jumps to her feet, averting her eyes from mine as she heads out of the basement. I watch her dart up the stairs, my gaze stalling when it reaches him coming down.

Kassian.

I eye him warily as he approaches, his steps leisure, like he's got not a care in the world. His hands are shoved in the pockets of his black slacks, his suit fresh and crisp, his shoes shining under the bright basement light. He looks completely put together... all except for the scratches on his face. Gashes mar his jawline, his cheek, before running down his neck. They still look enflamed, swollen, the skin glowing pink.

I look down at my hands, seeing the blood and filth caked under my nails.

Guess that was me.

"Good morning, pretty girl," he says, grabbing the metal chair and dragging it over beside the mattress, sitting down in it. He glances around, picking up the piroshki from where it lays on the mattress. "You do not want the food I made for you?"

"I'd rather have peanut butter and jelly."

He ignores that, unwrapping the piroshki and tearing it in half—a yeast roll stuffed with something, I don't know, but it smells so good that my stomach again clenches. "Cheese and potato, just as I remember you like it... no onion. Never onion."

He holds half out to me and I take it but don't eat it, despite the fact that my body is begging for calories. He can remember that I hate onions, but he can never seem to remember that I hate *him*.

"What did you do?" I ask, my voice trembling around those words. "Tell me you haven't hurt her... tell me she's okay, that you wouldn't *really*..."

I can't even bring myself to say it.

He takes a bite of the half of the piroshki he kept, chewing slowly as he regards me, before he motions toward where I'm sitting. "Are you enjoying your mattress?"

"I told you I didn't want it. I never asked for it."

"Oh, but you did," he says, continuing to eat. "Do you not remember? You *begged* me for it."

"I didn't."

I *wouldn't*.

There's no way I would beg.

"You did," he says again. "You said you were sorry, that you would be a good girl, that you would love me right... and you did. As soon as I had the mattress brought in, you showed me how

224

grateful you were for my generosity."

Tears sting my eyes. "You're lying."

A smile plays on his lips as he looks at me, eyes carefully scanning my face, before he says, "I can bring you the video, if you would like to watch."

I shake my head. "I don't believe you."

"You do not have to," he says, shrugging nonchalantly, "but it is true. You were so wet for me when we made love. I can still smell us in here... can you?"

Bile burns my throat, and I try to swallow it back, but it's rushing through me too fast. Hunching over, I dry heave, gagging over the side of the mattress.

Before I realize what he's doing, he's crouching down in front of me, his piroshki long forgotten as he smoothes my hair, like he's trying to console me. He grabs the chain around my neck, tugging on it as he pulls out the keys. I watch him warily as he unlocks it, unwinding the chain and letting it drop away.

"Come on," he says, meeting my gaze. "We need to get you washed up."

"Why?" I ask quietly. "What's the point?"

"You do not want to be dirty for the party, do you?"

"Party? What party?"

"Your coming home party," he says as he raises an eyebrow. "You did not think I would make the guest of honor miss her own celebration, did you?"

"But—"

Before I can finish my thought, his hand clamps down around my mouth, covering it, silencing me, as his other hand settles on the back of my head, pulling me closer. "I do not want to ruin the surprise, pretty girl, but I think you will be quite pleased with what I have planned. You remember how much fun we had at your *Sweet Sixteen*?"

My eyes widen, and I struggle against his grip, reaching up and grabbing his hands, trying to pry them away as I scream into his palm.

"Shhh, none of that," he says. "You have to be a good girl,

like you showed me you can be, and when it is all over, I will answer your question about what I did with our daughter."

He gives me time to calm down before letting go and standing back up. He offers me his hand then, extending it toward me. For a moment, I hesitate, just staring at it, before carefully reaching out, letting him pull me to my feet. My legs are weak, my knees nearly buckling. I look down, as he tightly grips my hand, seeing the bruises covering me—some old, some new, a kaleidoscope of purple and yellow, black and blue with subtle green hues, a splattering of blood like dark red paint.

I'm a fucked up rainbow.

I don't fight it. I don't fight him as he hooks up the hose and washes me. I don't make a peep, even when it stings, even when it burns, even when his hands are rough against a bruise or he gets soap in a scrape. The water is ice cold, and my teeth chatter, but I otherwise remain still, letting him do what he's going to do, the thought of getting out of this basement too tempting to ruin.

He wraps me in a towel once I'm clean, pushing me toward the metal chair, forcing me down into it. His hands are on my shoulders as he leans down to whisper, "Do not move from this chair."

Kassian leaves the basement.

It would be a lie to say I don't consider trying to run, but *running*, in my current state, is sort of out of the question. I could do it, sure, but I wouldn't make it far, maybe not even to the top of the stairs this time before I got caught. So I sit still, doing exactly what he told me to do, until the basement door opens again.

It's not him, though.

It's Alexis.

She descends the stairs slowly, carrying a small black bag, setting it down beside me. "He, uh... he told me to help you get ready?"

She poses it like a question, like maybe she doesn't really understand any of this, either. My gaze flickers to the bag, and I reach down, unzipping it to sort through the contents—hairbrush, makeup, clothing. I pull out the skimpy fabric, eyeing the see-through black lingerie, the lacy garter belt and thigh-highs to go along with it. I don't even have to look back into the bag to know there will be a pair of red six-inch heels to go with the outfit, and somewhere, mixed in among the makeup will be a tube of bright red lipstick.

He has a *type*, remember?

I ignore her, getting dressed on my own, lifting up just enough to slip the lingerie on. The brush keeps getting tangled in my hair, so I yank it, pulling out knots without any care. There isn't much I can do with it myself, since I don't have a mirror, so I don't object when Alexis jumps in and takes over. She does what she can... what that is, I don't know. Doesn't really matter, either. Kassian's hands will end up all through it later, gripping handfuls.

Whether he'll be doing it out of *pleasure* or *anger* is anyone's guess at the moment.

Alexis kneels in front of me, pulling out the makeup, going to work as she slathers foundation all over my face. Eye shadow, eyeliner, mascara—all black, just the way Kassian likes it. When that is finished, she grabs the red lipstick, but I snatch it from her hand, shaking my head as I throw it across the room.

I'm not wearing it for him.

She frowns, not moving from her kneeling position. "Where is he taking you? Do you know?"

"Home," I whisper.

The word sounds wrong. *So wrong.*

That place isn't my home.

Never has been, never will be.

Her eyes widen, panic flickering across her face. "He's taking you to the party?"

"He says it's for me," I say. "My own little homecoming parade before the big game."

"Oh God," she whispers, her eyes darting all around. "No, no, no... *ugh*, this isn't how it's supposed to happen."

My brow furrows. "What?"

"You're supposed to be *here*," she says. "This is where he's coming. This is where he thinks he'll find you."

227

"Who?"

"Scar."

The word is a hiss from her lips, like a curse springing from the tip of her tongue. *Scar.* My chest tightens at the sound of it. "Lorenzo?"

Before she can respond, I hear others coming. Alexis panics, springing to her feet and taking an immediate step back, smoothing her hands on the fishnets covering her legs.

Kassian makes his way down into the basement, followed by a few of his guys. My heart hammers hard as he approaches, the guys stopping near the exit, blocking it. *Back up.* He might be letting me leave this basement, but that certainly doesn't mean he's going to be putting any trust in me.

"*Suka,*" he says, stopping in front of the chair, nudging my chin to force me to look up at him. "You are still sitting there."

"You told me not to move," I point out.

He whispers, "good girl," as his gaze travels my face. His thumb sweeps across my dry lips, his expression tightening as he looks around the basement, eventually finding the lipstick before turning back to me. "You do not want to wear it?"

"Wear what?"

A smile flickers across his lips.

Strolling across the basement, he retrieves the tube of lipstick before returning. He's not going to let it go. *Figures.* He carefully puts it on me, and I play along, because I'm running out of options at the moment. Really, what other choice do I have here?

"Shoes," he says, pointing at the heels, ordering me to put them on in not-so-many words. *Ugh.* I glare at the shoes as I slide my feet into them, sitting still, not acknowledging him any further.

He inspects me before grabbing my arm, pulling me up out of the chair and shoving me toward his men. I wobble, my muscles sore, already out of practice with walking in heels, but I manage to stay upright.

"Take her to the car," he orders. "If you let her escape, I will kill every single one of you."

I scowl as hands grab me, clutching me tightly.

Yeah, they're not letting me out of their sight tonight, that's for sure.

Men filter out. I'm marched up the stairs, my gaze flickering back down, watching. Alexis tries to follow, but Kassian cuts in front of her, blocking her exit. "Where do you think you are going?"

"To the party," she says. "You told me I was going this week."

"Yes, well, I have changed my mind," Kassian says. "I have somewhere else for you to be."

Her brow furrows as two of Kassian's men come up behind her. "Where?"

"Right here."

The men grab her, and she struggles, but there's not much she can do. One pins her down, holding her there, as the other grabs the chain and winds it around her neck. My footsteps stall, alarmed, as she screams, but I can't help her. *Nobody* can help her. The men drag me out of the basement when I try to resist, pulling me through the club as they usher me outside to an awaiting vehicle. I'm shoved in the back of an SUV, one of the men shutting the door and standing guard beside it on the curb.

My gaze settles on the door on the opposite side, wondering how far I can get if I jump out and make a run for it through the street.

Fuck it.

I slide across the seat, shoving the door open to try, when Kassian appears in the doorway, blocking it. I immediately retreat as he climbs into the backseat beside me. "I am going to pretend you were opening the door for me."

"Of course," I whisper. "Just returning your generosity."

He settles into the seat, barking something in Russian to the others. A man gets in the front seat to drive as Kassian puts his arm around me.

"You will want to be careful, *suka*," he says, his voice low, a warning to the words. "I will be killing people you care about tonight. Do not make me kill *you* on top of it."

I pull away when he says that, swallowing thickly. "What?"

He cuts his eyes at me. "Do not look so surprised. You must have known this was coming."

"What are you talking about?"

"You let him come inside of you. Did you think I would let him live after that?"

"But—"

Before I can get anything else out, he reaches up, covering my mouth.

"Be a good girl, remember? After the fun is over, I will tell you what you want to know about your daughter, but not before we're done."

I blink rapidly when it strikes me what he's really saying.

He wants me to sit idly by while he kills Lorenzo.

He wants me to see it, to watch, as he gets his revenge. He's going to force me to obey him, to do nothing to stop him from killing everyone who tried to help me, and he's using my daughter as bait to make me be compliant.

He's making me choose.

Because he knows there's no choice.

There will never be a choice.

It will always be her.

I'll always choose her.

Before him… before Lorenzo… before myself.

Sasha's all that matters.

Tears sting my eyes as I look away. I can't stomach the sight of him. Not ever, but especially not right now.

"You don't have to do this," I whisper when he pulls his hand away.

"I know," he says. "But I am going to, anyway."

"Why?"

"Because none of my other lessons ever stuck with you," he says, putting his arm around me once more. "Maybe this is the one you will remember."

18

Lorenzo

"So let's go over the plan one more time."

I don't think I've ever heard Three sound quite as serious before as he does right now, saying those words. *So let's go over the plan one more time.* Never mind the fact that we've been through the plan a dozen times already, that we've analyzed and assessed every possible fucking scenario short of a hoard of goddamn Storm Troopers bursting in. Even the words *nuclear weapons* have been brought up. But yet, Three wants to go through the plan again, one more time, just to be on the safe side.

This girl of his from the club must have some real good pussy for him to be so concerned about all of us making it out of this… including *her.*

"I'll head to Brighton Beach and keep an eye on the house. Lexie should be on her way to the party with Aristov right about now. She's going to signal me when she finds the kid—flash a light or something. If she doesn't signal, I'm going to assume the kid's not in the house."

The others mumble in agreement.

"I'll ring you all when she signals," Three continues. "You'll hit the club, full-on ambush, at eight o'clock, whether she signals or not. Lexie said she'd make sure the keys to the basement were left on the bar in Aristov's office, but the key to the chain, well, he keeps that on his person…"

"I can pick the lock," Five chimes in. "Not a problem."

"And I'll keep on watching the house," Three says. "Probably won't take him long to be alerted to what's happening—

a few minutes, at most, but it should be enough time for you to get Morgan out. If he leaves, I'll warn you he's on his way. Lexie's going to try to stay behind… chances are, if you're hitting his club, he's not going to be worried about *her*… so she'll grab the kid and meet me outside once he's gone, and then we'll all meet up."

Once again, the others mumble in agreement.

It's a nice little plan, barring nothing goes wrong, but that's the problem with plans like this: something *always* does. People don't act like you expect them to, things don't happen the way you hope, and all it takes is one little hiccup before nobody fucking knows who's doing what anymore.

"All right, let's do this," Three says, standing up, the rest of the guys joining him on their feet. They say their goodbyes, hyping themselves up, nothing short of fucking chest-bumps as they go separate directions, ready to get this all started.

Sighing, I shove up off of the couch, getting to my feet, and stroll out of the living room behind them.

I leave this shit to them… the *planning*. They're good at it, at orchestrating schemes, timing shit to work to our advantage. It doesn't mean I'm not in charge, though, and they know it. They still yield to me at every corner. All I have to say is '*no*' and it'll come to a screeching halt.

I don't say a word.

Not now. Not yet.

I've got a bad feeling about it all, though.

Something's not right.

But I sure as fuck don't have a better idea, so I'll go with theirs until we hit a roadblock, and then I'll do what I'm best at doing—making shit up.

"You want me to drive your car, boss?" Five asks.

I hesitate, pulling out my keys, before tossing them to him. *Why not?*

I climb in the passenger seat, relaxing back, as we head south out of Queens, down into Brooklyn, making our way to Brighton Beach. We branch out different directions when we reach the area, Three making his way toward Aristov's house near the shoreline while the rest of us head to Limerence.

It's dark out, nighttime falling by the time we reach the club. We pull in down the block, parking as close as we can get, as the car carrying the rest of the guys parks across the street.

Five cuts the engine as I glance at the clock.

7:21 p.m.

Thirty-nine minutes to go.

Five glances at me. "You think this is going to work?"

"Which part?"

"Any of it."

Five might be the most cynical guy on my crew. Highly suspicious. He listens to his gut on everything, but the problem with his gut is it's all twisted up, making him a paranoid son of a bitch. I appreciate that about him, though. He won't sugarcoat or bullshit.

"It could work," I say. "Probably won't, though."

He frowns. "I don't think so, either."

"You got any other ideas?"

"None that won't get half of us killed."

"Same here."

"Might come to that," he says. "Only option might be guns blazing, whole shebang, a lot of people dead."

"I won't let it," I say, reaching into my pocket, pulling out my tin. Empty. *Damnit.* Still haven't gotten around to rolling any joints. "I won't let this take you guys down. It's my fight, not yours."

"*Bullshit,*" Five says, cutting his eyes my way as he pulls out a small bag of weed and a glass bowl, offering it to me. "No offense, but seriously... that's bullshit."

I take his weed, because *fuck it...* I need the relief.

"Before you came along, we were castoffs," he continues as I pack the bowl and snatch up a lighter from the center console, inhaling the smoke when I light it. "Me? Not enough Italian blood for the Italians, yet *too* goddamn Italian for everyone else. And Declan, nobody would have a damn thing to do with a pretty rich boy from Midtown who wanted to do this for the thrill. We're the fucking *Island of Misfit Toys*. So I think I can speak for the rest of the guys, too, when I say your fight is *our* fight. You gave us a chance to prove ourselves. We're not going to punk out now when you need us for something. That would just prove everyone right who said we were worthless."

I pass the bowl back to him, saying nothing, staring straight ahead at the club. There's nobody coming or going, I notice.

I glance at the clock.

7:33 p.m.

Twenty-seven minutes to go.

Nothing yet from Three, either.

Bad, bad feeling...

I watch in silence for a few more minutes, as Five and I pass the weed back and forth. The haze fills the car, surrounding us both, time steadily passing.

Tick. Tick. Tick.

7:45 p.m.

Fifteen minutes to go.

Nothing.

"You ever see *Return of the Jedi*, Five?"

"No."

His answer is unapologetic. Turning my head, I look at him through the darkness that shrouds the car, wondering what kind of monsters I've befriended if he's never seen *Star Wars*.

"If you survive tonight," I say, "we're going to have to do something about that."

"Whatever you say, boss," he says. "Any particular reason you're bringing it up right now?"

"Because, as Admiral Ackbar so nicely put it, *it's a trap!*"

Five cuts his eyes at me as I pull out my phone, making sure the son of a bitch is still on since it hasn't rang. "You think we're walking into a trap?"

"I sat out here the other night, watching this place, and in the span of thirty minutes I counted no less than a dozen people in and out. Tonight? Not a single soul."

"Could it be they're all at Aristov's?"

"Maybe," I say. "But if that's the case, there's no way Scarlet's here. He's not leaving her unguarded."

"So either she's not inside anymore or..."

"It's a trap," I say, calling Three's number.

He picks up on the second ring. "Yeah, boss?"

"Anything happening over there?"

"Seems pretty quiet," Three says. "A few cars, a few lights, but otherwise, nothing unusual."

"She hasn't signaled you yet?"

"No," he says. "I'm guessing the kid's not inside."

Or else it's another trap...

"Hold your position," I tell him. "Don't go into that house, Three. That's an order. You got me?"

"Uh, sure," he says. "You think something's wrong?"

"I *know* something's wrong," I say. "Were you aware Five here hasn't watched *Star Wars*?"

"*What?*"

"Seriously, I can't wrap my head around it, so I'm going to need a few minutes. Stay where you are, and call me if anything changes."

I hang up, tapping my phone against my cheek a few times, as if that'll help me think. Plan B. Plan C. Plan D. I'm quickly sliding my way right down to X-Y-Z, but only one idea is springing to mind.

Well, one idea that doesn't involve a grenade. Still haven't taken that off the table.

"When Han Solo rescued Princess Leia from the Death Star, you know how he managed it?"

"This sounds like it might contain movie spoilers."

I laugh under my breath. *Smart ass.* "He dressed up like the enemy. He put on a stormtrooper uniform and waltzed his ass on through, undetected."

"So, what, we need to become Russian? Not sure how *that's* going to work..."

"No, we just need to not be who they're expecting," I say. "We need uniforms."

I dial another number, waiting as it rings. And rings. And rings. I think maybe he's not going to answer, but finally, he picks up, his voice hesitant. "Gambini?"

"Ah, Jameson, how are you and the boys in blue this evening?"

"Was doing pretty good until you just called," he says. "You need something?"

"I need you to raid a place for me."

"What place?"

"This place Aristov runs down in Brighton Beach... *Limerence*."

He doesn't respond right away.

"You hear what I said, Jameson?"

"I'm hoping not," he says, "because it sounded like you were asking me to put together a raid on a strip club in Brooklyn, where I don't have any jurisdiction, without any probable cause."

"Well, it's more like a whorehouse..."

"There's no way," he says. "No judge is going to sign off on that."

"I don't expect you to get a search warrant. I just need you and the guys to, you know... go in, lock it down for me, so I can take a quick look around."

He curses under his breath.

"I can talk to the guys, see if we can work something out," he says. "When do you need this to happen?"

I glance at the clock.

7:50 p.m.

"In about ten minutes."

"You're joking," he says. "I can't even fucking get to Brooklyn in ten minutes, Gambini."

"Well, then, you might want to use the siren," I say. "I'll owe you one."

I hate those words. *I'll owe you one.* I hate owing anybody anything. But it does the trick, like I need it to, because he tells me to hold tight before he hangs up the phone.

"Uniforms," Five says. "Smart."

"Yeah, well, we'll see if it works."

Another few minutes go by, still seeing no sign of life around the club. *Light's on, but nobody's home.*

Eight o'clock comes and goes.

Nobody makes a move.

Plan officially fucked.

8:17 p.m.

I see the cars speed by, whipping in along the curb—two unmarked NYPD cruisers and an unmarked SUV, lights and siren off, trying to go undetected. The officers climb out, conversing, getting their gear together as Jameson stands along the curb, eyes scanning the neighborhood, falling upon me.

Instead of approaching, he pulls out his phone.

Mine rings seconds later.

"Only seventeen minutes late," I tell him.

"You're lucky we're here at all," he says. "Damn lucky one of Aristov's guys has an active felony warrant in the system, and the club is open, because it gives the guys some leeway to go right in, no judge needed."

"Well, let's hope the luck continues," I say, "because there might be a woman chained up down in the basement that needs to be set free."

He lets out a low whistle. "Not your woman, is it?"

I give him that one, not correcting him on her being mine. We both know who he means. "Yeah, that's what we're hearing."

"Jesus... you're *serious*? How the hell did he get her? Thought she was with you."

"Long story," I lie. It's sort of a simple one—my closest guy betrayed us, turning into a bigger rat than Peter Pettigrew in Harry Potter. Yeah, whatever... you're wondering how I know who that is, huh? Truth is, my brother's got a nerdy side. He read the books as a kid, wouldn't shut up about it. "Look, just go in, secure the building, make sure it's clear, then give me the signal so I can come take a peek."

"Got it," he says, hesitating before adding, "What's the signal?"

Sighing, I pinch the bridge of my nose, mumbling, "Do some jumping jacks, for all I fucking care. Just make something up. I'll know."

I hang up before he can respond, tossing my phone up on the dashboard to get it out of my hand before I snap the fucking thing in half out of annoyance.

8:21 p.m.

The plainclothes warrant squad rushes into the building, guns drawn. All is silent. No gunshots.

8:25 p.m.

Jameson's on his phone. He turns toward me in the car, not-so-subtly tapping the side of his nose.

"Is he on *coke*?" Five asks, watching.

"Wouldn't surprise me," I mutter. "Come on, that'll be our signal."

We get out, as do the rest of my guys, leaving the heavy weapons stashed in the trunks, since the police are now involved, small guns hidden on us just in case something happens.

There are a few guys inside the club, twice as many girls, all of them lined up along the wall, sitting on the floor with their hands visible. Officers stand guard in front of them, keeping them wrangled, as I walk right in and help myself to Aristov's office.

The keys aren't where Three's girl said they'd be, but I find them easily enough, tossed in a drawer. The basement door is here in the office, and I fumble with the keys, trying to figure out which one goes to which lock as my guys stand guard nearby.

Five is right behind me.

"Here," he says, snatching the keys from my hand. "Let me do this for you."

Under normal circumstances, I would've lost my cool over that, but being as I'm in a hurry, I let it go... *for now*.

He gets the door unlocked a lot quicker than I could, and I flick on a light as I pull out my gun, just in case I'm about to be ambushed.

It's quiet, and still, like nobody is here.

"Scarlet?" I call out as I head down into the basement, my

voice echoing off the barren concrete walls.

No answer.

I come to an abrupt stop at the bottom of the steps as I look in the shadows, being met with a pair of discarded red heels.

That's never a good sign.

Fuck.

Fuck.

Fuck.

Just inches from where they'd been kicked off in what looks like a struggle, I spot a pair of feet, the black pantyhose covering them ripped. They peek out from the bottom of a tattered blue blanket, but I can't see anything else, the rest covered.

I feel like the fucking Grinch as I stop here, staring at what's clearly a lifeless body. My heart feels like it's way too big, the only thing inside of me, each beat hard and hesitant, like it's squeezing the life out of my fucking chest.

"Boss, what—oh, whoa... *fuck.*"

Five rode the whole gauntlet of emotion with just that one sentence. Confusion. Shock. Distress.

He stalls there, taking my place as I step forward. Reaching down, I grab the blanket, pulling the top part of it down to look.

I exhale loudly—*too* damn loudly—the second I see the face. Three's pretty little brunette is chained to the concrete floor like a dog, makeup streaking her cheeks. She's not breathing. The chain is wound so tightly around her neck that it asphyxiated her.

She's alone, though.

Not that it makes it any better.

She's not supposed to be here at all.

She was supposed to be at the house.

She was supposed to signal Three.

She was supposed to get the kid out, but instead, here she is. And the worst part of all, I think, is that the sight of her is bringing me relief.

It could be worse. *A lot* worse.

It could be Scarlet.

For a moment, just a flicker, I truly thought it was, and the way that's making me feel inside? I don't like it. It has me all twisted up.

I lower the blanket back over the girl's face, covering her once more. I stand in silence, trying to come to terms with whatever this is I'm feeling.

"Is it...? Fuck, boss, I need you to say something. It's not her, is it? Is that Morgan?"

I glance at him. He looks legitimately concerned, like the son of a bitch might be getting emotional. "No."

His eyes widen. I see it in him, too. *Relief.*

"It's Three's girl," I say, heading for the steps. "Guess we know now why she didn't signal him."

Five blinks, the relief gone as he looks past me, whispering, "Fuck, this is going to hurt Declan."

I make my way out of the basement. Five follows me, right on my heels. There's no reason to linger any longer. What we came for isn't here, like I feared. I nod my thanks to the officers and head out the front of the club, out into the peculiarly warm night, empty-handed and out of luck.

I wish I could say I was also out of *fucks*, but no, those just keep on growing, simmering and festering. For the first time in a long time, I feel this strange twinge inside of me. It's hard to describe. It's a tightening in my chest. It's a tingling in my fingertips. It feels as if my lungs are trembling, like the weak punk bitches are trying to stop functioning. The woman has got me all fucked up here, flipped upside down and inside out.

It's like the striking of a match.

All it needs is that spark.

"I want you to keep an eye on my brother," I order the rest of my guys. "Five and I will go get Three."

Jameson stands there, eyeing me warily, as the men scatter. "That sounds like a math problem."

"It's some kind of *problem*, all right," Five mumbles.

"There's a dead girl down in the basement," I tell Jameson. "And for the record, before you ask, she was already dead when I got there."

His eyes widen. "She's dead?"

"It's not *his* girl," Five says, answering for me as I head toward my car. "It's somebody else's."

I climb in the passenger side, waiting for Five to hurry up, and snatch my phone off the dashboard. Nothing from Three. *Of course.* I dial his number. It rings and rings and rings before voicemail kicks in.

I hang up, trying again. *Nothing.*

"Fuck!" I yell, throwing the phone. It slams into the windshield so hard the damn thing cracks, the phone bouncing off, hitting Five as he gets in behind the wheel. It bounces off of him, too, tumbling to the floor by his feet, ringing shattering the tense air the moment it lands.

"Answer that," I say, "and tell Three I said he better not be dead or I'll kill him."

Five picks it up. "Boss, I don't think it's Declan."

He holds it up. Brooklyn number. I recognize it right away. *Aristov.*

I snatch the phone back to answer it. "Gambini."

"Ah, Mister Scar, I am sorry it has taken me so long to contact you. I have been quite busy."

"So it seems," I say. "What do you want?"

"To let you know that I have your reward," he says. "Feel free to stop by tonight, if you would like, so I can make sure you get what you are owed."

"Yeah, okay," I say. "I might just do that."

I hang up without waiting on his response, tossing the phone onto the dash again as I mutter, "Fucking Russians."

"Was that Aristov?" Five asks. "Why did he call?"

"To invite me over."

"Are you going?"

"What do you think?"

Five starts the car. "I think if you go, you're not going without us."

19

Buster was gone.

The little girl stood in the doorway to the den, staring up at the fireplace mantle. How long had he been gone? She wasn't sure, because she never came in here anymore. Panic flooded her, her eyes darting around. "Where did Buster go?"

The Tin Man stood in the middle of the room, turning his head to look at her. "Away."

"Where?" she asked. "What did you do with him? Why did he go *away*?"

"It does not matter," the Tin Man said, waving her off. "Buster is gone."

The little girl's stomach felt like it dropped to her feet. "No, Daddy! Get him back! *Please*!"

"No."

No. No. *No.*

"Please!" she screamed, running through the room. "I didn't do nothing! I *didn't*! I've been good! Don't burn up Buster!"

He stopped her before she could make it to the fireplace, before she could look. She had to see.

The little girl fought, but it was for nothing, because the Tin Man was too strong, like he was truly made of metal. He clamped his hand down on top of her head, the simple touch enough to stop her in her tracks. She grabbed his wrist, trying to pull his hand off, pushing against it with her head as she screamed, "Stop it! Don't do that! Let me go! I wanna *go*!"

"Where?" he asked, glaring down at her. "Where do you want to go, kitten?"

"Home!" she screamed, hitting his arm as hard as she could with a clenched fist. "I don't like you. You're *mean*. You talk ugly! You don't love me. Mommy loves me! I don't wanna be here no more, so *let me go!*"

He let go.

Just like that.

He let go so fast she stumbled, falling.

Before she could get back on her feet, he snatched her right up with just one arm and hauled her over his shoulder, carrying her out. He moved fast, heading through the foyer, disabling the alarm and yanking the door open to step out into the cool night.

The Tin Man shoved her into his car before getting in, driving away from the big palace as she started crying. "Where are we going?"

"Home," he said. "That is what you want. You say your home is not with me, that you want your mommy. So fine, I will take you home."

The little girl started shaking—the good way, this time. Home. She was going *home?*

"Thank you," she blurted out. She thought maybe it could be a trick, but she couldn't help herself.

He cut his eyes at her, his voice quiet as he said, "Anything for you, kitten."

Half an hour later, they pulled up in front of the familiar house. The little girl hadn't seen it in *so* many months, but she recognized it right away. *Home.* He parked out front and hauled her out of the car, motioning toward the house. "Go on."

The little girl ran right for it.

She didn't realize, until she reached the door, that it was all dark inside, no lights on. The Tin Man strolled along behind her, pausing on the porch, leaning against the house as he watched her try to open the front door.

Locked.

The little girl knocked and knocked and knocked, calling out for her mother, but there was no answer. She pounded on it until her fist ached, running around the outside to peek through windows, but she couldn't see anything.

"She's not here," the little girl said, "but she will be, I know it. She'll come home soon."

"We will wait," the Tin Man said, glancing at his watch. "We will stay here as long as it takes."

The little girl sat down on the porch.

Half an hour turned into an hour, which turned into *forever*. Hours... and hours... and hours. The little girl shivered, huddling in her shirt, her eyes heavy. *So tired.*

It was nearing sunrise when she almost fell asleep on the porch, leaning against the thick railing column, letting it support her. Her eyes were closed, resting, when she heard footsteps. Her heart raced, eyes snapping open. *Mommy?*

Not Mommy.

The Cowardly Lion stood on the pathway in front of her. He looked angry, not very *cowardly* anymore. He glared past her, at where the Tin Man still stood. "What are you doing?"

"She wanted her mother," the Tin Man said, "so we are waiting for her to come home."

That answer didn't make the Cowardly Lion any happier. "You know damn well her mother isn't living here."

The Tin Man said nothing.

The little girl glanced back at him. What did that mean? "Where's Mommy? Why doesn't she live here?"

"Look what you have done," the Tin Man said, his gaze fixed to the Cowardly Lion. "You have gone and upset her."

"This is not me," the Cowardly Lion said. "What you are doing here is *cruel*, Kassian."

"Her mother is the one that moved on. She is the one with a new life in the city, one without her daughter... new friends, new lover, new *everything*, and no Sasha."

The little girl frantically shook her head. "No, Mommy wouldn't do that."

The Tin Man looked at her. "Your mother is gone, kitten. I have tried to find her, but she does not want to be found. She is the one hiding now. But you do not like me. You do not like my home.

So here you are, where there is *nobody* to care for you."

He shoved away from the house, stepping off the porch, pausing in front of the Cowardly Lion.

"Do something with her," the Tin Man said, "since you cannot ever seem to find her *bitch* mother. Do you think you can handle that much, Markel?"

The Cowardly Lion stared him in the face, saying nothing.

The Tin Man shoved against him, knocking him out of the way as he headed to his car.

The little girl got to her feet to follow, tears falling down her cheeks. "Wait, Daddy!"

He shook his head as he turned to her, holding up a hand. "No, this is what you wanted. You thanked me for it. You are just like her. I hope you are happy. No Mommy. No Buster. And now, no *me*. No home. No love. No food. So good luck, my kitten, with *nothing*."

The little girl stood there, crying, as he drove away. She should be happy the Tin Man was gone, shouldn't she? So why did her insides feel so empty?

"Do not cry, sweet girl," the Cowardly Lion said, placing his hand on her shoulder. "You will be okay."

20
Morgan

The phone drops to the coffee table with a thud.

I stare at it as the screen goes dark, my fingers itching to reach for it, but I don't move. Legs pulled up, arms around them, chin resting on my knees, I just sit here on the floor near Kassian's chair, right by his feet, where he used to always make me sit.

Easy access, he says.

Always within arm's reach.

His hand presses against my hair, smoothing it, *petting* me, absently twirling strands around his fingers. My scalp tingles, even though I wish it wouldn't. I want no part of me to ever react to any part of him, but it's unconscious. I can't stop it. The nerve endings are traitorous, sparking from the gentle touch, no matter how cruel the man attached to those hands may be.

It makes me sick to the stomach.

Or *sicker*, rather.

His phone call with Lorenzo was enough to make me want to throw up.

"It will not be long now," Kassian says, his voice low. "The fun will soon begin."

I shake my head, whispering, "He's not coming."

"You do not think so?"

"He's smarter than that," I say. "He's not going to show up here just because you suggested it."

"Oh, I think you are wrong. In fact, I think he is already on his way. Maybe not for the money. Maybe not for *you*. But he will come, because he is not the type to turn down an invitation, and we both know that, pretty girl. He will show his ugly face soon."

The more he speaks, the more his grip on me tightens, the tingles replaced with pain as he tangles his fingers through my hair, fisting a handful. I wince as he tugs my head back, straining my neck, forcing me to look up at him.

"But maybe you are right," he says. "You will be lucky if he does not show. Because when he gets here, the first thing I am going to do is fuck you. Right here, like we used to, right where everyone can watch. I might even let him join, let him take you one last time, kill him while he is deep inside of that sweet pussy. Would you like that, *suka*? Being the last thing he ever does?"

I don't respond. I don't react.

Man, that makes him mad.

His cheek twitches. He shoves me away, nearly knocking my head into the table from the force of it as he slouches in his chair. I rub my sore scalp from where he pulled my hair, my face flushing when I glance around the room.

Everybody's watching us.

Watching *me*, rather.

Before I can dwell on it, I hear the front door open. The alarm is disabled as a thick accent echoes through the foyer. "*Vor!*"

Markel.

I tense, hearing a struggle, a *scuffle*, before Markel appears in the doorway. He's not alone, though, and parts of me viciously twist at the recognition, as Markel drags another guy with him. *Declan*.

"Ah, Mr. Jackson! How nice of you to join us!" Kassian waves into the room. "Have a seat. We were just waiting for your boss to make an appearance."

Declan struggles as Markel shoves him further into the room. His lip is busted, bleeding, the side of his face swollen. He fought, *hard*, but you can't tell it looking at Markel. He's all put together.

Well, except for his eye—still swollen and bloodshot, a milky haze coating it. *Oops*.

He shoves Declan down onto the couch across from me, his

eyes on my face. I can feel his gaze, even after I look away, my attention returning to Kassian's phone, discarded on the table just inches away. My heart is racing like a jackhammer, banging against my bruised ribcage.

"I have to use the bathroom," I whisper when Kassian's hand weasels its way back into my hair.

"No," Kassian says, barely paying me any attention as he snatches up a bottle of vodka from the table.

"I'll make it fast," I tell him. "I promise."

He ignores me, drinking, his eyes fixed on Declan.

"Kassian, I really have to pee."

My hand slips beneath his pant leg as I shift position, grasping his bare calf. It catches him off guard, me touching him. He reacts instinctively, shoving me off, throwing me right into the small table. I wince, the blow hard enough to rock the flimsy wood, knocking things off. Bottles tip over, and people scramble to grab them before the liquor spills out, while I catch myself on the edge of the table, grabbing the phone and slipping it behind my back.

I'm not wearing much, I know, but you'd be amazed where women can hide things. I slip the small phone right under my arm, tucking it in the band of the black bra, before holding my hands up in front of me defensively.

Kassian glares at me as I shake, genuinely fucking *shake*, because if he saw what I just did, I'm fucked. Literally, figuratively, every sense of that word and every which way it can happen. *Fucked.*

"Go," he says. "Before I change my mind."

I'm on my feet, scurrying away, but I don't make it from the room before he speaks again.

"Markel," he says. "Show the *suka* to the bathroom."

I stall near the door. "I remember where it is."

"I know," Kassian says. "I just do not trust you."

"But—"

"Either he escorts you," Kassian says, cutting me off, "or you go right here in front of us all. Take your pick. There is no other option."

Markel chooses for me, grabbing my shoulder and pushing me out of the room, his grip so tight I grimace the entire way down the hall. He shoves me inside of the nearest bathroom, feeling along the wall to blindly turn on the light. Stumbling, scowling, I grab the door to close it when his palm smacks against the wood, shoving it right back open.

He shifts his body into the doorway. Crossing his arms over his chest, he leans against the doorframe. He doesn't look happy.

"Well?" He raises an eyebrow. "You said you had to go."

"Can I get some privacy?"

"No."

"Seriously? Can you turn the *other* way, at least?"

"No."

My stomach drops. I just stand there, frozen.

"Stage fright?" he asks.

"This is humiliating."

"I have seen you in worse predicaments. So go. I'm waiting. Tick, tick, stupid girl... time is being wasted."

Rolling my eyes, I just do it. I didn't really *have* to go, but I force myself to so not to raise suspicion. Afterward, I stand there, taking my time washing my hands, buying myself a few seconds to think.

Groaning, Markel comes closer, shoving me out of the way as he steps over to use the bathroom.

I move away as soon as his back is to me, stepping out into the hall and pulling the phone from my bra. It's locked, so there isn't a lot I can do, trying a few codes but they all say *try again*. Kassian's too smart to use something I can guess.

Out of luck, out of time, I hit the '*emergency*' button. Can't do much besides call 911.

Not like it'll help me right now, but maybe they can trace the call.

I hit the button to end the call after I'm sure it connects, shoving the phone back into my bra as Markel steps out of the bathroom.

"You didn't wash your hands," I tell him, making a face.

"Give it to me," he says, holding his hand out.

He still doesn't look happy.

"Give you what?"

"Give it to me," he says again, his voice louder. "I will not tell Kassian as long as you give it to me *right now.*"

I stall, hesitating, about to say I don't know what he's talking about, when a soft buzz echoes around us. My chest starts vibrating. It's ringing. *Fuck.*

Before I can give it to him, he shoves me against the wall, patting me down and taking the phone out of my bra. I try to snatch it back, but Markel slams his forearm into my throat, pinning me there as he answers the call.

"Hello," he says, glaring at me as I struggle to take a deep breath. "Ah, yes, I am very sorry, but it was a mistake. Just a little girl playing on the phone, pressing buttons. There is no problem."

He hangs up on them, still glaring at me, saying nothing for a moment, just clutching the phone.

"You know how he is, Markel," I whisper. "You know what he'll *do.*"

"So why do you do these things? Why do you always have to *anger* him?"

"What choice do I have?"

"You could be what he wants you to be."

I look away from him when he says that. He knows I can't. He knows it's not right, that it's not *fair.* Markel may not be a saint, but he's not like his brother, either. There's compassion in him somewhere, and sometimes it feels like it's buried so deep it can't ever be unearthed, but other times, I see glimpses of it.

He takes a step back, removing his arm from my throat to slip Kassian's phone in his pocket.

"Where is she?" I ask, my voice trembling, hoping this is one of those moments. "Have you seen her?"

"Why should I tell you anything?"

"Because she's my little girl. I need to know that she's okay. I need to *see* her."

He tells me nothing, instead nodding toward the den,

wordlessly ordering me to go. My gaze trails along the floor as I cross my arms over my chest, making my way back to Kassian.

He's hunched over the table, snorting a thick line of snow-white powder when I step into the room. I hesitate, watching that, as Markel knocks into me from behind, moving around me to approach Kassian. Leaning down, he whispers, and my heart hammers hard, wondering if he's ratting me out. Kassian's gaze seeks me out as he listens to his brother, his eyes dark, *so damn dark*, his pupils massive.

Kassian says something in return, I don't know what, the words rushed and in Russian, like they're arguing. After a moment, Kassian groans, throwing his hands up, dismissively waving Markel away. "Fine. *Fine*! Go."

Markel reaches into his pocket, pulling Kassian's phone out, sliding it onto the table before stalking off. He slows as he passes me, walking so close his shoulder bumps mine, as he says, "I will see you later, *suka*. Be a good girl while I'm gone, and he will be nice."

Nice. That's not the word I'd use for it. He's erratic on coke, hot and cold. He either thinks you walk on water or he wants to bury you in the dirt.

There's no middle ground.

A smile lights his face as he looks at me.

My stomach sinks.

I'm walking on water at the moment.

I think I'd much rather want him to bury me.

Slowly, I approach, to take my seat on the floor, but Kassian grabs a hold of my hips and pulls me onto his lap instead. His arm snakes around me, shifting me in the chair, pulling me back against him as he relaxes, sipping from his bottle of vodka. I don't move, don't fight it, even as his hand caresses my stomach, even as his lips find my shoulder blade, kissing it.

I bite my cheek, squeezing my eyes shut.

Happy place.

A loud chime echoes through the house. Everyone grows silent. Reopening my eyes, my gaze meets Declan's across from me.

He doesn't look like he's afraid, but he's certainly not at ease, either.

It isn't until the chime rings out for the second time that anyone seems to realize what we're hearing. *Doorbell.* Kassian shoves me off of him, and I slide down onto the floor, taking my seat once more, hugging my legs. He sets his bottle of liquor down in front of me on the table before waving toward his minions. "Somebody answer that."

The guy closest to the door gets up and walks out, leaving Kassian here with Declan and I and two others, now that Markel is gone.

It's quiet. Almost *too* quiet. Nothing happens for a moment. The guy who answered the door doesn't come back. Did he *leave?* Nobody else seems concerned, though, so I try to relax, until out of nowhere I hear his voice—cool and calm, almost mockingly so. "No offense, Aristotle, but your parties kind of suck."

My eyes dart to the doorway, right to where he appears. *Lorenzo.* My heart beats so frantically my vision blurs. He's wearing black from head-to-toe: black slacks, black shirt, black combat boots. He looks almost sinister, standing there in the shadows, hands shoved in his pockets. He glances around at the men, gaze lingering on Declan, before he turns to Kassian, skipping right over me.

It's like I'm not even here.

Like I no longer exist to him.

My insides twist in knots, and I swallow thickly. I feel like I'm going to be sick. *Ugh.*

"Ah, yes, well, there are usually more women," Kassian says, reaching down to pat my head. "Tonight, we only have our little guest of honor, but she is quite enjoyable on her own. I am sure she would be more than happy to liven things up for you."

"I appreciate the offer, but I've already fucked her," Lorenzo says, those words nonchalant, but they hit me like a blow to the chest. "More than a few times, actually."

"So I have heard." Kassian fists a handful of my hair and roughly tugs my head up, so I'll look at him instead of Lorenzo. "But who has *not* fucked her?"

A throat clears nearby, a voice chiming in. "I haven't."

Declan.

Kassian loosens his grip on my hair. "Ah, yes, you have a thing for one of the others. *Lexie*. Seems she took a liking to you, also."

"Can you blame her?" Declan asks.

"Yes," Kassian says with a laugh, "I can."

Slowly, I turn my head again, my eyes shifting back to Lorenzo in the doorway. He's staring at me now, his expression blank, not a hint of emotion to be found anywhere. I so desperately wish I knew what he was thinking, wish I knew what was going through his mind. I wonder if he came here with a plan, if he knows what he's doing, if he realizes why Kassian told him to come. I wish he could hear my thoughts, so that I could warn him, so that I could thank him for everything he's done to help.

So that I could tell him to get the fuck out of here.

As he stares at me, his cheek twitches, the slightest hint of a frown tugging his lips.

"Sit, Mister Scar," Kassian says. "Have a drink."

Blinking, Lorenzo turns away from me again, looking to Kassian. "I'd rather we get business out of the way first."

"Fair enough," Kassian says, shoving out of his chair, leaning across me to grab a black duffel bag from the floor nearby. He drops it on the center of the table before sitting back down. "A million. It is all there. Every dollar I promised for her."

Lorenzo strolls into the room, coming closer... and closer... and closer, stopping so close to me that I can smell the faint hint of his soap as he leans down, unzipping the bag.

It's overflowing with cash. I can see that from here. Lorenzo shifts through it, but he doesn't bother counting before zipping it back up.

Snatching up the bag, he tosses it over to Declan, nearly knocking the wind out of the guy as it lands on his lap with a thud.

"Take that out to your car, Three," Lorenzo says.

Declan forces his way up off the couch, not one to disregard an order. The guys in the room look around, not sure if they're supposed to let him leave, looking to Kassian for some guidance. "What is the rush?" Kassian asks, waving them off. "*Sit.* Enjoy yourselves. No need to run off."

"I'm not running anywhere," Lorenzo says, grabbing Kassian's discarded vodka bottle from the table. He sniffs it before taking a swig.

Declan walks out, lugging the heavy bag with him. I can feel Kassian tense, his hand shifting to my shoulder, squeezing it hard, like he thinks Lorenzo might try to have me hauled out of here next.

Lorenzo steps over and drops down onto the couch, taking the seat Declan vacated. He looks at the guys on either side of him, assessing them, as he helps himself to the liquor. He seems at ease, more than he ought to, a fact that I know is ruffling Kassian.

His grip gets tighter... and tighter... and tighter.

I wince, trying to move from his grasp, trying to scoot to the right, out of his reach, but he isn't having that. His hand shifts once again, this time grasping the back of my neck as he leans down toward me, saying, "It seems you were wrong, pretty girl."

"Fuck you," I whisper.

He laughs at me, and I shudder at the feel of his breath on my skin.

"Eager, are we?" he asks, running his nose along my hair. "Patience, pussycat."

"So, tell me something, Jabba," Lorenzo says, interrupting. "You got the kid frozen in carbonite somewhere?"

Kassian pulls away from me, but he doesn't let go of my neck. "Jabba?"

"Yeah, you know, *Star Wars*," Lorenzo says. "You seem to have a Jabba the Hutt thing going on with your chained-up dancers. Quite uncanny, really."

"*Star Wars?*" Kassian's voice is incredulous. "I do not like all that space stuff, with those aliens and the *beam me up* nonsense."

Lorenzo coughs, choking on some vodka. Sitting up, he points the bottle at Kassian. "Did you seriously just...?"

"*Star Wars*," Kassian says, waving him off. "It is all so stupid."

Something happens in that moment. A flicker of rage flashes across Lorenzo's face. Before the last syllable even passes from Kassian's lips, Lorenzo *snaps*.

Flipping the liquor bottle around, he snatches it by the neck and swings hard, like a baseball bat, slamming the guy to his right in the head with it.

BAM.

The bottle shatters, glass scattering, vodka saturating the room as the guy falls limp. *Knocked out.* The guy to Lorenzo's left grabs him, to try to stop him, but there's not much he can do to ward off what's happening. Still clutching the neck of the broken bottle, Lorenzo turns, not hesitating at all as he lunges, *stabbing*, the jagged glass plunging through the side of the guy's neck.

The guy gurgles, gasping, panicked, and yanks the bottle out. Mistake. *Big fucking mistake.* Blood spurts from the wound, shooting out like a water fountain, not stopping even as he grasps his neck, holding tightly.

Lorenzo shoves the guy off the couch, unfazed as the blood splatters him.

Seconds. Mere *seconds*. If I would've blinked, I would've missed it all. Kassian reacts, shoving up out of the chair in alarm. His fingers wind tightly through my hair, forcing me to my feet, pulling me against him as he steps back, away from the table, putting some distance between the men. I cry out as pain radiates along my scalp, feeling like he's ripping out clumps of hair. His hands shift, arm winding around my neck, putting me in a headlock from behind, my body shielding part of his.

Lorenzo's on his feet, pulling a gun from beneath his shirt. He cocks it, aiming at Kassian. Aiming at *me*. My heart races.

"Hiding behind a woman?" Lorenzo asks. "Kind of a dick move, isn't it, Jabba?"

"Sentimental fool," Kassian says. "You would not risk hurting your precious *Scarlet*. You do not have the guts to pull the trigger."

BANG.

The moment Kassian says it, a gunshot lights up the room. I

scream, startled, my ears ringing as a bullet flies right by me. So close. *Too* close. Lorenzo didn't flinch, didn't move, not a flicker of emotion on his face when he pulled the fucking trigger.

Kassian shoves me, moving, trying to dodge the gunshot. Or maybe he's trying to throw me *into* it, I don't know. *I don't know.* All I know is seconds later, in another blink, there's movement. The guy on the couch, the one Lorenzo smacked with the bottle, comes to with a jolt, the loud bang rousing him back to consciousness.

Lorenzo doesn't notice. The guy is in his blind spot.

"Lorenzo!" I scream.

Kassian's hand clamps down on my mouth as he pins me against him, hissing, "Stupid girl, *shut up.*"

Lorenzo turns just as the guy hits him, fists swinging. *Oh god.* Lorenzo fires a shot that misses entirely, the bullet hitting the mantle over the fireplace, ricocheting my direction. I cry out into Kassian's palm, panicked, my vision blurring, struggling to break free but it's not working.

They start going at it, hitting, grabbing, the gun ripped from Lorenzo's grasp and kicked across the floor. My stomach drops. Lorenzo's at a disadvantage, not only because of his blind spot, but because Kassian's guys are *built* for this. They're trained to disarm, to subdue, to inflict pain...

"You see that?" Kassian whispers in my ear. "He is weak, your little plaything. He cannot save you."

Lorenzo puts up one hell of a fight, using everything he's got, but it isn't long until he's knocked down, dropping to his knees. Blood streams from his busted mouth as he breathes heavily.

My heart damn near stops.

"Aw, look at that, *suka,*" Kassian says. "Now you get to watch him take his last breath."

I struggle, flailing, kicking my legs, swinging my arms. I throw my head back, slamming into Kassian's chin, my elbow jabbing him in the rib, but it's still not enough.

Fuck this.

I bite him.

My teeth clamp down on his palm. He rips his hand away

from my mouth, cursing, and shoves me, throwing me to the floor by the fireplace.

I wince, my ankle twisting in the goddamn heels as I land... *hard.*

"Stay," he barks, glaring at me, furious. Turning away, he stalks over to Lorenzo, shaking the hand that I bit before he snatches the gun from the floor. He steps right in front of Lorenzo, raising the gun, pointing it at his forehead. "It is a shame it has come to this, Mister Scar. You and I could have been friends."

Lorenzo says nothing, just staring up at him, his tongue slowly running along his busted lip.

"But friends do not steal from each other," Kassian continues. "My friends do not try to take what is *mine.* I may let them have a taste, from time to time, but the *suka* belongs to me. She is not theirs, and she is certainly not *yours.* The stupid girl, she does not know what is good for her. She let you believe you could keep her, she let you have parts of her that were not hers to give away, and that, *Scar,* is why we can *never* be friends."

Anger flows through every syllable from Kassian's lips, his hand shaking as he grips the gun. He doesn't use them. He prefers his bare hands. But his finger is on the trigger, and I know he's going to pull it. Any fucking second, the gunshot is going to echo through the air.

No. No. *No.*

Frantic, my eyes dart around, my mind working fast, looking for a way out. Where are Lorenzo's guys? Where'd Declan go? Where are the others? Where's *Seven?* Why aren't they here, protecting him? Why is nobody doing anything to stop this?

Why isn't Lorenzo fighting?

It makes no sense.

It's *insane.*

A smile creeps up on Lorenzo's lips. It sends a chill down my spine. *Oh no. Oh god.* Why the fuck is he smiling? A light laugh escapes him as he spits blood on Kassian's shiny shoes, like none of this bothers him.

"You're right, Aristotle," Lorenzo says. "You and I could

never be friends."

As soon as he says that, I hear the front door of the house open. I don't know who it is. I don't know who's coming. All I know is that if somebody doesn't do *something*, this is it. It's all over.

He's going to die because of me.

I can't let that happen.

Kicking off the heels, I shove up to my feet, grabbing the first thing I can reach—the fireplace poker. I grasp it tightly in my sweaty palms, clutching it with both hands as I lunge right for Kassian, ramming it in his back. It doesn't go far in, the thick metal curving, my bruised body too damn weak to shove it through, but it pierces him enough to knock him forward.

His minion grabs me before I can do much else, ripping the poker out of my hand, out of Kassian's *back*, before he throws me across the room. The gun goes off as soon as I hit the floor, the noise harrowing in my ears.

BANG.

I scream, desperately turning.

Don't let him be dead.

I watch, eyes wide, as Lorenzo finally fights. He's on his feet again, twisting Kassian's arm, forcing him to pull the trigger again.

BANG.

The bullet grazes Kassian's shoulder, throwing him off enough for Lorenzo to get the upper hand. He snatches the gun back as Kassian staggers, stunned.

People swarm the room as adrenaline flows through me, the rush nearly making me black out. The first person I see, the first face I encounter, is one I haven't seen in a while.

Seven.

Behind him is Declan. Beside him, Frank. Declan and Frank carry guns, assault rifles, while Seven holds his hands up in front of him, almost defensively.

Lorenzo stands up straight, no hesitation, pumping a few bullets into Kassian's last minion, dropping the guy before he points the gun at Kassian.

"You see, the thing is," Lorenzo says, "I could never be

friends with someone who doesn't know the difference between *Star Wars* and *Star Trek*."

He doesn't pull the trigger.

No, he *swings*.

BAM.

Lorenzo beats him, slamming him in the face with the pistol, blow after blow, unrelenting. Lorenzo backs him up into the wall, hitting him so hard Kassian drops, sliding to the floor. His face is a streaked mask of red, blood pouring from him, coating Lorenzo's hand.

"Damn, boss," Declan says. "Just pop a bullet in the guy... would be more humane."

"No," I yell, my own voice surprising me. "Wait, you *can't*. Don't kill him!"

The guys cast me peculiar looks.

All except Lorenzo, who doesn't even look my way. I'm invisible again. His attention is on his guys, scanning them as his expression darkens. He raises the gun again, aiming, this time at *Seven*.

I have no idea what to make of that, no idea what's happening, but I don't have time to figure it out. Kassian's eyes are drifting closed, like he's going unconscious.

I rush over, dropping to my knees beside him, grasping his bloody face and shaking him. "Kassian, *look at me*."

His cold gray eyes meet mine.

"Tell me where she is," I whisper, my voice cracking. "Tell me where I can find Sasha."

He curves an eyebrow. "Markel did not tell you?"

"Markel? No. Tell me *what*?"

He says nothing.

I hear Lorenzo behind me, talking to Seven, his voice angry as he says, "What the fuck are you doing here?"

"Jameson called me," Seven says. "He was trying to get up with you. He told me about the club, and I just... I screwed up, I know, but I want to help, boss."

"Don't call me that," Lorenzo says. "You shouldn't have

come. I told you I *never* wanted to see your face again. Hell, I told *all* of you to get out of here. None of you listen!"

Kassian turns his head, glancing past me, at the guys.

I've lost his attention.

"Listen to me, Kassian," I say, making him look my way again. "Tell me where she is so I can go to her. If there's any heart in you at all, if you love her... if you love *me*, like you say... you'll tell me how to find her."

He reaches for me, his fingertips brushing against my cheek. He's wiping away my tears, I realize.

I'm crying.

"Always so beautiful when you cry," he says, his fingers tracing my jawline before running down my neck, his hand settling on my throat. "What is it you used to say? Face your fears and wipe your tears?"

"Yes," I whisper.

"Then wipe your tears, pretty girl," he says, "because the time has come to face your fears."

He grips my throat tightly, and I gasp, shoving against his chest to push away but he yanks me toward him instead.

"Oh, whoa, *whoa!*" Declan yells. "What the fuck?"

Someone grabs me, dragging me away from Kassian. I don't have to look to know it's Lorenzo. I can smell him, can *feel* him as he wraps his arms around me from behind.

Declan steps in front of me, taking my place beside Kassian, slamming the butt of his gun into his face. "Hands off, dickwad."

"That's enough," Lorenzo says, his voice firm.

Declan casts him a look that asks '*why?*' but he says nothing, stalling what he's doing.

"Get him out of here," Lorenzo says. "Put him in my trunk. And if you let him die, I swear to fuck..."

"Got it, boss," Frank says. "We'll keep him alive."

The guys snatch ahold of Kassian, pulling him to his feet. He sways, knees damn near buckling, not making it easy for them as they haul him away. The second he's out of my line of sight, panic rushes through me. I shove out of Lorenzo's grasp, darting after them.

"Kassian, *please!*" I yell, stopping in the middle of the foyer as they reach the front door. I'm not above begging at this point. "Please, tell me what you did with our daughter!"

Kassian stalls, resisting, fighting the guys as he turns to look at me. "You want to know where kitten is?"

"Yes!"

"I would take you to her, if I could," he says. "I would love nothing more. It would be my pleasure, truly, to choke the life out of you again, just like I did her."

"No," I whisper, dizzy, as I shake my head. "No, no, no... you *didn't.*"

"I did."

"Don't do this, Kassian. Don't... *please!*"

"Too late," he says. "So go to hell, *suka*... if you are lucky, maybe you will find her there."

My knees give out on me. The world spins as I drop. Lorenzo is there, grabbing me before I hit the floor, arms winding tightly around me, but he's not strong enough to keep me from falling apart.

I choke on a sob, crying, inhuman noise echoing from my chest as I struggle to catch my breath. My heart, I can feel it shattering. It hurts. *Oh god, it burns.* My lungs won't work anymore. They're nothing but ash, charred by flames. *No, no, no...*

"I've got you," Lorenzo says, his voice quiet as he holds me. "It's okay... *I got you.*"

The strength fades from my body as those words reach inside of me, gripping tight. Days of torture, weeks of sorrow, months of heartache catch up to me all at once. I collapse into myself, unable to find the words to tell him he's wrong. It's not okay. It'll never be okay. They just hauled my best chance to find my daughter out of that door, and my fear of never seeing her again is feeling more and more real.

On my knees, curled over, I hold onto myself, trying to keep from breaking but it's hard. *So hard.*

I don't believe it. I refuse to believe it. She's not gone. I'd know it if she was. A mother always *knows*. I'd feel it in my heart. A piece of me exists inside of that little girl, and it has to still be out there. It can't just be gone.

Who knows how long I lay here, just like that, how long Lorenzo kneels beside me, letting me cry. It feels like forever. Lifetimes pass. He takes off his coat, draping it over me, covering me up as he rubs my back.

He says anything for a long moment, consoling me in silence.

His hand stops moving eventually. I feel him tense, pulling away, putting enough distance between us that I lose his warmth, coldness creeping through me, ice in my veins.

"Morgan," he says, his voice quiet as he whispers my name. *My name.* "Open your eyes, baby."

I raise my head up when he says that, but I don't get far enough to look at him. I freeze when my gaze reaches the front door, still hanging wide open. Markel stands there, barely visible within the shadows of the front porch, but that's not what gets me. *No.* It's the small body just inside the entryway, a few feet in front of him, not far from where I sit. Bare feet, white nightgown, wild brown hair—longer than I remember, but everything else is so much the same. She stares at me, her dark eyes wide like she's seeing a ghost, like I'm a figment of her imagination. *Sasha.* She's not moving, not making a sound, but I can see her chest rising and falling fast, like she can't breathe very well.

"Sunshine?" I whisper, finding my voice.

Her bottom lip trembles, tears filling her eyes. "Mommy?"

I nod, opening my arms, choking on a sob at the sound of her sweet voice calling me that again. *Mommy.*

I don't have to say another word.

She runs right for me, loudly crying, flinging herself at me so hard she nearly knocks me back onto the floor. I wrap my arms around her, clinging to her, feeling her warmth. My heart. My innocence. The light of my life. I squeeze my eyes shut, and for a brief second I wonder if I'm dreaming. I wonder if I'll open my eyes and all of this will be gone. It's cruel, the thought that maybe it's just all in my head, but her voice washes over me again, and I push those thoughts away.

If this is a dream, whatever... I'm okay with *never* waking up again.

"You found me, Mommy," she says, her voice shaking. "You found me!"

I open my eyes again, pulling back just enough to look at her. She smiles as I wipe the tears from her flushed cheeks. I glance past her, around the foyer, being greeted by nothing more than silence.

The front door is closed now. Lorenzo is gone.

There's nobody here, nobody but *us*.

"I did," I whisper, smoothing her hair as I return her smile, looking back at her. "I promised, didn't I?"

21

Lorenzo

My life is a three-ring circus.

I like to think that I'm the ringmaster of it all, but I'm beginning to feel more like a fucking trained lion, one that's sick of jumping through hoops, seconds away from breaking loose and mauling *everyone*. The acrobats are all around me, bending over backwards, or hell... maybe they're more like a carnival freak show. Regardless, I know who the fucking clowns are.

One of them is currently indisposed in my trunk.

The other jumped in a car and sped away after dropping off a kid that was supposedly dead. I haven't exactly wrapped my mind around all of that yet, but suffice it to say, that particular bozo will get to live to see another day.

How many *more* days is really the question... the answer dependent upon what he does after tonight.

The one in the trunk, however, won't be so lucky.

"Christ, it feels like we ought to be halfway to *China* by now," Five mutters, sweat rolling off of him. He comes to a stop, leaning on his shovel as he pulls his shirt up to wipe his face. "How come *he* gets out of digging?"

Five motions toward my car.

"He's really in no condition to dig his own grave."

"I meant Bruno, not the Russian," Five says, pausing as he looks at me, his voice dropping lower. "Wait, shit, this *is* for Aristov, right? This isn't, you know... is it?"

I glance over at Seven as he leans against the side of my car, arms crossed over his chest, watching us in the darkness. Instead of humoring that with a response, I continue to dig, throwing shovelfuls of dirt aside. "The reason he's not doing it because I don't trust him."

"You don't trust him to work a shovel?"

"I don't trust him to take a piss right now. The jackass in the trunk has been more honest about his intentions, so no, I don't trust him with a shovel."

"Why's he here then?"

"Because I haven't killed him."

"Are you going to?"

"Maybe."

"Do you think he—?"

Sighing exasperatedly, I slam my shovel into the dirt and look at Five, cutting off his last question, because I'm not answering whatever it is. "Is this one of those *check yes or no* moments? You trying to pass me some notes here? Want to gossip like little fucking busybodies? Braid each other's hair? Be best friends forever?"

"My fault," he mutters, going back to digging. "Just trying to get on the same page."

"All the page I'm on says is *'they dug a fucking hole to bury the Russian in'* so that's what I'm doing."

He nods. "Got it."

We dig in silence until I'm satisfied the hole is big enough. Takes about an hour. My shoulders ache and my back hurts, not to mention my head is viciously pounding. It has been steadily thumping since I took those hard blows to the face hours ago, when the jackass beat the hell out of me before Aristov put my own gun to my forehead.

Yeah, it has been one fucked up day...

There was a second, a brief second, where I thought I might die tonight before Scarlet got her wits about her and decided to do something. I was counting on that, counting on her tenacity.

She didn't disappoint, but the pain in my head says it sure took her ass long enough.

Throwing my shovel up over the side, I pull myself out of

the hole, brushing the dirt from my clothes. Five follows my lead, but he struggles, crawling over the side, collapsing on the ground beside it.

"You're starting to whine more than Three," I tell him.

Five forces himself up. "I haven't said a word in forty-five minutes!"

"Doesn't mean I can't hear you complaining."

"Whatever," he mutters, not bothering to brush the dirt from his sweaty clothes. "That's who ought to be out here digging holes. *Declan.*"

"He's got other things to take care of," I say, popping the trunk on my car and opening it, my gaze meeting Aristov's as he forces his eyes open. He's barely clinging to consciousness. He's lost quite a bit of blood. Not from the bullet that grazed his shoulder, nor from the beating he took. No, it was the rod of metal that Scarlet rammed into his back. I don't know what she hit, but she must've hit *something.* "You look tired, Aristotle, but don't worry... we've got your bed all made up."

Grabbing him, I start yanking him out of the trunk. He doesn't fight, because he doesn't have much fight left in him, which means it isn't going to be *easy* for me, either. Five jumps in, helping me lug him out, dropping him to the ground between us.

Aristov groans, muttering something I don't pay attention to, because *fuck him.*

Would *you* give a shit about his final words after the things he's done, if he did them to *you*?

We haul him toward the hole, but the son of a bitch is heavy, *bulky*, dragging the ground as we pull him along. Seven shoves away from the car, coming toward us. "Here, let me help you, boss."

"I swear to fuck, Seven, if you call me that one more time, Five and I are going to be digging yet another hole tonight, and trust me when I say none of us want that to happen."

"I sure don't," Five mutters. "I'm *tired.*"

Seven grows silent, returning to his place beside the car, as Five and I drag Aristov the rest of the way and roll him into the hole.

He lands face-up with a thud.

I grab my shovel, scooping up a pile of dirt, instantly dropping it on him. He opens his eyes, looking up at me, but he otherwise does nothing.

What *can* he do?

Not a goddamn thing.

I know. *I know.* I've been there.

It might've been a world away, but I've lay where he's lying.

The pain... the pain had been intense. I can still feel an echo of it sometimes rattling around in my head. Otherwise, just like my skull, the rest of it became fractured, my memory a pile of puzzle pieces that will never completely fit together. Flashes and moments, like a fucked up flipbook out of sequence. I vividly remember my stepfather standing over me, panting and sweaty, his nose bleeding. I'd put up a fight, but it wasn't enough. He caught me off guard, swinging the metal shovel, hitting me right in the face the second I turned around.

I laid in the hole he dug behind the house, barely clinging to consciousness as I stared up at him in the darkness. My ears were ringing, and the man was talking, but I could barely make out his words. Something, something, something... *you brought this on yourself.* Alarms shrieked inside my skull, but I didn't make a sound. I didn't beg, or cry, or curse, even as he took the bloody shovel and picked up a pile of dirt, sending it raining down on me.

I closed my eyes as they burned, coated in blood. I waited for death. I knew it was coming. I waited... and waited... and waited... as he piled on the dirt.

Something jarred me eventually as I was yanked and dragged, the pain explosive as I forced my eyes open, looking up, expecting to see my stepfather, but it was another face I found. A guy, not much older than me. People were shouting into the night, fighting going on somewhere, as he knelt down, leaning over me. "Can you hear me?"

I tried to nod.

"Can you tell me your name?" he asked. "Can you tell me *anything?*"

I opened my mouth, my voice a broken whisper as I tried to speak. No idea if he heard me or if he understood, but he said, "My name's Ignazio. Just hold on, okay?"

Blackness took over then, more little flashes. It took a while for me to realize Ignazio had saved my life, pulling me out of a homemade grave and finding help.

"How long does it take?" Five asks, his question catching me off guard, drawing me out of the memory.

He's staring down at Aristov. The hole is only about four feet deep, six and a half feet long.

"What?"

"How long does it take to die this way?" Five asks. "Hours? Days?"

"More like minutes," I say. *Buried alive.* "Inhaling dirt, a thousand pounds of pressure on top of you. You'd suffocate."

"Sounds terrifying."

It is.

Within a few minutes, Aristov's no longer visible. He doesn't have an Ignazio to save him like I'd had. Less than an hour later, and the hole is again filled.

We kick stuff on top of it—leaves, tree branches, stones, making it blend in, so if anyone stumbles upon the area, it won't stand out. We're deep in the woods, an hour or so across the border in New Jersey, in the middle of fucking nowhere. He'll likely go undiscovered forever.

"I don't know about you, but I feel like I could sleep for a *month*," Five says as we toss the shovels in the blood-soaked trunk, adding dirt right on top of it, a forensic team's wet dream. "Probably could use a vacation after the night we've had."

"Florida's nice this time of year," I tell him. "You should take the trip down."

"Yeah?"

"Yeah, there's some work on the groves that needs done."

Five laughs, pulling out the car keys to head for the driver's seat. "It's not really a vacation if you've got me on the clock."

I shrug, getting in the passenger seat. I've never taken a

vacation from working, so I don't know what that's like. There's always stuff that needs done. Seven climbs in the backseat, staying silent, as Five drives us back into New York under the cloak of darkness, heading straight to my house in Queens.

The rest of the guys are here, waiting. Well, except for Three. He's still off handling things.

I dismiss everyone right away, not in the mood for company, needing some time to get my thoughts in order, but Seven lingers, standing on my front porch. As much as I'm still itching to gut him, I have to admit he's got balls. Big balls. Maybe *too* big, but still... it takes balls to stand here.

"What do you want, Seven?"

"A second chance," he says.

"Why should I give you one?"

"Because I want to make it up to you."

I shake my head. "That's not a good reason. I don't care what you *want*. Not anymore. So if you're looking for a second chance, come back when you've got a good reason as to why I should give you one. Until then..."

I wave him off.

He turns away, leaving without arguing.

My brother meets me in the foyer as soon as I'm in the house, my boots tracking dirt in along the floor.

"What happened?" he asks. "What's going on?"

"Nothing," I say. "I took care of it."

"You took care of it," he repeats, looking all around me, and I know what he's looking for: *Scarlet*.

"She's fine," I tell him. "She's with her kid."

His eyes widen. "You found her daughter, too?"

"Yes." I grasp his shoulder, squeezing it. It's all of the reassurance I can manage. "All's well that ends well, right? Or some other cliché bullshit. Whatever you want to hear right now."

"But—"

He's got questions, I know... *so many* fucking questions... but I'm not in the mood. "Not tonight, Leo. Let me get my head right before you interrogate me about this shit."

He just stands there, gaping at me, as I walk away, heading to my library. He doesn't try to follow, dropping it for the moment, going into the living room to report what he knows to his girlfriend, to set her pretty little head at ease that the world is a beautiful place again, that the sun will come out tomorrow and the flowers will soon bloom and they can sleep snug as a bug in a fucking rug tonight without worrying about monsters hiding under the bed.

Me? I'm exhausted, but there's no way *I* can sleep, not with so much weighing on me. Turning on the lamp, I run my hands down my face before fixing my attention on my still unfinished puzzle.

It has never taken me so long to do one before.

After grabbing a bottle of rum from the kitchen, I decide to dive into the puzzle, hoping the alcohol will numb my pain, hoping focusing on something else will keep my head from exploding. I don't know how much time passes, the night wearing away, but I'm feeling little more than a tingling sensation in my muscles when there's a knock from the doorway.

I glance over, seeing Three standing there.

"How'd it go?" I ask quietly.

"Okay, I guess," he says, stepping into the library, rubbing the side of his face. It's red, a hint of a bruise forming on his pale skin. "I had them checked out by a doctor. Neither seemed happy about it, but they're both okay, for the most part. Nothing seriously wrong. Some dehydration, a bit of malnourishment, a hell of a lot of bumps and bruises on Morgan, but that was obvious just looking at her."

"Tell me about it," I mutter. Her skin was a kaleidoscope of injuries, but the kind of shit that is just superficial. The real damage, I think, has to be rooted deeply in her, the kind of damage that fucks up somebody *mentally*.

I should've gotten to her sooner.

I'm a fucking failure.

I wavered and waited... and waited... and waited... so not to get her hurt. A lot of fucking good that did, huh? While I sat around, biding my time, he did what he did to her.

I can imagine, you know. I don't need anyone to tell me. I saw the way she looked.

Should've just tossed the grenade and ended it before it started.

"Anyway, so I booked them this suite at The Plaza," Three says. "This little pink poufy looking place. They do tea time and shit. Figured a little girl would like that, right? Cupcakes and pink shit and… tea?"

"I don't know," I mumble, looking back at my puzzle, picking up a piece. "I don't know anything about kids."

"You raised one."

"Pretty sure the one I raised was born more mature than me."

Three pauses to lean against the table. "I don't know shit about kids, either, clearly, because the little girl wanted nothing to do with it. Said some shit about it looking like another palace, said she wasn't doing it anymore, whatever that means. So Morgan gave me some address in Long Island, told me to take them there… some house they could stay at. They seemed, well… okay."

"Okay," I repeat.

"Yeah."

I snap my puzzle piece into place before picking up another one. "So, at what point did she hit you?"

He laughs lightly, rubbing his face again. "When I gave her the money. She didn't want to take it, got downright pissed, but then I told her what you told me to tell her, and well… she kind of got emotional, so I jetted out of there."

"You told her?"

"Yeah."

Go find your picket fence.

It's as good of a goodbye as any, I figure. She wants the fairy tale with the happy ending. All I have are bullet holes in a house with no soul. I knew she wouldn't want Aristov's money, but I took it for her. *A million dollars for Morgan.* That was the deal. I took it so she wouldn't go back to stripping, so she wouldn't resort to stealing, so she wouldn't ever have to pickpocket another motherfucker like *me.*

I took it because she deserves a shot at the kind of life she says she wants. Nothing will erase what he put her through, but maybe it'll ease her hurt just enough for her to move on.

"You okay, boss?" Three asks.

I cut my eyes at him. "I'm fine."

"You need anything else from me?"

"No," I say. "Not tonight."

"I'm gonna head home, then. I'll see you later."

He starts to leave, heading toward the door, as I sit down in my chair and run my hands down my face. *Fuck.* "Before you go..."

He glances back at me. "Yeah?"

"The brunette from Limerence, the one you, uh..."

"Lexie?"

"Yes."

"Oh, look, about her," he says. "I know she was supposed to be there tonight, that she was supposed to help, but she wouldn't have flaked intentionally, you know. I don't know what happened, but Lexie... she's a good girl, so if you could maybe cut her a break, I'd—"

"She's dead."

He stalls, his expression falling. "What?"

"She's dead," I say again. "When we hit the club tonight, we found her in the basement."

"Dead?"

"Yes."

He's quiet for a long moment, just standing there, staring at me, like he's not sure how to react. I can see it in his eyes, though. The sadness. The *pain.* He liked her, for whatever reason, and he's grieving. *Look them in the eyes if you want to know what they're not saying.* My stepfather used to stress that.

They say the eyes are the windows to the soul. Is it really any wonder why mine are fucked up?

"Well... that sucks," he says, running a hand through his blond hair, ruffling it up. "But hey, on the bright side, Bruno's back, so I guess we have snacks again, huh?"

I don't have it in me to tell him not to get his hopes up on that, because Seven might have shown up but I wouldn't call him *back*, so I just nod. He's deflecting. I'm not going to be a bigger asshole and call him out on it.

"Goodnight, boss," he say quietly, walking out.

I turn back to my puzzle, mumbling, "Goodnight, Declan."

* * *

"Lorenzo?"

"Yeah?"

"What are you doing?"

"What does it look like?"

When I get no response to my retort, my gaze turns to the library doorway, where my brother stands. He's staring in at me, watching me, his eyebrows raised.

"It looks like you're standing there," he says, "doing the same thing you were doing when I went to bed twelve hours ago."

I glance at my watch. It's shortly past noon. *Huh.* "You went to bed at midnight?"

"Yes," he says. "I said goodnight, remember?"

No. "Vaguely."

He stares at me some more.

"I'm still working on my puzzle," I tell him, turning back to it. "I'm almost finished."

I only have about five hundred pieces left out of the eight thousand that make up Michelangelo's painting on the ceiling of the Sistine Chapel.

"Have you even *tried* to sleep?" he asks. "I'm guessing not, since you still look like *that*."

I glance down at myself. I haven't even taken my boots off. I'm covered in dirt, sweat, *fuck*... even some blood. It's not very visible on the black fabric, but it still covers my hands, caked under my nails. "I haven't gotten around to it."

"You know sleep deprivation can kill you, right? I mean, it probably won't, but it *could*."

"I'm fine," I say, "but if it'll make you feel better, Pretty Boy,

I'll go to bed when I'm done."

"When's that going to be?"

"Tomorrow, maybe."

"Tomorrow."

"Maybe."

He grows quiet, but I can feel his judgment. Seems my answer isn't good enough for him for whatever reason. Sometimes I think he forgets I'm the adult here, that I raised his little punk ass and not the other way around.

Before he can try to lecture me, a chime echoes through the house. Instantly, I hear Melody's shrill voice as she panics in the living room, like she's traumatized by the sound of a doorbell.

Leo forgets all about our conversation, rushing away to console her.

I ignore it, going back to my puzzle, working on it in silence. I assume my brother answers the door, because a minute or so later, he's right back in the doorway. "Seven's here to see you."

"Good for him."

"Yeah, he rang the doorbell," Leo says. "Seems to think his open invitation has been revoked, so he's waiting on the front porch."

"Ask him if he's come up with a reason yet."

"Uh, okay..." Leo walks away, returning a minute later. "He says because he's sorry."

"Not good enough."

Leo leaves, once more returning. "He says he thinks he can still be helpful."

"Well, I think Valet parking is helpful, but that doesn't mean I can't park the fucking car myself."

And again.

"He says he'll do whatever you say."

"Tell him I say to come back when he's got something real to offer, because otherwise, I'm liable to shoot him in the fucking face."

Leo hesitates before walking away.

I focus on the puzzle, piece after piece after piece, and fall into a trance. *Tunnel vision.* There's a disconnect inside of me. My mind's working, my muscles moving, but I'm on autopilot. *A fucking robot.* My blinks get slower, my eyes burning, the world around me a blur as the day drifts away, darkness falling.

Leo keeps popping in, trying to engage in conversation.

Are you hungry? No.

You sure? Pretty damn positive.

Need something to drink? I've got my rum.

Are you almost done? I would be, if you'd leave me the fuck *alone.*

I scrub my hands over my face, groaning, squeezing my eyes shut, but I instantly regret it.

Whenever I close my eyes, I see her. *Scarlet.*

I see her smiling. I see her crying. I hear her laughter flowing through me, sending chills down my spine. The sound of her moaning creeps through my bloodstream, the face she makes in the throes of passion the pulse that spurs it on. Whatever this is I'm feeling, I want it to stop. I want it to go away. I want to stop fucking seeing her every time I blink. I want to stop fucking thinking about her every time I pause to take a deep breath. She's like an infection that's settling into my chest. I would rip out my own organs if I thought it might purge her from my system.

I need a witchdoctor to break the spell this woman has on me.

"Goddamn voodoo pussy," I mutter, snatching up the liquor bottle and tipping it back, guzzling the last of it before turning back to the puzzle. *Almost finished.*

You'd think it would be easier, since I'm nearing the end, most of it all filled in, but you'd be wrong.

Everything that's left looks the same.

Or maybe I'm just drunk.

Who the fuck knows?

The world around me is lightening again as I get down to a handful of pieces, the sun rising, another day dawning. I snap the pieces in place, looking at the lone jagged hole in the center of the puzzle, right there in *The Creation of Adam*, probably the most important part of the entire painting.

My gaze scans the table all around the puzzle, searching for the last piece.

Nothing.

"What the hell?" Annoyed, I feel around along the edges, hands skimming along the puzzle, thinking it has to be blending in, but I find nothing. "You have gotta be fucking kidding me."

I look around the table. I look *under* the table. I check my chair. I check inside the box. I search the bookshelves and all along the floor and every fucking place a puzzle piece could possibly be in this room.

"No, no, no," I chant, double-checking half those places, even patting down my own pockets, because it has to be *somewhere.* I'm exhausted, and aggravated, and I just want this goddamn thing to be done, to get it over with so I can move on. For months, I've been working on this puzzle, weeks of my life spent putting it together, and for what? Huh? To leave a hole in the center of the goddamn picture so for the rest of my life I have to live with the fact that I never finished what I started, that I never got it *done?*

"Motherfucker!" I yell, kicking the chair, sending it flying across the room, skidding right into the bookshelf with a bang.

"Lorenzo?" Leo's voice calls out from the doorway. "What's wrong?"

"His dick is gone!"

"His... *what?* What's gone?"

"His *dick,*" I say again, pointing at the damn hole in the puzzle, right there, cutting through Adam's crotch, cutting it *out,* so there's nothing in that spot. "God is breathing life into man, but his dick is gone, so what's the point?"

"What's the point?"

"Can't fuck," I say, anger building up inside of me, my fingers tingling, my chest burning, my face going hot. I'm *sweating.* "Can't even take a piss. He's just there, half a goddamn man... can't do a fucking thing for Eve like that, can he? No, he *can't!* Even his goddamn balls are gone. There's just... nothing. There's a fucking hole there, Leonardo, right where his dick's supposed to be, and I can't do shit about it!"

He steps into the library, carefully approaching. "You're spiraling, bro. I think you need to go lay down."

"Fuck you. And fuck lying down. I'm *fine*. Sleep isn't going to change a goddamn thing, is it? There's still going to be a hole, right fucking there. It's not going to just fix itself. It's pointless... all of it. All of this. I bust my ass trying to put it all together, but why do I bother? Fuck all of it!"

Something inside of me snaps, hitting me so damn hard it's like a punch to the chest, right in the sternum. It hurts. I almost lose my breath. Grabbing ahold of the table, I shove it, *throwing* it, flipping the fucking thing over, sending the puzzle flying. It breaks apart, scattering.

Leo freezes as I pace around. It's taking everything in me not to reach for my gun, to not put bullets through the table, to not blow holes in the fucking thing. Running my hands through my hair, gripping onto it, I kick at the puzzle on the floor, stomping on it as I pace, done... *so fucking done.*

"You're in love with her, aren't you?"

I cut my eyes at Leo. "What?"

"Morgan," he says. "You fell in love with her."

"You don't know what you're talking about."

"I think I do," he says. "You fell for her, and you're freaking out, because she's not here now."

"Fuck you."

"You do realize it's not too late, right?"

I turn away. I can't even *look* at him right now. I'm so damn angry that I'm liable to do something I'll regret if he doesn't stop running his mouth. "Get out."

"I'm serious," he says, not shutting up, not *getting out*. "You push people away. You push everyone away, and you're a real dick about it most of the time, but she's not *gone*, Lorenzo. She's still out there."

"I swear to fuck, if you don't *get out*..."

"You'll do *what*? Push me away, too? Sorry, bro, it might work with other people, but I *know* you. So lash out all you want...

yell at me, curse me, threaten me... I'm not going anywhere, *ever.*"

"Strong words for someone busy packing boxes to move the fuck out."

"It's not like that and you know it."

"Whatever."

"*Whatever,*" he says, mocking me.

I turn to him, stepping toward him, getting right in his face. He doesn't back up, doesn't balk. He doesn't even look afraid. "I might've raised you, Pretty Boy, but you're not a kid anymore, so don't think I won't knock you the fuck out."

He raises his eyebrows. "Strong words for someone busy freaking out *because* I'm moving out."

The little son of a bitch is mocking me *again.*

I shove against him, pushing him backward, forcing him out of my way. Without saying a word, I go around him, walking out.

"I'm serious," he says, calling after me as I head for the stairs. "You should go to her, *talk* to her."

"Fuck off."

"Get some sleep first, though," he continues, following me, stopping at the bottom of the stairs as I trudge up them. "And take a shower, too, because, *bro*... you're looking a bit like something out of a horror flick."

* * *

I know what you're thinking: this guy, he's *finally* going to get his shit together. He's going to wake up from a deep sleep, having dreamed about a different kind of life, or it's going to hit him like a ton of bricks when he's in the shower, washing up, rubbing one out. He's going to realize his brother was right. He's going to see that he's in love. And he's going to go after the woman, like some goddamn hero, and they'll live happily ever after, always and forever.

But this isn't some chick flick rom-com. John Hughes isn't directing. My brother's not fucking his girlfriend on my couch while watching this on my television.

That's not how this goes.

I sleep. I eat something. I finally shower. I mope for days, making everybody miserable. A week passes. My house is filled with boxes. My brother finally got the keys to his rinky-dink apartment.

Three pops in every day, keeping me updated.

The house Scarlet and her little Pearl went to turned out to be hers. Her *home*. The house she told me about... she still has it. You see, all along I thought men like ol' Mello Yello were milking her out of every penny, that they were stealing everything *she* stole, because she had nothing that I saw, but it turns out she was just hemorrhaging money trying to keep up with two lives—the one she'd been drifting through when I met her and the one she always intended to go back to.

She already had her picket fence.

She just needed help getting back to it.

She'd been paying the rent, been paying the utilities, keeping the place going even though she couldn't stay there, even though it wasn't safe, because she planned to one day have that life back.

She never lost hope, despite everything.

You have to respect that.

Or well, *I* do.

It's around dusk on Friday evening. The guys are out, doing what they do, making money and raising hell, everything right back to normal. My brother's at work. His girlfriend is... well, who the hell knows, but she's not *here*. It's quiet, so very quiet... not a peep in the house.

It's peaceful. It's boring.

I'm back to being bored out of my fucking mind.

After peeling an orange, I stroll out of the kitchen and head down the dim hallway. Just as I make it to the foyer, a chime echoes through the house. *Doorbell.* I divert that way, yanking the door open, coming face-to-face with Seven.

I sigh. *Loudly.*

"For your sake, I hope you've got a good reason," I say, leaning against the doorframe, "because it has been *way* too long since I shot somebody, and you're still hanging out on the top of my list."

He's quiet for a moment before saying, "Because we're family."

I take a bite of my orange, regarding him. "Because we're *family*."

"Yes," he says. "Family's not perfect. We make mistakes. We don't always like each other, don't always get along. So maybe I'm the black sheep of this family, and I deserve whatever happens to me because of it, but we're family, and when you're family, you deserve a *chance*."

I continue to eat my orange. "You know I killed my mother, right?"

"Yes."

I nod. "Just making sure."

"But that's different," he says. "Family's more than blood. Family is who we *choose*. So I'm not asking you to forgive me, not asking you to forget... I'm just asking for a chance to earn back your respect."

I stand in the doorway for a while, long enough to finish off my orange, neither of us saying anything until I'm done. Reaching into my pocket, I pull out my car keys.

"Come on," I say, stepping out onto the porch. "Let's take a ride."

If the guy was smart, he'd bail right now, run like hell at the suggestion, but he doesn't. Instead, he nods, taking my keys and heading for my car without questioning where we're going. *Guts*.

I give him the address.

He punches it into the GPS.

It takes us about an hour to get there, night falling by the time we arrive, darkness shrouding the neighborhood. He parks just down from the place, cutting the car off. I get out but don't approach, perching myself on the hood of my car.

White house, red door, quaint little picket fence in quiet suburbia. A stone walkway leads from the gate to the front porch, a trail of outdoor landscape lights illuminating it. The place is lit up, shining bright in the night, a soft yellow glow coming from a few of the windows. I'm not close enough to hear anything, but I can sense shadows as they move around inside.

Seven climbs out of the car, coming over to stand beside me. I don't know how long I sit here, just watching the house in silence, but it's long enough for the lights to flick off, one-by-one, until all that's lit up is the right top window. Scarlet's room, I imagine. I faintly catch glimpses of her as she moves around, brief flashes of her through the break in the dark curtains.

"You going to go say hello?" Seven asks.

I shake my head.

He's quiet, like he's trying to make sense of why we're here if it's not to visit her. I hope he doesn't ask, because I'm not in the mood to explain myself.

Just when I'm about to end this, to do what I came to do, so I can go back home and close this chapter, the phone in my pocket rings. I look away from the house, pulling the phone out to glance at it. *Blocked number.*

I'm not sure what compels me to press the button, to answer it, since I've never answered a blocked caller before, but I do.

Bringing it to my ear, I say, "Gambini."

The line is silent.

Without a word even spoken, I know it's her.

Call it my gut. It's just the feeling I get. I can sense her on the line, I know she's there, but she says nothing. Maybe there's nothing left to say. Maybe this is all it is, all it was, all it could *ever* be. Maybe this is the end of the story. Yeah, my gut says it should be.

But the traitorous heart beating in my chest isn't having that bullshit. It's angrily banging, begging me to do something, something my brain definitely doesn't agree with. My brain says *fuck that.*

"Tell me a story," she says finally, her voice barely a whisper.

"A true story or a fairy tale?" I ask.

"Surprise me."

"A long time ago, in a galaxy far, far away, Luke Skywalker—"

Laughter cuts me off.

I don't finish, because I'm pretty sure she already knows how it goes. Silence falls over the line again before she says, "I have a confession to make, Lorenzo."

"I'm listening."

"*Pretending* to listen?"

"No, I'm actually listening."

She sighs. "I don't really know how to say this, but I need to get it off my chest, and I just... I feel like you should know, that I should tell you how I really feel..."

"Just spit it out, Scarlet."

"I really love the prequels."

I hesitate. "You love the *prequels?*"

"Yes," she says. "The *Star Wars* prequels. I know a lot of people hate on them, but I really love them."

"I, uh... I don't even know what to say to that."

"Anakin and Padme's story was just so heartbreakingly beautiful, you know? *The Phantom Menace* is probably my favorite movie."

"Of the prequels?"

"Of the entire series."

I grimace. "You're kidding."

"Nope."

"Jesus, fuck, woman... and you call *me* crazy. You're insane. I just... what the hell is wrong with you?"

She laughs again.

The genuine kind of laughter.

I don't know that I've ever heard her laugh like that before, so lighthearted, like a heavy burden has been lifted off of her. I smile at the sound, even though she's lost her fucking mind.

"I feel better," she says, "now that I've confessed."

"Yeah, well, I'm wishing I wasn't listening," I tell her. "You should've saved that confession for a priest, someone who could help you get over that shit, because I don't even know where to begin."

She laughs some more before it all goes quiet.

"Thank you," she whispers after a bout of silence.

"You're welcome."

"I mean it."

"I know."

She says nothing else, although I can tell there's more she wants to. Whether or not she *should* is another question. Maybe I'm not the only one with a heart and a mind at odds.

"Goodnight, Scarlet," I say. "Take care of yourself."

Her voice is barely a whisper as she says, "Goodnight."

Hanging up, I shove the phone back into my pocket before pushing away from the hood and reaching into the backseat of the car, snatching out the filthy, old teddy bear I'd thrown there days ago after cleaning out the car. I walk away, finally approaching the house, my footsteps quiet as I go through the gate and navigate the walkway. Stepping up onto the porch, I prop the bear against the door where I know it'll be found.

Darkness falls over the rest of the house as I walk away, the bedroom light turning off. I climb straight into the passenger seat of my car, waiting for Seven to get in behind the wheel. A minute or so passes as I stare blankly at the dashboard, waiting for Seven to start the car, when I hear his voice. "Uh, boss..."

I close my eyes as I lean my head back against the seat, covering my face with my hands. "Not now."

"But—"

"Just drive the fucking car, Seven."

"Somebody's here."

Somebody's here.

I look at Seven, but he's not looking at *me*. His gaze is across the neighborhood, just past Scarlet's now darkened house, where her and her daughter are in bed, probably beckoning sleep. Somebody stands there, in the shadows, watching. I struggle to get a good look until they turn, a nearby streetlight illuminating them.

Markel. "*Shit.*"

I look from him to the house to him again. *You've gotta be fucking kidding me.* Instinctively, I reach for the gun in my waistband, even though I can't use it. I can't go shooting all willy-nilly in front of her house. The last thing she needs is to wake up to a dead

Russian in her front yard, his blood splattering her pretty little fence.

So I keep my grip on my gun, just in case I *have* to use it, in case he doesn't give me any other choice, and I watch him in silence, letting him make the first move.

Ten minutes pass.

Fifteen. Twenty.

He just stands there before walking away. *Leaving.* I watch as he gets into a black SUV down the street, starting it up to leave.

"Follow him," I say.

Markel drives straight to Limerence, parking out front and going inside. The place is dark, no lights on, no open sign lit. I'm not sure what Jameson did about the girl in the basement, if he did anything at all. I don't know what happened with all of the other girls, either, the ones who worked here every night, now that the man who controlled them is gone. It's possible Markel took over, but I don't know...

Honestly, and maybe this makes me an asshole, but I don't really care, either.

But I *do* care what happens to Scarlet.

I'm not going to let anyone hurt her.

"Wait here," I tell Seven. "I'll be right back."

I get out, still clutching my gun, and head inside the club. Dark and quiet, so quiet that the sound of my footsteps echoes through the vast space.

It feels *abandoned.*

I'm not sure where he went, so I start with the office, figuring that's my best bet, under the circumstances.

The door is wide open.

Markel sits inside, alone on the couch, holding a bottle of vodka. He takes a swig from it as he looks at me, not surprised by my presence. I know he saw me there, at the house. He would've figured I'd follow.

"I mean them no harm," he says.

"You expect me to believe that?"

"Ah, it doesn't matter what you believe, but it's true."

He shrugs me off, drinking in silence, like that's that.

"So, if you don't mean them any harm, why go there?"

"Why did *you* go?"

"Pretty sure that's none of your business."

He laughs. "I could say the same."

I stroll closer. Call it curiosity. Maybe it's boredom. But I take a seat on the edge of the couch across from him, wondering what his end-game is.

It's silent for a moment before he says, "*Limerence*. Do you know what the word means?"

"No."

"It's obsession, compulsion, when love is not love but something more... *dangerous*. It is an uncontrollable need, when you cannot live without someone. I always thought it was funny Kassian named this place Limerence, because that was how he felt about her. It was a sickness. I knew, eventually, he would grow so sick that he would kill them all... that is why I helped her."

"You helped her."

"I was supposed to keep an eye on her the night she escaped. I saw her. I knew what she was doing. And I knew it was her only chance. So I looked the other way, and I paid for that. He ordered me to find her, and I did, but I never told him. Every night, he sent me out looking. Every night, I would go to that house and I would see her."

"Why?"

He shrugs. "I was invested."

"That's why you went there tonight? *Invested?*"

He shrugs again.

"So, how'd he find her?" I ask. "If you never told him where she lived, how'd he catch up to her?"

Markel stares at me, frowning. I don't need him to answer to riddle that one out. *Kassian followed him.*

"He used to offer her to me," Markel says. "Whenever he left on business, he would have me watch her. As payment, I could take her, all night, do whatever I wanted. He just had one rule: *always* use a condom. That's why he planned to kill you, you know.

He didn't care if people used her for pleasure as long as they didn't leave any trace of themselves inside of her."

"That's a fucked up way to think."

He laughs humorlessly. "The nights Kassian left on business were the only nights Morgan had peace. It was the only time she smiled. That was pleasure enough for me, so I didn't touch her."

He takes a drink... a *long* drink... like he's a thirsty man guzzling water. He drains the rest of the bottle before sitting up, discarding it on the table between us.

"So many nights, he hurt her. Must have been hundreds of times. One night, he was worse than ever. He left afterward, and that night, instead of peace with me, she sought comfort. Maybe it was wrong, but I showed her love... and I broke my brother's rule as I did so." He shakes his head, looking away. "Nine months later, she gave birth."

Son of a bitch. "You think the kid is yours."

It suddenly makes sense why he'd look the other way, why he'd show up outside of her house night after night, why he'd do what he did to try to help them while still protecting his own ass.

"Well, this has certainly been enlightening," I say, standing up, "but I think I've heard enough."

"So you know I mean them no harm."

"What I know is that it doesn't matter what you *mean*, because you are as harmful as they come."

BANG.

BANG.

BANG.

I unload the gun, bullet after bullet, right into his fucking chest, not a second of hesitation from the first trigger pull to the very last, shot after shot lighting up the room, until the gun does nothing but click.

CLICK.

CLICK.

CLICK.

He slumps over, falling from the couch to the floor with a thud, no longer moving. No longer *breathing.*

I shove the gun away and walk out, keeping my head down. Seven still sits behind the wheel, driving away as soon as I'm beside him.

"Where to, boss?" he asks.

"Home," I say quietly. "It's over."

22

The Cowardly Lion lived in a gloomy castle.

Or so it felt like it to the little girl. It wasn't beside the beach, like the palace, although it seemed to be just as big. Maybe even bigger. This place was cold, and dark, and off on its own. *Isolated.*

Some of the flying monkeys stayed there, too, along with some women, a rotating door of people, which meant there was always somebody around to watch her. They didn't act like she was invisible. No, they acted like she was a prisoner, like a princess locked away in a tower.

"Hey, sweet girl," the Cowardly Lion said one night, appearing in the room she'd been kept in, where she'd been spending all day, every day, with nothing more than a mattress and a small television, letting her watch cartoons for the first time in months.

The people in the house were upset about something, yelling at each other about some club somewhere that maybe got raided by somebody or something. She didn't know. She didn't like their talking, so she just kept turning the volume up on the television.

She said nothing to the Cowardly Lion. Not because she wanted to be mean. She just had nothing to say to him.

"Are you not speaking to me?"

Nothing.

"Have I made you upset?"

Nothing.

Stepping into the room, he walked over, blocking her from seeing the movie on the screen. It was *Toy Story*, but part two, the one where Woody got stolen. She scowled, thinking he'd turn the volume down, but instead, he shut it off.

"Hey!" she said. "I was watching Woody!"

"Too bad," he said. "Maybe you should not have ignored me."

She let out a noise of annoyance that made him laugh, like he thought she was being funny. "I don't got nothing to say."

"You don't have to say a word," he said, "but you do have to get up and come with me, because it is time for you to go."

"Go where?" she asked, her stomach in knots.

"Go home," he said, leaving it at that.

Home. That word used to make the little girl's heart soar, but now her insides soured.

"I can't go. He don't want me."

"Who?"

"Daddy."

The Cowardly Lion gave her a sad smile. "I've spoken to him. He agreed that you could come home now. In fact, there is a surprise waiting for you, one that will make you *very* happy."

Buster, she thought. *Maybe he saved Buster.*

The little girl got up, leaving with him, quiet as they drove away from the dark castle, heading back to the palace. It was chaotic when they finally arrived, cars and people and noises all around.

"Shit, shit, *shit...*" The Cowardly Lion chanted, not even bothering to shut off the car, leaving it running when he pulled to a stop. "Come on."

Before the little girl understood what was happening, he yanked her out of the car, leaving the door wide open. Her heart raced wildly as she looked around outside. She didn't recognize the people she saw. They all watched them, frozen, like ice sculptures with wide eyes, holding guns.

Guns.

The little girl felt sick.

She thought she might throw up.

The Cowardly Lion dropped her to her feet on the porch, pushing on the front door. It was already cracked open—no locks, no alarm. The little girl had never seen it like that before.

Noises hit her from inside, strangled noises, gasping breaths. The little girl blinked rapidly, scared by the sound. Tears burned her eyes but she tried not to cry.

"Go on, sweet girl," the Cowardly Lion said. "Your surprise is waiting."

She walked into the foyer, taking small steps. Someone was crying, curled into a ball on the floor. The little girl crept closer, alarmed, as something inside of her got all tangled up.

A man knelt there, his face slashed with a big scar, but the little girl only vaguely noticed he existed at all. No, her attention was fixed to the woman hunched over. She could hardly believe it. Her eyes were cloudy from tears, but she could still see her so clearly.

"Morgan," the guy said, standing up. "Open your eyes, baby."

The woman looked, the sight of her nearly crippling, the little girl's knees going weak. *Mommy.* She was there, right in front of her, not asleep anymore. Her eyes were open, looking straight at *her.* "Sunshine?"

The little girl trembled. "Mommy?"

The woman opened her arms, sobbing, and that was all it took. Emotion flooded through the little girl as she launched herself right at her.

"You found me, Mommy. You found me!"

23
Morgan

Buster.

It's the first thing I see when I open the front door. It falls over, halfway in the house, halfway on the porch, the decrepit teddy bear propped up there. The moment my eyes meet it, my insides drop. My heart *stops*. Breath hitching, my gaze scans the area around the house, caught off guard.

It's near dawn, the sun slowly rising, lightening the quiet neighborhood. Nothing looks out of place.

No familiar cars.

No familiar faces.

No Lorenzo.

I left the bear at his house. I know. I saw it the morning Kassian showed up. It had been lying in the unmade bed, tangled up with the sheets.

Reaching down, I carefully pick it up before stepping out onto the porch, keeping the front door open behind me, to listen inside, in case Sasha wakes up. I just need some fresh air. I need *out* of there.

Coming back here was harder than I imagined.

Sighing, I sit down on the top step, hugging the bear as I stare out at the neighborhood. It's strange, you know. I lived here for years. We built a life in this house, found happiness within these walls, loved beneath the sloped, dark roof, and for months after it all fell apart, I yearned to be back here. But stepping inside now, all I feel is the heartache. I feel the void. The violence. The *pain*.

When I walk the halls, I feel the fear I felt that night, when

Kassian showed up at the front door under the cloak of darkness, and I told Sasha to hide. When I step into the kitchen, I feel hands around my throat, squeezing the life out of me, stealing my soul.

It doesn't feel like *home* anymore.

"Mommy?"

Sasha's voice is quiet, guarded, as it rings out behind me in the doorway. I turn my head, looking back at her as she eyes me warily. I didn't hear her approach. So much unlike the little girl who grew up in this house, who couldn't ever seem to tiptoe because she danced when she walked. She has always been good at hiding, but she'd learned to sneak around, learning to not make a sound. I can't even bring myself to dwell on how that came about.

"Hey, sunshine," I say, giving her a smile. "Somebody else wants to say hello, too."

Her eyes flicker around, alarmed. "Who?"

I hold up the bear. "This little guy."

She hasn't mentioned him, so I'm not sure how she's going to react. Maybe she won't care. Maybe Kassian stole that part of her, the part that believed in magic, the part of her that loved her bear like he was real. Maybe she won't want him. Maybe she'll be upset. Maybe she'll think he let her down, because she always believed the damn bear would protect us. Maybe... maybe... maybe... but I hope it isn't so. I need her to still have some of that innocence she deserves.

She looks at it, her eyes widening, as I hold my breath. It takes her a second before she even reacts *at all*. "Buster!"

She sprints out onto the porch, snatching the bear from my hand, before flinging herself at me, nearly knocking me down. I laugh as she clings to both me and the bear.

"Mommy, it's Buster!" she squeals. "He came back!"

"He did."

"Where did you find him?"

"Right here," I say. "He was sitting on the porch, waiting for us, this morning when I woke up."

She smiles, a wide kind of smile. Her whole face lights up. Sitting down beside me on the step, pressing up against me, she studies the bear in her lap. Her fingers run along the messy, dark stitches holding parts of the bear together. "Somebody gave him surgery. They saved him from Daddy!"

I try to keep a straight face, but I grimace. *Daddy.* The man never deserved that title.

"Or," I say, nudging her, "maybe Buster saved himself."

"Maybe," she agrees, pausing before adding, "but he didn't give himself his surgery."

"How do you know?"

She gives me a look, like I'm being ridiculous. "Because he can't."

"Why not?"

"He doesn't have no thumbs. He only has his paws."

"Oh." I glance at the bear. Can't really argue with that logic. She was always too smart for her own good. "Well, in that case, somebody else certainly gave him surgery, but it looks like he still needs some more work."

He's still missing his right eye.

Needs a good scrubbing, too.

He's *filthy*.

"Daddy didn't like Buster," she says. "He put him in his fire because he said I was being bad, and then I couldn't have him back until I said I loved him, but then he didn't even believe me when I did, so I never got him again."

She frowns, poking her bottom lip out.

I have no idea what to say, how I'm supposed to handle this, how I'm supposed to explain it to her so she'll understand. I was never exactly equipped to be a mother, but this is so out of my realm of expertise. I'm terrified of messing her up, of her growing up traumatized. I don't have a little Dr. Phil in my pocket to walk me through these things, so I'm just going to be real with her, because honesty is the best policy, right?

"You didn't deserve that, sunshine," I say. "Everything he did, no matter what it was, it wasn't your fault. You're not bad, and he shouldn't have done those things, okay?"

"Okay," she whispers.

"I'm serious," I tell her. "And you don't have to call him 'Daddy.' You can, if you want, but you don't have to. You don't have to call him anything."

"He told me I have to."

"I figured, but you don't."

"But what if he gets mad?" she asks. "What if he takes Buster away?"

"He won't," I say. "I promise."

"But—"

I gently grasp her chin, tilting her face up. "No *buts*. He'll never get mad at you, never take Buster, never show up here again... he's gone, sunshine. *Forever*. So you can call him whatever you want, or you can call him nothing at all. It's okay."

She stares at me for a moment. "Did he never get his heart or something?"

My brow furrows. "What?"

"Tin Man," she says. "That's what he was called. I heard you say he had no heart, like the Tin Man in that movie."

My stomach sinks. "Uh, I don't know. Maybe he had a heart, but he didn't show it to me, so I couldn't see it. But it doesn't matter, because it's all over. We won't have to play Hide & Seek anymore, okay?"

"Okay," she says, "because I don't want to play *ever*."

"Me, either." I smile. "What *do* you want to do?"

She shrugs.

"Come on, there has to be something," I say. "We'll get out of this house, just you and me."

"And Buster, too?"

"And Buster."

"Can we go eat hot dogs? And ride that big wheel thing? You know, the one that goes whoosh, whoosh, whoosh with the lights and the music?" She holds her hand out, making circles. *Ferris wheel*. "They have one at that place with the beach..."

Coney Island.

"I, uh... sure. If that's what you want."

She nods.

"Well, then... how about we go get dressed and make a day of it?"

She throws herself at me again. "You're the best, Mommy!"

My stomach is in knots as she gets up and runs into the house. Coney Island isn't where I'd choose to be, but whatever makes her happy.

Where I'd choose to be, if I had a choice, is at a white house with a picket fence surrounding it... just not *this* one.

* * *

We spend the entire afternoon down in Coney Island, riding rides and playing games and stuffing our faces full of hot dogs and ice cream and cotton candy. She's glowing, like a weight has been lifted off of her small shoulders, so much my little girl again, carefree and happy. *Not broken.*

I'm not going to say she's over it. That's a lie. She may *never* get over a lot of what happened, but she'll learn to live with the memories she can't forget, because she's resilient.

She's definitely *my* child.

It's early evening when we stroll through nearby shops, her lugging Buster under her arm in a headlock, as I carry her new little friend—a strange looking rainbow-striped monkey she won shooting clowns with tiny water guns. We end up in a little bookstore, aisles piled high with used books. Sasha stays where I can see her, never leaving my line of sight, as she scours through stacks of children's books. I pick up a book of fairy tales, flipping through it to see if Sasha might like any of the stories when one catches my eye.

The Juniper Tree.

I know that one.

Well, I remember it, vaguely.

Lorenzo told me the story.

His favorite fairy tale.

Leaning against the shelf, I skim the story, realizing quite quickly Lorenzo did a horrible job of summarizing. He stopped midway through, never telling me how it ended. Some stories don't have happy endings, he'd said.

That lying son of a—

"Mommy?"

I glance up from the book, looking at Sasha. "Yes?"

"Can I have this?" she asks, holding up a book, this one also about fairy tales, but hers has pictures and color and is made by *Disney,* unlike the crazy shit I'm reading. "Please?"

I probably don't have to tell you that there's no way I could ever tell her *no* right now. No matter what the girl asks for, it's a resounding '*hell yeah*'. If I can't afford it, I'll fucking steal it, but being as the book has a price tag of a dollar, I think we'll be just fine.

Lorenzo made sure of that.

Lorenzo.

I glance back at the book I'm holding, closing it as I tell her, "Of course you can have it. Come on, let's get out of here."

I pay for the book I'm holding, as well as Sasha's, and we head out of the store, making our way back to the boardwalk, strolling along it as I hold her hand.

She's as happy as can be, as she somehow convinces me to let her take her shoes off and play in the sand (yeah, right... like I'd tell her *no*, remember?), making a little makeshift campsite as she sets up Buster and Mr. No-Name Monkey and tries to read her book to them.

Newsflash: she's only five, which means she can't really read, so she's just making up some nonsense.

Still better than the bullshit half-story Lorenzo told me.

"Come on, sunshine," I say as time wears on, wanting out of there before sunset, still not sure how safe it is for us. "Time to get going."

"Home?" she asks, looking up at me, her expression falling. "Do we have to go home, Mommy?"

I frown. I don't think she likes being there any more than I do now, the bad overshadowing so many years of good. "Uh, no, not if you don't want to. Would you rather go somewhere else?"

She nods. "Buster doesn't like that house so much now."

"He doesn't? Why?"

"He didn't like when you were sleeping in the kitchen."

Sleeping in the kitchen. "He saw that?"

"Yes, he got scared 'cuz you didn't wake up when we tried to wake you."

"You tried to wake me?"

She nods.

"You came out of your hiding spot that night to try to wake me?"

She nods yet again.

"And that's how *he* found you?"

Yet another nod.

"We don't have to go home," I tell her, "so tell Buster not to worry. We can go somewhere else."

"Where?"

I think about that for a moment, looking at Buster, as I pull Sasha to her feet. "How would you like to go meet the person who did Buster's surgery?"

Her eyes widen. "Really?"

"Really," I say, picking up Buster. "He's a friend of mine. He's not the best at stitching, but he's got something else going for him."

"What?"

"Unlike the Tin Man, I *know* he's got a heart."

* * *

The sun is setting as I step through the gate of the small picket fence in Queens, leading up to the house. Sasha clings tightly to my hand. I can tell she's nervous.

Fuck, *I'm* nervous.

I've been putting off coming here, not because I haven't wanted to. I *have*. I've put it off because I'm not sure *he* wants me here, and that kind of rejection sucks serious balls. Lorenzo walked away a week ago without even saying goodbye, like he could just easily dismiss me from his life, and Buster showing up on my porch this morning... well, that's just a cherry on this fucked up sundae I call life. Buster's presence felt like severing ties.

I don't accept it.

Stepping up onto the porch, I raise my hand to knock before hesitating, my fist in the air, my gaze drifting to the doorknob. *Fuck it.* I grab it, turning the knob, finding it unlocked.

Of course. I push the door right open. I've never knocked before, and I'm not going to start now.

The moment I step inside, pulling Sasha into the foyer, voices halt, eyes turning toward me. Leo and Melody stand in the living room doorway.

"*Morgan!*" Melody gasps, lunging right for me as Sasha shifts herself behind me, ducking out of sight. "Oh my god, I can't believe you're here!"

"Hey," I say, patting her back as she clings to me as tightly as Sasha had. "It's good to see you."

"Me?" Melody shoves out of the hug, tears brimming her eyes. "Look at *you*! The last time I saw you, oh god, Morgan... I thought... I mean, I didn't think you were going to... you're frickin' alive! I thought for sure you were dead! I thought that Russian *asshole*—"

"Mel," Leo says, cutting her off, coming between us as he pulls his girlfriend away. "Not the time for that, babe. Little ears are listening."

Melody looks at him with confusion. "Little *what?*"

"Ears," he says, diverting her attention as he motions to where Sasha peeks out from behind me.

Melody glances down, her expression shifting, from confusion to shock before jumping right to excitement. No hesitation, she drops to her knees in the foyer, making them eye-level. "Hey there! I'm Melody! What's your name?"

"Sasha," she says quietly, stepping out in the open, like she's decided she likes Melody. Not surprising, since they're both little *firecrackers*.

"Sasha," Melody says. "That's such a beautiful name!"

"Thank you," she says. "Mommy gave me it."

"Your mommy has great taste."

Leo makes a noise, half-scoff, half-laugh, that draws our attention. He holds his hands up defensively right away. "Hey, I'm not disagreeing. Just imagining my brother's reaction to that statement."

Melody rolls her eyes before turning back at Sasha, scanning her, attention settling on Buster clutched under her arm. "Hey, I remember this guy! Bruiser or something, right?"

Sasha laughs, the lighthearted sound warming me. "He's Buster."

"Buster," Melody repeats, moving on to the rainbow monkey. "And who's this one?"

"He doesn't have his name yet," Sasha says. "We just got him today."

"Huh, he needs a name," Melody says. "A *good* one, something as awesome as he is."

"Leo," Leo chimes in.

"No," Melody says, "not happening."

Leo shrugs it off, as Melody and Sasha chatter back and forth, the attention turning to the book Sasha's holding. Melody takes it from her, expression lighting up. "Oh, *Cinderella*, she's totally my favorite princess!"

"Do you wanna read it?" Sasha asks, her voice a little louder than it had been. "We can!"

"Hell yeah," Melody says, standing up, holding the book, going pale when she realizes what she said. "*Oops.*"

"Can Melody read my book, Mommy?" Sasha asks, looking up at me as she tugs my hand. "Please?"

"Of course," I say, gently pushing her toward Melody. "Go ahead, it's okay. I'm not going anywhere, I promise."

She must trust that, and she must *really* like Melody, because she grabs her hand and lets her take her into the living room without second-guessing it. I turn to Leo once they're out of earshot, seeing him grinning as he watches his girlfriend.

"She's great with kids," Leo says.

"I see that. You going to give her one of her own soon?"

He laughs incredulously, turning toward me. "Not until

we're married."

"Strong morals?"

"More like scary ass brother," he says. "He'd whip my ass if I didn't do it the right way."

He probably would, I think.

"Speaking of your scary ass brother," I say, glancing around, surprised he hasn't appeared. "Where is he?"

Leo's expression falls. "Library, I guess."

"You *guess*?"

"Yeah, he, uh..." Leo laces his hands together on top of his head. "He's pissed off at the world, touchy... *twitchy*. It's been pretty unbearable."

I sigh.

I wish I could say I was surprised.

"He got home last night, and I don't know... something seemed different," Leo continues. "I know he's dealing with a lot, with me moving out and with what happened with you, but he was just next-level *whatever*, talking about packing up and going back to Florida."

My stomach drops. "Florida?"

"Yeah, he said he's got work to do down there, but I don't know... feels kind of like he's running, which is very much *not* Lorenzo."

Yeah, that's not Lorenzo at all.

"So, the library, you said?"

I step by him, heading down the hallway.

"Uh, yeah, but he's not really feeling... *hospitable*."

The door is closed. I see that as I approach. Not a stitch of light filters out from the crack beneath it, which means if he's in there, he's just sitting in the darkness, all alone. I glance back at Leo, and it's as if he can read my mind, because he gives me a small smile and points toward the living room, saying, "I'll keep an eye on our girls."

"Thank you," I whisper, barely making a sound, before I turn to the closed library door and take a deep breath.

This time, out of respect, I knock.

There's no sound inside, no footsteps or voices, not a peep at all, like he isn't there.

I knock again.

Nothing.

A third knock is again met with silence, which tells me I could knock all night and he wouldn't answer.

Knocking's pointless.

So instead, I grab the knob and open the door.

He moves fast, reacting.

Right away, I hear a gun cock.

Within seconds, it's aimed at my chest from across the room.

I don't move, just standing in the doorway, staring at him. He's sitting in his chair, glaring my way, his chest rising and falling harshly, nostrils flaring.

He's *furious.*

Shadows cover him. I can barely make him out as darkness shrouds the house, night falling around us. He's dressed in all black, blending into his surroundings. He hasn't shaved in a few days, and I don't know if he's been sleeping, because he looks every bit the *scary ass brother.*

But I'm not afraid of him.

"I knocked," I say. "You didn't answer."

"And that didn't tell you something?"

"It told me a lot."

"Yet there you stand."

"Would you rather I have went away?"

He says nothing.

He's not going to answer that question.

After a minute or so passes, he lowers the gun. That's all the answer I need from him. He's not going to shoot me. If he were, he would've done it *way* back at the start.

Carefully, I push away from the door and stroll into the library, coming closer to him.

I notice right away that the table is turned over, puzzle pieces scattered all along the floor around him. Wordlessly, I grab the table, flipping it back onto its legs. It's a pain in the ass, *heavy*, but I manage to get it upright again without any help—which is good, because he doesn't look like he planned to offer any. I pick up the lamp next, plugging it back in before setting it on the end of the table.

As soon as I turn it on, Lorenzo dramatically winces.

I laugh at his reaction, perching on the end of the table near him as I look around. "What happened to your puzzle?"

"Adam's dick disappeared."

My brow furrows. "What?"

He runs his hands down his face, grumbling, "A piece was missing."

"Oh." I look at the mess, my chest tightening, not mentioning the fact that it probably got lost the night he fucked me on top of it. "That sucks."

He laughs bitterly as he tilts his head back, slouching in the chair, stretching his legs out, covering his eyes with his forearm. The gun rests on his thigh, in his lap, his free hand on top of it, keeping it securely in place as his leg steadily moves back and forth. *Antsy.*

"There's more to the story," I say quietly after a moment.

His arm shifts, his eyes meeting mine.

"*The Juniper Tree*," I say, holding up the book I bought to show him. "The little boy is reincarnated into a bird, which is born from the tree. The bird sings a song, rats out the stepmother, and she dies as punishment for killing him, before he's once again reborn into a kid."

Lorenzo blinks a few times, his voice completely flat as he says, "That sounds like bullshit."

"Better than the story you told me."

"I like my version better."

"Do you?" I ask. "*Really?*"

Another question that goes unanswered.

"Didn't think so," I whisper.

He sits up. *Fast.* So fast it catches me off guard. I freeze in place as he shoves out of the chair, gripping the gun tightly so it doesn't fall to the floor. He doesn't aim it, doesn't even raise it, instead slamming it down on the table beside me as he stalls in front of me. "What do you want from me, Scarlet? Huh? Haven't I done *enough* for you?"

"You've done more than enough, but—"

"But," he says, cutting me off. "There's always a but, isn't there? Nothing's ever good enough as it is; we have to tack on a fucking *but*."

I stare him in the face as I set the book down on the table. He's struggling hard to control himself right now. I don't know what's gotten into him, but something has him teetering on the edge.

"Are you okay?" I whisper, pressing my palm to his scarred cheek, my thumb gently stroking the rough skin.

He doesn't like that.

At all.

Instantly, he pulls back, moving out of my reach, anger flickering across his expression. He leaves the gun on the table beside me as he clenches his hands into fists, like he's about to punch something, like he might find that so much more satisfying at the moment than pumping bullets through whatever it may be.

Not *me*, though.

He won't hit me.

You might be sitting there thinking I'm stupid, that I'm insane for thinking that way. A few minutes ago, the guy had a gun aimed at me, so what makes me think he'll keep his hands to himself?

Well, it's simple, really... it's what I told Sasha.

He's got a heart in his chest.

I see it when I look him in the eyes. I see the agony he feels. He's tortured, twisted, all tied up in knots. He's busy beating himself up inside. But most people don't see that, because they don't *look* at him. They turn away from the surface, terrified, because what he shows the world can be downright fucking scary. But if they just took a second to really see him, they'd know what I know.

They'd believe what *I* believe.

And what I believe is this man is far from being a monster. I've lived with monsters. I *know* them. And maybe, on the surface, Lorenzo falls into that category. Legally defined, he might be a serial killer, or maybe a *spree* killer... I know he has killed. Who knows how many lives he's taken—I'm not trying to justify that. Psychologically, they'd probably diagnose him as something *dangerous*, but I believe the world is wrong about him.

Because I see what they don't bother looking for, assuming it must not be there.

I see his conscience. I see his compassion.

I've listened to the heart strongly beating in his chest that he desperately tries to silence to keep everyone from hearing.

"Why are you here?" Lorenzo asks, an edge of anger to his voice, his tone almost *accusatory*. "What do you want?"

"I don't know," I say, because it's true... I don't know. I could list off reasons all day long as to why I might be standing here, but I'll never know which was the reason that put me in this room. Gratitude. Guilt. Regret. Longing. Maybe it's all of those, or maybe it's something more, something *deeper*. "I just... don't know."

He looks away from me, scrubbing his hands over his face as he starts to pace. "Why are you doing this to me? Huh? Why can't you just *stop*? Why can't you leave? Just go the fuck away?"

"Is that what you want?"

"Yes!"

He yells the word so loud that I cringe. Oh no, his hands won't ever hit me, but his words might. It's like a punch straight to the chest.

"I want you *gone*," he says. "I want you out of my life. Out of my *system*. I don't want to spend another goddamn second thinking about you, wondering about you, *worrying* about you. I don't want to look at you, don't want to see you or smell you or taste you or hear you. I don't want this. Do you get that? I don't want *any* of this. It's driving me fucking insane. I can't sleep. I can't eat. I can't *think*. I hate this, whatever this is... whatever this bullshit is that I'm feeling because of you. Make it *go away*."

I just stare at him, because I don't know what to say to that.

I don't know much of anything right now except what I'm feeling, and even *that* is hard to comprehend.

"You want the fairy tale," he continues. "You want the happy ending. You want the little boy to be a fucking bird so he can fly away and make everything okay, but I can't do it. I've told you that. It's not me."

"I know."

"So why the fuck are you *here*?"

"Because I love you anyway."

It's like the world stops at that moment.

I wish I could say it was beautiful.

Wish I could say the sun shined and the flowers bloomed and the birds sang. Wish I could say there were fireworks, that there was happiness, that the stars aligned just right. But this isn't *Mary Poppins*. I'm no goddamn *Cinderella*. The fairy tale I'm sitting in the middle of right now isn't made by Disney.

There's not a symphony playing in the background.

The word is meek when I say it, barely a whisper. I hadn't meant for it to come out. It wasn't something I planned to say to him. I've never said it to him before, struggled admitting it even to myself, but it's true, the truest syllable I've ever spoken.

Love.

I love this dangerous, menacing asshole.

I can very easily stand on my own two feet, but the thought of losing him makes my knees go weak. The thought of not having him around makes my chest ache. I can breathe without him. I don't *need* him. He'll never complete me, because I'm *already* complete. But yet so much of me is now tangled up with so much of him that the thought of living the rest of my life without him around makes me feel cold inside, like he gives me my warmth.

"Don't," he says, or more like he *growls*, still not looking at me. "Don't fucking say that."

"It's too late," I whisper. "I already said it."

"Don't do this to me." He shakes his head, still pacing. "Why are you doing this to me? Why couldn't you just fuck off and go find your picket fence?"

"There's one right outside."

His head turns, his gaze shifting my way when I say that. "*Not* that one."

"Well, I mean, you didn't exactly specify..."

He doesn't look amused by that. He looks like he wants to run outside right now and set the fence on fire before ripping it out of the ground.

"What do you want, Morgan?" he asks after a moment, his voice low. "Just... tell me what you want from me. I can't stand here and do this with you."

"You named me," I say. That's not the first time I've heard him call me by my real name. *Morgan.* "You only name what you keep, remember?"

He just stares at me.

"So I'll go away, if that's really what you want, if that's what will make you happy. I'll leave you alone, Lorenzo. You'll never have to see me again, and you can forget I ever said what I just said. We can pretend I didn't mean it and go our separate ways. But... you named me. And maybe it's stupid of me to believe this, and I'm not trying to make shit weird, but it makes me think you might feel the same way. So if that's true..."

I trail off, and he says nothing. His expression is blank, a mask of nothingness. I give him a moment to respond, to think about what I'm saying, but it gets to be too much eventually.

I'm bearing my heart to him, when so much of me is hardened not to, and he's not reacting.

Maybe I'm wrong.

Maybe he's trying to spare my feelings here.

Pushing away from the table, I turn to leave. If he wants me gone, I'll go. I'm not going to push him. I make it a few steps before he reaches out, snatching ahold of my wrist.

I glance at his hand before looking at him.

The world stops yet again.

This time, it's not quite so ugly.

He doesn't say anything.

What, did you really expect him to?

Have you been paying attention *at all?*

He's not a man of emotional declarations. He shows you he cares through his actions. And words... they're just *words*, remember? Letters and syllables. Kassian told me he loved me so many times that those words don't have half the meaning as Lorenzo clutching my wrist does as he stops me from walking out of his life.

He stares at me.

I wait for him to speak.

"The prequels are some of the worst movies ever made," he says eventually, finding his voice. "You'll never convince me otherwise."

"Come on, they have General Grievous. He's *badass.*"

"Yeah, but they also have Jar Jar Binks, who should've never been created."

"I thought he was kind of funny."

"He's an abomination."

"And what, like *we're* not?"

His serious expression cracks for just a moment as he pulls me to him. He lets go of my wrist, instead cradling my face as he leans down, gently kissing my lips. It's soft, and sweet, a few simple pecks, as I close my eyes and grasp his forearms, savoring the moment.

I've missed this. Missed *him.*

It's only been a week since I've seen him, two weeks since I've kissed him, but a lifetime of hell passed within that time. I try to deepen the kiss, eager for more, groaning into his mouth, when a small voice calls out.

"Mommy?"

The sound startles me.

Lorenzo pulls away. *Fast.*

I turn, seeing Sasha in the doorway, her eyes bouncing between me and Lorenzo, alarmed. Leo's behind her, just out in the hallway.

"Sorry, didn't mean to interrupt," Leo says. "It got quiet, so I figured it was safe, and she said she was thirsty, and I wasn't sure what she was allowed to drink, and well, the kitchen is this way, so..."

"It's okay," I tell him, so he'll stop stammering, before motioning to Sasha. "Come here, sunshine."

She approaches, and I kneel beside her. She eyes Lorenzo suspiciously, looking up at him, while he stares down at her like he thinks she might bite. They're both damn nervous. It's kind of cute.

I mean, there's a chance one (or both) of them might freak the fuck out any second, but still... *cute*.

"Sasha, this is Mommy's friend, Lorenzo. He helped me when I was looking for you, helped me *find* you."

"And did surgery on Buster?" she asks quietly.

"Yeah, he's the one who sewed up our Buster," I say. "That was nice of him, wasn't it?"

She nods.

"And Lorenzo, this is—"

"Your little Scarlet Letter," he says.

"Uh, yeah, that's one way to put it," I say with a laugh. "You said you wanted to know what a mini-me was like, so here she is."

Neither of them says anything right away.

They just stare at each other. *Assessing*.

It's like they're sizing one another up, getting a read on the competition, gauging whether or not they'll be willing to share my attention. I'm not at all surprised when it's Sasha that cracks first, but the words that fly from her lips nearly knock me on my ass.

"How did your face get all hurt?"

She points at him, right at his face, at his *scar*.

Lorenzo blinks at her.

Oh god.

"Sasha, baby, you know we don't—"

"It's fine," Lorenzo says, cutting me off, his gaze on her. "You want to know what happened to me?"

She slowly nods before cutting her eyes at me, like she's worried *I'm* going to be mad. Not *him*, no... she's not worried about him. If she were, she wouldn't have asked that. I'm the scariest one in the room, apparently.

Lorenzo hesitates, like he's considering how to answer, or even if he still *wants* to answer. But eventually, he says, "I got hurt a long time ago by a very bad man."

"What kind of bad man?" she asks.

"The kind that liked to call himself my dad."

Her eyes widen. "My daddy is mean, too."

"I know," Lorenzo says. "I'm glad he never hurt you like I got hurt. I tried to make it so he couldn't."

She processes that, her brow furrowing, before she says, "Will your face get all better?"

He shakes his head. "It's stuck like this."

"Does it hurt?"

I see Lorenzo's cheek twitch.

I think maybe he's done entertaining questions, but he answers before I can chime in.

"Sometimes," he admits. "The eye hurts. It doesn't really work anymore."

"It got broken?"

"Yes."

I'm not sure if she understands the concept, since his eye is still there. It still blinks and moves, looking pretty normal except for the lighter coloring.

She frowns, but it only lasts for a moment before her expression brightens. She holds up her bear, as if he's never seen it before. "Maybe you can give yourself surgery like Buster! His eye got broken, too."

"I think that's enough for now, sunshine," I say, squeezing her in a hug before standing back up. "Go ahead to the kitchen and find something to drink. You can have anything but the rum."

Leo laughs from the hallway.

She starts to leave when Lorenzo clears his throat.

"It's nice to meet you, Sasha," he says.

"You, too, Mommy's friend," she calls back as she runs out of the library.

Sasha. He called her Sasha.

He used her name.

My eyes sting. I can feel the tears welling up. There's a lump in my throat that's getting harder and harder to swallow down.

As soon as she's gone, Lorenzo looks at me. "I swear to fuck, Scarlet, if you start crying right now, I'm going to throw you out of my goddamn house."

"I'm sorry, I just—"

"Don't apologize to me."

"Ugh, okay. I'm not." I try to shake it off, clearing my throat. "That was just really nice of you. I didn't expect you to be *so*..."

"Nice?" he guesses. "I'm not an asshole, you know. Well, I am, but not *that* much of one. I was a kid once. I remember what it was like when adults were assholes. I'm not going to do that to her. Besides, she's *yours*, so I didn't really expect her to make this shit easy for me. Her mother sure as fuck doesn't."

No, I guess I don't.

Pausing, I reach up, pressing my palm to his cheek again. He grimaces but doesn't move, doesn't pull away, although I can tell part of him wants to. "Do you, uh...?"

"Do I *what*?"

"Do you at least like *The Force Awakens*?"

He stares at me. "I haven't seen it."

"Wait, what? How can you call yourself a fan if you haven't even seen the new movie?"

"I've been a bit busy lately," he says. "Dealing with you has taken up *a lot* of my free time."

"Oh, whatever. That's bullshit. You had enough free time to put together a gazillion piece puzzle. You've got time to watch a movie, and you know it. I'm just... I'm ashamed of you. Legitimately ashamed."

"I'm guessing it's good, then?"

"Oh, I don't know." I shrug. "I haven't watched it. Been too busy."

Lorenzo pulls my hand away from his face and laughs.

Genuinely *laughs*.

24

Lorenzo

The seven deadly sins and I are on a first-name basis.

Gluttony. I don't deny myself anything.

Greed. I want it all, everything there is.

Pride. I'm full of it, every inch of me.

Sloth. I'm a lazy son of a bitch.

Wrath. I've got an itchy trigger finger.

Lust. Pretty sure this one goes without question.

Last but not least, the one they call '*envy*'. I don't find myself feeling jealous very often, not anymore, but as I stand in the doorway to my living room, staring at the little girl asleep on my couch, I feel a twinge of it. At barely three-feet tall, not even forty pounds, she's tiny, but something about her just *fills* the room, like her personality can't fit in that minuscule body.

She's just like her mother. It's *eerie*.

I know what you're probably thinking: *this dumb son of a bitch is jealous of a five-year-old.* And you'd be right. But I'm not jealous for the reasons you're thinking, so knock that shit right out of your mind. It's got nothing to do with Scarlet.

I'm jealous because the kid's asleep.

Not just dozed-off, dainty sleep, either. I'm talking sprawled out on her back, hanging halfway off the couch, mouth wide open, snoring and drooling kind of sleep, the kind where you can shake her and she's not waking up.

The kid is practically comatose.

I've never slept like that in my life.

Just one night of that sleep would probably cure me of every problem I have. I'd wake up the next morning feeling like Mr. Rogers, welcoming motherfuckers to my neighborhood.

"I should probably get going," Scarlet says. "Get her to bed... it's been a long day."

"No, *stay!*" Melody says right away. "I mean, I know it's not my house or anything, but it's so late, and she's already asleep... there's no reason to drag her out of here right now, right?" She looks to Leo. "*Right?*"

Leo shrugs. "It's not my house, either."

They both look to me as if I'm going to contradict that, as if I'm going to kick them out on their asses.

"You know you can stay," I tell Scarlet. "*Mi casa es...* everybody's fucking *casa.*"

"She can sleep in my room," Leo says. "Mel and I can take the couch tonight."

"Don't be ridiculous," Scarlet says. "I'm not taking your bed from you. We can just crash right here."

"Besides, who-fucking-knows what the two of you have done on that bed, what kind of '*monkey see, monkey do*' shit you play when you get naked," I say. "It would take us until sunrise to sanitize the mattress to make it safe for her to sleep on."

Leo shoots me a look. "Are you kidding me? She's asleep on a couch you supposedly stole from a *strip club.*"

"One that I thoroughly sanitized."

"You sprayed it with *Lysol.*"

"Which kills 99.9% of germs."

"Pretty damn sure syphilis falls into that .1%, bro."

"What the hell do you know about syphilis?"

"I took a health class."

"That *better* be all you took when it comes to syphilis."

"Guys," Scarlet says, cutting in, physically stepping in front of me before I can question him more. "Seriously, I'm fine right here."

"*I'll* take the couch," I say, looking at Scarlet. "You can take my room."

"But—"

Grievous

"Enough with the fucking *buts*," I tell her. "My bed's big, it's comfortable, you've slept in it dozens of times before. Besides, it's not like I'm actually going to be doing any *sleeping*. So just... take her to my room."

She scowls but doesn't argue, walking over to pick up her daughter. The kid sleeps right through it, not even opening her eyes as Scarlet carries her from the room and takes her upstairs.

I stroll into the living room, toward the couch.

"I can't get over how stinkin' *cute* she is," Melody says as I approach. "Like, whoa, she looks just like Morgan. That's got to be a mind-fuck for her."

"Right?" Leo grins, looking at his girlfriend. "Can you imagine a little Mel running around?"

As soon as my brother says that, I reach over, smacking him on the side of the head. "Don't get any ideas. You better be wrapping it every single time."

He winces, grabbing his head. "Jesus, bro... I am."

"Good. I'm not ready for you to make me an uncle."

"Aw, Uncle Lorenzo," Leo says with a laugh. "You know, you're always talking about how you raised me, which would kind of make you *Grandpa*, wouldn't it?"

I glare at him, shoving him over to sit down on the couch. "Get the fuck out of my face, Pretty Boy, before I lock you in a tower until you turn thirty-five."

Rolling his eyes, he stands up, grabbing Melody's hand to lead her out. "Come on, Mel... lets go defile this mattress of ours some more."

I groan as he flicks the light switch, turning the lights off on me on his way out. "I swear to fuck... wrap it up or I'll rip it off."

"Noted," Leo hollers back. "Goodnight, bro."

Goodnight.

Sighing, I lay down on the couch, not bothering to even take my boots off. There's no ceiling fan in here, a fact I'm just now noticing. I'm not even sure how to force myself to fall asleep anymore without incessantly watching the fan blades go round and round and round until I pass out.

315

Fuck.

I lay here for what feels like forever, analyzing the plain white ceiling in the darkness. *Tick-tock. Tick-tock. Tick-tock.* I'm going out of my fucking mind.

Digging in my pocket, I grab my tin, pulling out a freshly rolled joint and lighting it. Dropping the tin and the matches onto the coffee table, I lay there on my back, covering my eyes with my left forearm and smoking in silence.

I hear the floor creak after a while and move my arm, peeking over, my gaze instantly meeting Scarlet's in the shadows. Before I can even greet her, she climbs onto the couch, sitting right on top of me and straddling my waist. Wordlessly, I hold out the joint, and she grabs it, no hesitation, taking a deep drag, drawing the smoke into her lungs before passing it right back. I watch her in the sliver of moonlight filtering through the nearby window, watch as she tilts her head back and closes her eyes, slowly exhaling. She's wearing only a pair of black underwear and a too-big black t-shirt. *My* shirt, I realize, straight out of my closet.

"Stealing from me again?" I ask, my free hand slipping beneath the shirt and coming to rest on her slim waist.

She smiles, looking down at me. "Just borrowing it."

"Did you ask?"

"Can I wear it?"

"Fuck no."

She laughs as I tuck what's left of the joint between my lips to grab the shirt. Her hands go up, letting me pull it off and toss it onto the coffee table.

No bra.

Reaching up, I palm her tits, squeezing them, tweaking her nipples, watching as they perk up, growing hard under my touch. She snatches the joint right from my lips, smoking the little bit that's left.

After caressing her chest, my hands trail down her stomach, my fingertips tracing the scar beneath her belly button.

"He didn't want to take me to the hospital," she says quietly, discarding the remnants of the joint.

Grievous

I meet her gaze, raising an eyebrow curiously.

"He said women gave birth at home all the time, that I'd be fine, that I didn't need a doctor—I just needed to *be a woman*. So I gave birth on a mattress in the basement of Limerence... there, not at home, because he didn't want to have to listen to my screams."

Soundproof.

"You did it alone?"

"Some of the girls were allowed to check on me, but for the most part..." She trails off, a soft smile on her lips. "I was by myself when I had her. He came down after it was over. Took her, cleaned her up."

She averts her eyes. I can tell there's more to the story. Hell, I *know* there is. My fingers graze along the scar again. "So where did this come from?"

"He took me to a hospital afterward," she says. "Markel convinced him to. I was sick, hemorrhaging blood. I ended up needing a hysterectomy. That's when they, you know—"

"I know," I say before she has to explain.

She can't have kids anymore.

Makes sense why she told me she couldn't get pregnant. I took her at her word, pretty sure only a fool would risk making a baby with *me*, but I figured she just put herself on some potent birth control, given the life she was living. Never crossed my mind to think she might've had that choice ripped away from her when she was still just a teenager.

He stole more from her than I realized.

"I'm sorry," I say quietly, those words from my lips before I even think about what the hell I'm saying.

Her eyes instantly meet mine. "Did you just—?"

"Apologize," I say, letting out a laugh. "Sure as fuck sounded like it, huh?"

She smiles as she leans over me, pausing with her lips just shy of mine. "Thank you."

She kisses me, slow at first, soft, before her lips grow frenzied. My hand drifts lower, sliding between us. I stroke her pussy through the thin fabric separating us before my hand slips

317

beneath it. She lets out a soft moan as I rub her clit, closing her eyes and shifting her hips.

Fuck, she's so wet... so warm... so soft. I grow rock hard as she grinds against me for more friction, taking what she wants. Breaking the kiss, she pulls away, tilting her head back. Her palms press against my chest as she practically fucks my fingertips, my free hand caressing her side before grasping her ass, squeezing it.

Her breathing gets heavier, turning into pants and moans. It doesn't take long at all, a minute or so, before her breath hitches, her fingernails digging into my skin, clawing at my chest.

"Fuck," I groan as I watch her come, her muscles twitching, jaw going slack, chest rising and falling fast. My free hand moves yet again, roaming, caressing, my fingertips swiping along her parted lips as I mumble, "You're so goddamn beautiful."

Her eyes open, and she looks down at me, leaning closer, her voice shaky as she says, "It's been so long since somebody said that and I actually *felt* it."

She kisses me again before I can respond, deeply, feverishly, as I reach between us, undoing my pants. I pull my cock out, stroking it, giving her a moment, before pushing the fabric separating us aside.

No hesitation, she slides right down onto me.

She moves slowly, and I don't push her, don't rush her, don't flip her over and shove her face into the couch and fuck her—although, come on, you know part of me *wants* to. No, I let her take her time, let her do this how she wants, how she *needs*. She wasn't just tormented emotionally—her body has been through hell. Remnants of bruises still pepper her pale skin, fading but visible. So I just lay here, my hands gentle as they explore, running through her hair, gripping it, holding on.

I can feel it building inside of me, twisting, tightening, as I kiss her breathlessly, my lips never leaving hers. My chest fucking aches at the sensation.

"Fuck, I'm going to come," I groan into her mouth, my hands sliding down her back, grasping her ass as I buck my hips. I know, I know... *take it easy, asshole*. I just can't help myself. I slam into her a few times, her cries echoing through the living room, as I let out a fucking growl, pleasure rippling through me. *"Fuck."*

As soon I stop moving, Scarlet lays down on top of me, nuzzling into my neck, her breasts pressing against my chest. I wrap my arms around her, stroking her back, still balls deep inside her pussy.

It's a strange sensation.

Cuddling.

We're fucking *cuddling.*

What the hell happened to my life?

Scarlet reaches up, her fingertips grazing along my jawline, stroking the scruff I need to shave.

It doesn't last long before it grows uncomfortable.

She's covered in body fluids—hers and mine.

"Ugh, I'm all sticky," she grumbles, lifting up so I finally pull out. I miss her warmth right away, as she gets to her feet and pauses in front of me. She snatches the shirt up off of the coffee table, tugging it back on as I eye her in the moonlight, seeing her thighs are slick with juices.

She stares down at me, and I can tell she has questions. She's going to want details on everything that happened. It's inevitable, I know… I'll have to tell her about the dead girl in the basement, have to tell her what I did to the Russians, have to tell her about Seven, but I'm not in the mood. And maybe that's selfish, maybe it makes me *allergic to feelings*, but I'd much rather use my mouth for something other than talking right now.

She yelps as I tug her to me, my hands on her waist. Ducking my head, I trace my tongue up her inner thigh, tasting her, licking it off. She whimpers, grabbing ahold of my hair, *"Oh god."*

Go ahead, cringe if you must. Scoff and say no, nada, not doing it, *nope*. Do whatever you want, I don't care, but me? I'm not afraid of body fluids. I'll drink every last fucking drop she has to give.

She stands there, gripping onto me as I nuzzle into her pussy, licking, sucking her right through her underwear, but the position gets awkward real fucking quick, I get a kink in my neck, so it's either stop or—

"Fuck it," I groan. *"Come here."*

She squeals as I pull her back onto the couch, yanking her up, bringing her pussy right to my mouth as I lay down flat. She laughs, bracing herself there, straddling my face, as I tongue-fuck her right to orgasm.

"Oh fuck, *Lorenzo*," she whimpers, arching her back as she comes, grinding against my mouth, no shame at all. She will ride my face if it means she gets off, and fuck if that doesn't turn me on.

She stalls when the pleasure fades, looking down at me, her face flushing. She *blushes*.

Filthy fucking woman has the nerve to look innocent.

I push her off, sitting up, and she laughs as she falls over onto the couch. Before I can pull myself together, there's a noise above us on the second floor, somewhere in the vicinity of my bedroom. *Shit.* Scarlet gets to her feet, quickly leaning over and kissing me... just a peck on the corner of my mouth. "I've gotta get back to bed."

"Seriously?" I call out as she starts to leave, just like that. "You just fuck my face and run?"

"Yep."

I hear her laughter again and then she's gone.

I desperately need a shower, but that's out of the question, so I instead wander into the kitchen, doing what I can with what I've got to clean myself up. Afterward, I drop back down onto the couch, staring up at the blank ceiling again, my eyes heavy.

Finally tired.

* * *

You know that feeling you get whenever you're being watched? That skin-crawling, nagging sensation, like you can feel their gaze as it penetrates you, sliding along your insides. Hair stands on end. Goose bumps spring up. It's eerie. You know somebody's there. You can feel it in the air.

That's what I wake up to, the sensation so strong it forces

me conscious. My heart races, my fingertips tingling from the rush of adrenaline, as my mind starts screaming *'attack, motherfucker, attack.'*

My eyes snap open.

The second they do, I see someone else's eyes.

Curious little brown eyes.

Right fucking there.

I shove up, startled, sitting up so damn fast I get dizzy. Everything goes black for a second before coming back. Blinking, I look at her, the little Scarlet Letter just standing there a foot in front of the couch.

Sasha.

"Jesus," I grumble, scrubbing my hands over my face, trying to wake the hell up. She's standing there, staring at me, like it's the goddamn *Children of the Corn* up in here. "What are you doing?"

"I'm hungry."

She says that shit so matter of fact, like that's a perfect reason to be staring at me at *whatever* o'clock. The room is dim, like the sun isn't even fully shining yet. "What time is it?"

She shrugs.

Doesn't even look for a clock.

Hell, can she *read* a clock?

Sighing, I search through my pockets, not finding much, suddenly aware I've got drug paraphernalia sitting just to the left of the kid, splayed out on the table. I snatch it up, shoving it away.

We're off to a great start.

"Where's your mother?" I ask, looking around.

"Sleeping."

"Sleeping," I say. "And you're just, what... roaming around my house? Why?"

"I'm hungry," she says again.

"So you stare at me instead of eating something? What kind of sense does that shit make?"

She shrugs. *Again.*

I blink at her, thinking maybe if I wait she'll figure out what she's doing, but we're talking about Scarlet's kid. Should've known better. She'd probably stand here all goddamn day waiting for me to get *my* shit together and make sense of things for her.

"I, uh... okay. You want some food?"

"Yes, please."

Please.

She whipped out the manners on me.

Who can say *no* to that?

Well, hell, *I* easily could, but I'm not going to.

I shove to my feet, stretching before strolling out of the living room, heading down the hallway to the kitchen. The kid follows me, right on my heels, marching along like we're part of a goddamn parade or something.

It's way too early for this shit.

5:27 a.m.

That's what the clock in the kitchen tells me.

"What are you hungry for? What do you want?"

I don't have to look at her to know she's shrugging. Her silence gives that away. I glance around the pantry, scowling. Seeing as my brother is moving out in a matter of days, he hasn't bothered going to the store, which means we're running short on shit that's convenient, unless the kid likes raisins.

"You like raisins?" I ask, glancing behind me as I hold up a bag of trail mix, most of the mix part gone, leaving half a bag of pretty much just raisins at this point. Sasha slides up onto a chair at the kitchen table, so damn short her legs dangle, and makes a face at my question, clearly not a fan. "Yeah... me, neither."

I look at the bag again before tossing it in the trashcan.

"You don't have any allergies, do you?" I ask, realizing I should've probably asked that first.

"What's that?"

"Allergies, you know... some people are allergic to peanuts, which means peanuts can kill them, so they can't eat them. You got anything like that? Anything that can kill you?"

"Lots."

Shit. "Really? Like what?"

"Guns."

I look at her, brow furrowing. "Guns?"

"Guns can kill people."

The little walking, talking *PSA* stares at me, not being a smart ass about that at all, simply answering my question. I almost forgot what it was like dealing with a kid. *Almost.*

"Allergic to guns... got it," I mutter, moving on to the fridge. "No foods that can kill you?"

She hesitates before saying, "Porridge."

"*Porridge?*" What the hell? "What kind of porridge?"

Again, she hesitates, before saying, "All the kinds."

I glance at her, eyes narrowed. "You're telling me porridge will kill you if you eat it?"

She nods adamantly.

I'm pretty sure she's bullshitting, but I can't call her bluff. She's only five, for fuck's sake. If I try to make her eat some, to prove she's lying, I might accidentally kill her, and we can't be having that.

Besides, it's not like I have the shit around here to make porridge. What do I look like, Oliver Twist?

"No porridge, then. I won't ever feed you it."

She grins, a smug little smile. *Manipulative little shit.*

"Okay, look, kid... I'll be straight with you. We've got bologna, we've got fish sticks, and we've got a bunch of shit to maybe make a salad in here."

She makes another face.

Doesn't sound good to me, either.

"You don't have breakfast?" she asks. "Lucky Charms?"

"No, but I can probably make pancakes."

Her eyes widen, her expression brightening.

Ding, ding, ding.

"Pancakes, it is," I say, gathering what I need. Truth be told, I could make pancakes in my sleep with how often I've made these things for Leo.

Sasha kicks her legs impatiently as I whip up the batter, her heels banging against the legs of the chair.

"You want some kind of something in these pancakes?

We've got..." I glance around. *Shit.* "Looks like we have some chocolate chips."

She gasps. "Can I? *Please?*"

"Yeah," I say, grabbing the bag of chocolate chips, dumping the whole fucking thing in the batter.

As I wait for the pan to heat up, I grab a tangerine.

"Can I have some of that, too?" she asks, watching me.

I grab another tangerine and walk over, rolling it to her on the table. She picks it up, eyeing it warily, clutching it tightly as her gaze turns back to me. I peel my tangerine, tossing the scraps on the counter, and pull out a segment to eat as the pancakes start to cook.

"Ugh, how do you do this?" she grumbles.

I look at her as she claws at the tangerine, poking a hole, her finger going right through it as juice drips out onto the table. "Never peeled a tangerine before?"

"I don't know," she says, frustrated. "I just wanna open the orange."

Laughing under my breath, I walk over again, taking the tangerine and starting to peel it, showing her how to do it so she can finish the rest. "It's a tangerine, not an orange."

"It's not an orange?"

"It's more of a mandarin," I tell her. "They're all citrus fruit, but tangerines are smaller than a normal orange."

She glares at it, looking skeptical. "How does it taste?"

"Like an orange."

She gives me a look that says, '*Are you fucking kidding me? What was your point?*'

I'm so preoccupied with the tangerine that I burn the first pancake, having to toss it out. I focus after that, still trying to wake up, stacking up nearly a dozen pancakes on a platter. As soon as they're finished, I grab some plates and turn around, freezing when I look at Sasha.

The kid's a fucking *mess.*

Juice drips from her chin, smeared on her face, even somehow finding its way into her unbrushed hair. Tangerine covers the table in front of her, clinging to her shirt, like she fucking bathed in the juice. She licks her fingers, not at all bothered, her eyes lighting up when she sees the pancakes. I slap a few on a plate in front of her, ignoring the tangerine as I give her a fork.

Sitting down across the table, I hand her a bottle of syrup, watching as she drowns the pancakes in it and dives right in. I eat some, just folding the fuckers over like tacos, not bothering with silverware.

If I thought she was a mess before, it's got nothing on her *now*. Mess on top of mess on top of mess. Sticky syrup and melted chocolate cover her—on her hands, on her face, on her clothes. I watch incredulously as she drops her fork and jumps down out of the chair, licking her fingers once more. My gaze follows her as she heads straight for the fridge, leaving a chocolate covered handprint on the door handle as she opens it.

She doesn't say shit. Not a goddamn word.

She reaches right inside, helping herself to a Capri Sun.

"Give me one of those," I say, holding my hand out, a sticky juice pouch landing in my palm.

"You're welcome," she says right away, even though I hadn't thanked her, and I almost feel a twinge of guilt over that—over forgetting my manners—until it strikes me she hadn't thanked me for the fucking pancakes.

Yeah, I know I'm petty.

You don't have to tell me.

Pulling the little straw off the back of the pouch, I take the plastic off and aim for the hole.

I miss.

Every fucking time.

I stab the air, I stab the pouch, I stab *myself*. I'm about to lose my cool and throw the fucking thing when I hear Sasha laugh. My gaze darts to her. She's sipping her drink. She got her straw in the hole, no problem.

"I can do it," she says, launching herself across the table, grabbing the straw from me. I surrender it, pushing the juice pouch at her. She shoves the straw right in before giving it back. "There you go!"

My gaze flickers between her and the Capri Sun. "Thanks, shortcake."

She smiles widely, her voice soft as she says, "You're welcome."

"*Oh my god.*"

A voice cuts through the room, coming from the doorway, catching both of us off guard. Scarlet stands there, wide eyes watching us.

"Mommy, I ate chocolate in pancakes!" Sasha says, turning toward her, nearly falling out of the damn chair as she tries to shift out of the way, to show her mother her breakfast.

"I see that," Scarlet says, strolling closer, grasping the back of the chair as she looks her daughter over. "Looks like you're *wearing* it, too."

Brow furrowing, Sasha looks down, like she can't fathom what the hell her mother's talking about. Plucking off a piece of pancake that's stuck to her shirt with syrup, she pops it right into her mouth. Scarlet laughs with disbelief, hauling her out of the chair and onto her feet. "Why don't you go find a bathroom and wash up?"

Sasha doesn't argue, trudging out of the kitchen. Once she's gone, Scarlet slips into the chair across from me. I can tell she has shit she wants to say, so I just sit here, waiting her out, sipping from my juice pouch, knowing she'll get to it eventually.

Her voice is quiet when she finally speaks. "What are you doing, Lorenzo?"

I glance down at myself, just as confused by that as Sasha had been about wearing her breakfast. What does it look like I'm doing? "Sitting here."

"No, I know that, I just mean... what are you going to do now?"

"Probably keep sitting here for a while."

She smiles softly. "What's your plan?"

"For today?"

"For *every* day."

"For every day," I repeat, not sure how to answer that. "I've never been good at making plans, Scarlet... even worse at keeping them. I kind of just get up and go and hope for the best."

"Any idea where you might be *going*?"

"Depends."

"On what?"

"On how long it takes you to quit beating around the fucking bush and tell me what it is you want," I say. "Because the rate you're going, I might not ever make it out of this chair."

She makes a face at me, like I'm being a pain in the ass, but I'm not a mind reader. I'm not in the business of making assumptions, so while I could *guess* what she's getting at, I need her to just be straight.

For her sake.

For my *sanity*.

Because there's a kid off somewhere in my house, probably flooding my fucking bathroom, and she needs us to be on the same page about this. If there's going to be a 'we', it's not just 'her' and 'me', since there's also a little 'she' that has to be factored in somehow.

A little 'she' that complicates shit greatly.

"I'm just trying to figure out where I fit," Scarlet says. "Trying to see if there's even a place in your life for me."

"For you *both*, you mean."

She nods. "I know this isn't what you signed up for, Lorenzo. That's why, when Declan gave me your message, I tried to respect it, and I still will. I understand if we don't fit in your life. It's okay. But I just need to know. Because if we don't fit here, I have to figure out where we do. She's been through too much for so much of her life to be uncertain. She deserves to *belong*."

"So do you," I say.

Scarlet doesn't react to that, just staring at me, waiting for something more.

"Look, *your* plan is what matters here," I tell her. "Don't try to squeeze yourself into somebody else's life, like you're just a guest in their universe. Because yeah, that's fitting, but that's not belonging. I could fit my cock in a million holes, but that doesn't mean my cock has any business being in any of them. So why don't you tell me what *your* universe looks like, Morgan... what life looks like for you and Sasha... and then we'll decide if I belong there."

She stares at me for another moment, like maybe she doesn't know what to think, before finally, she says, "I just need it to be a place where we can be ourselves—where she can be who she is, and I can just be me. I don't care if there's a picket fence. I don't need a boy to turn into a stupid bird. I just... I want to be happy."

"What makes you happy?"

"You do," she says quietly.

I think about that, those words bouncing around in my skull. "How do you feel about Florida?"

"Florida?"

"Nothing permanent, just maybe get away for a while, you know, decompress. The guys can handle business here. It'll give my brother a chance to do his own thing without me looking over his shoulder and breathing down his neck, and it'll give us a chance to test the waters a bit."

"Florida, huh?"

I nod. "Florida."

Scarlet's quiet for a moment, staring off into space, before Sasha comes running back into the kitchen, not much cleaner than she had been.

"Hey, sunshine," Scarlet says, grabbing the girl, pulling her toward her. "How do you feel about Florida?"

"What does it have?"

"Uh, sunny skies." Scarlet glances at me. "Alligators, maybe? Help me out here."

"Beaches," I say. "Oranges."

"*A lot* of oranges," Scarlet says. "Oh, and *Disney World* is in Florida, too."

Sasha's eyes widen. "Can we go, Mommy? *Please?*"

"If you want to go, sure."

A grin lights up her face as she leans over, cupping her hands around Scarlet's ear, whispering something to her.

Whatever it is makes Scarlet's smile grow, a laugh escaping as she says, "Of course."

The kid lets out a squeal as she runs away, literally *running* in my house, yelling, "I'm gonna tell Buster!"

She's gone in a blink.

I stare at Scarlet in silence for a moment before curiosity gets the best of me. "What did she say?"

"She wanted to know if *Mommy's friend* could come with us to Florida," she says. "She likes the way he makes his pancakes and she thinks it's funny that he doesn't tie his shoelaces."

Brow furrowing, I glance down at the loose laces of the combat boots I'm wearing, the ones I never bothered to take off at bedtime, before I meet Scarlet's gaze again. She's still smiling, radiating happiness. *Warmth.*

"When she comes back, you tell her I said she's not half-bad herself."

25

"Wake up, sunshine," a voice called out in a raspy whisper as the little girl was shaken, roused from a deep, dreamless sleep.

The little girl peeked her bleary eyes open, blinking a few times as she gazed at the face beside her. "Mommy?"

Her mother smiled—a big, wide kind of smile. It wasn't the kind of smile the little girl saw every day. This smile glowed with happiness, almost vibrating with excitement, as her mother whispered, "We're here."

Here.

It took the little girl a moment to get it, a moment to understand what her mother meant, to remember where '*here*' was supposed to be. She sat up straight, moving so fast the seatbelt locked in place, trapping her in her booster seat. Groaning, she impatiently tugged at the seatbelt, looking around outside the windows of the car, but it was *so* dark, and all she could really see were the shadows and the trees.

Lots and lots and lots of trees.

Whoa, *so* many trees.

"Can I see them now?" the little girl asked. "Can I see Woody and Buzz?"

Her mother laughed, unclipping the seatbelt so the little girl could climb out of the car. The ground was hard, mostly dirt, with patches of green grass leading to a brown house.

"Not tonight," her mother said, "but I promise, after we get settled in, we'll go see them."

"You two have fun with that," another voice said as a car door slammed.

Mommy's friend.

The little girl thought he might be *her* friend, too, but she hadn't asked him. He was nice to her, though. He made her pancakes whenever she wanted them and never ever tried to feed her porridge, not even once in the weeks that she'd been around him. The little girl and her mother had stayed at his house with him back in the city before everything was put in boxes and they got into his car to drive the whole way to Florida.

'Home... *for now*,' her mother kept calling it. She said if the little girl didn't like the place, if it didn't make her happy, they wouldn't stay long, but with Woody and Buzz being nearby, how could she *not* like it?

It was like a dream come true.

"Oh, come on," the little girl's mother said. "You know you want to go, too. I mean, it's freakin' Disney World. Who doesn't want to go to the *Happiest Place on Earth*?"

He raised his hand.

The little girl laughed.

"They have Star Wars stuff," her mother said. "Rides and stormtroopers and souvenirs."

"And Woody and Buzz will be there," the little girl told him. "You don't wanna see them?"

He looked at her, pausing in a patch of grass. "I'll pass, shortcake, but thanks. I have plenty around here to keep me busy."

The little girl glanced around. The air smelled sweet, and all the trees were filled with oranges. It reminded her of an enchanted forest, like the ones from the fairy tale stories.

She turned back to him. "Like what? What are you gonna do?"

"Pick oranges," he said. "Eat oranges."

"Real oranges? Or you mean like them tangerines?"

"Both."

"Oh."

It was quiet for a moment, as they stared at each other, before his expression cracked and he laughed. It wasn't a mean laugh, no, so she didn't mind his laughter. His laugh sounded happy.

He turned to her mother, shaking his head. "She's so much like you, it's terrifying."

"Starting to think you're in over your head?" her mother asked.

"Pretty fucking positive I'm *so* in over my head that nothing short of decapitation is getting me back out of this one."

Her mother laughed, yet another happy sound, as she reached for him and wrapped her arms around his neck. He kissed her then, a messy kiss, all sloppy and noisy and wet. The little girl scrunched up her nose. It kind of looked like they wanted to eat each other's faces off.

It wasn't at all like the way the Tin Man had kissed her mother that night in the kitchen.

Maybe *this* was love, the little girl thought. Maybe love made you kiss all messy. Maybe love made you hungry for faces. Maybe he loved her mother, and maybe her mother loved him back. Maybe they loved each other like the little girl loved Buster.

"Buster," she gasped.

The sound of her voice made them pull apart, breaking the kiss. *Oops.*

"He's in the car," her mother said, "right where you left him."

The little girl rushed back into the car, snatching up Buster and pulling him out. There were other people around now, approaching to greet them, people who worked on the orange groves. Her mother had told her all about them. *Not flying monkeys.*

"Come on, sunshine," her mother said, taking the little girl's hand. "How about we go on inside and find you a bedroom while Lorenzo takes care of things?"

The little girl smiled.

She liked how that sounded.

A new bedroom, in a new house, with her mother and Buster... *and even their new friend, Lorenzo.*

Acknowledgments

Shout out to the makers of Capri Sun for that sharp ass little plastic straw that really does hurt like a bitch when you get stabbed with it. To all the orange growers, who are pretty damn awesome for making OJ possible, even though I have this weird aversion to pulp that Lorenzo would probably kill me for. To George Lucas for creating *Star Wars*, and to Disney for resurrecting *Star Wars*… and to both for not suing me for anything I say about *Star Wars* (I swear, I really do like *The Phantom Menace*).

Acknowledgments are the hardest part for me to write. There's always this crippling fear that I'm going to forget someone instrumental, because so many people are vital to the writing process, and I'm afraid they're going to think I'm an ungrateful twat (when really, sometimes my brain just clocks out). But for real, you all know who you are. I love you.

About the Author

J.M. Darhower is the *USA Today Bestselling Author* of paranormal/erotic/romantic suspense novels about the baddest bad boys and the ladies who love them. Fangirl at heart, J.M. is obsessed with books, music, and all things Marvel, especially the glorious Sebastian Stan. She spends her days in a tiny town in North Carolina, churning out words and chasing down Pokémon.

Printed in Great Britain
by Amazon

20305053R00195